For Aish and Meg

With thanks to:

Mr Dennis Remoundos
Dr Bernadette Lavery
The NHS
The Churchill Hospital, Oxford
GenesisCare Oxford

100% of the author's proceeds from this sale of this book before the 1st July 2023 will be donated to

Breast Cancer UK

Copyright

First published in Great Britain in
2022 by Antony Guntrip
Copyright (c) Antony Guntrip 2022

The right of Antony Guntrip to be identified
as the Author or the Work has been asserted
by him in accordance with the Copyright,
Designs and Patents Act 1988.
Cover design (c) King_of_Covers at Fiverr.com
Cover photography (c) Hans
Maeckelberghe at Unsplash.com

All rights reserved.

No part of the publication may be reproduced,
stored in a retrieval system, or transmitted,
in any form or by any means without prior
written permission of the publisher, nor be
otherwise circulated in any form of binding or
cover other than that in which it is published
and without a similar condition being
imposed on the subsequent purchaser.

antony.guntrip@gmail.com

Also by Tony Guntrip

Identity

Sticks and Stones

*Identity/Sticks and Stones plus
two short stories box set*

TONY GUNTRIP

1881

One

The Royal Highland Hotel, Edinburgh
Saturday 31st December

Porter, in his traditional role of self-appointed Master of Ceremonies, rose unsteadily to his feet. 'Musketeers – we stand on the cusp of a new year, when surgery will take a few more blinking, faltering steps into the light – as will we, since by some miracle we have all qualified to wield scalpels on the living instead of the dead. Without further ado I implore you to raise your glasses to The Year of Our Lord Eighteen Eighty-Two!' He held his glass aloft, which signalled the others to cheer noisily.

Ballantyne slapped his palm on the table, barely able to make himself heard above the din. 'Objection!'

Porter squinted at him, rocking gently on his heels. 'You *object*, D'Artagnan? On what grounds, Mister – sorry, *Doctor* Ballantyne?'

The small group – sufficient to fill the private dining room which had hosted the ceremony for the previous six Hogmanays – fell silent. 'We will hear your objection, Ballantyne. Pray continue, sir.' Porter slumped back onto his chair, spilling most of his burgundy as he did so.

'Thank you, George,' said Ballantyne. 'Since this august institution came into being, our first toast has always been to our most noble Queen.'

Porter struggled back to his feet and slapped his own wrist. 'Of course! I beg the collective forgiveness of the assembled members.'

With slurred murmurs of assent the other newly-qualified surgeons rose as one.

'My fellow Musketeers,' continued Porter. 'To our beloved and rotund Queen, Victoria, and all who sail in her – Victoria Regina Magnificat!'

'And all who are in her,' replied some of the others,

Ballantyne and Robertson abstaining from the chorus of disloyalty. They fell back into their seats.

Porter waited for the scraping of chairs to subside before he resumed. 'There is no need to rise again, gentlemen – or should I repeat *doctors* – as I once more propose Eighteen Eighty-Two.'

A chorus of 'Eighteen Eighty-Two!' filled the small room.

'Which brings us to our seventh – and thankfully final – Hogmanay awards ceremony. Please try not to weep or rend your garments until the end.' He pulled a tattered scrap of paper from his pocket. 'Our first award this evening is for the least effort in both academic and practical lectures. The winner is Monsieur Treville: Charles Gordon.'

The assembly stamped their feet and rattled their cutlery whilst Gordon busied himself counterfeiting appropriate outrage.

'Secondly, for his unstinting efforts in the consensual eradication of virginity in Edinburgh and its environs – oh gosh, it's me.'

Feet were once again stamped in approbation, as Gordon shouted 'Male or female?'

'I fear that I am not that discerning,' replied Porter.

'You are remarkably successful with the fair sex for one so ineffably ginger,' slurred Priestley.

'I cannot be held responsible for my beauty, Athos. It is an affliction I must bear.'

'Touché,' said Priestley.

'Next, for research into the effects of the continuous application of excess alcohol, with only himself as a subject, Arthur Robertson!'

Robertson smiled and held aloft his tumbler of cordial.

'Aramis,' asked Porter, 'can we not prevail upon you to drop your vow just once, on this, our last night together?'

'I regret not, Porthos,' replied Robertson. 'Only through God's strength have I maintained it over these endless years in your company, and it would be a great pity to fail so close to the end of my torment.'

'For the love of Pete,' said Porter. 'You can loosen your corsets just this once, surely?'

Robertson shook his head in feigned apology.

Porter rolled his eyes and continued. 'Therefore, I propose an additional toast for Aramis: To temperance.' Porter waited whilst everyone took another deep draught. 'With Aramis demurring Douglas Priestley is therefore awarded the Queen's Medal for alcoholic gallantry in his stead. Arthur Robertson is instead named the recipient of the most pious surgeon of Eighteen Eighty-One, a title which he has taken in every previous year of our studies.'

Porter took another mouthful of his burgundy. 'It's just as well that God's on his side, because he's not going to save a soul with his own efforts. A blind beggar with the DTs would make a better anatomist. Nevertheless, I have no doubt that he will enjoy his missionary position amongst the savages of the dark continent.'

Robertson refused to take Porter's bait.

'Two awards remain. A drum roll, if you please.'

The five doctors obliged.

'The next award is presented to Edward Ballantyne for his unstinting dedication to sleep research. Our young D'Artagnan is rarely observed with his eyes open for more than sixty contiguous minutes, so we are indeed honoured that he is still with us – and conscious – this evening. Let us hope that when he begins his preposterously low-paid career as an army surgeon there is sufficient enemy action to keep him awake.'

Ballantyne waved away their applause, which continued until Porter rang his glass with a knife. 'Which brings us to our final award–'

'Careful, George,' said Robertson.

Porter raised his hand. 'It's not what you think, Aramis. The prizes are awarded by the committee without fear or favour, and fall where they may. It is not for us to question them. I am merely the humble mouthpiece. Our final award goes to Doctor Nathaniel Blacklock, who for a record-breaking seventh year–'

The room fell silent, heads swivelling between Porter and Blacklock.

Blacklock rose, throwing his napkin onto his plate. 'I, for one, have never found these so-called "awards" amusing,' said Blacklock, almost in a whisper. A thought occurred to him. 'They are puerile and serve no purpose beyond Porthos's overwhelming desire to hear himself pontificate. These past seven years have been often educational, occasionally entertaining, but rarely convivial.' He took another sip of wine. 'Some of you have been friendly, some less so. As I look around I realise that I still regard each of you as mere acquaintances – in a couple of cases you are to all intents and purposes still strangers to me. But this is no longer of any import. This evening is our last together, and from this point our paths diverge. I have no doubt,' he continued as he rose and put on his topcoat, 'that the five of you will continue your career journey together as friends. I will take a different path, freely chosen. Independent.' He strode to the door and took his hat from the stand. He considered saying something else but thought better of it and walked out into the throng of New Year's Eve revellers, beyond the confines of the private dining room.

'Nathaniel!' shouted Robertson. 'Don't be such a humourless fool! Come back. Porter's an idiot. Please!'

Blacklock strode on without acknowledging the call.

When Porter called at Blacklock's lodgings to apologise the next morning, the landlady informed him that Blacklock had left. He had provided no forwarding address.

1894

Two

60 New Square, Lincoln's Inn Fields, London
Monday 8th October

Blacklock had been waiting since six forty-five a.m. in the anteroom of his solicitor's office for an appointment arranged for quarter past seven. He checked his watch for what seemed like the thousandth time – it was now eight, and he had another tedious pathology lecture – from both his and, he suspected, his students' perspective – to deliver at nine-thirty. A moment later Marlow bustled in, trailing a hint of the day's oily yellow fog with him.

'Ah, Nathaniel, so sorry I'm late old man. I was waylaid by ... well, something or other. Anyway, follow me.'

Marlow bustled to his chambers, pausing only to request that Sullivan, his clerk, deliver "two hot beverages, immediately, if not sooner."

Once inside his office Marlow gestured to a chair. 'Sit, Nathaniel, and take the weight off.'

Marlow slipped off his not-quite-threadbare overcoat and slumped into the chair, elbows on his blotter, fingers steepled. 'Any news?'

'None. I had rather hoped that you might have some,' said Blacklock, failing to disguise his concern.

'Nothing which one might consider useful. I have a missive somewhere – Sullivan! Bring in Doctor Blacklock's file should you ever deign to bring us those drinks.'

Sensing a brief halt to proceedings and unwilling to engage Marlow in small-talk Blacklock tried to look out of the office window. In spite of its decades of accumulated filth he could make out the seething mass of dark grey humanity scurrying past, like so many indistinguishable ship rats.

'Coffee, sirs, and Doctor Blacklock's file,' said Sullivan,

who had somehow entered the room without disturbing Blacklock's reverie.

Marlow thumbed through the wad of papers. 'Ah, here it is – a letter from the head of the disciplinary committee at your beloved Royal College of Surgeons. Listen: "*Further to your letter of the 3rd instant I regret to inform you that in all cases of internal discipline within The College, its status as a private organisation permits it to enforce its rulings in camera. Furthermore, no legal representation is recognised by said disciplinary committee. Please remind Doctor Blacklock* – as if we don't know who you are – *that should he persist in trying to mount a legal challenge to either his suspension or the authority of the committee or the aforementioned process the likelihood is that his current temporary suspension would be escalated to a full and irrevocable exclusion from The College, with the consequent termination of his capacity to legally practice surgery throughout the United Kingdom and such parts of The Empire which fall within its compass.*"'

Marlow sat back and sipped his coffee. 'I fear, Nathaniel, that that might be considered somewhat conclusive. If I try to help you then you're threatened with the end of your career.'

Blacklock ran his hands through his hair. 'Leaving me to churn out barely adequate lectures in pathology to uninterested students.'

'Precisely. As a friend I would say that you're wasting your money retaining me on this case. As a solicitor I would offer to appeal to the RCS on your behalf but that might be ruin for you and leave you only mouldering cadavers for company. I really don't know what the best course of action for you might be.'

'I wish they would just bloody decide,' sighed Blacklock. 'Please excuse my immoderate language. This limbo is almost worse than permanent exclusion. The other day I overheard a couple of my students in conversation and one said that I am only allowed to work with the dead because I cannot make them any worse. Frankly, Abraham, I am a laughing stock.'

Marlow redirected his gaze to the papers on his desk. 'It's been ... eight months. They have to make a decision soon. Their own procedural limit is eighteen months. If you like I could send one more letter to remind–'

'No, best not. They hold the whip hand and I would prefer not to rile them any further than I already have.' He snorted. 'By the time of the wedding I will either be a surgeon again or a poverty-stricken lecturer-cum-fool.' He slapped his hands on his thighs and stood up. 'Right, Abraham – it has been a pleasure of sorts but I must return to the hospital. I have a listless mob to address on the subject of dissection of the head and neck – the subject a maid who tripped over her apron at the top of some servants' stairs. The majority of my students either do not care or are too stupid to learn a damned thing. Most yearn only for lucrative private practice and are frankly unwilling to listen to someone who may not be a surgeon for much longer.' He held out his hand. 'Thank you for trying.'

Marlow rose and smiled uncomfortably. 'Good luck.'

Blacklock finished his drink and headed out into the ochre gloom, an appropriate mirror for his mood.

Three

The School of Medicine, Prince Albert's
Hospital, Fulham, London
Monday 8th October

As Blacklock approached the School of Medicine, still angry from his meeting with Marlow, he was surprised to find a large crowd gathered in the redbrick quad. People of all ages were milling around; he spotted several members of his first class of the day talking together. He looked about him and saw several other groups, also engaged in deep conversation. The Principal, a man of few words and less practical value, was talking to a police constable, mopping his pale and perspiring face with an enormous handkerchief. Everyone was too engrossed to notice Blacklock as he passed among them, walking ever more slowly as he approached the grand steps which marked the entrance to the hospital's medical school. He became convinced that some desperate tragedy must have occurred, but the fabric of the building appeared intact and apart from the scattered whispering groups everything seemed to be in order. He mounted the steps but found the door blocked by another constable.

'I'm sorry, sir, but you can't come in unless you are on official police business. If you don't bear a warrant card I must ask you wait down on the quadrangle until it is deemed appropriate to open the building again.'

'What has happened?'

'I'm not at liberty to say, sir.' He leaned forward and lowered his voice. 'You could ask anyone in the quadrangle, sir. They all know what's afoot. Bad news travels fast; disgusting news fastest of all. It's a bad do all around.' He straightened back up. 'Now, off you go.'

Uncertain what to do next Blacklock turned round and surveyed the crowd before him, searching for a friendly non-student face. It was at times like this that he wished he had expended more effort on socialising.

At last he spotted Miss Henry, the School of Surgery's secretary in a far corner, engaged in animated conversation with Miss Ellis, the Principal's personal secretary. He made his way quickly through the crowd.

'Miss Henry, Miss Ellis. Do you know what has happened here?' Remembering his manners he added, 'I am sorry – good morning.'

Miss Henry turned to him, her face wet with tears.

'Oh, Doctor Blacklock, it's terrible!' She began to sob again.

He reached out tentatively to touch her arm but thought better of it and withdrew awkwardly. 'There, there, Miss Henry, it cannot be as bad as all that, I am sure. Miss Ellis, can you tell me what has occurred?'

Miss Ellis, who was also crying but less effusively, said, 'Please walk with me a few yards. I wish to spare Miss Henry further distress. I'll be back directly, Camille.'

They walked a handful of paces away. 'It's the most awful thing, Doctor, and I can't recall anything like it happening before. One of the new cadavers has been ... desecrated.'

'*Desecrated?* How so?'

'It was the body of a young woman – a lady's maid, I believe – who fell down her employer's stairs–' She paused.

'I am familiar with ... her. Please go on, Miss Ellis.'

'Mr Jenkins was on his caretaking rounds at about five this morning when he discovered that the lock had been forced into the medical school cold storage room. He entered and - oh, I can't say any more. I'm sorry.' Miss Ellis's tears began flowing almost as plentifully as Miss Henry's before her.

Impatient to know what had happened but mindful of his conduct Blacklock didn't feel he could leave the women crying. Filled by a guilty frustration, he fought to hide his irritation.

He was on the verge of asking Miss Henry again as her

tears lessened, when three more secretaries joined them, relieving him, he felt, of his duties. With a muttered "excuse me" he left the group.

He surveyed the mass of staff and students, seeking someone with a firmer grip on their emotions. One of his pathology students, Levy, was peeling away from one of the student huddles. 'Mr Levy! Could I speak with you for a moment, please?'

Levy hastened over. 'Sir?'

'Do you know what has happened, Mr Levy? Our female colleagues are too distressed to tell me.'

'One of the cadavers, which I have heard only arrived on Friday, has been ... cut to shreds, sir.'

'What? How?'

'A young female, sir. I understand that her abdomen has been opened, her organs removed and ... strewn about. The caretaker has been taken to hospital – he collapsed with shock because he believed he had found a murder victim.'

'Yes, yes,' said Blacklock, failing to stifle his impatience. 'Do you know anything else?'

Levy shrugged. 'That's all I've heard, sir. The rumour is that the service door from the alley behind was jemmied.'

'Thank you, Mr Levy. You may go.'

As he watched Levy walk away Blacklock was approached by a weasel-faced man, in a gaudy plaid overcoat surmounted by a brown bowler hat.

'Are you Doctor Blacklock, sir?'

'I am. And you are?'

'Detective Sergeant Cargill, sir. From the Metropolitan Police.'

'Is this a police matter?'

'How could it not be, sir? Someone has broken in,' Cargill counted on his tobacco-stained fingers, 'which is offence number one. Said person has ... violated a dead body in the most despicable manner – offence number two – in a manner likely to outrage public decency. The Principal called us in.'

'I see, Sergeant. I teach anatomy and pathology here. Can I see the body? I might be able to discern something of interest to you.'

Cargill shook his head. 'I'm afraid not, sir. The body – and parts – have already been removed. Sir Edward Allam is the Force's appointed surgeon and will do ... whatever he does.'

'Perhaps I might assist?'

'Thank you for your kind offer, Doctor, but that won't be necess–'

Cargill was interrupted by a bellowing voice nearby. 'Doctor Blacklock, I would like to see you in my study at your convenience, please.' Principal Moore's voice filled the quad. 'It would be most appropriate if your convenience was now.'

With a curt smile Blacklock excused himself and walked as fast as he could – without appearing to rush – to Moore's study. The door was open but he waited for a formal invitation.

'Don't stand on ceremony, man. This is no time for niceties, Blacklock.'

Blacklock entered and sat down without further invitation, keen to avoid extraneous "niceties" which might further enrage the Principal. Moore stood and moved to look out of the window, hands clasped behind him, forcing his robes into a black fan like a peacock in mourning. 'I assume this calamity is the work of one of your trainee butchers, Nathaniel. Do you know which one? Who is struggling, furthest behind with his studies? Who is most likely to display perverted tendencies?'

'I–I,' stammered Blacklock.

'Come on man!' shouted Moore. 'Out with it. For God's sake, *the police* are on campus. It'll be in the papers this evening. Which one?'

'Of?'

'Your bloody students, man! It has to be one of your lot. No one else cares to dissect the dead.'

'All medical students, whether they study pathology or

not, have access to the body store. And–'

'And what?' snapped Moore.

'I am given to understand that the external door was forced open, so it need not be someone from this institution at all, let alone one of my students. In fact, sir,' said Blacklock with a flush of self-preserving inspiration, 'it might be better to let everyone know that so that they assume it is more likely the work of some sick-minded individual from beyond our walls rather than someone they share the campus with.'

Moore did not turn around but Blacklock sensed him becoming calmer. 'That's not the worst idea I've heard this morning.' He called through the door. 'Miss Ellis?'

'I believe Miss Ellis is in the quad.'

'Damn. Be a good fellow and send her in, will you? There's a good chap.'

Blacklock bit back his urge to reject Moore's fetch-and-carry orders. Discretion and a low profile were the order of the day. 'Of course, Principal, although I fear she is rather upset.'

He got up to leave.

'If Miss Ellis is unable to pull herself together send one the others up. One more thing, Nathaniel. If this does turn out to be the work of one of your butcher boys you'll be out. Understand?'

As he walked down to the quad Blacklock ran through his roster of students. It couldn't possibly be one of them, could it? Had he missed some alarming propensity towards this awful perversion? No one stood out in his mind, but he only really noticed the top and bottom ten percent of each class. The middle eighty percent merged into some shapeless mass of anonymity.

The quad was emptying now as people drifted away. It was clear that the police would not relinquish their grip on the premises in the short term. Miss Ellis was walking towards the gate with Miss Henry, whose shoulders were still betraying hitching sobs.

'Miss Ellis?'

The women stopped and turned in his direction.

'Miss Ellis, Professor Moore would like to see you in his study.'

A fleeting shadow of disappointment crossed her face. 'Thank you, Doctor Blacklock.' She sighed. 'Duty calls, Camille. I had better go back in. I am so sorry to leave you like this.'

Miss Henry waved away her apology.

'Miss Henry,' said Blacklock when Miss Ellis had moved beyond earshot, 'would you like me to escort you home? I have time on my hands.'

Miss Henry smiled. 'I am grateful for your kind offer, Doctor, but I shall be alright.' She pulled up her collar then freed her ornate French Plait with a shake of her head before continuing her journey.

Blacklock pursed his lips and headed for his lodgings.

Four

Fortnum and Mason's, Piccadilly, London
Tuesday 9th October

Although his cash reserves were already lower than he could ever dare to admit – even to himself – Blacklock remained committed to treating his fiancée Matilda in the same manner he always had, even though these regular afternoon teas at Fortnum's were already close to unaffordable. His innate prudence whispered frequently to his conscience but he chose to ignore it.

They were barely seated before Tilly brought up her favourite topic. 'Darling, how was your meeting last week with Mr Marlow?'

He continued to examine his menu, trying to form an honest yet optimistic answer. 'The same as the last one, and the one before that ... ad infinitum. He says we just have to sit tight. However, you should not concern yourself. The College's own rules say that a decision must be reached quickly.'

Tilly beamed. 'So I may not only be the most talked-about bride of the spring season, but my beloved husband will be practising again as a surgeon! Won't that be wonderful?'

'Without doubt you'll be 1895's most beautiful bride, my darling. We'll have to wait and see whether your second supposition comes to pass.'

'Oh darling, it simply *has* to!' She wrapped a blonde ringlet around her finger. 'I couldn't be married to someone who makes his living disembowelling the dead!'

'I understand.'

'Oh gosh, I'm teasing you, silly! I'd marry you if you were the person who empties the ward chamber pots!'

He smiled, his bubble of self-importance burst. 'I am sure that is not entirely true, Tilly, but I appreciate the sentiment.' He touched his water-glass to hers as the waiter approached, stepping carefully over the leads of a pair of yapping Pekingese at an adjacent table.

'Have mademoiselle and sir made their choices?'

Blacklock deferred to Matilda who made her selection quickly. 'And sir?'

'I know we are ostensibly here for tea, but I am ravenous. Is there any of the lunchtime soup left?'

'I believe so, sir. It is a most excellent chowder, the recipe recently imported from our American cousins.'

Blacklock smiled – he hoped – ingratiatingly. 'If I might break all the rules – most irregular, I know – I would be forever grateful.'

The waiter bowed, flirting with obsequiousness. 'Of course, sir. I shall check with the kitchen directly. Would you like a little something with it? The current house champagne is quite without equal in London.'

Before he could reply, Blacklock's financial conscience tapped him on the shoulder again and he changed his as-yet unspoken response. 'I think I will wait to see how I feel after my soup. Thank you.'

The waiter bowed again, even lower. 'As you wish, sir.' He bowed to Tilly. 'Mademoiselle.' He walked away.

'So, Tilly, while I have been hammering anatomy and decay into the unyielding heads of the uninterested, what have you been up to?'

'Papa gave me permission to go to Harrod's and I found the most wonderful frocks there. I only chose three because I don't want to be spoiled. You'll see that they're perfectly adorable! Oh, I also bought a delightful bright powder blue evening bag which is simply divine. All that for only twenty guineas!'

Blacklock winced, he hoped only inwardly. That was six weeks' pay as a lecturer – only two as a surgeon, but nevertheless – it seemed so wasteful for something he knew Tilly would only wear once or twice before boredom set in. He sighed but knew better than to say anything. Tilly continued speaking but in spite of his best efforts his concentration waned and his attention drifted elsewhere from the pretty mime that was his fiancée. The spinning kitchen door caught his attention at the moment their server appeared, bearing Tilly's afternoon tea and his chowder. The waiter deftly threaded his way across the busy salon, weaving left and right and appearing preternaturally adept at anticipating the vagaries of others' movements. Retelling the tale later Blacklock would swear that that was when time slowed down, for he could recall everything which followed in exquisite detail. As the waiter approached to within about four feet of their table, already beginning to bend to deliver their meal, one of the Pekingese took violent exception to a similarly miniaturised dog which had just entered the salon. Darting out, its lead stretched tightly across the path of the waiter who, unsighted by the tray, walked straight into catastrophe. He lost his footing and tumbled forwards. Before Blacklock could move the scalding soup coated his right hand. He leapt to his feet and seized a napkin from the table as anger, pain and fear battled for dominance.

'You bloody imbecile, man! What the hell do you think you are doing?'

Blacklock picked up the water jug and poured it over his hand, before holding both hands up to the terrified waiter. 'Do you know what these are?' he shouted, the salon falling immediately silent.

'I'm terribly sorry, sir, it was an acc–'

'I did not ask you how you felt, you bumbling incompetent! I asked you what these are!'

'Nat, please don't make a scene,' pleaded Tilly.

Blacklock turned to her. 'Be quiet, Matilda.'

'Hands, sir?' The waiter was confused.

'Not just hands, *idiot*, but *surgeon's* hands. They save people's lives. I cannot risk damage to them!' Blacklock was almost screaming now, ignoring Tilly's desperate pleas for calm. 'If I cannot operate, people could die. I could lose my career. All because you are obviously incapable of the idiot's task of carrying a bloody–'

'Sir! Please!' hissed the maître d', who had rushed over to the mêlée. 'Calm yourself – there are ladies present. Why don't you tell me what precipitated this outburst?'

'This ... this ... imbecile poured steaming chowder all over me! Look at my hands, man! My career depends on them and this fool came close to throwing that all away. For Pete's sake. I should–'

The maître d' positioned himself between Blacklock and the waiter. 'Fowler, leave us please. I'll speak to you later.' The waiter needed no second opportunity to flee to the relative safety of the kitchen.

'Crabtree,' said the maître d' to another waiter who was hovering indecisively nearby, 'please fetch Matron to attend to this gentleman's wounds. Now, Doctor Blacklock, please try to calm down. I appreciate that you are upset but I'm sure this was simply an unfortunate accident. Fowler's been with us for over twenty years and I cannot recall a single similar incident in all that time.'

The maître d's practised soothing tones acted to defuse Blacklock's anger. 'Of course, you are right,' said Blacklock, flopping back into his chair. 'I overreacted.'

The maître d' crouched down beside him, which was signal enough to the other patrons to resume their teas. Tilly mopped at silent tears. 'We'll move you to another table and you can resume your meal. Has anything splashed on your clothing? We will of course have them laundered at our expense.'

Blacklock checked his suit. 'I do not think so, but thank you for the offer. Tilly, shall we move over there?'

Tilly sniffed. 'If it's all the same, Nathaniel, I think I should really rather go home.'

'Of course. I will summon a hackney.'

'On my *own*, Nathaniel. Phelps will be nearby. My nerves have sustained a terrible shock and I need peace and quiet. You must excuse me.' With that she rose and flounced from the salon.

Blacklock, nonplussed, turned to the maître d'. 'My bill, please.'

'There's obviously no charge, sir. If you'll just wait until Matron arrives–'

'That will not be necessary. If I could have my hat, cane and cape I will also return to my lodgings.'

Blacklock dashed downstairs in pursuit of Tilly. He could not see her inside the store so ran out into the tumult of Piccadilly. Looking desperately about him he still could not locate her. He assumed that she had already left in one of her father's many anonymous black carriages which always shadowed their sojourns and had melded into the multitude of omnibuses, hackneys, barrows, dustmen and costermongers that jostled for dominance even as they choked the thoroughfare. Rejected and still angry, although unsure whether with himself or the waiter, he elected to walk back to his rooms to allow his displeasure to subside. The pavement twenty yards ahead was blocked by a trio of beggars. He slowed his pace as he approached them, waiting for a rare gap in the traffic to afford him the opportunity to cross to the other side of the street.

The stroll improved his mood to the extent that by the time he reached his lodgings in Stoke Newington, he realised that he had yet to eat. He headed to The Olde Bell and Unicorn, where the landlord was able to summon up some mutton and boiled potatoes, served with a diabolically rough red wine. This served to further improve his mood. On his return home he scribbled a couple of short notes of apology – one for Tilly, one for Fortnum's – which he despatched via messenger boys. He instructed the first boy to wait for Miss Caldecott's reply, but was not entirely surprised when he returned empty-handed.

Let her enjoy her tantrum. She will come round soon enough.

Five

The Caldecott Residence, 17 Belgrave
Square, Knightsbridge, London
Thursday 11th October

Phelps, the Caldecott family's driver, was grooming Sir Edmund's trademark jet-black four at the kerbside in front of their townhouse, which was naturally on the most expensive side of the square. He glanced up and nodded curtly at Blacklock. To the surgeon, for reasons he could not fathom, this represented some form of vital acceptance. He returned the nod whilst trying to maintain the separation from the servants which he felt his status merited.

Blacklock pulled the bell chain which sounded deep within the house. Through the stained glass door he saw Watson, the butler, approaching in his ridiculously ponderous manner, only for Tilly to appear from a nearer doorway and race to open the door.

'Oh Nathaniel, do come in. I'm sorry I was so uncaring about that awful to-do in Fortnum's. Do you forgive your little Tilly?'

By this time Watson had arrived and Blacklock thought it inappropriate to respond in such childish terms in front of the staff. 'Of course I do, Matilda. In fact there is nothing *to* forgive.' He stepped inside, giving his hat and coat to Watson. He felt a passing embarrassment at their relative shabbiness but could not afford to replace them until he was either reinstated or married.

He followed Tilly into the Drawing Room. Her father rose from the table and coldly offered his hand. 'Blacklock.'

'Sir Edmund.' Blacklock bowed slightly.

'Matilda informs me that there was an unfortunate altercation in Fortnum's. I trust you are uninjured?'

Blacklock smiled. 'Indeed, sir. There was a little soreness

but it could have been far worse.'

Caldecott tutted. 'I am also given to understand that your behaviour was less than dignified. In fact, I am further given to understand your conduct fell well short of that expected from a gentleman.'

Tilly was standing behind her father, eyes wide open. She shook her head.

'It was a shock, sir, and my career, to all intents and purposes reposes in my hands. If I was for any reason unable to hold a scalpel with the greatest delicacy then tragedy might ensue.'

'As we well know,' smiled Caldecott, humourlessly. He pulled a gaudy full Hunter from his waistcoat. 'I must go. I am due at my club within the hour. Good evening, Blacklock. Goodnight, Matilda.'

'Good evening, sir.'

Caldecott turned and limped out. *Gout,* thought Blacklock. *Your lifestyle will catch up with you sooner or later.*

Dinner passed quickly, orchestrated with its usual military efficiency by Caldecott's army of liveried servants, ridiculous anachronisms from the previous century. Blacklock sensed that each of them was scowling at him, but only when just out of his field of vision. He realised that he was not listening to a word of Tilly's conversation. He justified his inattention by assuring himself that most of what she was saying was either vapid, irrelevant or both. He quickly returned to himself when she became insistent.

'So, what do you think?'

He groped for an answer to a question he had not heard. 'I ... am not sure.'

'You must have someone in mind.'

'For?'

'Your Best Man and ushers. You haven't mentioned a single soul that you wish to invite to our wedding.'

'Is it not a little early to consider such matters?'

Matilda snorted. 'People in *society* are extremely busy.

Without sufficient notice they may find themselves with prior engagements. One does not start an event in society by embarrassing one's proposed guests.'

'No one springs to mind. Starling, perhaps.'

'What about friends from university or medical school? You must have hundreds of acquaintances in Edinburgh. I would love to meet them. The tales they could tell of you – I am sure they would be deliciously off-colour!'

'No.' Images of the final awards ceremony filled his mind. 'There is no one worth inviting. Even if there was I have no way of contacting them. They could be scattered to the four corners of the earth for all I know.' *Or care.*

'Nat, you really *must* think of *some* people to invite, otherwise the church and the wedding breakfast will seem awfully one-sided. I am already having to cull people from my list. Papa is most insistent that numbers remain manageable.'

'Your father is a wise man, my darling. What is this new limit?'

'I am only allowed two hundred guests of my own choosing. The majority will be chosen from society by Papa's secretary.'

Two hundred is a minority?

'I think that between you and your father you should have quite enough guests. I shall ask Starling if he will be my Best Man and be content. It is not, after all, about the ceremony or the attendant celebrations. It is about our life together thereafter. Really, my guests or lack thereof are of no import to me.'

'As you wish,' snapped Matilda. 'I am sure it would be equally splendid with just the two of us and the vicar.' The cloud that passed briefly across her face told Blacklock everything he needed to know about the veracity of her statement. 'You might also care to invite some of your lavatory cleaning friends. Goodnight, Nathaniel. You must excuse me. I am very tired.'

Six

The School of Medicine, Prince Albert's Hospital, Fulham, London
Tuesday 16th October

At the moment of incision Blacklock's blade caught the lamplight overhead, searing a brief persistence onto his retina. He blinked and shook his head to clear it. Again, he brought the scalpel close to the victim's skin, and after a second hesitation he started to cut, across for a fraction of an inch and then down, feeling the skin pulling erratically against the blade in the way he knew so well. A little liquor of decomposition spilled from the wound as he continued his cut, but not enough to obscure his field of vision. As he reached the end of his planned section, he turned the blade again to make another minute cross-cut before returning the blade to its starting point at the upper end of the sternum. Pressing harder this time, he felt the microscopic fibres of the fascia beneath drag before they parted, forcing him to further increase the pressure. Slowly the slit in the blade's wake opened, widening as he continued.

A bead of sweat ran from his forehead and dropped silently onto the boy's pale skin, causing him to pause for a moment to watch as it quickened with gravity and rolled into the darkness below. His concentration was broken and he inhaled. Blacklock straightened up and stepped back from the table, out of the glare and fatiguing heat of the surgical lamps overhead. He rolled his neck and opened his shoulders, cursing his loss of stamina. He surveyed the spectators and chose the one trying his utmost to be unobtrusive. 'Mr Mowbray, tell me – do you see anything abnormal?'

'N–no, sir, I don't think so.'

'You don't *think* so? You are not here to think, Mowbray,

you are here to *know*.' He sighed, a little theatrically. 'Is there anyone else here more confident than Mowbray? Langan? Rice? Levy? Salvadori?'

'Sir?'

'Mr Levy. Excellent. So, pray tell what is abnormal here?'

'I think ... I mean, I know ... there is nothing abnormal.'

Blacklock raised an eyebrow. 'A brave choice.' He almost added "young man", but managed to stop himself. At forty he felt barely older than his students. 'Any more opinions, or – better still – facts? Who agrees with Mr Levy? Anyone?'

The group shuffled uncomfortably, all studiously avoiding eye contact. 'I see. Mr Levy, your colleagues here appear to be in the most profound disagreement with you.' He paused again. Seeing Levy start to colour Blacklock broke his own silence. 'Gentlemen, Mr Levy is to be congratulated. There is nothing wrong with what you see before you, barring of course the tragedy of a dead boy who had barely attained the age of fourteen years. Therefore, we must delve at least a little deeper.'

Blacklock picked up the scalpel once more and made a number of deep horizontal cuts which ran in each direction from the top and bottom of his central incision. Without hesitation he reached into the boy's chest and, starting with the uppermost, spread each pair of ribs in turn, either breaking them or tearing them free of the spine as he did so.

'Blacklock's ravenous this evening,' stage-whispered a student, veiled in the darkness beyond the lamps. A barely-suppressed ripple of laughter passed through the class.

Blacklock became still for a moment, which immediately halted the sniggering. 'Thank you.' He paused again as if expecting a challenge, but none came. 'Before we continue, I will warn Mr Salvadori that I will be most happy to dispense with his sparkling wit if he is unable to contain it. I am sure such comic genius must be a terrible cross to bear, but you must endeavour to do so.'

Silence.

'Very well. We will continue. If we are to determine

the cause of this boy's death, remember that in surgery one seeks to limit one's impact; in pathology one strives for the clarity, knowledge - the truth, if you like. You will never have a better chance of "doing no harm" than with a patient whose soul already reposes elsewhere.' He stood back, holding his scalpel high. 'If you will step forward, one by one, you'll see that the young man's heart appears to be in excellent condition. Apart from the inevitable deterioration which time inflicts on the dead all seems well. With a few cuts, this–' Blacklock was working fast now. He removed the heart and placed it in a stained porcelain bowl. '–is removed, exposing the lungs to scrutiny. They are best examined, like most of the organs, outside the body.' In a minute or so he had freed them. 'Does anyone see anything untoward? Excluding you, Mr Levy.'

'It's obvious, sir.'

Blacklock sighed. 'Mr Salvadori. Please share your insight.'

'The human body functions more effectively with the heart fitted internally. I believe the cause of this boy's demise to be heart-in-bowl syndrome.'

'Good day, Mr Salvadori. It is time you left us. Do not return to my lectures until next week.'

'But–'

'No. I gave you fair warning – more than you deserved, given that you have established this tedious and repeated pattern of behaviour ever since you started in this class – but for all your alleged intelligence you could neither heed my advice nor rein in your impulsive petulance. The other students will gain more by your absence. You can discuss the matter further with Principal Moore, when you are called in to explain the report I shall lodge this evening. Now get out. Unlike you there are some present who wish to learn.' He stared at Salvadori, who stood his ground and stared back.

'I said, you tiresome oaf, that it is time for you to be anywhere else but in this lecture.'

Salvadori's jaw clenched briefly before he collected his briefcase and sauntered to the double doors. He paused when he reached them.

'Whatever it is, Salvadori, you can share it with your sycophantic chums later. You have wasted enough of your colleagues' time. Just leave.'

Salvadori pulled back his shoulders and left the room.

Blacklock waited a few seconds before he spoke. 'Does anyone else care to join our resident comedian or might we be permitted to continue this lecture without further interruption?' He looked at each student in turn, eyebrows raised. 'Good. I ask once again: does anyone see anything untoward?'

'They – the lungs – seem discoloured, sir,' said Langan. 'A section would be more useful.'

Blacklock offered the student the scalpel. 'Be my guest. Cut through the lobe of your choice and tell us what you see.'

Langan applied the scalpel to the exposed right lung, but initially the gelatinous tissue refused to yield.

'Be more assertive, Mr Langan. You need to remember that you are the master here.'

With renewed effort Langan managed to cut cleanly through a lower lobe, revealing the blackened interior of the lung.

'Aha! Thank you, Mr Langan. What do we now see? Any ideas?'

Levy stepped forward. 'Such ... gross corruption. How long has the boy been dead? A month?'

'Two days. You may wish to consider a new hypothesis. Perhaps a new question. *Think*, man. Where does a doctor start?'

'What do we know of the patient's recent history?'

'Bravo! Very good, Mr Levy. History is no less critical to your examination with the deceased. I can tell you that this boy worked illegally as a chimney sweep.'

Levy smiled triumphantly. 'I believe he died from

prolonged exposure to soot, which would corrupt the lungs, or perhaps smoke inhalation although I see no burns. No. I think he died from the accumulation of soot in the lungs.'

'An interesting conjecture. Would you care to examine the body further?'

For the first time in the lecture Levy looked uncertain. 'I don't ... no. I believe there is sufficient evidence to make a determination.'

Blacklock nodded. 'Thank you for your decisiveness, Mr Levy, you may step back.' Folding his arms, Blacklock asked, 'Any further theories?'

The usual silence ensued.

'Alright, I appreciate that it is difficult under these artificial conditions, particularly in front of one's peers. What if I do this?' He took the boy's head between his hands and leaned it over until the ear touched the shoulder. With a grinding click a bone projected from the side of the neck, tenting the skin. 'And now?'

'H–his neck,' stammered Langan. 'It's ...'

'Broken? Indeed. Do you care to reassess your position, Mr Levy?'

Levy's mouth opened and closed soundlessly as if he was an automaton with a broken voice-box.

'No matter,' said Blacklock, 'and I apologise – I was being grossly unfair, albeit for good reason. I hope that the point I have made with Mr Levy's help is that you should assume nothing until you have completed your examination. Often the first cause of death you determine is indeed the correct one but to *assume so* is to do your patient, their grieving relatives, yourself and our entire profession a grave disservice. Poor John Colter here – yes, he had a name – stumbled over a broken kerbstone on Marret Street and was fatally – and unluckily – struck by a speeding hackney. Mr Levy was right, I think, in concluding that this poor soul would have eventually perished from the noxious effects of his labour but this broken neck caused his expiration. He died instantly – a blessing.' He stood back and removed his blood-stiffened apron, which he exchanged for his coat from a nearby peg. 'Good day, gentlemen.'

Seven

The School of Medicine, Prince Albert's
Hospital, Fulham, London
Friday 9th November

Blacklock rubbed his hands together with false glee in an attempt to engender something more than a passing interest in the lecture within his students. 'Good morning, gentlemen. I understand that for undergraduates nine a.m. on a snowy morning may seem obscenely early but should you eventually move on to actually practise in any branch of medicine you will quickly begin to relate to time as a strictly abstract concept – as you will lunch, dinner and in your early years perhaps even blessed slumber itself.'

His remarks drew no response from his class.

'Very well, we shall begin. Today we are joined by the mortal remains of Mr Jack Cox, who passed away yesterday evening.' He drew back the sheet covering the body. 'What do we observe?'

One hand was raised.

'Mr Monkton. What do you see?'

'A slim male of perhaps thirty years, outwardly in good health.'

'Very good. Pray continue.'

'There is a pronounced distension of the abdominal wall which corresponds – approximately – to the fundus.'

'A promising start. Why "approximately"? Surely you can do better than that?'

Monkton continued uncertainly. 'Because the stomach is the most mobile organ, sir?'

'I see. Was that a question or a statement? Come on, be bold man.'

'A ... statement, sir.'

Blacklock clapped his hands. 'Bravo! Someone who

listens in anatomy lectures. What would you do next, Mr Monkton?'

'Dissect the abdomen.'

Blacklock nodded. 'Would anyone do anything else before wielding the scalpel?' He looked around. 'Mr Levy? Perhaps you might wish to leap into action, your scalpel flashing like Zorro's blade?'

Levy looked at the floor.

'Sound and palpate the abdomen to determine if there is an increase in internal pressure or perhaps areas filled with fluid,' said Salvadori.

'Good, Mr Salvadori. Thank you. Gentlemen, Mr Salvadori is correct. In these early hours post-mortem there has been insufficient time for the gases of decay to pressurise the internal cavities. Gastric pressure at this stage would likely be perimortem. Who would care to examine Mr Cox?'

Salvadori pushed forward and began the examination. Blacklock almost reached out to stop him, but with no other volunteers another moment of conflict would be pointless. Salvadori suggested that there was no untoward internal pressure. Blacklock concurred, having examined the cadaver before the lecture.

'The musculature of the abdomen, especially in a fit young man, can be difficult to dissect,' said Blacklock. He opened his instrument case and withdrew his favoured Number Three scalpel. He began the dissection without delay, narrating as he worked. 'To dissect the abdominal muscles we start with a vertical incision from the ensiform cartilage to the pubes – thus. Can somebody tell me what to do next, please? Anyone? Come on.'

When Levy spoke it was almost in a whisper. 'A s-second incision from the umbilicus to the outer edge of the fifth or sixth rib?'

'Are you sure, Mr Levy?'

After a moment of hesitation Levy committed. 'Yes.'

'Excellent.' Blacklock made the incision. 'Next?'

'It's obvious. A third cut from midway between the umbilicus and the pubes,' said Salvadori.

'How far, and in which direction? Specificity is critical in medicine.'

'Transversely outwards towards the anterior superior iliac spine, and along the crest of the ilium as far as its posterior third.'

'I have to admit that that is an excellent approach, Mr Salvadori. Well done.' He put his scalpel to one side. 'Now, gentlemen, we reflect these flaps from within outwards, in the direction of the muscular fibres ... there.'

He looked up. 'With the exception of Messrs Levy and Salvadori, who can tell me what they would do if the abdominal muscles were too slack to work with? Mr Rice, perhaps? Mr Mowbray?'

'One could–' started Salvadori.

'No, Mr Salvadori. You will let someone else answer. I believe I asked you in plain English not to share your knowledge on this topic? I will thank you to desist from any further interruptions until the class ends.' He paused. 'Messrs Rice and Mowbray are clearly somewhat taciturn today. Mr Langan?'

'I th-think that–'

Langan stopped when he saw Blacklock's raised eyebrow.

'One could inflate the peritoneal cavity via the umbilicus.'

'Good. See how far a little belief gets you? Now, come here and tell me what you see.'

Langan walked slowly forward, swallowing hard as he did so. Blacklock thought he looked even paler than usual; more cadaverous than the man split open on the table.

'I think the small intestine is dead sir.'

'Why?'

'It is blackened and seems distended. Everything else appears healthy.'

'Alright.' He held out the scalpel. 'Dissect out the offending section with a two inch margin and we will take a closer look.'

The scalpel glittered as the overhead light struck it, betraying Langan's trembling hand.

'There is no need for nervousness, Mr Langan. The patient's condition cannot be made worse.'

Langan smiled humourlessly.

'Have you taken coffee this morning, by any chance?'

'Yes sir.'

'Aha! Another opportunity to learn. In a surgical context, it is a wise practitioner that avoids such stimulants before operating. Steady hands are a must. Continue.'

At the periphery of his vision one of his audience stepped away into the shadows. Blacklock pursed his lips as the student's breakfast spattered noisily onto the tiled floor.

'Be sure to clean that up, whoever you are. Those that clean in our wake have a difficult enough task, and they are not our slaves. Who was that, anyway?'

'Brewer, sir. I'm sorry.'

'Do not waste your noxious breath on apology. You do both yourself and our patient here a grave disservice. If you persist in these ... eruptions may I suggest you reconsider your career choice? If this pantomime is repeated I will stand you down for two weeks. Do I make myself clear?'

Before Brewer could reply someone stage-whispered, 'I hope I puke soon.'

A few students sniggered until Blacklock stopped and slowly raised his head. 'I beg your pardon, I did not quite hear that. Would you care to repeat it?' The only sound was the hiss of the gas lamps. He scanned the students, briefly making eye contact with each one in turn. 'One of you is feeling terribly witty this morning. Who is it?'

All the students lowered their heads.

'Mr Brewer.' Brewer, still wiping his face with his handkerchief, stared at Blacklock, terrified. 'Please step outside and locate Mr Jenkins, who will be pleased to provide you with a mop and bucket so that you might tidy up after yourself. I for one find the odour of your partially-digested breakfast unpleasant.'

Blacklock waited for the door to close. 'Well, this is fun, is it not? Someone is quite the entertainer – a regular Dan Leno – and verging upon humorous.' He paused. 'But not in here. How many times must I remind you, gentlemen, that this is a place of respect for the deceased. These people – these *individual human beings* – were God's creatures, as much as you and I, replete with their share of hopes and desires.' He slammed his fist onto the table. 'They are not the piglets and calves you have toyed with before. I am sure that some of you may even be viewed with some affection by your parents, though I fail to see why. So were the people here, and those you will serve every day of your working life. Most are only here as donated specimens – such as Mr Cox – because their families cannot afford to bury them. *They cannot afford to say goodbye.*' He took a deep breath before lowering his tone. 'Who wished that he might become nauseous?'

No one spoke.

'If you consult your predecessors in this course you will discover that I am an exceptionally patient man – except when someone gives me just cause not to be. Has our resident comedian lost his tongue?'

The silence gave him his answer.

'It seems our nauseated companion has taken a vow of silence – a relief for us all.' Blacklock checked the wall clock. 'We are a little short of time, I am afraid, as a result of these myriad interruptions. To hasten proceedings I shall dissect the dead intestine.' He took his scalpel from a grateful Langan and began to split the section the student had removed. After a few inches the scalpel stopped. 'Interesting.' He tapped the tip of the scalpel on the obstruction. 'What do you hear?'

'Metal?'

'Ah! You *are* alive, Mowbray. So good of you to join us. Metal, you say? Let us see.' He slit the sample, and picked out the cause of the blockage. 'Any suggestions as to what this is?'

'It looks like a gold sovereign,' said Mowbray.

'Correct,' said Blacklock. 'Mr Cox here – in life – enjoyed a rather ... distant relationship with the law and was not above a little petty larceny to refill his coffers. On Wednesday he was caught red-handed, as it were, but in what clearly proved to be an unwise course of action elected the swallow the proceeds of his latest venture. He may well have hidden the evidence – until nature took its course – but alas his bounty became lodged in his gut and he died before help could be summoned. A cautionary tale for us all.'

The remainder of the lecture proceeded uneventfully. Blacklock demonstrated correct abdominal closure then dismissed the class. 'Mr Salvadori – I require you to attend my rooms at 9 p.m. sharp this evening–'

'But–'

'But?'

'It's the first ball of the semester, sir.'

'I am aware of that, Mr Salvadori, but I find myself rather concerned about this strange desire you have to voluntarily vomit and I believe that we must get to the bottom of it before you could possibly consider gallivanting. I am sure you will agree.' Blacklock stared implacably at the student.

'Yes sir,' replied Salvadori, unable to hold Blacklock's gaze.

'Are there any final questions before we close for this evening?'

A student he didn't recognise – therefore of middling capability – raised a hand. 'Yes?'

'Sir, I noticed that your primary incision was shaped somewhat like the letter S. I wondered why?'

Blacklock blinked. 'Was it?' He glanced back at Cox's chest, frowning at his own work. 'So it was. Never mind – just an old medical school habit. Anyone else?'

Silence. 'Excellent. Class dismissed, with the exception of Mr Brewer. Thank you again Messrs Levy and Langan for your valuable contributions.' The class filed out, Salvadori ensuring he was last out so that he could slam the door.

Brewer approached Blacklock, seemingly intent on studying his shoes.

'Mr Brewer, does your nausea stem from the sight or the smell of the deceased?'

'I am ashamed to say it's the smell, sir.'

'Many moons ago I was afflicted with a similarly unreliable stomach. Might I suggest a little petroleum jelly mixed with camphor or menthol, liberally applied to the moustache before the class commences? Such precautions served to tide me over until I developed sufficient strength. Do not abandon your career, regardless of what the more unkind members of the class may say. You have promise and it would be a great pity to waste it.'

Salvadori attended Blacklock's office at the appointed time. It was in darkness. An envelope was attached to the door, addressed to the student. He tore it open and held the note within up to a nearby lamp.

Mr Salvadori,

Thank you for your attendance this evening. I trust your stomach has settled. The ball started at 8 p.m., but try not to worry about what you may have missed so far. Latecomers are very strictly not admitted. I trust this period of rest and recuperation will aid your concentration in future lectures.

Dr. N. Blacklock

Eight

The Olde Bell and Unicorn Inn, Shacklewell
Lane, Stoke Newington, London
Friday 9th November

Blacklock checked his watch and smiled. 'At this precise moment, Jon, one of the most troublesome students it has been my misfortune to encounter should be learning a lesson without my even being present.'

Jonathan Starling, destabilised by the Unicorn's cheap and awful red wine, frowned. 'Well done. I think. How?'

'It does not matter but suffice it to say that he should be exceeding unhappy and consequently unlikely to disrupt my lectures again. Honestly, Jon, he has been driving me to distraction. Rich, spoilt, and entirely uninterested.'

Starling held up his filthy glass. 'To teaching!'

Blacklock touched his own glass to it. 'What has been happening in the helter-skelter world of the only actuary I know?'

'So glad you asked. Today was like any other Friday, which is to say like any other weekday. I arrived about eight, consulted myriad tables in order to upset some people with their proposed premiums and satisfy others. A light lunch around midday, followed by more tables and a deal of challenging arithmetic. If I revealed any more of the excitement I am confident you would quit butchery and join the inner circle.'

Blacklock rolled his eyes at Starling's butchery comment, which he made at least weekly. 'I do not doubt that you are right. I assume that the excitement continues unabated and unchanged next week?'

It was Starling's turn to roll his eyes. '*Every* week, Nate.' He upended the wine bottle, only for a slug of brown sediment to slide into his glass. 'Another bottle of landlord's best red passes beyond the veil. One more?'

'I think that unwise.'
'As do I. Another?'
Blacklock nodded.

Nine

Blacklock's lodgings, 64 Pellerin Road,
Stoke Newington, London
Saturday 10th November

Blacklock's head felt like it had been danced upon by a particularly weighty Suffolk Punch when he was awoken by the combination of dawn light splintering through his blinds and the calling of a paperboy. 'Extra! Extra! Read all about it! Jack's back! Jack's back!'

He pulled his pillow over his head, cursing the sun, but it did not provide sufficient sound insulation to drown out either the boy's caterwauling or the excited babbling of those gathering about him in the street immediately below his first floor window. With further curses he levered himself upright and shuffled to the window. The crowd was dispersing but still too loud for this time of the morning. The paperboy walked past, his sack empty, smiling as he tossed a coin.

'I say, boy–,' called Blacklock.

'Sorry, sir. Sold out. I've 'ad a good day.'

'What is the story?'

'Ain't you heard? Jack's back!'

Blacklock shook his head, half in confusion and half to clear it. 'Jack who?'

'Who'd'you think? Jack Tar? Jack Be Nimble? Jack the Ripper, of course. Killed some doxy down Whitechapel. G'day, sir.' The boy continued on his way, whistling loudly.

Jack the Ripper? How could that be?

Blacklock's disbelieving horror was quickly subsumed by the luxury of a day of solitude spent reading copies of The Lancet which had accumulated into drifts around his cramped room. So complete was his immersion in his reading that he forgot all about the sensational news until he was making his way home with a small loaf for lunch from a bakery in Catman Street. His highlight of the day had been Tilly's acceptance of his apology and an agreement to meet the following evening to take a stroll on the new Thames bridge.

Every newspaper shared a similar headline, designed to instil fear into the uneducated. He did not think too deeply on the subject but nevertheless purchased an evening edition of the Daily News to address his mild curiosity. He read the story over a supper at The Unicorn. There was little substance but much speculation, disguised as fact, although it was clear to even the most disinterested observer that there were certain similarities with what he knew of the Ripper era. Sir Edward Allam had been more circumspect in his language, which was possibly why his measured words did not appear until halfway down page five – presumably because they were unlikely to sell more newspapers or induce the appropriate levels of panic required to sell the morning edition of the same newspaper to the same customers. Blacklock approved of his restraint.

Blacklock stared at the dreadful red wine as he swirled it around the cracked glass.

'Penny for your thoughts, Doctor Death?'

Blacklock smiled in spite of himself. 'Jonathan Starling. How are you? Grab the least filthy glass you can from the bar and help me to kill this bottle before it turns the tables and kills me.'

Starling did as he was told and returned with a glass no less cracked and certainly no less dirty than Blacklock's. Starling drank deeply, winced, and put the glass down.

'Does the Unicorn's extensive array of vintage wines merit its own listing in your risk tables?'

'No, but you make an excellent point. I will bring up this dangerous omission with the publishers forthwith. To death-doctoring!'

'We prefer to call it pathology, you imbecile. To awful ...

whatever the hell is that you do.'

'So what do you think, Nate?'

'About?'

'The return of Jack, of course.'

'Anything is possible, although where has he been?'

'I heard a theory that he had just spent half a dozen years in prison for something else and has recently been freed so is once again at liberty to ply his trade.'

Blacklock snorted. 'I assume you read that in a Penny Dreadful?'

'I must protect my sources, Nate.'

'You are a bloody actuary, Jon, not a reporter or a policeman. The only thing you ever read are tables of risk, and only find them salacious when some proposed activity is dangerous.'

Starling took another drink. 'Christ, this wine doesn't get any better, does it?' He put his glass down and leaned forward. 'I resent these smears on both my profession and my reputation, Nathaniel Blacklock. If you do not retract them this instant I shall demand satisfaction - and I would not be a merciful opponent. There would be no coup de grâce. You would suffer.'

'I am sure I would,' muttered Blacklock. 'Would you read actuarial tables to me until I murdered myself?'

'You're familiar with my methods, Death. I see I must devise something more cunning.'

'Do not waste your time. You are puny and cannot defeat me.'

Starling shrugged. 'If you say so.' He picked up Blacklock's paper. 'I still think Jack could be back. He wouldn't be the first villain to go to ground.'

'It does not matter. That conundrum is the concern of the Metropolitan Police Service. I met one of their number – Carver, I think his name was – and I was not filled with confidence. Wait, that does not sound right - Carter? Cargill? That is it. I do not think he would have a snowball's chance in hell of catching Jack if he has come back. He could not catch a cold. In the meantime I think more wine is called for.'

Starling returned quickly with another bottle. 'Is there any other news? How is the fair Matilda? Still fragrant and lovely and life-enhancing?'

'Of course. As a matter of fact I am taking her to the Tower Bridge tomorrow evening. She has not been and I must confess I am also rather keen to experience it. I have of course admired it from ground level but I hear that one must climb to the top for the greatest effect. Have you been?'

'Not yet. I'll wait a while for the thing to settle in before I visit the top. I've walked across it at road level and that's bad enough. At the centre you can look straight through the gap and see the water.'

Blacklock laughed. 'You are too cautious, my friend. Live a little. Take a risk for once. Try to think less like an actuary and more like a human being.'

'I resent that remark, Death. We're onto our second bottle of godawful red wine in the most dubious inn this side of ... well, almost anywhere. And–' He stopped short.

'And?'

'Nothing.'

'Come on man, spit it out.'

Starling continued, noticeably less animated. 'And I don't think I would want to be under the knife of a hungover surgeon. Sorry. Not thinking.'

'That is alright. No need to walk on eggshells.'

'Any news from the–'

'None of it good. Drink up. We will talk about something else.'

Ten

Tower Bridge, London
Sunday 11th November

Blacklock checked his watch for the tenth time in as many minutes. *Where had she got to this time?* The queues to climb the stairs to the upper walkways seemed endless and he began to regret suggesting the bridge for this excursion, for he had no doubt that she would be dressed in clothing entirely unsuited to the ascent – if she came at all.

He was on the verge of leaving when she stepped from one of her father's anonymous black carriages, forty-five minutes late. 'Darling, I'm so sorry. What must you think of me? I was about to depart when I mentioned my destination to Papa and he suggested – very forcefully, if I may say so – that I wear my riding costume to afford some protection from the crowds.' She turned to her driver. 'Phelps, could you wait?'

'With all respect ma'am, not here.'

Blacklock thought he detected a hint of exasperation in the driver's voice.

'The bridge is far too busy to block by waiting,' continued Phelps. 'They'd probably call the old bill on me. I'll find somewhere along there, in Butler's Wharf. Do you know it, Doctor Blacklock? It's about four hundred yards off.'

'I do not, Phelps,' said Blacklock, still a little discomfited by the use of the driver's surname only. 'However, I am certain we can find our way. Good evening.' He offered his arm to Tilly, who wove hers through his. 'Shall we go?'

'Yes.' She stopped and peered skyward. 'Are we going all the way up there?' She pointed at the freshly-painted walkways far above, thronged with sightseers.

'We are. I understand the views are wonderful.'

Tilly looked nervously at him. 'I understand now why they call it Tower Bridge.' Before he could correct her misunderstanding she said, 'Come on. Let us go before my courage fails me. Do you think it safe?'

'Of course, Tilly.' He thought a white lie appropriate. 'I would not risk you with anything I thought otherwise. By the way, the bridge is named for its proximity to The Tower of London, not because of its height.'

Tilly rolled her eyes and walked ahead of him to join the queue for the climb.

Once they had purchased their tickets it took almost half an hour to complete the ascent, climbing one step at a time as the glacial queue snaked up the spiral staircase. The atmosphere grew close, and Tilly – not alone – complained that she may faint if she did not get some fresh air soon.

Any faintness, real or imagined, was forgotten as they finally stepped out onto the broad open walkway. Tilly bolted into the open air, like a cork from a champagne bottle. In the time it had taken them to make the climb the sun had dropped almost to the horizon, and the sudden cooling had evidently driven those less hardy from the bridge.

'We must be a thousand feet up, darling,' she said.

'One hundred and forty-three, actually,' replied Blacklock, quoting from a nearby poster.

Tilly took Blacklock's arm again, this time with real pressure, and pulled him along. 'London's beautiful!'

He surveyed the panorama through eyes more jaundiced. The East End was wreathed in yellowish smog produced by the cheap coal they burned there. The once-gilded monument to the Great Fire, now soot-stained like the rest of the city, still managed to catch the final rays of the setting sun and even Blacklock had to admit its magnificence.

A large clipper was approaching from downstream. They

watched as it dropped anchor while a small steam tug was swiftly tethered to its bow. A gong sounded far below. Through their feet they could feel the vibrations of some hidden machinery of immense power growling into action. At the next instant the crowd below cheered, followed by those on the walkway as the gigantic bascules began to lift. Briefly Blacklock felt as though he was falling, although of course the bascules were tilting upwards, towards him. In a few moments the bridge was open.

With a tinny whistle the tug huffed into action as it pulled its enormous cousin – slowly at first, then quickening – through the bridge. The watchers on their level held their breath, sure that the mast of the vessel would strike the walkway, but it passed harmlessly below them with a clearance of several feet. Some of the crowd expressed their disappointment that there had not been some calamity, thus depriving them of their role in a potential naval disaster.

Throughout this Tilly clung ever tighter to Blacklock's arm. 'Thank you, darling – this is simply the most exciting evening.' As they continued to watch, the road decks rotated swiftly back into position and traffic seethed across the bridge once more.

'I have nothing to say, Tilly, that would not be the most profound of understatements. This is more magnificent than I ever could have imagined,' replied Blacklock.

'That's 'cos you ain't 'ad me, lovey!' squawked a woman's voice from the shadows, followed by the raucous laughter of her companions.

Blacklock blushed to his boots. 'Come, Tilly, we must be getting along.'

'Ooooh, hark at him,' said the same woman. 'He thinks he can make her come just because he commanded her to! He must be very blessed in the bedroom department.'

He took Tilly's arm and virtually dragged her to the centre of the bridge where the crowds were sparse and there were fewer shadows to hide undesirables.

'Was she...' asked Tilly, in a hoarse whisper, 'was she ... fallen?'

'I believe so, my dear. I had heard rumours that such women frequented the bridge but I assumed that by now a constable or two would have been stationed up here to deter such offensive verbal attacks on innocent passers-by. I am minded to write to the Chief Constable tomorrow.'

'Don't worry on my account, darling,' said Tilly. 'Papa says it takes all sorts to make a world. And I must add that rubbing shoulders with such ne'er-do-wells has made the evening even more memorable, although I should be ashamed to admit such thoughts to anyone but you.' She shivered. 'I think it is time for us to head back down to earth and find Phelps. I find myself rather chilled here, although I beg you to bring me back when the weather is more clement.'

'We shall fix our return date as soon as possible. I often thought that had I been better at mathematics than biology I would have liked to pursue a career as an engineer such as Brunel, or as an architect like Wren. This confirms it. My arm, Miss Caldecott?'

They had covered no more than twenty paces before a booming voice called, 'Pathos? Is that you?'

Blacklock stuttered briefly in his step before continuing with renewed vigour. The exit staircase was only fifteen yards distant.

'I say! Hello there! Pathos!'

A milling crowd queued for the narrow door, slowing their pace.

'Is that gentleman talking to you, Nat?'

'No more so than the previous woman, I am sure. Why is everyone so *slow*? Have these people never seen a staircase before?'

They managed another couple of steps before a powerful hand clasped Blacklock's shoulder. 'It *is* Pathos! Our sixth Musketeer!'

Blacklock gave up his hope of escape and turned, a false

smile in place. 'George! What a pleasure!'

The red-headed giant pumped Blacklock's hand hard. 'What a coincidence! How long has it been? Seven years? Eight? I thought it was you and I shouted but you couldn't hear me.'

'I am sorry, George. One cannot hear anything above this hubbub. And it has been six years since Leeds.'

'Apology accepted and duly disbelieved.' He turned to Tilly as if seeing her for the first time. 'And who is this fine vision of womanhood?'

'This is Tilly – Miss Matilda Caldecott. My fiancée,' he added as if this would invoke some form of magical protection. 'Tilly, this is George Porter. We studied together in Edinburgh and later we were briefly reunited at Leeds General Infirmary.'

Porter bowed elaborately and kissed Tilly's hand. 'Miss Caldecott, I have never been more charmed. Fiancée, eh? Pathos is a lucky man.'

Blacklock squeezed her hand to signal their need to make their excuses but her expensive schooling had imbued her with an excess of politeness.

'I'm very pleased to make your acquaintance, Mr Porter. Do you have a family, sir?'

Porter laughed uproariously, which Blacklock found unseemly. 'I may have, Miss Caldecott – one can never be too sure of such matters. If there are any Miss or Master Porters running wild I haven't met them yet.' He laughed again. 'Where are you practising, Blacklock? I'm at Barts. I'm surprised I haven't seen you at The College-'

'Which is where we can continue this conversation at a later date, George. I am sorry but Tilly and I must rush off – we have another engagement. Good evening, George.'

'Don't be so hasty, Pathos. I'm dining alone this evening at Bateman's, on The Strand. I would consider it a personal honour if you would both dine with me. At my expense, of course.'

Blacklock tried to walk on. 'As I have already said,

another time, George. I must get Cinderella here home before her coach turns into a pumpkin.'

Porter was undeterred. 'Miss Caldecott, please talk some sense into this fiancé of yours. I haven't seen him for so long, and when I do he's found himself the most charming companion.'

Blacklock felt Tilly weaken. 'We'd be delighted, Mr Porter. Ignore Nathaniel – he can be such a grump sometimes. If you don't have a carriage you may share mine.'

Realising the battle was lost Blacklock said, 'Alright. We accept, George. Our carriage is waiting at Butler's Wharf.'

Tilly placed her cutlery daintily on the side of her plate. She had hardly touched her meal.

'You've barely eaten anything, Miss Caldecott,' said Porter. 'It is fortunate that you are in the company of two doctors who will be able to revive you should malnutrition get the better of you.'

She blushed deeply. 'Mr Porter, I have eaten more than enough. The portions here are overly generous and I wish to stay slim for my nuptials.'

Porter inclined his head, smiling. 'As you wish.'

'Why did you call Nathaniel Pathos? *Oww!*'

Blacklock had meant to tap Tilly's shin gently under the table but misjudged his movement. 'I am so sorry Tilly, I can be so clumsy.' He turned to Porter. 'George, what happened to you after you left Leeds?'

'Not so fast, Nathaniel. I do believe that Miss Caldecott had a question. Have you not told her the tale of the Six Musketeers?'

Tilly clapped her hands joyfully. 'No, he hasn't! Have you some terrible secret, Nathaniel? As your wife I should know every detail about you!'

Blacklock sighed. He was beaten, and shrugged carelessly to indicate as much.

'Nathaniel,' mocked Porter. 'I'm appalled that you should hide what must surely have been one of the highlights of your life – present company excepted.' He leaned conspiratorially towards Tilly before he continued. 'The story starts two decades ago on the wet and windy streets of Edinburgh...'

'Get on with it, if you must,' said Blacklock. 'Spare us the melodrama.'

Porter laughed. 'Once upon a time there were six medical students–'

'*Six?* My goodness! Nat said he had no friends at all at medical school. And he was a *Musketeer?*' said Tilly.

'We styled our little group of friends so. There were five of us who were already established musketeers – technically trainee surgeons, but where's the romance in that? The Three canonical Musketeers are Porthos, Aramis and Athos. I – Porter – became Porthos. Arthur Robertson – 'AR' – naturally became Aramis. Charlie Gordon became Athos even though we couldn't forge even the most tenuous link to the text. We co-opted M. Treville and D'Artagnan as monikers for Edward Ballantyne and Dougie Priestley respectively. In the book a poor fourth musketeer joins the group, who is D'Artagnan from Gascony. By now Nathaniel here had attached himself to our little group as the sixth member, so naturally his nickname should have been D'Artagnan – the fact that D'Artagnan is of ... humble origins was a perfect match. However, Priestley was already D'Artagnan so we invented Pathos to reflect our new friend Blacklock's less fortunate background. From that day forth we were The Six Musketeers. In retrospect it all seems rather childish but at the time we considered it terribly dashing.' He paused, but Tilly said nothing. 'So that's the tale in a nutshell. We were the terrors of the taverns, the beasts of the bed–.' He cleared his throat. 'The terrors of the taverns.'

Blacklock was relieved that the most damaging parts of Porter's narrative seemed to pass Tilly by without the need for further explanation.

'Then where are the others now, Mr Porter?'

'I'm afraid, Miss Caldecott, that I have lost touch with

them. Arthur Robertson was mad-keen on God and left the profession immediately after graduation to become a missionary somewhere on the Dark Continent, I believe. I don't think his limited skills would have been missed, least of all by his patients. A rumour circulated that he had returned to England – Brighton? Bristol? I don't recall. Priestley was an alcoholic even when we knew him and therefore presumably either died in a gutter somewhere or still lives in one. I dimly recall that Ballantyne became an army surgeon and disappeared almost immediately to a warmer but far-flung corner of The Empire, so I would be very surprised if he hasn't found himself with a cannonball in his vitals by now. Gordon – I've no idea, just as I had no idea about young Pathos here until this evening. Anyway,' he beamed – 'so ends the tale of the five and a half Musketeers, idealists who flew like Icarus only to fall and break on the rocks of reality. It's a crying shame, but there you are. Youth is a wonderful thing if you meet life head-on.' He turned back to Blacklock. 'I don't think you said where you are practising.'

Blacklock considered lying but there was no opportunity with Tilly present. He sighed. 'I am working as a pathology lecturer at Prince Albert's. My surgical licence has been temporarily suspended by the College–'

'*No!*' breathed Porter. He turned to Tilly. 'Nathaniel was the best of us. What on earth happened, man?'

'My appeal is still outstanding and therefore you will understand that I cannot discuss it.'

'Quite, quite. How long?'

'That's immaterial–'

'Nine months!' exclaimed Tilly. 'It's a dreadful strain. My poor Nat seems to have aged ten years in that time.'

'Nine *months*?' echoed Porter. 'That's an outrage, Blacklock. You must consult a lawyer. My family retains an excellent fellow–'

Blacklock raised his hand. 'I have done so, to no avail. The College doesn't recognise legal representation for disciplinary matters.'

Porter puffed out his cheeks. 'A rum do indeed. I assume a patient died?'

'For the last time, Porter, I cannot and will not discuss this with you or anybody else.'

The combination of his outburst and scarlet blush told Porter all he needed to know.

With a forced calm Blacklock continued, 'Now, Tilly, I think it is time to let George enjoy his dessert in peace. Good evening, George. Come along, Tilly.'

Eleven

The Caldecott Residence, 17 Belgrave
Square, Knightsbridge, London
Sunday 18th November

Sunday morning was traditionally marked by the Caldecott household's day of empty ritual. Blacklock had risen early in order to black his boots and hat and brush as much dust as possible from his ageing suit. His one collar was almost beyond use, but Sir Edmund had presented him with one of his staff's cast-offs so that his prospective son-in-law would not appear too down-at-heel during the Sunday services, which were required attendance for all ranks above under-maid within the Belgrave Square residence.

Watson ushered Blacklock in a few minutes before the carriages were due to depart.

Sir Edmund was already bellowing. 'Watson! Watson! Where is my half-crown wallet? We've only minutes before we leave.'

Blacklock exchanged a glance with the butler, whose trepidation was clear as he spoke. 'Sir, with the utmost respect, of course, are you sure you do not mean your threepenny wallet? The morning service is low church.' The butler's hands were shaking.

'What?' Sir Edmund shouted. '*What?*'

'It's the low service, sir. You normally take threepenny pieces for that.'

'Of course,' huffed Caldecott. 'You know very well what I meant. The threepenny wallet, obviously. And the dice.'

Without comment the butler retrieved them from the drawer in the console table, where they were always kept. 'Sir Edmund.'

'Good.'

Caldecott rolled the three dice. 'Six. Excellent. That'll keep the paupers on their leprous toes.' He counted out six threepenny pieces from a shimmering velvet bag. 'We shall be free of them early today. Before we leave it seems that my luck is running so I shall also throw for evensong.'

He rifled through the drawer again. 'Is the half-crown wallet here, Wat–. Ah, yes.' He picked up the dice and rolled them again. 'Sixteen? Far too much. I refuse to waste two pounds on beggars.' He rolled again. 'Seven. That's better.' He counted the coins into a second wallet. 'You do not build or maintain wealth by giving money away, Blacklock.' He checked the hall clock. 'Come. The Lord does not appreciate tardiness.'

'Is there any news on a constituency, Sir Edmund?' Blacklock detested such sycophancy but wanted to finish the conversation on a higher note.

'Not yet. The Chairman of the party tells me that the sitting MP in Peterborough North is not long for this world so I should be a shoe-in there. I don't even know where the dashed place is – somewhere in Suffolk I think – but I don't expect to be there very often, if at all.'

'Would you not move there?'

Sir Edmund laughed. 'Good Lord, no! I couldn't run my businesses from *there.* Besides, there's probably no society worth the name within a hundred miles.'

The Caldecott household's six-carriage convoy made its way slowly to St. Aidan's. Even though Phelps was leading Sir Edmund's carriage on foot the journey only took a few minutes, the church being perhaps eight hundred yards from the house.

As they approached the poor, separate lines of women and men held out their hands for alms. Even from the second carriage – Blacklock was not yet eligible to ride in the first with Sir Edmund and Matilda – he could hear Caldecott commanding them to wait in an orderly fashion. 'Patience is a virtue, my friends. There's plenty to go round.'

He doled out his alms. 'My goodness! I only have six coins on my person. I am sure there will be more next Sunday.'

The unlucky majority moved away, afraid to show any disappointment.

Blacklock patted his pocket – there was a handful of loose change. His driver, whose name he could not recall, opened the door and dropped the steps to allow the doctor to alight. A couple of optimistic stragglers looked at him, their expressions mixtures of hope and tragedy. 'I am sorry but I have nothing. Perhaps next week.'

He walked quickly past them and into the church to join Tilly in her pew, which was immediately behind her father's front row position. There were a few minutes to spare before the service was due to commence. Blacklock surveyed the congregation. A frisson passed through him – people were looking at the Caldecott family, huge benefactors of the church, and despite all its associated superstition *he was part of the Caldecott constellation.*

The rector, who looked long overdue for his own appointment with his maker, struggled up the three steps into the pulpit. With palsied hands he fumbled his spectacles into position. From his vantage point Blacklock could see the morning sun as it shone through the lenses. They were so marked by greasy fingerprints that he doubted they assisted the clergyman at all. 'We shall start with hymn number–.' He hesitated to squint at his notes. The verger had already posted the hymn numbers of the pillar next to the pulpit and around the church. 'One hundred and eleven,' announced the minister with an air of triumph. 'All Things Bright and Beautiful.'

'Chas Darwin made them all,' Blacklock stage-whispered to Tilly, who responded with a silent but wide-eyed admonishment.

Caldecott's voice boomed above all. *As if God himself was auditioning for piety*, thought Blacklock. Tilly sang very well, years of expensive schooling in trivia including such instruction. Blacklock struggled to concentrate, his mind wandering widely as he waited for this, the first act of the weekly pantomime, to pass. *Did anybody actually believe?*

They retook their seats as the hymn finished. Tilly squeezed his hand surreptitiously. He turned and smiled his smile of forbearance, which she returned with a comical frown, a co-conspirator in his heretical performance.

The rector was by now mumbling more-or-less incoherently, rambling across diverse topics of faith and duty. Blacklock itched to consult his watch, aware that in the afternoon they would all repeat these roles learned by rote, simply in a different building with a better – i.e. wealthier – congregation, where Sir Edmund was not yet the Father of the House.

The service dragged on – thirty minutes, an hour. At one point Sir Edmund delivered a reading with great vigour, to which Blacklock made an effort to pay especially rapt attention, ensuring he made eye contact with Caldecott whenever possible.

When the reading had ended Blacklock found that his mind roamed freely once again, trying to identify any evidence which might help his case with the College.

At last the Sunday morning torment ended and the entourage processed in equally stately fashion back to Belgrave Square. A light lunch was waiting; it would not do to nod off during the afternoon's cathedral service. Blacklock managed to snatch a few moments of stilted conversation with Tilly, although the bulk of the lunchtime discourse, such as it was, consisted of Sir Edmund's usual self-aggrandising commercial monologue.

'I have decided, Blacklock,' he said in closing after Tilly had left to change, 'to release you from this afternoon's commitment. You are free to leave.'

Blacklock's immediate joy was quickly tempered. A display of such generosity had to have more value to Caldecott than the recipient.

'Thank you, Sir Edmund, but I am more than happy to

attend the service with Matilda and you. It is always an honour.'

Caldecott rolled his eyes. 'I see I must make myself clearer. I was trying to spare both Matilda's and your feelings but I deem your attendance at such a service as an adjunct to the Caldecott family inappropriate until your professional standing is restored. You are welcome at the low church morning service as ever but I regret that where the cathedral service is concerned the Caldecott family must obviously cleave to a higher standard. You may go. I will inform Matilda of my decision and your opinion when she returns.'

'But surely I–'

'No, Blacklock. My decisions, within and without this house, are irrevocable. Good day.'

Twelve

The School of Medicine, Prince Albert's
Hospital, Fulham, London
Friday 23rd November

Blacklock stood back from the cadaver, which had its ribs splayed. 'In this case, and perhaps unusually, you can clearly and immediately ascertain the cause of death. Mr Buchan here was a sixty-seven year old gentleman and – as you can see – excessively corpulent. When we opened the abdominal cavity it was literally awash with blood. Observe his aorta – note how distended and loose it is. The tear you see was not the result of clumsy scalpel work when making the incision. The aorta had developed an aneurism – carrying so much weight for so many years is hard labour – which burst due to the thinning of that vessel's walls. The saving grace is that the patient succumbs in very few minutes, sometimes less. He suffered far less than his good lady wife who witnessed his demise, helpless to prevent it. Mr Mowbray, do you think that any form of clinical investigation prior to this catastrophic event would have–' He stopped as the door to the laboratory opened. Miss Henry entered.

'Yes?' he snapped.

'I'm sorry to interrupt, Doctor, but there's a gentleman to see you.'

'Please have him wait until the end of my lecture, Miss Henry.'

Miss Henry looked over her shoulder into the corridor. 'I don't think that will be possible. I suggest you may prefer to step out and see him.'

Blacklock pursed his lips. 'I am *teaching*. He can either wait or bring his business in here.' He turned back to body.

'Doctor Blacklock,' said Miss Henry who had by now crossed the room, 'please accept my word on this occasion that you must see the gentleman immediately, and outside.'

Blacklock sighed as he wiped his hands on his apron. 'Very well. Gentlemen – please continue to examine the body, but do not touch. I shall return directly.'

As the door closed behind him Blacklock hissed 'This is most irregular, Miss Henry. It will not do. Do I make myself clear?'

'As crystal, Doctor. However, since your visitor is a policeman I thought it better that you meet him out of sight of your students, which I also thought *would not do.* I hope I make myself clear.'

Before Blacklock could respond they passed through the double doors which opened into the surgical school's reception area. A gimlet-eyed man got to his feet as they entered, his dusty brown bowler held in both hands. 'Doctor Blacklock. I'm Ser–'

'Yes, yes, Sergeant Carter. I remember you. I presume you have some progress to report with respect to the desecration of the cadaver?'

Miss Henry turned away and walked back towards her office.

'That is no longer an active case, Doctor. And the name's Cargill. I'm here on another matter – I'm sure you know what that would be.'

'I am sorry, Sergeant, but I have no idea.'

'Ah, well. The short answer is that Sir Edward Allam has had a severe turn overnight and has ... passed beyond the veil.'

Blacklock frowned. 'You mean he is dead.'

'If you wish to be so blunt, yes.'

'So?'

'We - that is, Her Majesty's Metropolitan Police – are investigating the murder of a young woman from Whitechapel.'

'I am fully aware of that, Sergeant. Every newspaper hawker from here to Dover is shouting about it. I still do not understand–'

'We need a new police pathologist and you have been recommended to us, sir.'

'By whom, may I ask?'

'I don't know, sir. I've just been sent to get you. Or rather, ask you.'

'I will need some time to think about it, Sergeant Cargill.'

Cargill looked away and tutted.

'There is no call for such rudeness, Sergeant.'

'I'm sorry, sir. No rudeness intended. I was just imagining my Inspector's reaction.'

'I cannot help that. It is a problem beyond my control. I am a surgeon first and foremost, saving lives, and an educator second. I cannot easily make space in my life for a third role. Good day.'

Blacklock turned on his heel.

'Thank you, sir. Please communicate your decision to me, care of Leman Street Station.'

Blacklock raised his hand in acknowledgement without turning back, then stopped in his tracks. 'I assume this is not a voluntary position.'

'Beg pardon, sir?'

'I presume that I will be compensated for my pains if I am to take this role?'

'Of course, sir.'

'In that case, please inform Inspector Duncan that I accept on a trial basis. It is also contingent on my being able to fit my police duties around my lectures. Finally, I can only accept this position as an interim appointment because I expect a change in my primary role soon. I will meet your Inspector ..?'

'Duncan, sir.'

'Please inform your inspector that I will meet him at Leman Street Police Station at seven prompt on Monday morning. Good day to you.'

He pushed back through the double doors, leaving Cargill frowning.

On the way past reception Blacklock encountered Miss Henry. 'Thank you for your considerate handling of what could have been a delicate situation – your judgement was impeccable. I am grateful not to have to explain a visit from the police, even entirely innocent, to my students. They only hear what they want to hear, much like most dogs.'

Miss Henry nodded, smiling. 'Always pleased to help, Doctor Blacklock.'

Thirteen

Leman Street Police Station, Shadwell, London
Monday 26th November

'Ah! Professor Blackmore. So good of you to join us. Tea, Cargill – pronto.' Inspector Duncan motioned to a chair. 'Sit.'

Blacklock sat. 'It is Blacklock. Doctor Blacklock.'

'Yes, yes, very good,' huffed Duncan. 'You're a detail man, I suppose, which is appropriate for this sawbones thing you do. I assume Cargill outlined the job? Allam was very good but never going to last forever at his age, especially with so much port and brandy on board. I'll give the old bugger one thing, though: he knew our game almost as well as he knew his own.'

'I see.' Blacklock was determined to remain aloof. 'I thought I would only be required to understand medicine. Perhaps a little about the human body. I did not expect to have to learn your job too.'

Duncan's mask of affability fell away. 'I think we need to understand each other–'

The door opened and Cargill almost tiptoed in with two teas in tinplate mugs. 'Leave 'em on the desk Cargill, then get out.'

With his back to Duncan, Cargill rolled his eyes and left.

'Where was I?' asked Duncan.

'I think you were about to lecture me on our need to understand each other?' Blacklock did not want to throw this chance away but equally he did not expect to be treated like a scullery maid in the Caldecott household.

'Right,' said Duncan, gulping his tea then wiping his mouth on the back of his hand. 'You may think you're awful clever, and not fit to mingle with those that work in the street, but you're dead wrong. I do my research and happen to know that you're already in a spot of bother with the

College of Surgery or some such and aren't doing much of anything at the moment. Your shoes are worse than mine, and if your hat hasn't been polished with boot black then I'm a monkey's uncle. Don't pretend you can take or leave this job, Prof.'

Blacklock swallowed hard and then took some time to calm himself and gather his thoughts before replying. *How much does this man know?* 'My personal situation, Inspector, is not of your concern and if we are to work together I will thank you to keep your opinions to yourself. Do we understand each other?'

'Of course, Prof. I think we see each other pretty clearly.' The glint in Duncan's eye told Blacklock that they both understood that the scales were weighted in the Inspector's favour.

'Very good. Did the Sergeant mention my query with reference to compensation?' Blacklock blushed and despised himself for it.

Duncan attempted a smile which became a leer. 'Yes.'

'And?'

'Well, as with so many things in these difficult times it depends.'

Blacklock sighed, already tired of Duncan's idiotic games. 'On?'

'Whether you take the job on a permanent basis or temporarily. Temporary means we'd pay you per corpse - piecework, if you will. Thirty bob a body. Permanent and we retain you whether there's a stiff or not – fifteen bob a week. I don't want to play games. I want to know where I stand. Sir Edward managed to limit himself to just one job, God rest his soul.'

'But he was no longer a working surgeon.'

They both realised what Blacklock had said. Duncan simply raised an eyebrow.

Blacklock, uncharacteristically flustered, went on. 'What I mean–'

'I know full well what you mean, Prof.' He smiled

humourlessly. 'The notice period is ninety days. You could take the retainer and give notice if – sorry, *when* your surgery career restarts. What do you say to that?'

'An interesting question, Inspector. Before I answer, please tell me whether Sir Edward had completed his work on the poor girl from Whitechapel?'

Duncan's predatory smile returned. *The fish was hooked.* 'Why do you ask? Keen to sign on?'

Blacklock smiled back. 'Keen to "understand your business". I need to know whether there are any loose ends, so to speak.'

'You're out of luck, Prof. Sir Ed had finished his work and submitted his report before he died so there are no easy pickings for you.'

Blacklock nodded. 'I simply wanted to verify that the family of the victim of the putative Jack The Ripper would not have to wait longer than necessary for the body, that is all. My answer, Inspector, is no. I do not wish to work for or with the police. The compensation is frankly derisory – as surgeons we train for seven years, but we never stop learning and refining our craft. Thirty-nine pounds a year does not come close to buying that experience.' He rose and picked up his hat, suddenly wary of the boot polish he had used to black it. 'Good day, Inspector. I sincerely hope that you find someone to fill the post.'

With a calculated flourish he turned without waiting for a response from the dumbfounded Inspector.

As he stepped from the office, closing the door behind him, Cargill started from his desk.

'When do you start, Doctor Blacklock?'

'I do not, Sergeant.' He almost shared his distaste for Duncan with Cargill but opted for diplomacy. 'Unfortunately it would be too much of a commitment from my already stretched schedule. Thank you for your kind consideration and I wish you luck with your search. Perhaps we will meet again.'

Fourteen

The Caldecott Residence, 17 Belgrave
Square, Knightsbridge, London
Sunday 9th December

Blacklock brushed the dust from his hat, patted down his topcoat, buffed his toecaps on the calves of his trousers, straightened his cravat and walked up the steps to the front door of Tilly's father's house. He checked that he had a few coins for the poor. Impression set, he rang the bell which sounded faintly in the bowels of the almost-mansion. He smiled as he heard the butler's stately progress telegraphed by his heeltaps across the tiled floor. The door swung open.

'Dr Blacklock. Good morning.'

'Watson, so good to see you. You're as radiant as ever.' He made to step past the butler but the old man sidestepped with unexpected agility to fill the doorway, making passage impossible.

'I'm sorry, Doctor, but your entry to the house is not permitted.'

'Really? Oh dear? Is Miss Caldecott unwell? If so, I am a doctor after all–'

'No sir. She is, to the best of my knowledge, perfectly healthy sir.' Watson handed Blacklock an envelope from the small console table beside the door. 'I have been instructed to give you this missive, sir.'

It was simply addressed to 'Doctor N. Blacklock' in Matilda's flowery hand. Before he opened it he sniffed it – no perfume.

'Will that be all, sir?'

'I – er – are you sure I cannot come in?'

'Completely and absolutely, sir. Good day.' With that, Watson shut the door emphatically but stopped short of slamming it in Blacklock's face.

Blacklock half-walked, half-staggered down the steps and crossed the road to the iron railings opposite. He inspected the front of the envelope, then the reverse as if there might be some hidden clue he had missed. There was nothing. He reluctantly hooked a finger under the flap, broke Tilly's vivid red wax seal, and withdrew a single sheet of paper.

Dear Doctor Blacklock,

It is with regret that I must sever our engagement, effective immediately. Please do not attempt to contact me again because my decision is irrevocable.

Regards,
M C D Caldecott (Miss)

He flipped the page for a clue, or perhaps a punchline to accompany this terrible joke, but it was blank. *Irrevocable? Wasn't that her father's word?* *Regards?* He shoved the letter back into the envelope and fell back against the railings which surrounded the small garden-cum-park in the centre of the square. He glanced up at the house to see Tilly looking back at him from an upper window. Her expression was unreadable.

'Tilly!' he shouted as he sprinted across the street, heedless of a fast-approaching hansom. 'Tilly, please!'

She turned away from the window and walked back into the depths of the house.

I must speak to her! He diverted towards to the steps but Phelps blocked into his path. 'That would not be a good idea, sir. I think the best thing for you would be to head for home or to an inn to drown your sorrows.'

'But you cannot–'

'I can, Doctor, and I am. Sir Edmund and Miss Caldecott are both most insistent that you be kept away, and that's my job. I don't wish to use force to do so.'

'Are you *threatening me*, Phelps?'

Phelps smiled. 'Of course not, sir. Why would a humble servant like me threaten a gentleman such as yourself? I've never heard such a thing.'

Blacklock's shoulders slumped in submission.

'Now, if I were you sir, I would take myself along to The Olde Bell and Unicorn, order myself a bottle of my favourite red wine and see if I couldn't cheer myself up. What do you say?'

'Alright, Phelps. You win.' He thrust his hands into his pockets and walked slowly away, knocked far off centre by this turn of events.

He was half a mile away before it occurred to him to question the fact that Phelps knew the name of the inn he frequented when it lay far off in another borough.

Fifteen

The School of Medicine, Prince Albert's
Hospital, Fulham, London
Monday 10th December

After a sleepless night Blacklock wandered distractedly into college, racking his memory to recall where he had left off at the end of his previous lecture, which now seemed to be in a land lost in time where he and Tilly were together. Hell, he had been *engaged* at the end of his last teaching session. For once he found himself gloomier than the fog.

On his bench in the laboratory a terse note requested the pleasure of his company in the Principal's office. Sighing, he checked the clock. It was twenty minutes before his lecture started, which allowed sufficient time to see Moore and get back.

Miss Ellis smiled briefly as he entered.

'Good morning, Miss Ellis.' He showed her the note. 'Do you know what this is about?'

She shrugged noncommittally. 'Please go straight in, Doctor.'

'The way my life is going I suppose I am about to lose my position,' he joked, turning away without pausing and missing the secretary's horrified expression.

Principal Moore looked up as Blacklock entered. 'Please sit down, Doctor Blacklock.'

Alarm bells began to ring at Moore's unaccustomed formality.

'I won't beat about the bush. I have received a complaint about your conduct.'

Blacklock was almost too tired to register surprise. 'From whom?'

'That's irrelevant.'

'That is *preposterous*, Principal! What is the nature of the complaint? Who made it? How can I reply to it if I do not know its nature?'

'Did you purposely humiliate one of our students in front of his classmates?'

'No. Absolutely not. I will not deny asking testing questions, but I believe I am fair to everyone.'

Moore drummed his fingers on the desk. 'Did you ... engineer a student's exclusion from the term ball?'

Blacklock shook his head in disbelief. 'Salvadori.' *Of course.*

'Did you or did you not engineer circumstances such that he was refused entry?'

Blacklock squeezed his eyes shut and ran his fingers through his hair. 'Inadvertently, yes. I called him for a disciplinary consultation after an incident in my lecture.'

'A consultation which you chose not to attend yourself?'

'I was unfortunately delayed.'

'And yet you managed to leave a note on the door of your rooms. Interesting chronology.'

Blacklock had been caught in his own lie. 'Alright. Yes, Principal, I made him miss the ball because he behaved appallingly in my lecture *again*. He is continuously, incredibly, constantly disruptive. The boy is incorrigible.'

Moore sighed. 'It is a teacher's lot to rise above such things. I wish *you* had, Blacklock.'

'So do I, now.'

'Were you aware that Salvadori's uncle is on the board of governors for this institution?'

'Oh for God's sake! Really?'

'There is no need for profanity, and I will thank you to refrain from such utterances in my presence.'

'I apologise unreservedly, Principal,' replied Blacklock, hoping that his response sounded authentic.

'I could suspend you without remuneration or remove you from your post without notice.'

Blacklock bowed his head. 'I know.'

'But that would leave me without my lecturer in human pathology, and the students would suffer. What would you do in my situation, Nathaniel?'

'What if I apologise to Salvadori?'

'You will obviously be doing that anyway. The question is what *else* I should do.'

All Blacklock could hear was the blood rushing in his ears. He shook his head.

'I think a final written warning will suffice, with the expectation of flawless behaviour for a year hence. What do you think?'

'Does my opinion matter?'

Moore smiled humourlessly. 'Not a great deal. You can accept the warning, or resign, or be dismissed. Salvadori has friends in high places which is unfortunate for you. If you had managed to rile any other student there would probably have been no repercussions.'

Blacklock held his hands up in surrender. 'Alright, Principal, I accept the warning. Can I go now? I would hate to be late to my lecture and attract a further complaint.'

'A wise decision. You head off. The paperwork will follow in due course.'

Blacklock rose to leave.

'One more thing, Doctor Blacklock. I should not have to say this but clarity is everything. There are to be absolutely no reprisals against Salvadori, or indeed anything that could be construed as such, even in the most twisted of interpretations. Please do not put either of us in that position.' Moore turned back to the papers on his desk, dismissing Blacklock by ignoring him. Blacklock's audience was over. Briefly uncertain, he nodded awkwardly and left Moore's study.

Miss Henry glanced up as he re-entered the surgery faculty. 'I hope the meeting was satisfactory, Doctor Blacklock.'

He pursed his lips. 'I still have my position, so I suppose

so.'

She smiled, so fleetingly that he thought he might have imagined it. 'I'm so glad, Doctor. Here is the letter the Principal mentioned.'

Sixteen

Blacklock's lodgings, 64 Pellerin Road,
Stoke Newington, London
Saturday 15th December

Blacklock was awoken from a night of fragmented dreams by hammering on the external door which separated the central stairwell serving each bedsitting room from the street. A voice called up at the windows. 'Professor Blackmore! Professor Blackmore, come quick!'

He donned his robe before shuffling downstairs to the door, silently praying that his landlady and the other tenants had not been disturbed. The clock in the hall read a minute or two after four. 'What do you want? It is the middle of the night.'

'Messenger, sir. I've got a note from the Leman Street Station, sir. From Inspector Duncan.'

In his state of undress Blacklock had no desire to open the door. 'I surmised as much. Can you read it out, please?'

'No sir. Sorry sir. Can't read.'

Blacklock tutted. 'Slide it under the door.'

The sealed notepaper duly appeared below the door. He reached down and unfolded it. The hand was uneven, the quality of the line blotchy. *Dear Blackmore. Attend Leman Street soonest. Your expertise is needed. Thirty-five bob. I. K. Duncan.*

Blacklock needed no second invitation. He opened the door. 'Please wait here a moment.' He returned to his room and came back with twopence to tip the messenger. 'Please inform Inspector Duncan that I will attend as soon as I am dressed.'

The boy vaulted down the steps and into the darkness beyond.

Blacklock dressed quickly and carelessly. A glance in his corroded looking glass made him hope fervently that he met no one he knew – he had not even bothered with a cravat. He placed his surgical instruments case into his Gladstone and dashed into the night.

Seventeen

Leman Street Police Station, Shadwell, London
Saturday 15th December

A small but vocal crowd was gathered at the entrance to Leman Street Station. Blacklock forced his way through, only to find his way barred by the biggest police constable he had ever seen. 'I must enter, officer, I have been called.'

'Look mate, that ain't going to happen. No press.'

'I am not press. I am Doctor Black–. Blackmore. Inspector Dun–.'

'Well why didn't you bloody well say so then, and save us both a lot of time?' The constable stepped aside to allow Blacklock to pass. The crowd surged behind him but the giant easily held them back.

Sergeant Cargill was smoking in the bleak corridor beyond. 'Doctor Blacklock, this way, please, and hurry. The Inspector ain't renowned for his patience.' Cargill led the way past cells and huddles of uniformed officers then down a steep staircase into the cell-lined basement.

'Surely she isn't here, with the *criminals*?'

'No, sir.'

Set into the wall at the far end of the cells was an ancient door, more broken than intact. Cargill took a candle stub from a box on the wall and lit it before he opened the door. 'There's a spiral staircase here, Doctor. Proper wicked. Watch your step or you'll break both our necks.'

The steps were worn, their edges rounded. Damp from the walls seeped onto them, rendering them doubly treacherous. The very atmosphere felt thicker than air, miasmic. The bottom of the staircase opened onto what appeared a long tunnel – another candle guttered ineffectually in a sconce on their left. On the right they passed a row of disused cells, like barred stables. In the poor light Blacklock caught glimpses of their contents: abandoned furniture, tarpaulins, wooden barriers and many specialised items beyond his capability to identify. The knots of uniformed officers split to allow Cargill to pass.

The penultimate cell was illuminated by an oil lamp close to the wall, its wick badly trimmed. The smoke streaked the distemper with soot before pooling above them against the curved brickwork.

The body lay on a rough wooden table.

Duncan was leaning against the wall, arms folded. The butt of an extinguished cheroot hung from his lip. 'Blackmore, about bloody time. Got a fresh one for you.' Once again Duncan's eye shone with an unpleasant glint, something akin to glee. 'Whaddya think?'

The oil lamp with its soot-blackened mantle was wholly inadequate for medical purposes – barely sufficient to reveal the profile of a body. A girl or woman – it was hard to discern which – lay at the periphery of the flickering light, her torso covered by a filthy blanket which had evidently been hastily retrieved from a nearby cell.

Sensing Blacklock's disapproval Duncan said, 'It was all we could find to protect her decency, Prof.'

'Is it possible to improve the ventilation down here, Inspector? With the damp and smoke it is difficult to breathe, let alone concentrate.'

'Nope. Sorry Prof. This level ain't really been used since it was condemned back in – oh, sometime around late sixties or early seventies, I reckon. I'm pretty sure Prince Albert was dead, anyway. There used to be vents to street level but they was always filling with horseshit, especially when it rained, so we gave up on the place.'

'It feels like an oubliette.'

'A what?'

'Never mind.' Blacklock fought the impulse to start his physical inspection. 'When and where was she found?'

'Somewhere in Whitechapel.'

'*Somewhere in Whitechapel?* What does *that* mean? Why

is she even here?'

'The chap that found her – a passing costermonger – carted her to the nearest charity hospital but there was clearly nothing to be done, so they turned him away. To his credit, he took a barrow and brought her here. There was nothing we could do to prevent that.'

'Is the crime scene being secured?'

'Two things, Prof. One – you're just a half-legit knife for hire, so you do what I tell you when you're on my shilling, or thirty-five shillings in this case. Two – I'm the bleedin' copper, don't try to tell me my job. Stick to those rules and we won't fall out.'

Blacklock pulled back the top portion of the blanket and studied the face of the young woman, and the faces of the young policemen looking on, suddenly interested in lurking in the noxious damp of the station sub-basement. Incensed, he decided that they could discover what they wanted to know of female anatomy in the fumbling dark – this was not the place to sate their curiosity. 'Could you all leave, please? The post-mortem examination is about to commence. There is no need for extraneous observers.'

He waited until they had slunk away before peeling back the fetid covering.

His breath stopped. The girl was rent open like something in a slaughterhouse. 'What animal ..?' He looked away, drew breath and tried to regain his sense of detachment. 'You sick bastard!' Blacklock surprised himself by using such language out loud, even if he was the only one to hear it.

'God bless her soul,' whispered Duncan, so quietly that at first Blacklock did not believe what he had heard.

'Prayer is the last resort of the uninformed, Inspector. Pointless superstition.'

'But there might be something to it. It can't do any harm for this poor girl.' Duncan spat on the floor and walked out.

Blacklock sighed as he withdrew a pad and pencil from his bag, committing to record what he saw as faithfully as possible. He had just started sketching when Cargill returned.

'Sir, the – Jesus Christ! What sick shit did that?' hissed Cargill. 'Oh my God. It's Jack, ain't it?'

'I do not know, Sergeant Cargill. I need to complete my examination and sketches. Even then, I obviously will not know who is responsible. Only what they did and why or how they caused her death.'

'Sorry sir. Anyway, the photographer has arrived – he is setting up his processing equipment in Cell 7 at the moment.'

'Photographer? *What* photographer? Who asked for one?'

'Oh yes, sir. The work of the police pathologist is always photographed now, to help with their reports. Sir Edward started the practice a while back.'

Blacklock was uncertain, vacillating between the accuracy of a photographic record and the dignity of the victim. 'Very well, Sergeant, the photographer is permitted to record the injuries. If I sense anything less than gentlemanly discretion in his manner I shall eject him. Please pass that message on.'

'What message would that be?' asked the photographer, shuffling in with a large wood and brass tripod.

Blacklock found his Irish accent almost impenetrable, but bit his tongue. 'That you treat this victim – any victim – with the utmost respect, sir, and do not take any images for ... titillation.'

The photographer nodded curtly, diverting his gaze from the body. 'Naturally. You determine what, if anything, is to be recorded. The compositional choices are yours. Francis McCormac, at your service. Friends call me Frank.'

Blacklock offered his hand before realising how bloody it was. 'McCormac. Nathaniel Blacklock. Doctor.'

'Shame about Allam kicking it. He was a good old stick.'

'I am sure he was, although since we never met my knowledge of him and his working practices are minimal.'

'I can help you out. Let me get the rest of my gear set up and I'll be ready when you are, Doc.'

Before Blacklock could correct this overfamiliarity McCormac left. He took a deep breath then turned back to the murdered woman and began to assess her injuries.

'Doc?'

Blacklock fought his rising impatience. 'What now, McCormac? I am trying to work and your continual interruptions are extremely unhelpful.'

'I'm sorry, Doc. I just wondered whether I might be able to assist in any other way? Not medically, you understand, but I have a very legible and fast writing style. You could dictate your views instead of losing your concentration ...' Seeing Blacklock's frown he trailed off.

The doctor looked back at the appalling remains. 'Thank you for your kind offer. It would be very helpful under other circumstances, I am sure, but–'

'But?'

'But without medical training I am sure you would stumble over key words and phrases and despite your best efforts slow everything down.'

'Try me. A few sentences. You have nothing to lose.'

Blacklock surveyed the photographer for several moments. 'Why are you so keen to assist, Mr McCormac? One would have thought your photographic skills sufficient support.'

'Where were you in '88, Doc?'

'I was a General Surgeon at Leeds Royal Infirmary. Is that relevant?'

'My cousin was Mary Guiley.'

Blacklock shook his head.

'Still no idea?'

'I am afraid I have no more time for these guessing games, McCormac. If you will permit me to continue my work we can complete this aimless discussion another time.'

McCormac stood his ground. 'Mary was the third victim

of Jack. Her husband lost his mind and murdered himself in '90. I want to see Jack hang, Doc, and would do anything to further that cause. The police never acknowledged that she was a victim but we knew better.'

Blacklock's irritation dissipated instantly. 'I am sorry for your loss,' he replied automatically, then kicked himself for such a trite response. 'I am sorry, I meant–'

McCormac smiled to ease Blacklock's embarrassment. 'It's alright, Doc, It seems that nobody has quite the right words for such occasions.' He clapped his hands together. 'Do you want to begin? I assure you that I can keep up.'

'Of course,' said Blacklock, keen to move the conversation on. 'We start at the head... No obvious injuries. Opening the collar we have – oh. That *is* odd.'

McCormac turned to him, pencil poised.

'The victim's throat has been cut, but there is very little evidence of bleeding. There are only a few trivial bloodstains.' He stopped and peered more closely. 'I believe this wound is a post-mortem injury. Only just, perhaps, but I do not think her heart was beating when this cut was made.'

As if returning from a distraction he asked, 'Have you got all that?'

'Verbatim.'

'Really?' He glanced at McCormac's pad. His eyes narrowed. 'Is that... Pitman writing?'

'Shorthand? Yes, it is.'

'You must leave, McCormac – if indeed that is your real name. I will not have this poor woman's death splashed across whatever tawdry rag it is that you work for.'

'I am not a reporter.'

'Sergeant!' bellowed Blacklock.

Cargill bustled in.

'Sir?'

'Please escort this ... individual from the premises.'

The sergeant glanced at McCormac and back to Blacklock. After a slight hesitation he said, 'May I ask why?'

'I believe him to be an imposter. I think he has infiltrated from the press.'

Cargill's brow furrowed. 'I don't think he is, sir. Mr McCormac assisted Sir Edward on many occasions.'

'He can write *Pitman*, Sergeant. That must be proof enough?'

'Of course I can,' said McCormac. 'I trained as a journalist before I discovered photography. I can assure you that everything I said is true.'

Blacklock began to realise the gravity of his error and coloured accordingly. 'I am merely trying to ensure that this tragic woman is accorded the respect she deserves.'

'And so she shall be,' said McCormac. 'I think you can go now, Sergeant. I should have been clearer with Doctor Blacklock.'

Blacklock cleared his throat and mumbled an apology. 'Let us get on, shall we?'

The victim's chest, back and arms displayed no signs of trauma, so Blacklock moved onto the wound site and began to dictate. 'The instrument used at the throat and abdomen appears to be the same. It must have been a very sharp weapon with a thin, narrow blade at least 6 to 8 inches in length, probably longer. The injuries could not have been inflicted by a bayonet of any kind. They could have been done by such an instrument used for post-mortem purposes - ordinary surgical cases might not contain such an instrument. Perhaps something used by a slaughterman, well ground down, might have caused them. Knives used by those in the leather trade would not be long enough in the blade. There are indications of anatomical knowledge.'

He glanced up and caught McCormac looking too. 'I will thank you to avert your gaze unless you are engaged in photography.'

McCormac shrugged and turned away.

'A further incision has been made from the navel down to ...' He fell silent.

'What?'

'Nothing, McCormac. Just...' He became still and silent, more mannequin than surgeon. It was unmistakable. The victim had been opened with an Edinburgh Incision. *Had she been murdered by a Musketeer? Porthos?*

'Are you alright, Doc? You look quite pale,' said McCormac.

Blacklock's mind was racing too fast to permit reply. He breathed deeply to regain some control. 'I felt a little faint, McCormac. I must have turned around too quickly.' He took another breath and pretended to continue his examination. Safe in the knowledge that there would be no further scrutiny of the body he moved quickly through the exposed abdominal tissues, even though he was preoccupied with the killer's identity. He allowed McCormac to expose a couple of plates before closing the wounds as well as he could.

Meanwhile, the photographer quickly transcribed his Pitman into English, the resulting notes proving remarkably accurate.

'Well done, McCormac,' said Blacklock. 'Most impressive. I hope we will work together again.'

McCormac looked at the body, now covered by the cleanest sheet they could find. 'I hope not, Doc. If I never saw such a spectacle again it would be too soon.'

Eighteen

The Olde Bell and Unicorn Inn, Shacklewell
Lane, Stoke Newington, London
Sunday 16th December

Starling slammed a large glass of whisky down on the inn table. 'Drink that, Nate. You look like you need it. I called at your lodgings earlier but you weren't there. I wondered whether this whole Tilly thing–'

Blacklock waved his hand impatiently. 'Never mind that. Her loss.' Blacklock picked up the glass and cradled it. 'I have spent most of the day on a problem I feel may prove insoluble.'

Starling sat down. 'Fire away.'

'You must give me your word that you will not tell a soul.'

Starling frowned. 'Of course. Goes without saying.'

Blacklock took a deep breath. When he spoke, his voice was barely a whisper. 'I do not know what to do, Jon. The incision on last night's murder victim was made by one of the others from Edinburgh. There's no doubt.'

'The others? Which others?'

'My cohort at medical school. The so-called Musketeers.'

Starling examined Blacklock before looking out of the inn window. 'Think logically, Nate. Perhaps the practice has spread, which would simply make it coincidence. Or, one cut looks pretty much like another and you were tired. You told me yourself how poor the lighting was down there.'

'The practice, as you call it, was limited to the six of us. It became a habit - one of my students noticed me doing it the other day, and I had not done it intentionally. We believed it reduced post-surgical wound infections.'

'And you kept that to yourselves? What about the–?'

'Hippocratic Oath? I know. We concluded that better survival rates would be good for our careers, so we did not share our belief with anyone else.'

Starling examined his own whisky intently. 'That's shameful. Nevertheless, you should go to the police with this.'

'I cannot do that.'

'Why ever not? Of course you must!'

'Think about this, as I already have. If I go to Cargill, he will go to Duncan, who is itching to make an arrest – he strikes me as a glory seeker. Four of my confederates are innocent. If I name any of the others he will simply apprehend the first one he can and have them strung up in some God-forsaken prison yard. Their innocence or otherwise will be completely irrelevant. You are a professional probability man. There is a four-fifths chance of an innocent man dying – and the guilty one escaping.'

Starling looked at Blacklock. 'Tricky. And it's a five-sixths chance.'

'Why?'

'Mathematics, that's why. Because you are also one of the set that makes that incision. If you tell Duncan you will also be a suspect – *and* the closest to hand. Not a position I would wish to voluntarily place myself in.'

Blacklock puffed out his cheeks. 'I had missed that joyous nuance. Trust a mathematician. What am I to do, Jon?'

'Isn't it obvious, Nate?'

'If it was I would not be asking for your advice.'

'If you are unwilling to trust the police then you will have to discover which of your erstwhile colleagues is the new Jack.'

'That is a ridiculous notion. I am not a police officer.'

'I know, but equally I see no alternative. How many of your new police chums do you expect to do the correct thing when there's a mob baying at their door? Or would they simply do the most expedient thing? Professionally speaking the least risk to your life and prospects is best served by not involving the police until you have irrefutable evidence against one of the others. Unless it *is* you, of course, in which case you can happily implicate whomever you dislike most. In my own self-interest I would also point out that you have a life insurance policy with us, which we would much prefer not to pay out on. It lapses without payment if you're executed. Nothing personal.' He smiled. 'Another drink, Blacklock of The Yard?'

'So that is the best plan you can come up with?' asked Blacklock when Starling returned from the bar. 'I become Sherlock Holmes?'

'No offence, Nate, but I don't think you have the brainpower. Logic's not your strong suit.'

Blacklock struggled to focus on Starling, The whisky was exacting its toll. 'I take exception to that. And besides, I have met several detectives lately and believe me, their collective intellect is no match for mine. On a bad day, barely a match for yours.'

Starling glared back. 'Alright, so be it.'

Blacklock said, 'Share your plan, Watson.'

'Later, Nate.' He squinted at his friend. 'You are having a little difficulty thinking at the moment. Besides, it doesn't require any intellectual leap to determine that the culprit is obviously this Porter fellow. He's in London, after all.'

'I do not believe it could be him.'

'On what basis? Please show your working.'

'Porter was – is – a great surgeon. Back in Edinburgh he used to take time away from his own studies to assist us all. Yes, he was brash and louche and more than a little unreliable – especially where women were concerned – but his heart is good and I believe that at least professionally his moral compass is genuinely true. We had a falling out in Edinburgh, the details of which are immaterial, and we lost touch afterwards. We were reunited, quite by accident, when Leeds General Infirmary employed us both – quite independently. As the only Scots on the staff we naturally spent time together and I discovered to my surprise that he had matured, at least a little. I saw him smuggle unfortunates from the free queue on more than one occasion when there were officially no beds available for charity cases. He once saved a man – in the street – whose abdomen had been rent in a knife-fight with little more than a nail and a shoelace to stitch the wound. It was not cosmetically pleasing, of course, but a life saved is beyond price. For all his bluster and obvious turpitude he is fundamentally a decent man. That said, if I had a sister I would rather send her to the moon that allow her to spend an hour alone with him.'

'Really?' asked Starling.

'I would obviously not quite go to that extreme but my sentiment holds true. Women do seem easily swayed by his dubious charms. Suffice it to say that he has broken many more hearts than he has repaired. I am pleased that I have no sister which frees me of that concern. However – to answer your question – I cannot think him capable of anything like this. It has to be *one* of the others.' Blacklock yawned expansively. 'I must get to my bed.'

Starling shook his head as bare-headed Blacklock weaved his way to the door, ricocheting off other drinkers, who, similarly inebriated, shrugged off his minor assaults. He turned to Starling, almost falling over in the process, saluted and turned back. He opened the door, and Starling could see past Blacklock into the night beyond. Huge drops of rain fell across the doorway, and further out the rain slanted in the street light. He waited for Blacklock to return but oblivious to the weather the doctor struck out for home. Starling smiled to himself, picked up Blacklock's shabby topper and set course for his own lodgings.

Nineteen

The School of Medicine, Prince Albert's
Hospital, Fulham, London
Tuesday 18th December

Blacklock smiled and rose as McCormac entered his college study, his preferred meeting location given the demeaning nature of his own lodgings. 'Francis, please take a seat. May I offer you some tea?'

McCormac's eyes narrowed. 'No thank you, Doc.' He cocked his head. 'I don't like this. How did you find me?'

'I told the sergeant that I wanted to check some details in my report against your photographs and he gave me your address.'

'I brought the prints with me.'

'I am afraid I do not want to see them. They were the best ploy I could come up with. I'm sorry.'

'So what do you really want?'

'It is all perfectly innocent, I assure you. I will get straight to the point. When you said you trained as a journalist, how much did you complete?'

'Assuming you mean "of the course", I graduated. Why?'

'Did the course cover investigation?'

McCormac frowned but said nothing.

'I am sorry, Francis, I really am not making myself clear. Do you think you could locate a particular individual?'

McCormac shrugged. 'It depends, of course, on how much information one has to begin with, and how keen the quarry is not to be found. Hiding is considerably easier than finding.'

'And if they do not know anyone is looking for them?'

'In that case, it could – should – be relatively simple.' McCormac paused for thought. 'So. No more prevarication. Who are you looking for and why?'

Blacklock quickly précised Porter's summary of the other

Musketeers' histories.

'That's not very much, Doc. I can't search the Empire to find your army doctor, but a Scottish missionary in Bristol or Brighton shouldn't present too much of a challenge. The alcoholic could be most difficult of all. There's not much documentation for deadbeats. Why do you want to find them?'

'It's a private matter, Frank.'

'I see. Tell me anyway. Any knowledge you have will make my task easier.'

'It's not that simple.'

'So?'

'You would not understand.'

McCormac rolled his eyes. 'Try me.'

Blacklock sighed. 'I cannot. There are risks–'

'Then I can't help. If I don't have the full story I've got one arm tied behind my back.' McCormac got to his feet. 'See you around.'

'Please, Francis – Frank – my position is impossible. I do not know where to turn.'

McCormac sighed and sat down again. 'Just spit it out, man.'

Blacklock slumped back in his chair and exhaled. 'It may be possible - let me stress, *possible* - that one of my old medical school cohort is the murderer of the young woman we examined on Saturday. Only poss–'

'*What*? You have a name for the Ripper? We must go to Dun–'

'NO!' Blacklock rubbed his temples. 'No. It is one of five individuals, I believe, and revealing just one of them would be tantamount to murder. You claimed you would do anything to obtain justice for your cousin. Would you want revenge at the cost of justice for someone else? I ask because I know that I am taking a huge risk in entrusting you with this information and I hope you will appreciate the gravity of the situation and conduct yourself accordingly.'

McCormac sucked his lips. He looked at the back of his

hands as if he might find inspiration in them. 'Alright. Do you have a picture? A group photograph from your graduation, perhaps?'

'I do not have one here but my aunt may have. I shall telegraph her immediately.'

'Whoa! There's no rush. Why should I do this for someone who only three days ago tried to throw me out of my legal employment because I can write shorthand?'

Blacklock studied McCormac carefully. 'Is it all true, the story you told me about your cousin?'

'Absolutely. I'd swear on the Bible if there was one to hand, but you don't strike me as that sort.'

'I need to find the survivors from my cohort and sort the innocent from the guilty. I cannot do that on my own – I would not know where to start. You have the skills and motivation to help catch the perpetrator.'

'How can you be so certain it's any of these friends of yours?'

'There were certain ... tell-tale characteristics in the butchery which indicates to me that the crime can only be the work of one of five individuals.'

McCormac sat forward in his seat. 'But in that case ... it could just as easily be you!'

'Of course not. Others might think so, if this information comes to light, so I am trusting you at the hazard of my life. If this information falls into the wrong hands an innocent man could die.'

McCormac said nothing for several minutes, mainly looking anywhere but at Blacklock, occasionally staring intently at him. 'I'm not sure I can help.'

'Why not?'

'Wasn't there a hoo-hah a couple of months ago at the college where you lecture? Didn't a body–'

'Yes, a parlourmaid's body was mutilated. What of it?' said Blacklock irritably.

'Did she bear the same hallmark, whatever it is?'

Blacklock sat up. 'A good question. I do not know. Allam

examined the body when it was removed from The School.' He frowned. 'Wait ... Were you called to photograph the remains? If the pictures are of sufficient quality–'

'Let me stop you there, Doc. I was not called. No one was. Because the poor girl was not murdered, our mutual friend Duncan deemed such recording an 'extraneous expense'. Only Allam's notes will exist. His sketching capabilities were negligible, which is how I got involved with all this is the first place.'

'Damn!' said Blacklock before recovering. 'I apologise, but it is all so frustrating. The mark we are looking for is so subtle that it is vanishingly improbable that Allam would have spotted it. If his drawing was as bad as you claim there would be nothing to see.'

'It was worse. I was being generous about Allam's artistic abilities, being unwilling to speak ill of the dead.' McCormac became serious once more. 'Do you *actually* believe that one of your colleagues was Jack?'

Blacklock flinched as if he had been struck. 'I hope to God not but I am not sure of anything anymore. Will you help? Please, Francis? I am a proud man and not in the habit of begging but I need someone with your training on my side.'

McCormac exhaled loudly. 'I'm still not sure, Doc. Whether my skills are sufficient for what you require, I wouldn't know. I am also not convinced that you have told me everything I need to know. I must see all of your cards if I'm to help. This is a risky occupation for me too. I would be conspiring to conceal evidence in a murder enquiry, if I'm not already doing so. I shudder to think what the penalty for that might be.'

Blacklock sighed. 'I know of nothing else I can say to persuade you.'

'Why were you suspended by the RCS?'

'How do you know about that?'

'There are few secrets in a police station, Doc. Duncan probably wanted everyone to know to keep the upper hand. He's a nasty piece of work. So?'

Blacklock looked at the floor. 'I killed a patient – or rather, more accurately, a patient died after I operated on her.'

'I'm sorry, Doc. But why are you only suspended? I thought you would have been struck off, or even jailed?'

Blacklock snorted. 'Surgeons have some licence in the eyes of the judiciary. My patient – a young lady called Mary Banville – was admitted with crippling stomach pain. I can still recall her screams, even though they were almost drowned out by those of her mother.' He sighed. 'She was quickly etherised, ending her screaming and calming her mother. I opened the abdomen and found a diseased artery to her kidney, which I removed. Regrettably there was a very unusual malformation of additional veins which I inadvertently severed. She passed away before I could control the bleeding.'

McCormac looked confused. 'Would she not have died anyway?'

'In all probability. However, Mary died as a result of *my* intervention and therefore I bear "last touch responsibility". Usually such investigations are a formality but for some reason which I cannot fathom the College seems to be taking an especial interest in the case.'

'So you're telling me that it's an occupation hazard?'

'It is not always seen that way. From the mother's biased perspective Mary was alive when she entered the theatre and ... well, never came out. She complained and shouted and wept to anyone and everyone who would listen and something had to be seen to be done. Therefore I was suspended by the College and cannot practise until that suspension is lifted. The only bright spot is that her family is too poor to launch legal action.'

'And you call that a "bright spot"?'

Blacklock shrugged. 'You know full well what I mean. It would be just another complication which I did not need.'

'But you yourself just said the she would have died anyway if you had not operated, so any trial would have cleared you.'

'Your confidence in the judicial process is touching but naïve, Francis. Jurors are laymen, and laymen cannot possibly understand the complexity of what we do. If I were *actually* judged by a jury of my peers – a dozen surgeons – I would be practising today.'

McCormac bit his lip. 'But ... in effect ... surely you *are* being tried by your peers within the College, and yet ... you're suspended. I don't follow.'

'Ha! Those that would seek to judge me still believe in bloodletting with leeches. The twentieth century is around the corner and surgeons are still treated like witches, even by their supposed peers. It is preposterous.'

McCormac nodded thoughtfully.

'So, are you going to help me, Francis – Frank – or not? If not for my sake, then for your cousin? The young woman killed on Saturday – Jenny Greaves, I am told – suffered terribly at the hands of whomever did this, be that Jack or his facsimile.'

McCormac massaged his temples between his thumb and forefinger. 'Alright, alright. My mother and stepfather live near Bristol. I am due to visit them for Christmas anyway, and I will see if I can track down your associate while I'm there. My stepfather and I don't see eye to eye on anything so it'll be a pleasure to have an excuse to get out of the house.'

Twenty

The Olde Bell and Unicorn Inn, Shacklewell Lane, Stoke Newington, London
Thursday 20th December

'Nate, can you explain this latest madness in words of one syllable, or preferably less?' asked Starling. 'You are telling me you have persuaded a police photographer to run off to Bristol on a wild goose chase to find one of your Musketeers? How much have you paid him? You keep telling me you have no money, yet here you are trying to set up your own police force. What's next? Charming the leaves from the trees as an encore?'

Blacklock shook his head. 'It is not like that, Jon. He also has a vested interest. I helped him understand that we are aligned in our pursuits.'

'You "helped him understand", eh?' He took a deep draught of his ale, their joint finances not even running to the Bell's wine. 'Was it manipulation or blackmail?'

'That is not fair, Jon, and I think you know that.'

Starling shook his head noncommittally. 'Do I? Don't be so sure. It's one of them, no matter how you might try to window-dress it. Are you setting another of your agents after Porter?' The light dawned in his face. 'Wait ... Am I one of your "agents" now?'

'No, Jon. For one, I do not have "agents", and two, I am very unhappy about the way you are painting this. I intend to investigate Porthos myself.'

'You do? How? Which of your imaginary investigative skills are you going to bring to bear?'

'If you are going to do nothing but mock you should leave now.'

'Sorry, Nate, but can't you see that you are taking this all too far? Six weeks ago you would have laughed at anyone behaving as you are.'

Blacklock shrugged. 'But a lot can change in a short time.'

They drank in sullen silence for a few minutes.

'So tell me about your plan to find Porter.'

'I am not minded to do so, Jon. I do not think you are feeling particularly receptive.'

'Alright. I promise to give you the fairest hearing I can.'

Blacklock examined Starling, his face expressionless. After a further pause, he continued guardedly. 'He practises at Barts, I assume as a General Surgeon because he showed no interest in specialisation – beyond debauchery – when we were in Edinburgh. His improvement was only marginal, several years later in Leeds. As far as I can see I just need to station myself outside Barts' staff entrance and wait for him to appear.'

'Great plan,' groaned Starling. 'Is that the whole thing?'

Blacklock shrugged. 'Yes, I am afraid so.'

'Won't he recognise you?'

'Not if he heads into the East End. There are precious few street lamps, and those that exist are filthy and shed virtually no light. I have walked through there on occasion – very rare occasion – and conclude that one could very easily remain completely anonymous. Like Jack, I suppose.'

'It is not a great scheme, Nate. What about your teaching?'

'Porthos – Porter – is mortal, just like you and me. I can assure you that when one spends any prolonged period standing in theatre one is good for nothing afterwards. George Porter will be no different. In fact, given my current employment I am likely to be to be far less tired than he.'

Starling laughed. 'You can be quite persuasive when you choose to be.'

'Hmmm. Perhaps. Ask Matilda.'

'Alright. Maybe not with fair maidens, but in general?'

Blacklock smiled.

'So, Nate, when does the surveillance commence, and – I cannot believe I'm saying this – can I be of any assistance in this mad scheme of yours?'

Blacklock smiled more broadly. 'I wondered whether you would ever ask! I might keep the Starling arrow in my quiver–'

He broke off as a familiar figure approached the table.

'Doctor Blacklock, I'm so glad to have found you.' The visitor turned to Starling. 'So sorry to interrupt your libations, sir, but I have business of a personal nature to discuss with the good doctor here. I hope you might be persuaded to excuse us for a couple of minutes?'

Blacklock held up a hand to stop Starling, who was already on his feet. 'It is quite alright, Mr Phelps, there are no matters which cannot be discussed in front of my friend Starling here.'

Phelps raised an eyebrow. 'In the normal way of things, sir, I'm sure that's correct, but I bear a confidential message which I have undertaken to deliver under conditions of the strictest privacy.'

'Mr Phelps, Jon, is Tilly's father's driver.'

'Oh, I *see*,' said Starling. 'In that case it's clear that someone has reconsidered their position, which is obviously a very private situation. I need to absent myself for a few minutes anyway – too much volume in ale – so I will leave you to it. Pleasure to meet you, Mr Phelps.'

'Likewise I'm sure, sir.' Phelps watched as Starling weaved his way through the drinkers to the lavatory. As he turned back to Blacklock his smile vanished. 'This is a simple message, Doctor, so I will keep it quick. Lay off, alright? Sir Edmund will not stand for Miss Matilda's being distressed so you can cut out your antics now. Understand?'

'No ... what? I do not know what you are talking about.'

Phelps leaned forward across the table. 'Don't give me that old bullshit, Blacklock.' He lowered his voice to a whisper. 'You are only going to get one warning. After that, things could get more ... difficult. You're only getting a bleedin' warning now on account of Miss Matilda's past fondness for you. Do not make me or one of my less even-tempered associates come back to discuss this again. Do I make myself clear?'

'Not at all, Phelps. Apart from the not so thinly-veiled threats I do not have the slightest idea what you are talking about.'

'You've been seen, Blacklock, so don't come the innocent with me. It won't wash, me old china.'

'I am telling you Phelps – Mr Phelps – that I have not been near the Caldecott residence since Miss Caldecott so unceremoniously terminated our engagement, which you witnessed. I swear on my li–'

'On your life, Doctor Blacklock? Please don't be so melodramatic. I'm sure it won't come to that.' He nodded at Blacklock's hands. 'However, you are real fond of the tools of your trade, aren't you? I'm a reasonable man, Doc, and I work for a reasonable gentleman. You leave Miss Caldecott alone – let's say I don't find you within half a mile of Belgrave Square – and your hands won't suffer any more unfortunate accidents. It wouldn't be a bit of hot soup, neither. Do we understand each other?'

'But I have not–'

'Do we understand each other, Doctor?'

Blacklock shrank in his chair. 'We do, Mr Phelps, although–'

Phelps cocked an eyebrow.

'Although, Mr Phelps, I genuinely have not been anywhere near the house. If you catch someone lurking, do whatever it is you do to people *to them*. It will not be me.' Over Phelps's shoulder Blacklock saw Starling zigzagging back. 'Here comes Starling. Please look after Miss Caldecott.'

Phelps nodded almost imperceptibly as Starling reached them. 'Goodnight, Doctor Blacklock. A pleasure, Mr Starling.'

Starling waited until Phelps had left. 'So? That was all most mysterious. What did he want?'

'He warned me to stay away from Tilly.'

'But I thought you were? Surely you haven't been

harassing the poor girl?'

'Of course not! What sort of a man do you think I am?' He pulled his watch from his waistcoat. 'I am about done-in, Jon, and I am sure you must have a thrilling morning with your slide rule in prospect. What do you say we call it a night?'

'As you wish, Nate. Don't forget my excessively selfless and generous offer to assist with your detective pastime. I might get to despatch some awful villain with said slide rule.'

Twenty-One

St Bartholomew's Hospital, City of London
Sunday 23rd December

Two freezing evenings – enlivened only by the imaginative and athletic propositions of wandering whores – elapsed before Blacklock finally glimpsed his quarry. His sanctuary was within the porch of an inn across the road from the hospital. The inn was long-abandoned, haphazardly boarded up with bills posted upon the walls. At least the roof was intact, protecting him from the fitful snow, although the broken windows offered no respite from the icy wind. His fingers and toes were painfully numb and he shivered so much that he almost missed the moment when Porter emerged from the south entrance, wearing a broad-brimmed felt hat and a dark cloak, sensible apparel on such a bitter evening. When Porter had passed, and Blacklock was sure that he had not been seen, he stepped from the frigid shadows and began to follow.

As they threaded their way through the dark courts and alleys, Blacklock keeping about twenty seconds behind his quarry to maintain a manageable number of people between them, it occurred to him that he did not know where Porter lived, and it was conceivable that he might simply follow his old comrade home and freeze stupidly outside whilst Porter sat comfortably at his own fireside. *What a fool I must be!*

They soon reached a point in Old Nichol where the streets were so narrow and labyrinthine that Blacklock became certain that he would not be able to find his way out of the maze, a thought which oppressed him. Whom could he ask? How might he explain himself?

The balance between the opposing follow and retreat thoughts was tipping overwhelmingly towards retreat when Porter stopped at a recessed doorway in the narrowest of alleys. Blacklock was almost thirty yards behind him, but the area teemed with, it appeared, hundreds or thousands of near-identical men, women and children, scurrying who knew where. Most individuals reflected their surroundings – filthy, noisy, restless. Occasionally a pathetic child flower-seller would pass, bright carnations serving only to highlight their dire circumstances. The proximity of so many *bodies* in such confined thoroughfares made Blacklock feel both physically sick and not a little frightened. He would be sure to bathe whenever he eventually returned to his rooming house, whether or not Mrs Mason had any hot water available.

He was wrenched from his reverie when a sliding panel in the door opened, a pale golden glow illuminating Porter's face, spotlighting him amongst the milling crowd. He leaned forward and spoke a few words. The door opened, spilling more warm light into the alleyway. This time the passers-by glanced in, as if keen to discover the secrets within. The door closed as quickly as it had opened, plunging the alley back into darkness.

Screwing up his courage Blacklock moved down the alley, wanting to dawdle but unable to do so, caught as he was in the flood of humanity coursing over every square inch of whatever Godforsaken place this was.

As he approached the door he stepped smartly to the right to find himself in the doorway recess, like Porter had been moments before. A rising shame filled his throat. Fear of discovery, the thought of having to answer for the conduct that had brought him here. Paralysed, he simply stared at the door.

An authoritative voice startled him. 'For God's sake, man, are you going to knock on the bloody door or not?'

'S–sorry.'

The doorway was so narrow that there was no room to permit the gentleman behind – who undoubtedly *was* a gentleman – to pass. He tried to think but as his did so an arm clad in an expensive camel coat reached past him and rapped on the door. Horror-struck, Blacklock was pinned to the spot, waiting for the sliding panel to open. A second later it did. 'Who's there?'

Blacklock's throat constricted, rendering him unable to utter a sound.

'It's Jof,' said the gruff voice over his shoulder. 'I cannot answer for this mute statue of an idiot blocking the doorway.' The door opened.

With that, Blacklock felt a shove in the back which propelled him across the threshold. He passed through a beaded curtain into a small vestibule.

An elderly but immaculately-dressed woman contemplated him, arms folded. 'Yes?'

Before he could reply she looked over his shoulder. 'Jof! Please come through. I believe Vanessa is free at the moment.' The blunt man barged past him. 'And you,' said the woman, glaring at Blacklock, 'what do you want?'

'I ... do not know.'

'What are you doing here then? Only men with particular and refined tastes find their way to our humble premises. Were you invited by someone? Were we recommended to you? Do you have a card?'

Aware that telling to truth at this juncture could only prove damaging, he struggled to find an alternative. 'I ... am lost. I wonder if you could direct me to ... Long Acre?' He blushed.

The previously stern woman smiled. 'You aren't lost at all, are you, my dear? You're nervous. Bless you.' She reached out and took his hand. 'Come with me. I'm sure we can find you an understanding companion. Is this little adventure a Christmas present to yourself?' She drew back the velvet curtain behind her and led him into a lounge area beyond. Blacklock gasped as he saw perhaps half a dozen women and girls reclining shamelessly in their foundation garments. The nearest of them, a petite woman of perhaps forty turned and smiled at him around a cigarillo which was clenched between her teeth. She patted the couch. 'Why don't you come and sit down next to Auntie Maggie and tell me exactly what you'd like to do. It could be exciting for both of us – a handsome gent like you.' She peered over the arm of the chaise. 'Looks about a size twelve boot to me, girls.'

The others laughed raucously. 'You're a lucky girl, Mags. A twelve!'

'I do not see what relevance my size of my foot has–' He stopped, suddenly and acutely aware of the subtext of the conversation, and horrified by his own naïvety. Aflame with embarrassment and driven almost to apoplexy by his innate politeness he mumbled an apology and fled back through the curtains to the street door, which was unforgivingly locked. He fought desperately to free himself but was unable to do so. Tears of anger and shame pricked his eyes, blurring his vision in the already dim light and making escape seem like an ever more remote possibility.

An elegant hand, placed gently on his arm, moved him to one side. The brothel's madam easily undid the locks and opened the door. As she stood to one side she said, 'Don't worry, darling. It's not only women that make nervous virgins. We will welcome you back when you're ready.'

He blundered back into the alley and the mass of bodies flowing through it. He was convinced that people were looking at him, smirking, aware of where he had been and judging him accordingly. Caught in the flow, a leaf in a brook, he was carried eventually to a quieter court. He rested his head against the rough brickwork, blessedly cool where the fog had condensed upon it.

He did not know how long he spent there, but when he eventually felt calm enough to retrace his steps he noticed that no one paid any attention to him. Each was intent on their own journey.

Twenty-Two

*The School of Medicine, Prince Albert's
Hospital, Fulham, London
Monday 24th December*

Blacklock inhaled deeply and surveyed his students. 'Welcome back. I trust you are all well rested.'

The only response were the usual lifeless murmurs. 'Well, what an enthusiastic brigade you are. Nevertheless, it is Christmas Day tomorrow and a time of goodwill so let us try to remain good-humoured and well-mannered today. Any questions before we commence with the structures of the leg?'

A hand snaked lazily up.

'Mr Salvadori?' Blacklock fought every urge to comment further.

'Has anyone been apprehended for this mutilation of the lady's maid in the cold store?'

'Not that I am aware of. Anyone else?' he asked, in a tone so cold that no one would dare have another query. He waited a few moments. 'Good. Let us begin.'

He lifted the cloth which covered the examination table. 'An unusual pathological specimen today, because the donor is still alive. The poor unfortunate attempted self-murder at Monument Station on the City and South London Railway. Miraculously, as some of a religious bent might say, the intense electrical current cauterised most of the major blood vessels contemporaneously as the locomotive severed the limb. The chap – one Samuel Smith – is senseless on opium to ease his suffering but at the moment is still very much alive.

'Did he give his permission for his limb to be used in this manner, Nathaniel?' asked Salvadori.

Blacklock pursed his lips. 'Doctor Blacklock, Doctor or Sir are the only acceptable forms of address for the teaching staff in this institution, Mr Salvadori. Would you care to rephrase your question with appropriate respect?'

'No, *Nate*, I won't. Did this man give his permission or not for you to pilfer his leg?'

'Salvadori, I–'

'Mister Salvadori, if you don't mind, Blacklock. It's a more appropriate level of respect. Don't you agree?'

A few barely-suppressed sniggers stoked Blacklock's anger but he nevertheless managed to force a smile. 'The gentleman, by trespassing on railway property, was already in something of a legal minefield. I believe he donated his leg at the point of illegal entry. Now, if we can stop this infantile nonsense we might perhaps try learning something. Do you think that might be a sound idea?'

Salvadori glared at Blacklock, the others at their shoes.

'Excellent. Perhaps – with *Mister* Salvadori's permission – we might begin?' Blacklock picked up his Number Three scalpel and started an incision at the top of the thigh. The cut was difficult to start cleanly because the skin was charred at the margin. With grim concentration he had managed to hack about an inch down the front centre of the thigh, in line with the femur, when the door of the laboratory swung open.

'What now? I am trying to–. Oh. Welcome, Principal.' The students followed suit with a mumbled greeting.

'So sorry to interrupt, Doctor Blacklock. I have just learned of the extraordinary circumstances by which this limb came into our possession and I thought I would see the miraculous artifact for myself.' He bustled across the room. 'Do carry on. Pretend I'm not here.'

Blacklock calmed himself before resuming the stubborn incision.

'Doctor Blacklock, sir, may I ask a question?'

Blacklock glanced up. Salvadori was grinning.

'Be my guest, Mr Salvadori. This is a teaching institution, so feel free.'

'Thank you, Doctor Blacklock. Sir, how deep should the

initial incision be when working with a solid section, like a thigh, as opposed to something with an underlying void, such as the chest?'

Blacklock opted to complete the incision before answering. 'Please observe, Mr Salvadori. You can see that my cut is between one-sixteenth and one-eighth of an inch deep, perhaps a little less. One seeks to separate the tissues without disturbing any underlying structures until you are quite ready to do so. We are not operating. Time is on our side. We do not have to rush our work.'

'Thank you, Doctor Blacklock. Most informative, sir.'

Blacklock nodded curtly before continuing, riled equally by Salvadori's games and the Principal hovering nearby. The students were distracted both by the presence of Moore and their colleague's antics, so he slowed his dissection to regain control, but also in an attempt to bore the Principal into leaving.

It worked. After a few minutes of valueless occupation Moore said, 'Right-o, gentlemen. The mechanics of the august institution need constant lubrication and I confess that I am but the humble engineer who wields the oilcan. I can see how engrossed you are so I will leave you in peace. Carry on, Doctor Blacklock.'

As the door closed behind the Principal, lecturer and students alike breathed a sigh of relief.

'Who would like to take over?' asked Blacklock. 'It is about time that one of you demonstrated your skills. Who has completed their theoretical studies on the structures of the ... knee?'

Salvadori's hand shot up, alongside a couple of others.

'Mr Harris,' said Blacklock, offering the scalpel.

Harris started to speak. 'I would split the–'

'I was first,' shouted Salvadori, suddenly a dissatisfied infant.

'I chose Mr Harris, Mr Salvadori. You never miss an opportunity to remind us of your knowledge and prowess, but once in a while I need to assess others. The world needs more than one pathologist. Mr Harris–'

'It's alright sir,' said Harris. 'I don't mind if Salvadori would rather do it.'

'A generous offer, Mr Harris, but not your decision. Please continue. Split the skin over the patella, remaining mindful of the ligaments underneath.' As he handed over the scalpel Blacklock scanned the other students and was gratified to see that Salvadori was seething, although he was careful to suppress any expression which might be interpreted as glee by the irate student.

The lecture continued uneventfully once Salvadori had been reined in.

When Harris stood back from the leg, which he had dissected with some skill – and then attempted to close with less success – Blacklock ushered them back into their seats. 'That piece of work from Mr Harris concludes our studies for this year. Take time over Christmas to reflect on what has gone well for you. Think also about that which you have found more difficult, but do not dwell there; the tools of a complete surgeon's armoury mature at different times during their education, and it is of only of real importance that everything is in place when you stand over your first patient, ready to make your first incision. You will never feel as ill-qualified and incompetent as you do at that moment.'

The students remained silent.

Blacklock drew out his watch. 'We have twenty-five minutes of this lecture left but seem to have reached a convenient point at which to stop. I propose, unless anyone objects, to give you that brief time to start your Christmases a little early. We reconvene at nine sharp on the second of January. I wish you a Merry Christmas, gentlemen.'

Twenty-Three

Whitechapel, London
Thursday 27th December

Another three evenings of lonely, cold and intermittent surveillance elapsed before Porter, followed at a discreet distance by Blacklock, next beat a path to the East End. Since the last visit had ended with such humiliation - although, thankfully he had avoided discovery by Porter – Blacklock was determined to maintain a more circumspect distance, especially as they neared the brothel. Unwilling to risk such exposure again, he watched from the end of the alley as Porter approached the door – and walked straight past. *What?*

Eager not to lose sight of his quarry Blacklock tried to force his way down the narrow path faster than those ahead of him, but his efforts were doomed at the outset by the dense mass of people ahead. Realising that the flow would take its own sweet time to break free from the alley he resigned himself to the frustrating shuffle of the crowd, eventually being ejected into another dark yard, identical in all respects to those he had already passed through. He could not see Porter. Looking around he spotted a small upturned crate. He climbed onto it, giving himself a useful height advantage over those around him but it seemed that Porter had gone. The yard had two exits, in addition to the route by which he had entered. The human traffic was fairly equally split between the two, so on a whim he selected the leftmost path.

The slum he entered was even more labyrinthine than any he had visited so far. There were many exits left and right, some into lanes so narrow that they could only be traversed sideways on. The mud – and worse – was almost ankle-deep, the fetid stink an additional insult to the senses.

He continued shuffling forward, into the narrowing lane beyond, hemmed in by others ambling in the same direction like so much herded livestock wandering blindly into the slaughterhouse. When the path split and he anticipated relief from the crush, others joined to replace those that had left. Every byway was full to capacity or beyond with grim-faced, filthy humanity going from nowhere to nowhere. Turning back was impossible, the flow too strong even if he could recall how to reverse the route he had chosen through the maze. Slowly, but nonetheless surely, a non-specific feeling of dread came upon him. This area of slum felt beyond the reach of the law, of all that was decent. He had not seen anyone who represented any form of authority, not even a constable. Hawkers in doorways offered pathetic wares, mostly perished vegetables which Blacklock would not have considered feeding to a dog.

Distracted by these matters he failed to notice when he took a turn away from the residential area and found himself enclosed by looming warehouses and derelict hovels. Although not in direct sight of the river he could both smell the rank water and hear the bustle of activity from it. Hopelessly lost in streets which had probably never even seen a hansom he followed his senses toward the river, hoping to board a passing steamer or even persuade a boatman to take him upstream to a point he recognised from which he might navigate his way home.

Further ahead, sparks carried by the biting wind flew from a night-watchman's brazier. *He* would be able to help. Newly confident, Blacklock picked up his pace, buoyed by the thought of escape from this sewer.

'Not so fast, sir,' called a mocking voice behind him. 'Got somewhere to go all of a sudden?'

Blacklock stopped and turned. 'I am sorry but you must have mistaken me for someone else. Please excuse me.'

'Why? What have you done?' More than one voice joined in raucous laughter. 'We ain't gonna excuse you, chief. Call me Mr. Smith. Bet you've got a fine watch in that there waistcoat. My burly friend here is an amateur horologist. What say you give him a look-see?' More laughter.

'I do not have a fine watch, or indeed anything approaching one,' replied Blacklock, his voice not as commanding as he would have liked.

'We'll be the judges of that, friend.' A figure advanced from the shadows into the half-light. Blacklock could still not discern his features. 'Now, we don't want to hurt anybody – specially not a fine gentleman such as yourself – but we have to make a living. Why don't you make things easy on all of us? Empty your pockets, hand over any jewellery you might have – don't forget cufflinks and tiepins – and we can all happily go our separate ways. I'm a reasonable man. What do you say? It's just business. You'll understand that, I'm sure.'

Blacklock felt himself trembling and was glad that there was not enough light to betray him. 'I have nothing, gentlemen.' He heard something click – a flick-knife, perhaps? Adrenaline surged and he turned to run, only to find his path blocked by more menacing silhouettes.

'You ain't getting away, friend, so you have a choice. The hard way, or the easy way. Trust me – you don't want the hard way.'

Without warning the assailant before him punched him in the stomach. He could not recall ever suffering so hard a blow. His breath departed and he sank to his knees, gasping.

'Slugs, that wasn't very kind, nor necessary. Not yet, anyway. Say sorry to the gentleman.'

'Sorry. Just warming up.' laughed the thug.

'Sorry, chap,' continued the ringleader, 'but my friend seems a little overeager this evening. Perhaps he's on a promise. If I were you, friend, I would give up my gear and be glad to walk away. Slugs has given you fair warning and next time he's liable to break something.'

Blacklock, still winded, struggled to his feet. He raised his fists. 'Look, I–'

Slugs hit him again, driving out what little breath he had regained. He fell onto his back, helpless.

'Calm down, Slugsy. Give our friend a chance.'

The man calling himself Smith loomed over him. 'So, friend. What say you?'

'I have noth–' He stopped as a boot settled uncomfortably over his hand.

'Enough of your games. I am more than willing to break a few bones until I get what I want. A finger at first, then perhaps a rib, a jaw, *your bloody head*, if I have to. I have also observed that people with broken heads don't swim too well.'

'No, no.' Blacklock thought he might weep. 'Let me up and I will give you everything. Please.'

The boot grazed across his hand before he was lifted roughly to his feet. 'Good decision. You're a bright boy after all. Now give.'

Adrenaline overcame common sense. Blacklock punched the oaf called Slugs in the stomach with all the strength he could muster. Slugs doubled over before instantly standing back up, laughing.

'That wasn't very friendly, friend. Not at all. A gentleman such as Slugs might take offence to your intent to do him harm. You'd better apologise before we decide to add you to Old Father Thames's flotsam. If you want to see the sun come up you had better play nicely.' He paused before he sighed. 'Go on, Slugsy. Introduce yourself properly.'

The fist hit Blacklock's jaw before he even saw Slugs's hand move and he once again landed on his back. 'Last chance, friend,' said Smith.

'Alright.' Blacklock pushed himself into a sitting position against the wall. He fished the fob watch from his waistcoat, a couple of guineas from his jacket and the gold cufflinks Tilly had given him for his birthday, piling them onto the ringleader's outstretched hand. 'Good boy. That wasn't so difficult, was it? Pleasure doing business with you. Goodnight.'

Smith had taken no more than half a dozen steps before there was a sickening sound of breaking bone and he fell to the ground. Before Blacklock could react, the creature known as Slugs was similarly dispatched. The others ran away, leaving a single figure standing, who turned and walked slowly towards the petrified doctor. 'No, please ... they already took everything I had.' He hated how pathetic he had become.

'I think,' said the stranger, 'that we had better get you back up town before you manage to find any more trouble, Doctor. What do you say?'

Blacklock, confused by this turn of events, could not answer.

His apparent saviour bent over the ringleader and, although it was difficult to see in the fading light, rifled through Smith's pockets. Seemingly satisfied he straightened up and returned to Blacklock. 'Your watch, your cufflinks and two guineas. I found another four guineas to cover my expenses, so you don't need to thank me, Doctor.'

'Who are you?'

'Come on, sir, it hasn't been that long has it? Phelps, sir. I am glad I was able to assist.'

'But ... but ... why are you here?'

'Coincidence?'

'No.'

'Of course not. Truth be told Sir Edmund has asked me to keep an eye on you. A gentleman's been seen hanging around the family residence, as we discussed previously, and Sir Edmund was of the opinion that you were the culprit. We have been unsuccessful in apprehending the person near the house so we decided to ... observe you. I was pretty sure I had made the case clear to you when we chatted in the Unicorn but the guvnor wasn't convinced. I must say I'm very surprised to find you whoring around the East End but each to their own–'

'I was not–'

'No one ever is, Doctor. I'm sure you're just another victim of circumstance and I didn't see you enter a brothel a few nights ago. Mind you, you were only in there eight minutes which is fast work by anybody's standards. I expect you'll improve with practice.'

'I was–.' Blacklock stopped himself. If Porter was hiding from the law, Caldecott's private militia would surely be able to track him down have little compunction about execution. 'Well, you know how things are, Phelps.'

'Maybe I do, sir, and maybe I don't. Come on, let's get you out of here. You've had enough thrills for one night. Perhaps you should confine yourself to the Unicorn for a few days. You'll be safer there.'

'And easier to keep an eye on?'

Phelps shrugged. 'Without a doubt, sir, if someone had a mind to do so.'

Twenty-Four

Blacklock's lodgings, 64 Pellerin Road,
Stoke Newington, London
Saturday 29th December

'You summoned me, my liege.' smiled McCormac. 'How can this humble Irishman serve the great Doctor Blacklock– Whoa! What's *that?* The good doctor now carries a cane? Quite the dandy, aren't we?'

'It is a swordstick, Francis. I ran into a little difficulty a couple of evenings ago and want to be better prepared should it happen again.'

McCormac picked up the swordstick. 'Ebonised oak with ivory inlay. Very stylish.' He twisted the latch. 'How long is the bla–? Blood and sand! How big is this feckin' thing?'

'Twenty-two inches.'

'Jeez! You could run someone through with this and they wouldn't even feel it...'

Blacklock tutted. 'Did you find Robertson?'

'Yes, thank you, Doc, I did have a nice Christmas, My mother is very well, thanks for asking. No, my stepfather wasn't in a good mood. My sister is with child, which left my ma in tears at every available opportunity. I see you're frowning, Doc. It's called conversation. Small-talk. It's how civilised human beings interact. You might want to try it sometime.'

Blacklock remained impassive. 'I am sorry that I do not share your need for inane discussion, Francis, but I might remind you that women are dying and that *you* committed to helping me. I do not think we have time for these irrelevant debates. Do you?'

McCormac snorted. 'Charmed, I'm sure. Robertson left Bristol in '91. I've heard third-hand that his wife died and he had some kind of breakdown. Got a crippled kid, too – consensus says a girl. Apparently he was heading for

London. By the way, he was practising medicine. I'm sure you told me he went off to be a missionary or somesuch.'

Blacklock puffed out his cheeks. 'I suppose people can change, but ... he was never destined to be a surgeon. He really did not have the aptitude. I wonder what changed his mind, and what field he is in? Do you know where he is now?'

'No forwarding address – at least, that's what they told me.'

1895

Twenty-Five

The School of Medicine, Prince Albert's
Hospital, Fulham, London
Friday 4th January

'Why won't you let us do *real* pathology, *Nate*?'

Blacklock rolled his eyes; Salvadori was probing again. He decided to let the pathetic name-calling pass.

'Perhaps you might be more specific, Mr Salvadori? What do you mean by "real", exactly?'

'What about that whore that was killed before Christmas? We could have worked on the post-mortem. We might have actually learned something, which would be verging on a unique event in this class.'

Wise and Heard, who were developing into Salvadori's idiot sidekicks, sniggered loudly.

'Well, well, the Salvadori we have all come to know and love returns. What a wearisome way to start a new year. One, whether the victim was a prostitute or not, you had better learn some respect if you intend to continue in this field. She is a *victim*. That is all you need to focus your mind on, no matter how small and useless it might be. Second, you only get to practise "real" pathology, as you call it, when you are appropriately qualified – not a moment before. The cadavers we use are donated to us. They are never part of current or future criminal proceedings. Frankly, Salvadori, your chances of qualification diminish with each of these petulant outbursts. You may well impress the most moronic of your peers, who have nothing to lose because they are such poor students who will never amount to anything, and are only here because their parents continue to throw good money after bad and pay their fees. They would be more usefully occupied as staddle stones, or perhaps gateposts. You, however, have at least a modicum of talent, Salvadori, which you seem intent on squandering on these tiresome pantomime performances.'

Salvadori blustered but was unable to speak.

'Furthermore, Salvadori, your continuing disruption of these classes has gone on for far too long and I will not tolerate it.'

'You have to, *Nate*. You have to take your licks or Moore will dismiss you.'

'On the contrary, Salvadori, I believe Principal Moore has both the integrity and the intelligence to see you clearly for the spoiled brat you are. Leave this lecture, and do not return. You will fail this part of the curriculum. Good day to you.'

Salvadori reddened. 'You haven't heard the last of this, Blacklock. I'll make damned sure you regret what you've done.'

Blacklock smiled benignly. 'I do not doubt that you will try to do just that. However, the greater good is served – certainly in this class – by your departure. I would not be surprised if the remaining students learn twice as effectively in your absence.' He turned back to the heart he was pinning open on a board. 'Please be so kind as to shut the door on your way out.'

Salvadori slammed the door so hard that one of the small panes inserted as peepholes shattered.

'What a tantrum,' muttered Blacklock, hoping that the humour would distract the class from his trembling hands.

He managed to avoid Moore as he left in the evening. His working assumption was that Salvadori would run directly to the Principal, but the ramifications of that could wait for the morning.

Starling did not appear at The Unicorn to share his sorrows, so Blacklock resigned himself to a sleepless, alcohol-free night – and met his own expectations.

Twenty-Six

The School of Medicine, Prince Albert's
Hospital, Fulham, London
Monday 7th January

Blacklock fretted over his clash with Salvadori throughout the weekend, day and night. Dawn broke on Monday and Blacklock was barely rested. He washed and dressed carelessly and even chose to forgo Mrs Mason's always excellent breakfast. He counted his remaining funds, which amounted to four weeks' rent and enough to eat and drink, albeit occasionally.

Daylight at least put his problems in perspective. Salvadori had been a brat. Blacklock would relate his side of the story to Moore, tender a hollow apology to said brat and get on with the day. He managed a smile as he walked to the college, marvelling at his own ability to weave a magnificently complex nocturnal melodrama from such insubstantial threads.

On arrival his laboratory was locked – Jenkins had obviously lost track on his rounds or was running late. Blacklock was convinced that such an oversight had occurred before. He turned for the caretaker's lodge to find Moore approaching.

'Ah, Blacklock...'

'Principal. I must get my key before the students arrive – Mr Jenkins has forgotten to unlock my rooms this morning.'

'He ... err ... hasn't forgotten, I'm afraid.'

Blacklock felt a fire ignite in his stomach and travel up through his throat before reddening his face. 'Has he not?'

'No, Nathaniel. I'm sorry but dismissing Salvadori from your lecture on Friday was both uncalled for and unprofessional.'

'You were not there, Principal. His behaviour and attitude were beyond the pale. I have many witnesses who–'

'It's not a bloody court of law, man! I'm sorry but you can't deny that you weren't warned. Salvadori has rattled his uncle's cage, who has threatened to withdraw his funding for the new library.'

Blacklock's tone grew cold. 'I see.'

Moore looked down, unable to meet Blacklock's gaze. 'It is with great regret, therefore, that I must ask you to tender your resignation.'

'Why? Because you lack the balls to dismiss me?'

'No. On the contrary, it is to spare your record a dismissal so that you might find it easier to obtain another position, although with language like that you will find it most difficult.'

'Oh, I–'

'However, you have made your opinion very clear, Nathaniel. You are dismissed with immediate effect. You will be paid until the end of the month as a gesture of our goodwill. Collect your belongings and be clear of the college precincts before ten a.m.'

'What will I do?'

'I have no idea. Perhaps a little time to reflect and improve your behaviour will prove beneficial. Good morning.' Moore turned and walked quickly away.

Blacklock watched him leave, then remained in the same spot for several minutes.

Twenty-Seven

The Olde Bell and Unicorn Inn, Shacklewell
Lane, Stoke Newington, London
Monday 7th January

'So what did you steal when you cleaned out your laboratory?' asked Starling.

Blacklock was very drunk. 'Nothing, Jon. I collected my personal surgical instruments and my writing case and left.'

'*What?* With all that equipment going begging? You should have taken a microscope or something in lieu of notice. In future, if someone fires you and tells you to collect your stuff without supervision they *want* you to fill your pockets because they feel guilty. It's a universal law.'

'That is quite a theory, Starling. Utter tosh, of course. One must retain at least a vestige of self-respect.'

Starling put down his drink and stared at Blacklock. 'You listen to me, Nate. You're out of work because some jumped-up little shit didn't like being told what to do, so ran crying to his uncle and the next thing you know you're done. Hardly fair, is it? Perhaps you could sue him for defamation of character or something?'

'Your drink is talking volumes, Jon. None of it sensible, but it is fun to watch anyway.'

'What will you do? How long until your suspension is reviewed?'

Blacklock sighed. 'That? Perhaps never. They seem to be able to change their own rules as they see fit. I do not hold out any hope.'

'So what will you do?'

'In the short term I will have to go cap-in-hand to Duncan and take the police shilling. It should pay enough to cover my board and lodgings until–'

'Until what?'

Blacklock paused, then laughed. 'Do you know what? I do not know. For the first time in my adult life I have no plan, no map to follow. At this rate I could see out the rest of my days as a jobbing pathologist. My uncle would turn in his grave. All those tuition fees wasted.'

'Not if you can catch the new Ripper. You will still be saving lives, albeit more indirectly than you might have otherwise intended.'

Blacklock massaged his temples. 'I have a shortlist of five candidates, if you recall. I suppose I will now have more time to observe Porthos. Porter.'

'I'll take a turn, if you like.'

'Why? You thought this was all a big joke.'

'You seem to be having quite a thrilling time of it. When I offered my services previously you rejected them. And I know you will not believe this – but actuarial tables are not very exciting'

'No?'

'No. Hard to credit, but true. Unless 1895 brings some huge and unexpected actuarial crisis I will still be consulting the same tables a year and thirty years from now.'

'How many "actuarial crises" have there been so far?'

'None. It is not a profession given to crises.'

Twenty-Eight

Leman Street Police Station, Shadwell, London
Thursday 10th January

'Good morning, Sergeant. My name is Doctor Nathaniel Blacklock.'

The desk sergeant did not look up from his work. 'Bully for you. Want a medal?'

'I have an appointment.'

Blacklock lingered uncertainly until the sergeant sighed and said, 'With? I'm not a bloody mind-reader.'

'Inspector Duncan.'

'Time?'

'Eleven a.m.'

'Alright. Sit. He's out. Don't know when he's getting back. Or if.'

Blacklock opened his mouth to thank the desk sergeant but decided not to waste his breath. An ancient wall clock ticked lazily behind the desk. It read ten forty. Blacklock's watch read ten forty-five, so whichever was more accurate he still had time on his side. He turned away from the counter with a half-smile. The waiting area was furnished with mismatched old dining chairs, most of which were occupied with people he would have expected to find in the cells.

At the end of one of the rows there were three consecutive unoccupied chairs, so he selected the middle one. He sat down, nervously fiddling with the brim of his hat. No one waiting wanted to make eye contact with anyone else so people stared at the floor, scraped their fingernails, picked invisible lint from their trouser legs, or if wealthy enough compared their pocket watches with the station clock.

As the time crawled around to eleven ten an old woman

shuffled in. The sergeant glanced up, half smiled then returned to his busy work. She was carrying a large coal sack in each hand, which were filled to capacity with her worldly goods. The only remaining free seat was next to Blacklock. The woman smiled – she had no teeth – and limped over. 'Hello, dearie. My, aren't you a smart fella?'

'Thank you, madam.'

'You a doer or was you doed to?'

It took Blacklock a couple of seconds to understand the question. 'Oh, neither. I have an interview with Inspector Duncan. For a position, I mean.'

'Ain't you the lucky one? He's a good 'un, that one. He lets me sit in here when it gets too cold for me old bones.'

'Is that why you are here now?'

'Yes. I should get a little bit of shuteye. They changes shifts in a couple of hours and the afternoon desk sergeant's a mean little bugger. He'll have me thrown out then, so I gets in early to try to get warmed right through.'

'I see,' said Blacklock, praying fervently that his name would be called soon. He feigned an interest in his newspaper, keeping one eye on the clock and the other scanning for a free seat. He did not want to smell like the old woman when he met Duncan.

'What job you arter?'

'Pardon?' His fascination with his newspaper had become genuine.

'You said you was here for a job.'

He saw no reason to lie or patronise. 'I hope to gain employment as a pathologist.'

'A what?'

'A pathologist. I'm a surgeon by training but I also work with the deceased to try to understand what killed them.'

'Good with a knife, eh?'

'Yes.'

'You're a cutsmith then. If you'd said that first I'd've understood.'

'I have never heard that word before.'

'Aintcha? Where you bin? A pickpocket – good with their fingers – is a fingersmith, right? Good with a knife – a cutsmith.'

'But I use my knife to help. I am not a ... ruffian.'

The old lady exploded in cackling laughter. 'I can see that for myself, dearie, even without eyeglasses. You're pure as the driven snow!' She laughed again and clapped her hands. 'Not a ruffian!' Her laughter lessened but occasional snorts and guffaws continued.

The clock ground its way round to eleven forty-five before Blacklock summoned the courage to complain and approached the counter.

'I am sorry, but–'

'Why? What have you done?'

'Nothing, but–'

'Don't bloody waste my time apologising then. Allow me to use my mystic powers to answer your questions. No, I haven't forgotten you're here. No, I don't know where Inspector Duncan is. Yes, I will be sure to tell him you're here when he returns. Does that about cover it?'

'Yes,' stammered Blacklock.

'Then sit down. You're making the place look untidy.'

Blacklock understood at a logical level that getting affronted was not going to help his cause, but it still required great self-control to avoid sniping back. He smiled and nodded before returning to the only spare chair, next to his erstwhile companion. Feigning a cold he pulled out his handkerchief to use as a mask.

The old woman stared at him but said nothing, which shamed him enough to drop the pretence and return the handkerchief to his pocket.

'Connors,' shouted the sergeant. 'Come through.' An elderly gentleman in hard times rose from a seat at the other end of the row and made his way through the low gate which marked the entry to the station interior.

Blacklock eyed the vacated seat, but it would be so

transparent if he moved that he would feel contemptible. As he committed to staying where he was Duncan burst into the station, barking orders at Cargill, who was following to heel.

'Any messages, Sergeant?'

The desk sergeant nodded at Blacklock.

'Ah yes, Prof. How are you? Listen, I've about ten minutes work to finish with Cargill here and I'll call you through. Chin up.' Without waiting for acknowledgement he marched off.

I can last ten minutes.

Almost an hour later a harassed Cargill appeared at the gate. 'Doctor Blacklock? This way.'

Duncan's office was chaotic, as if someone had ransacked it. The inspector smiled unkindly as Blacklock entered. 'Well, look what the cat's dragged in. Cargill, it seems that our favourite prof has deigned to grace us with his presence. Should we bow, Blackmore? Is that the proper form?'

Cargill, clearly uncomfortable, bustled out.

'So, to what do we owe this pleasure?'

'Well,' said Blacklock, clearing his throat. 'I have reconsidered your offer and have decided to accept the position.'

'Ain't we honoured? You've *reconsidered*. How kind.'

Duncan stopped speaking and half-smiled at Blacklock, who in turn did not want to be forced to speak first.

The silence strung out for several long moments before he gave in. 'Yes, Inspector. I thought about the role and how interesting it could be, and I also feel that I could bring fresh thinking to the task because my medical knowledge is more ... modern than Sir Edward's was.'

Duncan steepled his fingers. 'I see. Something fresh, eh?' He sat back. 'Thank you for your interest, but I'm afraid that the job's gone. I can't stand capricious prima donnas at the best of times. Cheerio. I'm sure a man of your unmatched intelligence can find their own way out.'

Blacklock felt his face burning. 'B–but–. Alright. Thank you.' He stood up and had opened the office door when Duncan said, 'Unless...'

Blacklock spun round, appearing much keener than he had intended – desperate, perhaps. 'Unless?'

'The fella ain't started yet. If you was cheaper than him – let's say ten bob a week – I could kick him into touch.'

'I thought the compensation was fifteen shillings per week?'

'It was, but it's a buyer's market now. Supply and demand. I've got more surgeons lined up than the average hospital. Take it or leave it, Blackmore. I recall you was very decisive last time you was in here.' He pulled a half-Hunter from his pocket and flicked it open. 'I like decisive people on my little team. You've got one minute to decide, once and for all. No second chances. What's it to be, Prof? You in?'

Blacklock pursed his lips. 'It seems that you have me at a disadvantage, Inspector.'

'That's what policing is, Prof. Keeping as many people as possible at a disadvantage. You're learning quickly.'

Blacklock snorted. 'Alright. I have little choice but to accept your terms.' He held out his hand.

Duncan shook it peremptorily. 'Excellent decision, Prof.'

'It's Doctor. Blacklock.'

Duncan shrugged. 'I'll send a constable across with your contract, which I would like signed and returned immediately.'

'Of course. When do I start?'

'When there's a body. The Great Unwashed public can't afford to start you on its payroll when there's nothing for you to do now, can it?'

Blacklock shook his head in dismay.

'I don't know how desperate you are for cash, Prof, but if someone meets an untimely end this evening I might have to send you to the gallows. I don't like coincidence.' He laughed but Blacklock did not join him.

'What will you tell the other candidate?'

The inspector smiled broadly. '*What* other candidate?'

'He is a bastard, Jon. An unconscionable bastard. I do not believe that Duncan has a single redeeming feature.'

'It seems to me, Nate, that you're more than a little inept at picking your battles. He saw you coming on this one. Has the contract arrived yet?'

'No.'

'Well, when it does don't forget you can always refuse to sign it. You're not a slave, or indentured, or a prisoner.'

'And do what?'

'I don't know. Go back to Scotland?'

'With a butcher on the loose here, who happens to be someone I know?'

'I'm not saying it's the right thing to do, only that you always have options.' He took a deep draught of the cheap ale. 'Even if those options are unpalatable, like this ditchwater mein host claims is beer. On the other hand, any word from the divine Miss Caldecott?'

'What do you think?' sneered Blacklock.

'Sorry to hear that she has yet to regain her senses. Salut!'

'Salut!'

Twenty-Nine

St Bartholomew's Hospital, City of London
Saturday 19th January

As he became inured to the freezing evenings Blacklock found it easier to maintain his vigils outside Barts. In truth, apart from Porter's occasional brothel visits he saw nothing to otherwise incriminate him. However, the nagging doubts in his mind ensured that he sustained his surveillance of his old acquaintance. Unless something occurred elsewhere – Blacklock did not want to admit to himself that the event which would clear Porthos could be the murder of another woman - while he was observing him, Porter's innocence would always remain open to question.

At the end of the working day the roads and paths around Barts were frenetic but Porter consistently used the same door to exit, which Blacklock assumed was the one closest to the surgeon's changing room.

Porter was certainly not a man for post-labour niceties with his colleagues. The shift finished at seven p.m. and Porter always emerged within five minutes.

This evening Blacklock was puzzled by Porter appearing a few minutes later than usual and walking down the steps dressed not in his normal attire but full evening wear. He stopped at the edge of the pavement and peered through the traffic, before smiling and waving at someone Blacklock could not see. Following Porter's gaze, Blacklock saw a smart brougham.

Retelling this episode later to Starling he could not remember whether he saw Phelps or Matilda first, but that detail was immaterial. Tilly jumped down from the carriage and modestly gathering up her long dress ran to Porter, who took her in his arms and spun her around.

Blacklock was nauseated by the spectacle, his mind surging with what seemed a million conflicting thoughts. *How long had they been carrying on like this? Did Tilly break their engagement to be with Porthos?*

He held his hand to his chest and took gulps of the filthy air, trying to moderate his breathing as they climbed joyfully into the carriage. Phelps whipped the lead horse and the carriage started with a jerk. Realising it was going to pass close by his position Blacklock took a step back into the shadowy doorway which had long served as his makeshift observation post. As the coach-and-four passed Phelps looked directly at him and mimed a sympathetic shrug, mouthing 'sorry' as he did so. How did Phelps know he was there? Since the attempted robbery by the warehouse Blacklock had looked carefully for anyone following him but had seen no one. Presumably a man of Caldecott's wealth had many dubious acquaintances who, like Phelps, could be called upon to perform such criminal activities.

As the coach moved out of sight Blacklock slumped against the great oak door, its rivets digging into his back. It was a perverse relief that he could feel them when he felt so numb and unmanned.

One terrible vision after another crowded his thoughts like a succession of horrific magic lantern slides. *Tilly and Porthos laughing at his expense as they deceived him; everyone in his miniscule social circle knowing the truth but keeping it from him; Caldecott clapping Porthos on the shoulder and anointing him his heir apparent; the engagement notices in The Times; the wedding – where would it be? St Paul's? Westminster Abbey? Caldecott's abused body quickly succumbing to his extravagantly unhealthy lifestyle and Porter, his fortune assured, setting up his court in Belgrave Square.*

His thoughts ran on like this for several minutes, scenario after humiliating scenario running one after another, each more grandiose and ridiculous than the last.

Until one last vision brought them crashing to a halt. *It was vanishingly improbable that Porthos was actually a murderer – but would he harm Tilly in another way? Surely not.* He pulled at his hair in desperation. The dilemma was magnified by this realisation. One passing notion was to follow Starling's advice and share the evidence he had which would see Porthos in court before he knew what had hit him – but how would that help? Tilly would be free again, but at what cost? He pushed the thought away, berating himself for allowing it to occupy his mind, even for a second.

He paced the streets aimlessly for another half hour, not only failing to reach any form of conclusion but actually confounding his thinking further, before he turned reluctantly for home.

There could be no question of returning Duncan's contract unsigned. The murders had to be solved and he knew that no one cared as much for justice as he did, with the possible exception of McCormac.

His walk home was haunted by the fears of the harm which might befall Tilly at Porthos's hands, until he happened upon a solution which could possibly serve to keep her safe whilst affording him the time he needed to make his determination of the monster.

Thirty

The Caldecott Residence, 17 Belgrave
Square, Knightsbridge, London
Sunday 20th January

He made doubly sure to confine himself to the shadows as he approached the square. Phelps seemed to have supernatural vision and tonight Blacklock almost wanted to be seen, but only on his own terms, so he decided to move in darkness across the ornamental gardens in the centre of the square, which would permit his covert approach to within a few yards of the house.

He clambered awkwardly over the railings which surrounded the residents' private garden, catching his foot and falling into the fortunately thornless bush below. A doorman from a nearby house shouted something but he could not make it out.

It was perhaps two hundred yards across the unlit miniature park to the Caldecott residence. After waiting for a couple of minutes to ensure that he had not aroused any unwanted curiosity he disentangled himself from the undergrowth and realised immediately why he was fundamentally unsuited to such adventures, particularly when undertaken in an unplanned manner.

The park was pitch black and he had nothing with which to light his way. He knew that this ersatz Eden contained perfect beds of roses, annuals and trees; a pond or two. The centrepiece was a Roman fountain, apparently a replica of something unearthed in Pompeii. In short, the next few minutes promised to be unnecessarily hazardous.

He closed his eyes tightly, then opened them wide hoping that they might adjust more quickly. They did not.

With his swordstick outstretched like a blind beggar he walked slowly towards Tilly's house, expecting at any moment to crash headlong into some thorn bush or water feature. Every few steps he stopped to regroup. His heart raced and his jaw ached from clenching his teeth. He took a deep breath and exhaled slowly. Like any surgery, this simple walk required thought, planning and care. There were no dragons or bearpits or flaming pits to negotiate, just a straightforward London park – and a tiny one at that. Through innumerable trees shone the attenuated lights of the huge houses. He stared into the darkness at his feet, willing his eyes to compensate at least a little. After a moment he raised his head, ensuring that he did not look high enough to encompass the lights beyond the park. When he squinted he believed that he could discern some details in the yards ahead. Holding his breath again he took a tentative step, then another. He almost fell at the transition between border and lawn but regained his balance.

He recalled from pleasanter times that this imitation oasis was dotted with random statues – nymphs, absurd cherubs riding dolphins, mermaids – all manner of romantic nonsense entirely misplaced in the capital of the Empire. He had paid precious little attention to these fancies then, engrossed as he was in his courtship. He paused briefly as he recalled how Tilly had called everything "delightful", an attitude he had historically chosen to find charming whereas he thought most of the drab grey trinkets a waste of concrete. He regretted his inattention now.

Arms still outstretched he chanced another few paces which passed without incident, unwarranted confidence growing.

The turf underfoot transitioned to fine gravel. If he was crossing the centre of the gardens a fountain stood directly ahead, surmounted by a statue of Diana.

He crouched down, favouring a first contact with his swordstick over his shin. After a couple of steps he struck the familiar flat rim of the fountain where he had sat for hours with Tilly in the previous couple of years.

Halfway.

He felt his way around the obstacle and set out into the darkness again.

'Going somewhere, chief?'

The voice stopped his breath and almost his heart. 'What?' This felt like the wharf all over again. He turned the knurled trim of his swordstick in readiness.

'We don't often get folks strolling through here at night.'

Blacklock felt the perspiration beading on his forehead. 'I s–suppose not.' He checked that the swordstick was free of its sheath.

'Y'see, it's residents only.'

'I am sorry. I–'

'And we're residents. Night-time residents, anyway.'

'I understand.'

'Got a light?'

'Sorry, I do not smoke.'

'No matter. Got somewhere to put your head down?'

'Pardon?'

'Somewhere to sleep? I can help you find a spot.'

'N–no–sorry–'

'Don't be sorry. There's no shame in a life on the road. Some of us weren't meant to be all cooped-up in 'ouses.'

The tension began to ebb from Blacklock. Whilst not among friends he did not think he was in immediate peril either. 'Thank you sir, but I have accommodation, for the time being at least. I am just on my way elsewhere, albeit via a rather foolish route.'

'You sure 'bout that?' The voice in the darkness had an edge of suspicion. 'If you've been robbin' the folks hereabouts, or got intentions to, you'll have me and several others to answer to. Y'see, the gentlefolk around here generly turn a blind eye to us as long as we only show our mugs just as the gardens are about to close and take our rubbish away with us when we leave, which has to before dawn. If you been thievin' there ain't no place for you here.'

'I have not. I really, truly have not. I took this stupid shortcut because ... my fiancée lives across there and I wanted to surprise her, so did not want to be seen. It is just a prank that has misfired.'

'If you say so. If your fiancée *does* live over there, what's the number?'

'Eighteen.'

'Alright. What's the family name at eighteen?'

'The Caldecotts. Watson is the butler, Phelps is the coachman.'

'Very good. And the young lady's name?'

'Tilly – Matilda.'

'Hmmm.' The invisible figure in the darkness was thinking.

Blacklock tightened his grip on the swordstick, double checking that the blade was still unlatched.

'Alright fella,' continued the disembodied voice. 'This time I'll believe you. One thing, mind–'

'Yes?'

'You don't go around givin' people's details to strangers you meet in the park. You'll never know what shenanigans they might have in mind. Now gimme your 'and and we'll see if we can't get you out of here.'

With some misgivings Blacklock held out his hand which was instantly enveloped is a hugely powerful fist.

'My, ain't you a dainty one.'

Blacklock smiled.

'Gotcha,' said the voice, now a menacing whisper. 'You can't escape now.'

His heart missed a beat as he realised that he could not unsheathe the swordstick with one hand.

'Only joking. You, my friend, are far too trusting of strangers. You ain't been on the streets long, 'ave you? First rule here is don't trust no one. Second rule's the same as the first. Got it?'

'Yes.'

Throughout this conversation they kept walking, his

guide deftly avoiding the myriad obstacles that cluttered the park as though it was daylight. When they arrived at the fence opposite the Caldecott house his guide became visible in the light from the street lamp. He was a full head taller than Blacklock, and twice as wide.

'Thank you, Mr...'

'Stewart. Paulinus Stewart. At your service.'

'Thank you, Mr Stewart, both for the safe passage and the advice. My name is Nathaniel.'

'Ah! God's gift.'

'Pardon?'

'Nathaniel, in the Bible. That's what Nathaniel means. Not a religious man, then?'

'Not to any great depth, I'm afraid.' He reached into his pocket and found a threepenny piece. 'Perhaps you can use this–'

'No thank you. No charity required. Just remember what I told you.' Stewart nodded at the tall railings. 'You goin' over?'

Blacklock scanned the immaculate street. 'Not yet. I need to see Phelps alone as part of my surprise. Have you seen him?'

'There's been no coaches in a while. The wheels make such a racket on the cobbles, they'd wake the dead.'

Blacklock was about to thank and dismiss his guide when an all too familiar carriage rounded the corner. 'Thank you, Mr Stewart.'

'Paulinus to you.'

'... but I can see him now. Once Miss Caldecott is inside the house I will speak to Phelps.'

'I'll wait to help you over the fence. Your entrance weren't the most graceful I ever see.'

They watched in silence as the carriage pulled up. Phelps jumped down and walked smartly around to the pavement side and opened the door. The coach rocked as someone exited and Blacklock felt immediately sick as Tilly appeared on the house steps. She was perhaps only thirty yards distant and yet he dared not speak. As she reached the door Watson opened it and the great house swallowed her. *At least she's alone.*

'Come on then,' said Stewart. He made a stirrup with his hands and boosted Blacklock effortlessly onto the top of the railings, from where he hopped down without drama. 'Thank you, Paulinus.' He smoothed his suit and walked nonchalantly over to where Phelps was tending the horses.

'Good evening, Mr Phelps.'

The driver turned slowly to face him. 'Well, if it isn't the great Doctor Blacklock. I distinctly recall very strongly advising you that you shouldn't be seen here. Especially by me, sir. Miss Caldecott–'

'I know. It is you I wish to see.'

'Alright.' It was the first time Blacklock had ever detected any uncertainty in Phelps's voice. 'Your wish is granted. Say your piece.'

'It's about Porthos. Porter.'

'Uh-huh.'

'Please keep a careful eye on him.'

'Why?'

'I ... cannot explain my reasons but please believe me when I say that it is incredibly important that you do so.'

Phelps laughed. 'I'm sorry, Doc, but I can't take account of your green-eyed monster. Doctor Porter called on Miss Caldecott and they've been stepping out for a few weeks now.' He took a step towards Blacklock. 'You have seen what I can do when I'm on your side, and when I am not. Trust me when I tell you that you are perilously close to crossing over to the wrong side of that line. I'm not without sympathy, I get it. You're upset, and between you, me, and the gatepost things could have been handled better where you're concerned, but what's done is done. You ain't going to win her back, especially by stalking her. That's likely to end very badly for you. Understand?'

Blacklock sighed in frustration. 'This has nothing to do with what went before. Please, I beg, do not leave him alone with her.'

Phelps grabbed Blacklock by the lapels. Something gave within his coat. 'Last warning. This has nothing – sweet Fanny Adams – to do with you. Now skedaddle before I put you in a hospital through the customer entrance. Go on. Bugger off.' He pushed Blacklock roughly backwards.

'Look. Just bear in mind what I said. I was not following Tilly, I was following Porter, and it might still be that I had good reason to do so.'

Phelps reached into the front of the coach and extracted a long club from the footwell. 'You know what my friendly persuader can do, Blacklock. It's saved your bacon, but you do not want to be on the receiving end. If you ain't a hundred yards away in the next thirty seconds, I promise you are going to find out. That ain't gonna be fun for either of us but much worse for you. I suggest most politely that you fuck off, *sir*, and don't let me even smell you within a mile of here.'

Defeated, Blacklock walked backwards for a few paces before he turned and half-walked, half-ran until he cleared the square, his sights set on The Unicorn.

Thirty-One

Blacklock's lodgings, 64 Pellerin Road,
Stoke Newington, London
Monday 21st January

Blacklock slowly regained consciousness into a brutal hangover – eyes too big for his head, shielded in turn by eyelids lined with carborundum paper. *What did I do?*

It required great concentration to tease out the threads of memory. The Unicorn loomed large, and being ejected from it. He looked down at his clothing. He was still dressed. One of his lapels had hung by a couple of threads, and his sleeve was out at the elbow. *What's that?* An address was scrawled on the back of his hand: Flat 7, 25 Barnabas Street. *Who?*

A flood of disjointed memories overwhelmed him – Tilly with Porter, a giant helping in a park, Phelps ignoring his pleas and threatening to assault him.

Did he threaten me?

The preceding evening became a sickening kaleidoscope. The traitor Porter had stolen his fiancée. This was not something a gentleman could accept without repercussions. He rolled onto his back with an arm covering his eyes. There must have been something else later, someone shouting at him? Perhaps it was the landlord of The Unicorn. He pulled his arm back and squinted at the blotchy address on the back of his hand, faint as an old sailor's tattoo. Barnabas Street? He thought hard but nothing came to mind.

Thirty-Two

Barnabas Street, Kensal Green, London
Monday 21st January

Barnabas Street was better than a slum, albeit by the slimmest of margins. Every window seemed to be open, and at every open window a mother screamed or a baby cried, rendering Blacklock's hangover insufferable. The cacophony was exhausting and he felt distressed just being there. Number 25 was no better than its neighbours. The front door was open – he noticed that the jamb was recently splintered, newly-exposed wood shining white through the old like bone through a gash.

He bounded up the stairs, keen to minimise his exposure to this damned neighbourhood. He rapped on the flat's flimsy door.

'Blacklock?'

'Yes.'

'Come in. It's open.'

McCormac was polishing a large lens in a brass mount. He looked up and smiled. 'It lives! The monster has risen.'

Blacklock smiled sarcastically. He sat on a rickety chair next to the dining table, which was stacked high with an untidy pile of cardboard and paper folios. 'Now, why am I here?' asked Blacklock, idly browsing through the portfolios.

'So that I can explain, once more, exactly what I explained last night to a drunken oaf in The Unicorn.'

'I received some bad news and was drowning the subsequent sorrows.'

'Oh?'

'My fiancée – *ex*-fiancée – is already stepping out with someone new, to whom I inadvertently introduced her.'

McCormac grimaced. 'Tough break. How careless.'

Blacklock tutted as he stood and walked around the

tiny room, filled to capacity with photographs and what he assumed to be the ephemera required for their creation. The chemical odours made his eyes water, which he dabbed delicately with his handkerchief. More portfolios on a shelf caught his eye. He selected one at random.

'No,' cried McCormac. 'Not those ...'

It was already too late. Blacklock gaped at the nude woman before him. 'What on earth? This woman is naked!'

'Well spotted,' replied McCormac, lowering his voice. 'Have you considered studying anatomy? I also have a sideline in natural portraits.'

'*Natural*-? These are ... pornographic! There is no need for this!'

McCormac smiled. 'Keep your hair on, Doc. It's just another way of dragging in a few bob.' He turned on the spot, hands aloft. 'Look at this place. Ain't a palace. I'd be on the feckin' street without the little bit I make from the discerning gentlemen who, unlike you, appreciate a little natural beauty.'

'But ... "natural portraits"? I have never heard such nonsense. These are simply lascivious.'

'Before you judge, get yourself along to The National Gallery. Plenty of flesh on show. Is that more worthy because it takes longer for a Pre-Raphaelite to paint a picture than make a photograph? Are you similarly affronted when you read a printed book, rather than one written by some poor scribe bent over a desk with a quill? No, you aren't. You don't object to mass production of books, and you don't object to nudity as long as it's in a gallery. That smacks of hypocrisy.'

Blacklock considered a counterargument but came up short. 'Did you rehearse that?'

McCormac laughed. 'Not recently. I memorised it years ago.'

'My point stands. Does Duncan know what you do? Does *your mother* know how you make a living?'

'No, and no. And I intend to keep it that way. Like I said,

it's just a little artistic sideline. Nobody gets hurt.'

Blacklock frowned and closed the portfolio before unceremoniously shoving it back onto the shelf. 'I feel like I should wash my hands. So what *did* you want to tell me?'

'That your friend Robertson is in London, somewhere south of the river when last heard of. He moved back with his daughter about a year and a half ago.'

'Divorced? Abandoned?'

'A widower.'

'Poor chap. But you could find out his address, I presume?'

'I went to the forwarding address but it was a burned out shell. A neighbour told me that the tenant and a child escaped the blaze uninjured but no one knows where they went next.'

'It should not be that hard to find him, assuming he is still practising. There cannot be more than a dozen decent-sized hospitals in London so like anything else it is simply a matter of elimination. If we check each–'

'*We*? Who are "*we*", exactly?'

'You. Me. My friend Starling. If we check one each per day we could track him down by the end of the week.'

'And?'

'And we – one of us, at any rate – follow him until there is an opportunity to intervene should he engage in horrific conduct.'

'Let's assume we do find him. How do we avoid alerting him? If someone was asking around for you don't you think you would find out? Somebody would be sure to tell him, and–'

'He would go to ground.'

'Precisely.'

'Dash it all.'

'Then *we*...'

'Yes?' asked Blacklock, too eagerly.

'I don't know. To observe even a single hospital takes a lot of manpower. So many shifts, so many staff, so many patients, so many entrances and exits. And I can't live on fresh air. Or live in it. I have rent to pay too.'

Blacklock sighed. 'That is alright. I can cover that for a short time from my wedding fund. I have no use for it now.'

'Well ... it's your money. And so a dream dies. What next?'

'No idea. How do I find someone without asking?'

'Surely all practising surgeons registered somewhere?'

'Yes. With the RCS.'

'And does that registration include their current place of employment?'

'Ye– oh my God. You, McCormac, are a genius.'

'I would be if I knew how to gain access to that register. Think, Doc. Do you know anyone who has access?'

'No.'

'Are you sure?'

'Yes.'

'Alright. Let's start from the beginning. Why do people need to access the register?'

Blacklock sighed again. 'To check a surgeon's bona fides.'

'And when do they do that?'

'When you apply for a new position. I do not understand why you are asking me all this.'

'Bear with me.' McCormac rolled his eyes. 'And who would verify these details?'

'The appointing supervising surgeon.'

'*Really?*'

'Of course. Who else?'

'Are you trying to tell me that a busy surgeon personally checks the register?'

'Well, no ... his secretary.'

'Aha!' McCormac clapped his hands. 'Progress.'

'It is?'

'You can be pretty slow on the uptake, Doc, for someone who's supposed to be bright. You do *not* need to persuade a senior surgeon to do this for you.'

'No?'

'No. You need to persuade *a senior surgeon's secretary.*'

Blacklock frowned. 'I still do not follow. Persuade a secretary to do what, exactly?'

'For God's sake, Doc, keep up! You find a friendly secretary who will *pretend* that Robertson is applying for a new position. She checks the register and she will have chapter and verse on him. I assume your address is on the register?'

Blacklock smiled broadly. 'You *are* a genius, McCormac.'

McCormac beamed. 'That's the second time you told me that in as many minutes. And you were right both times. I should get it in writing.'

'If only I knew a medical secretary, which I do not.'

'You're hard work this evening, Doc. Work your way back through each post you've had. Did you ... have relations with any of the secretaries, or will they all detest you as much as the rest of us?'

'I *did not* "have relations" with any of them! Matilda is – was – my first such ... arrangement.'

McCormac laughed. 'Don't tell me you're a bloody virgin too!'

Blacklock shook his head, but his reddening face spoke volumes.

'Alright, I'm sorry Doc. Let me rephrase this using the smallest number of syllables I can. Do you know *anyone* who works as a medical secretary and doesn't actively dislike you? I think it safe to assume that there are none you have loved and left.'

Blacklock started counting off roles on his fingers. 'Edinburgh, no. Aberdeen, no. Leeds ... no. London ... no.'

'Excellent. Anywhere else? What about the medical school?'

Blacklock slapped the table. 'Of course! Perhaps Camille–'

'Camille?' McCormac raised an eyebrow which went unnoticed by Blacklock.

'Yes. Miss Henry might be willing to help. I do not believe she agreed with my dismissal.'

'Don't forget to add Priestley to the mix while you're at it.'

Thirty-Three

Maggie's Tea Shop, August Street, Fulham, London
Wednesday 23rd January

'These are for you, Miss Henry.' Blacklock blushed as he handed over a small bouquet. An elderly lady at an adjacent table smiled encouragingly.

'Thank you, Doctor Blacklock.' She held them up to her face and inhaled deeply. 'They're lovely. The freesias are especially wonderful.'

'I – I regret that I do not know one bloom from another. Please – sit down.'

She took her seat in the small tea house a few hundred yards from the medical school.

'How are you?' asked Blacklock.

'Have you found a new pos–'

They started speaking simultaneously, then halted and laughed.

'After you, Miss Henry, please.'

'I wondered whether you have found a new position, Doctor?'

'Nathaniel, please.'

'You may call me Camille.'

He nodded. 'I have found some temporary employment as a pathologist with the Metropolitan Police Service – just until other outstanding matters are resolved, you understand.'

Miss Henry nodded. 'Of course.' She poured her tea painstakingly, then swirled in a little milk. 'Why did you wish to see me?' A little colour came to her cheeks.

Blacklock cleared his throat. 'I hope to beg a favour of you.'

'You may ask. I cannot guarantee that I will acquiesce.'

He moved to his much-practised speech. 'I am trying to track down a couple of old colleagues who, I believe, might be able to help with my ... licence suspension by the College, although they must have moved around the country in various posts and we have sadly fallen out of touch. If I could only contact them then I think I may be practising again in no time.' He handed her a slip of paper bearing Robertson's and Priestley's names.

The hint of blush left Camille's cheek. 'I don't understand how I can be of assistance.' She looked at the table.

'It is rather awkward and I hate to impose–.' He waited for interruption or encouragement but there was none. 'If you could ask the College for references for them, the registrars would confirm their addresses and where they are currently employed so that I might track them down and seek their help.'

Camille picked up a napkin and dabbed at the corner of her mouth. 'But I don't need a reference.'

'I know, but – Camille – I have exhausted all other avenues and I had hoped – perhaps forlornly – that you might be willing to tell a trivial white lie to assist my case.'

Camille exhaled. 'I see.' She stood and slipped into her jacket. 'Thank you very much for the tea, Doctor Blacklock, but I cannot help you. I do not wish to be complicit in such a deception, but more than that I am bitterly disappointed that you would even think for moment that I would. Please give these flowers to someone else. Good day.' She left the paper on the table.

Blacklock rose. 'I am so sorry, Camille, I should never have–' He was cut short by the tea room door slamming behind Miss Henry, its tinny bell jangling.

Thirty-Four

McCormac's lodgings, 25 Barnabas
Street, Kensal Green, London
Wednesday 23rd January

'Francis, given your undoubted journalistic skills I find I must beg a final favour of you.'

McCormac narrowed his eyes. 'Must you, indeed? What is it this time, Doc? And will there ever be a *final* favour?'

'I need to find out what happened to Ballantyne. I presume a man of your talents could lay your hands on such information.'

'No.'

'*No?*'

'Correct. No.'

'Please, Francis, consider your cousin. This action would further narrow the field of suspects.'

'I'm sure it would, Doc. Surely he would be listed on the Register too? Couldn't you ask your lady friend?'

Blacklock blushed. 'Miss Henry feels unable to render assistance, and I do not have access to others with appropriate skills – which we have established that you do.'

'He was an army man, wasn't he? Ask yourself: Where are the military service records?'

'Something else I do not know. But you–'

McCormac looked to the heavens. 'This is precisely why you stand to lose the few friends and allies you have left, by constantly asking them to perform these "small services" for you when *you have no idea what's involved*.'

'I did not mean to cause offence, Francis. Your skill in such matters is vastly superior to my own and I thought–'

'You didn't *think!*' exclaimed McCormac. 'That's one of the many problems you have – if you're not slicing into some poor soul's gizzards you assume that everything else in life is simple. It feckin' isn't.'

Blacklock held up his hands. 'I apologise once again. I seem to have accidentally stoked your inherent Irish volatility. I certainly did not mean to imply that everything beyond the operating theatre is simple. Some of it is not.'

'Hmmm.' McCormac sighed. 'Alright. Why don't we *both* think about this? I'll even start for you. The Military Records Archive is housed in a vast basement underneath the buildings which flank Admiralty Arch.'

'Good. That is a start.'

'Please bear in mind that my knowledge is second-hand here,' continued McCormac. I have never been there personally. If someone cares to access the service record for an individual they must present themselves at the Archive in person, with identification. You then complete a chit and with luck some minion ambles into the depths before returning like a conquering hero with the record, which you then get to read under their beady eye. You can't take anything away but you can take notes.'

'You know a great deal about the process for someone that claims to have no first-hand experience.'

McCormac shrugged. 'You're an astute man, Doc, at least some of the time. You might have noticed my accent, which isn't as welcome in London as it is in Dublin. I was turned away as soon as I opened my mouth.'

'Could you pretend–?'

McCormac laughed humourlessly. '*This is ma Scots accent, thank ye.* Convincing?'

Blacklock shook his head.

'*The Duke of Northumberland and I take tea and cucumber sandwiches on the terrace at precisely three o'clock.* English any better?'

At this point even Blacklock was forced to laugh. 'Only in a pantomime.' He sighed. 'Who else could do this?'

McCormac stood and leaned over the table. '*You* have to do this.'

'But I cannot–'

'Cannot what?'

Blacklock thought for a moment or two. 'You are right, Francis. Perhaps I can. I have my passport, so–'

'No! No no no! You're feckin' clueless. You can't go *as yourself*. What right or need would a surgeon have to examine Ballantyne's records? You need to *be someone else*.' McCormac sat down again. '*Think*, Doc. Who might need access? I'm struggling here.'

'A journalist?'

'No. Never welcome anywhere.'

'A solicitor?'

'Less welcome than a journalist.'

'A detective?'

'No, that's too–.' McCormac paused. 'Hold on. There might be something to work with here.'

Blacklock fell silent, unwilling to interrupt McCormac when he was scheming.

'*A private detective.* I assume Ballantyne was Scottish?'

'As Ben Nevis.'

McCormac pulled on his lower lip, deep in thought. 'A *private inquiry agent*. Fewer false documents to procure...' He exhaled. 'Alright. A private inquiry agent, acting on behalf of ..?' He massaged his temples. 'On behalf of the family, to ... to find out what happened to him for ... his son. The army wouldn't help anyone trying to build a case against them–'

'But he did not have a son. As far as I am aware he never married.'

McCormac rolled his eyes. 'It doesn't bloody matter what *we* know. We have to construct a story compelling enough to get you in and simple enough for you to remember. Obviously a challenge.' He grinned. 'No offence.'

Blacklock raised an eyebrow. 'None taken.'

McCormac jumped to his feet again and began pacing around the tiny room. 'The need for information mustn't threaten the Army because it will simply close ranks – no pun intended. My experience tells me that you really aren't cut out to be even a fake detective. Come on Doc, help me out here. What skills do you have that you can always rely on under pressure?'

'My medicine.'

'That's all well and good but useless unless the clerk happens to be having a stroke when you arrive, but otherwise not in the least bit feckin' useful.'

'Are you sure, Francis?'

McCormac stopped pacing. 'What? Don't tell me you've had a thought. Perhaps I should sit down to recover from the shock. Go on.'

Blacklock affected comedic outrage. 'I am sure I could be convincing as an army surgeon. I would only be partly lying, rather than trying to complete a total deceit.'

'Makes sense, I suppose. Do you know anything specifically about army surgery?'

'People are all the same, soldiers or not.'

'Alright.' McCormac sat down. 'Why would one army surgeon want to look at another's record?'

'Because he's an old friend ... and ...' He sighed in frustration. 'I do not know. Subterfuge is evidently not my strong suit.'

McCormac, staring into the middle distance, appeared not to hear him.

'I said–'

McCormac held up his hand. 'Shhh!'

The men sat in silence, McCormac apparently in some form of trance and Blacklock simply perplexed.

The Irishman broke the deadlock. 'You are an army surgeon ... now retired and working for ... an eminent journal ... and you've been despatched, since you were an old friend ... to determine whether Ballantyne should be proposed for ... no, awarded ... some rare prize. That *could* work. You lot love awarding each other prizes. It has a ring of truth.'

'But what if there is no such award?'

'For God's sake, man, it *doesn't matter*. They are not going to bother checking, I guarantee you that much. You will be representing an organisation that wants to make the army *look good.*' He sat back. 'That's brilliant, even if I say so myself.' He smiled. 'By Jove, Watson, I think we've cracked it.'

Blacklock also smiled. 'I see what you mean about your command of accents. That was truly dreadful.'

McCormac rubbed his hands together with glee. 'Now you need a name. Nathaniel Blacklock isn't going to cut it. You want to be instantly forgotten.'

'Do you have a copy of the Dublin Journalist's Almanac of False Identities?'

McCormac sneered. 'My copy wore out. Ignoring that slight, Doc,' he said, picking up a pencil stub and a scrap of paper, 'what's the most common Scottish surname?'

Blacklock shrugged. 'How on earth should I know? McDonald, perhaps?'

'That'll do. Christian name?'

Blacklock shook his head. 'James?'

'Good. Hello, Doctor James McDonald. I'm pleased to make your acquaintance. You have such a common name, Doctor, I'm sure there must be untold thousands of your countrymen with the same one. You must be very difficult to seek out at short notice, and doing so would require more effort than any poorly-paid clerk would be willing to expend.'

Thirty-Five

Admiralty Arch, St. James's, London
Saturday 26th January

Blacklock walked through Admiralty Arch at precisely eleven fifteen on Saturday morning. McCormac had reasoned that since the Records Office closed at midday everyone would be keen to start their weekend and therefore perhaps a little less diligent than they might be forty-eight hours earlier or later. He patted his breast pocket again, confirming that his false passport, courtesy of one of McCormac's shadier contacts, had not fallen out or simply vaporised during the journey. He could feel his heart racing beneath it. In his left jacket pocket was a card holder with a few cards bearing the legend "Dr James McDonald, Scottish Medical Gazette". At the photographer's insistence he had nothing about him with which he might inadvertently reveal his own name.

He passed easily into the building. The first guard had been much more interested in his newspaper than the whys and wherefores of Blacklock's quest. The hallways, wastefully wide with polished mahogany floors and needlessly tall whitewashed walls were almost empty. His steps echoed throughout the cavernous building. He encountered only a few other people, bustling to and fro with briefcases or stacks of folders tied with ribbon. No one paid him the slightest attention, not even deigning to return his nervous smiles. At one point he managed to take a wrong turning and had to ask for directions, but the surly minion simply pointed the way with an impatient grunt.

At length he found the Records Office which had been consigned to the basement, in common with all repositories of its kind. The door was ajar. He mopped his brow to remove the film of moisture which had formed there.

He entered the dreary anteroom, with its dull walls of nondescript green, was an assortment of rickety chairs which must have been old when Wellington was a boy. Behind a grille-covered window in the far wall sat a man of similar vintage. He wore the immaculate red uniform of a Chelsea Pensioner, in stark contrast to his surroundings.

He did not look up.

Blacklock swallowed hard. 'Excuse me, sir. I would like to consult the record archive, please.'

'Name?' barked the old soldier, as if he was still on a parade ground.

'Black–'

'What?'

Blacklock coughed to clear his throat, suddenly grateful that the old soldier was not looking at him as his face burned and his forehead glistened again. 'McDonald. James McDonald. Doctor.'

The soldier consulted a slip of paper on the desk. 'You ain't on the list, Jock.'

'On the list?' Blacklock's voice cracked like an ageing choirboy.

'No appointment.'

'I apologise, sir. I did not realise I needed one. I have just arrived on the overnight express from Edinburgh.'

The soldier shrugged. 'Good for you.' He finally made an effort to glower at Blacklock. 'What do you want to see?'

'The service record for Doctor Edward Ballantyne.'

'Purpose?'

'The ... Scottish Medical Gazette wishes to make an award recognising his valuable service to Queen and Country; I have been despatched to–'

A second, equally elderly pensioner shuffled in.

Blacklock swallowed again, his mouth unaccountably dry. '–to obtain details of his conduct for a ... scroll which will be hung in ... the chapel.'

'But you still ain't got an appointment.'

'What's up, Len?' asked the second old soldier.

'Another one without an appointment, Perce. Seems that bloody Pelham on the entrance gate can't be arsed to check the list. I should go down there and–'

Percy smiled and rolled his eyes at Blacklock. 'Len, it's already five-and-twenty to. Don't bother with that – there's not enough time and we'll both miss our lunch if you start all that again.' He looked back at Blacklock. 'No appointment?'

'Unfortunately not. I can only assume a letter was mislaid somewhere. I am deeply sorry for any inconvenience.'

Percy shrugged. 'It happens. Identification?'

Blacklock slid the counterfeit passport across the counter, aware that his hand was shaking. Percy examined it minutely. A rivulet of cold sweat ran down Blacklock's spine.

Apparently satisfied Percy pushed the passport back. 'Regiment?'

'I do not know. He joined up after we left medical school–'

'Not *his*. *Yours*. I need to check that you've served, otherwise we'd have every Tom, Dick and Harry in the place.' He laughed. Blacklock did his best to do likewise.

'The ... er ... Gordon Highlanders.'

'A fine, proud regiment.'

'Indeed,' replied Blacklock. 'The best of the best.' It was the only Scottish regiment he knew. 'At least, north of the border,' he ad-libbed, a quick political move to pacify the two Englishmen before him. It was clearly time to use the emergency line McCormac had provided. 'Do you have any plans for this afternoon, sir? After all, you are nearly done for the day.'

Percy looked at the clock. 'Good gracious. I had no idea how late it had become.' He started for the door at the back of the office, then halted. 'By the time I've checked your service record there won't be any time for you to read the file. Why do you want to see it?'

'They want to give the bugger some award or something,'

said Len.

'Then I shan't detain you any longer than necessary, Doctor,' said Percy. 'Please take a seat at a reading table. Now, whose record did you wish to see?'

'Doctor Edward Ballantyne, born sometime between '54 and '56.'

'Alrighty.' Percy shuffled away, leaving Len to mutter dark imprecations about the manner in which all the policies and procedures were going to hell in a handbasket.

Blacklock backed towards the chair, acutely aware that he was now perspiring freely, right through his jacket. The clock chimed the quarter. As Len occupied himself noisily tidying the desk, Percy returned. 'Only one Edward Ballantyne, so easy to find. Killed in action. That's what the cross stamped on the record means.'

'I had heard as much,' said Blacklock.

'You'd better read quick, Doctor. Len doesn't like to be kept late on a Saturday.'

Len tutted.

The file was not particularly thick, not more than twenty pages.

'Ten minutes,' warned Len, scowling.

Blacklock made furious notes in his pocketbook – Ballantyne's end was sadly dramatic but pointless – and left before the two old soldiers, keen not to walk the endless corridors with them, exchanging imaginary military anecdotes.

'So what happened to Ballantyne? Dead?' McCormac had clearly made his mind up.

'Very much so. He was posted to India and served uneventfully until he went on a bathing party. He was in the centre of a large river when the native guard spotted a crocodile. He raised his rifle and discharged the weapon, slightly wounding one of the other bathers. Ballantyne, apparently believing that the party was under attack, attempted to swim to the other side of the river but was swept away. The guard was summarily executed, before it was determined that the trigger mechanism on the ancient rifle he had been given was faulty. Ballantyne was not seen again and presumed dead. Ten days later a crocodile was killed and Ballantyne's head and torso were discovered inside it, partially digested. He is comprehensively dead.'

'Good.' McCormac blushed. 'Sorry, Doc, I meant–'

'I know what you meant, Francis. It does serve to simplify matters.' He shook his head, as if to clear it. 'And then there were four.'

Thirty-Six

Whitechapel, London
Tuesday 29th January

Blacklock followed the constable through Whitechapel, almost running to keep up. They had abandoned their hansom when the lanes became too intricate and too crowded to permit passage, although Blacklock suspected that the cab driver's fear of plunging any deeper into the labyrinth played a large part in his decision. As he glanced at the faint hobnail-grazes on his hand, still lingering from the attack a month before, he found himself more than a little inclined to share that view.

The night was bitterly cold, with three inches of snow on the ground. In the few places where it remained pristine Blacklock could imagine a better East End, but such areas were few. In most cases the snow had been trampled to filthy slush in the now mainly deserted streets. The combination of weather and time – he had been dragged from his slumber shortly after three a.m. – had sent most people to their beds, or what passed for them. Knots of the curious endured the cold, but melted into the darkness when the constable blew his whistle.

'How much further to go, constable?' Blacklock's lungs were seared by the cold, and the breathlessness that accompanied that made it more difficult to match the constable's brisk pace.

'A couple of minutes, sir, no more.'

After four or five further turns through the giddying maze they entered a yard which was thronged with people, in stark contrast to most of their journey.

'Come on you lot, make way,' shouted the policeman. 'Break it up before I decide to break some 'eads.'

The crowd dutifully parted in response to the threat. Blacklock was astonished to see several street vendors offering whelks, jellied eels, hot pies and even the ubiquitous chestnuts. Commerce never failed to miss opportunity.

In the far corner of the yard the crowd became so dense that it was necessary for the officer, with Blacklock in tow, to manhandle people aside to make headway.

The crowd had gathered around the entrance to a tenement. Many of its windowpanes were broken; those intact were so coated in soot that they were almost as opaque as the walls that held their rotten frames. The slurry which covered every street, court and yard within a mile flowed unchecked into the hallway, as if the street door did not exist.

Blacklock was startled when he saw the body of a small girl embedded in this mire, but was quickly relieved to see that the small figure which lay face down, half-buried, was a large doll. He followed another uniformed officer up several flights of stairs, again barely cleaner than the street.

'Nearly there, sir,' said the officer, breathless. 'She's in the fourth floor back.'

The final landing was a mass of uniformed officers milling aimlessly, serving no apparent function. 'This here's the doctor,' said his escort. 'Let him through.'

'He's a bit bloody late then,' said one. 'There's bugger all he can do now.' Several officers laughed. Blacklock's look of disgust did nothing to stop them. They shuffled around to let him pass into the dark room at the end of the landing.

A handful of candles had been lit and some police lanterns also burned smokily, although the sum of their output was insufficient to support any form of practical examination.

Blacklock stood at the threshold of the room, suddenly grateful for the inadequate lighting. The mass of blood, which he knew would be livid scarlet in daylight was reduced to a muted brown, although its extensive spread was nonetheless abundantly clear.

The woman lay on a litter on the floor, there being no

bedframe or other furniture in the room. At her side was a large washbowl, full of inky liquid that he knew would also be red in daylight, like the bundles of cloth next to it.

Her eyes were closed, a minor blessing. As he surveyed her injuries he prayed that she had been unconscious or better still already dead when they had been inflicted, even though the blood flow spoke for itself. He reminded himself that his duty was to examine her but he still felt like a voyeur, both unfit and unwilling to be present.

With an unconscious shudder he picked up the nearest lantern and moved as close as he dared to the woman's abdomen, which again had been cut open, although on this occasion to just one side. A quick glance up at her neck confirmed his first fears – it had been cut post-mortem. *Why do that?* He struggled to comprehend what form of sickness could drive such behaviour.

He resumed his preliminary examination, hoping forlornly that there would be nothing to incriminate his cohort. His fears were justified. The first slash – no, not a slash but an *incision* – bore the unmistakable signature of a Musketeer. *Porthos?*

He gingerly lifted the flap of flesh which concealed the area of devastation.

'Blackmore! What do you think? Is it our man?' Duncan's booming voice made him start but he hoped that his movement had gone unnoticed in the gloom. 'Possibly, Inspector. There are undoubtedly many similarities to the previous victim I examined, but this is hardly the place to make a final determination.'

'And I'm not the one who got arsey last time because the body had been moved. You can't complain this time, can you?' He entered the room. 'Jesus. What a bloody mess. No pun intended.'

'I will need photographs of all ... this. Can you arrange that, please? I assume that would not fall into the category of "extraneous expense", Inspector?'

Duncan sniffed. 'Of course not. I'll get McCormac here for

daybreak. Anything else?'

'No.'

'Good. I will have the body moved to Leman Street when McCormac has done his work. I expect you there no later than eight, and your report by three.'

'But–'

'No buts, Blackmore. This is serious work, not slicing bodies up in front of bored college boys. I've had three toms slashed on my watch and I don't need another. Do I make myself clear?'

'As you wish. I will be there at the appointed time, but my examination will take as long as it takes.' He stood up. 'Please find a sheet to cover her. Your idiot PCs have done nothing but gawp since I arrived. Afford her some dignity, Duncan.' He pulled on his hat and pushed past Duncan and the gathering of uniformed officers. He immediately realised that he had been somewhat petulant but it was already too late to go back.

When he reached the door into the yard the constable on point stood aside. A small girl, no more than three years of age was sitting in the mire, playing joyfully with the doll which a few minutes earlier had been trampled into the mud.

He had walked perhaps a hundred yards beyond the margin of the crowd when he realised that he was once again alone and lost in the East End, at night. He unconsciously massaged his grazed hand while he considered his options. Although no news had filtered back to him, he felt certain that Phelps had killed "Mr Smith". He had scoured the newspapers in vain, and concluded that his attacker's cohort had taken their leader somewhere for care, or perhaps simply thrown him into The Thames. Of course, there would be many more such thugs in this part of London. After a couple of minutes of indecision he elected to swallow his pride and ask for assistance from one of the many officers swarming over the area. He did not want to have to revisit the woman's room, where Duncan would no doubt be holding court.

Thirty-Seven

Leman Street Police Station, Shadwell, London
Wednesday 30th January

The post-mortem examination, such as it was, became a straightforward affair. 'The victim died of exsanguination, Inspector. As with the previous victim, the throat was cut after death.'

'Why would he do that?'

'Or she. Make no judgements without evidence.'

'For God's sake, Blackmore, the man's some form of fucking pervert.'

'As you wish.'

'Anything else? Something concrete?'

'Did any of your myriad officers locate the missing organs?'

'*What?*'

'Some of her small intestine, some of the large.'

Duncan kicked a chair across the room. 'Fucker! Now he's collecting trophies. The sooner this animal is strung up, the better. I'd do it my bloody self–'

'Inspector?' Cargill stuck his head around the door.

'What now, Cargill?'

'There's a crowd outside and the uniforms are struggling to keep them contained. Could you come up and speak to them? I've tried and they won't listen.'

'Well there's a fucking surprise.' Duncan stabbed a fat finger at Blacklock. 'Blackmore – you're coming with me.'

Seconds later Duncan stood in front of the wall of uniformed officers, Blacklock at his side, bemused at the circumstance. The crowd was deep enough to fill the street, with wings of people extending perhaps fifty yards to left and right. There was no obvious leader, although some men had forced their way to the front to shout abuse more directly at the police.

Blacklock wondered what was going to transpire between Duncan and this mob, which was clearly barely able to contain its collective anger. He chose not to stand alongside the Inspector, who was the main target of the taunts, but further back, closer to the line of uniformed police. He waited for Duncan's voice to boom out, trying to cow the crowd. Duncan did not make a sound nor even any gestures calling for quiet, or of apology, or supplication. Instead he folded his arms and looked at them all. Initially the crowd ignored him and continued with their almost riotous behaviour. Some spat, close to but not at Duncan. Blacklock's boots and trousers were not so fortunate. As he watched the crowd nearest the Inspector stopped their caterwauling and fell as silent as Duncan; still the Inspector did not react.

The quietening rippled through the crowd until only the most vociferous persevered. Eventually they too found themselves overwhelmed by the silence.

Duncan waited for a few more seconds of quiet to elapse before he spoke. 'Thank you, ladies and gentlemen.' Blacklock could not recall Duncan speaking so quietly, even in a simple conversation. 'I understand how alarmed you must be by these killings within your community. You have my word that I and my officers are doing all we can, but we need your help. Whitechapel is a warren, and a village. Have you seen any outsiders? Don't think that sharing what you know with us is grassing. This is bloody murder we're talking about, not the odd billfold pilfered from a West Ender's jacket. Not only that, but murder of one of your own. Is it Jack? I hope not, and don't think so. Is it some sadsack, copying him for whatever perverted reasons these lunatics have? Probably. Professor Blackmore here –,' he pointed at Blacklock '– is the man charged with telling me what happened to these poor women. It ain't pretty.'

All eyes turned to Blacklock, as did Duncan's. Was he expected to speak? His mind emptied and initially his jaw flapped open to nothing but comic effect. The mob remained silent and the weight of expectation unbearable. It became clear that Duncan would leave him out to dry, and enjoy the process. He looked at the Inspector who simply grinned back. He cleared his throat and started to speak, but stalled. He coughed again. 'Ladies and gentlemen. It is clear that these heinous crimes are horrific, and the recent occurrences I have personally investigated since the death of Sir Edward Allam are the work of – sorry, *appear* to be the work of – the same perpetrator. Furthermore–'

'It's Jack, ain't it?' shouted a woman lost in the depths of the crowd, which was followed by murmurs of agreement.

'I do not know. I was not here when those horrific events occurred. There are superficial similarities, obviously, but the important thing is that the person carrying out these murders is apprehended.' He sensed that the crowd was becoming restive. 'Inspector?'

'Thank you, Professor.' He smiled at Blacklock and for once the doctor thought the expression was sincere. 'People, you have my assurance that every available police officer is working on this case. The force didn't get Jack last time around, but this time have no doubt that we'll get him. We already have a number of suspects and with your assistance will perhaps find others. I will not rest until this evil is erased from our midst.' His tub-thumping delivery seemed to warm the crowd, even producing a smattering of applause. 'When I know who has done this,' Duncan continued, 'I will tell you all. And I *will* know who has done this, or perish in the attempt.' A few cheers rang out. 'Now return to your homes. Watch over your families. Watch over your neighbours and communities. Don't fear the stranger, but watch him closely. This is no time for mob rule. We – your police – will see justice delivered. Goodnight and thank you.'

The crowd shouted for more but Duncan turned away from them, triumphant. He collected Blacklock on the way back through the blue cordon. 'Give 'em what they want, Prof, even when you don't have it.'

'They are not that stupid. Surely you cannot lead them on for too long?'

'It's easier than you think, Prof. As long as you tell them what they want to hear they'll keep listening. We're what – ten weeks into this mess? In '88 Edmund Reid kept them at bay for the better part of a year, and although there was a bit of a to-do at the Commercial Road nick – hopefully we've had ours tonight – that was about it.'

They were joined by Cargill as they made their way towards the back of the station. Duncan's sermon continued unabated. 'We feed them enough to satisfy their hunger and they stay happy. If we can catch the maggot that's doing this, so much the better. We'll flood the district with bobbies for the next few nights but we can't keep it up indefinitely. Their wives and wages won't put up with that for too long – a week or two at most. Next we'll see them start patrolling for themselves. We'll make a lot of noise disapproving of that, of course, but we won't stop them. I just hope this all burns out before that kind of fever really takes hold.' He pulled out his watch. 'Bollocks. I'm late seeing the old man.' He walked off, cursing loudly and calling for a hansom.

'The old man?' asked Blacklock.

'Commissioner Wren,' replied Cargill.

'Ah, was all that true?'

'Yep. It's all about managing the community. As soon as he gets a likely suspect in his sights we'll either arrest him if the evidence is good or if it's not he'll leak the name to one of his snitches.'

'Why would he do that?'

'Saves a trial. Saves collecting evidence.'

'That is outrageous. Surely he would not–'

'Solomon Thurber.'

'Who?'

'Solomon Thurber. A few years back there was a bloke playing with little girls, if you get my drift. Duncan was convinced it was a chap called Solomon Thurber, who was definitely a bit simple but I thought he was otherwise harmless. Anyway, Duncan leaked his name when we couldn't get any decent evidence. Next thing you know Thurber washes up on the bank at Southwark, half beaten to death then thrown into the water with his hands and feet tied. Poor bugger never stood a chance.'

'I did not hear–'

'You wouldn't. The Met made sure of that. Anyhow, a few weeks after that there's a fella found hanging from a tree in Regent's Park, and in his pocket there's a full signed confession for all the crimes and more that Duncan had fingered Thurber for.'

Thirty-Eight

Blacklock's lodgings, 64 Pellerin Road,
Stoke Newington, London
Monday 4th February

At length Blacklock fell into ennui, a state at least partly driven by his pressing need to reduce his expenditure and consequently curtail even the simplest of diversions beyond his lodgings. Mrs Mason had demonstrated some sympathy by reducing his rent a little, but the trail of daily calculations in his pocketbook told the story of both his looming penury and his preoccupation with it. His surveillance of Porter had further depressed him, his quarry now spending almost every evening with Miss Caldecott – as Blacklock now thought of her, determined as he was to brick up that period of his life.

He had some income because a few days after he had returned his signed contract to Duncan – albeit grudgingly – there had been a sizable brawl at an unlicensed drinking house which had left two men dead. Duncan was overjoyed when Blacklock had concluded, from the shape of the knife wounds, that they had killed each other – a neat solution. When Blacklock had the temerity to suggest that the knives could easily have been placed in the dead mens' hands by a third party Duncan had shouted him down, explaining that everybody who had been in the inn at the time had the opportunity to make a statement. That the place was empty by the time the hue and cry had attracted a police presence was evidence enough that the community would be satisfied with the outcome of the investigation.

Several days passed with no work, and more often than not with no human contact at all. When they did meet Starling had quickly grown tired of paying for almost everything, and McCormac had swiftly followed suit.

As yet another featureless day ran its course, his afternoon slumber was disturbed by the postman, bearing a special delivery letter. He scrutinised the handwriting on the envelope - there was no return address - which was definitely female, but not Tilly's exuberant hand. Partly from habit he lifted the letter to his nose to check for perfume, before chastising himself for his misplaced optimism.

Dear Doctor Blacklock,

Much against my better judgement I have performed the office you requested.
Doctor Arthur Robertson is practising as a diagnostician and pharmacist at St John's Hospital in Vauxhall. He lives at 84 Grenville Street, in the same locale. The College claims to hold no record of Douglas Priestley.
I trust this information assists you with your appeal.

Sincerely,
C Henry (Miss).

His unanticipated disappointment at Miss Henry's perfunctory tone caught him off guard, momentarily eclipsing the information the letter contained. He read it, needlessly, a few more times but try as he might could detect no warmth. However, Miss Henry had performed a vital service and he made a mental note to send her some more flowers – particularly freesias – when he could afford to do so.

Thirty-Nine

St John's Hospital, Hampstead, London
Monday 4th February

Energised by this intelligence Blacklock got dressed – something he only did these days when he had a rare appointment outside his accommodation. It was five thirty; Robertson would probably be at St John's. Blacklock was unfamiliar with their working patterns but every other medical institution finished its non-emergency work at seven. He consulted his dog-eared London Gazetteer. The hospital was about five miles distant – a ninety-minute brisk walk. Robertson's claimed accommodation was a further couple of miles out of town. He struck out with renewed determination.

He walked quickly, hoping that the exercise would clear his head. A hansom would have delivered him there in a fraction of the time, but the troubling facts were that he had nothing better to do and could not afford to fritter away money on such luxuries.

The streets were pleasant enough, with London doing what London did best and making its way in spite of its chaos and disorganisation.

St John's was a much smaller hospital, occupying just a couple of three storey buildings, quite unlike the sprawl of St Thomas's or Barts. It enjoyed a prospect over parkland, enabling Blacklock to sit in relative comfort on a bench to observe the staff entrance. He invested in a copy of *The Times* and flirted ineffectually with the paper whilst preoccupied with the comings and goings across the street.

As he sat down a nearby clock struck the quarter – fifteen minutes to seven.

'My Word! I don't believe it! Is that *you*, Pathos?' The voice came from behind him, turning his guts to ice. A figure walked round and stood before him. 'It *is*! 'Of all the coincidences! How are you doing old man?'

Robertson had lost weight but was still recognisable. Blacklock mumbled something which he did not understand himself before regaining a measure of composure. 'I am very well, Arthur. How are you? What brings you all the way down to London? What happened to the missionary work?'

Robertson glanced at his watch before answering. 'So many questions! My faith was tested and I'm sorry to say found wanting. Actually, I came *up* to London – I've been in Bristol for a while. Listen, old man, I really have to go. I'm on duty in a few minutes.' He pulled out his notebook, scribbled a few lines and then tore the page out. 'Here's my address. I'm working night shifts at the moment – we're terribly short-staffed – but we really must get together. It will be just like the old days.'

He called over his shoulder as he walked across the road. 'If we only knew where Porter or Priestley were at least four of us would be reunited, so far from home!' He was shouting by the time he reached the end of the sentence, before dissolving into a series of hacking coughs.

Blacklock slumped back, disappointed at how easily he had been caught out.

He examined Robertson's handwriting, which was little more than the series of untidy zigzags it always had been. The address he gave tallied with the one on the reference Miss Henry had obtained although there was no point in going there now. He sorted through everything Robertson had said. *'If we only knew where Porter or Priestley were, at least four of us would be reunited!'* Blacklock's eyes widened. *Gordon is here too, and Robertson knows where.*

Blacklock set off for home – with Robertson working all night there was nothing to be gained from waiting like some overly faithful hound.

'So you're telling me at least four remaining suspects are in London?' asked Starling.

'Yes. At least *three* suspects.'

Starling rolled his eyes. 'You know I'm right, Nate. So what are you going to do next?'

Blacklock rested his head against the back of the chair and closed his eyes. 'I do not have the slightest notion.'

'Alright. Who do think is the most likely perpetrator... Porter?'

'Porthos would certainly not be at the top of my list but in truth –,' he paused, trying to construct his next statement – 'I was never really part of their circle. He was the loudest so you could not miss him. I suppose in retrospect Robertson and Gordon were somewhat in his shadow.'

'And where were you?'

'In *their* shadows, at best. With Priestley and Ballantyne.'

'I thought as much.' Starling clapped his hands then rubbed them together. 'Right. You think it is either Robertson or Gordon. We know where Robertson is, and from him we can find Gordon, or – more easily – Duncan can. If you want my advice I would hand all the names to the police and let them sort the whole bloody mess out. You will have done all the hard work for them. Everybody wins.'

'But–'

'But?'

'I hate to sound like a broken gramophone but Duncan simply will not care who actually did this and who did not. He will just parade one of them in front of a tame magistrate who will pass the case onto Crown Court, who will hang him on the strength of Duncan's testimony and my "evidence". He has admitted as much to me. With a case like this it is only about public profile. Duncan would probably hope to be a Chief Inspector by the end of it.'

'Ignore him. What can *you* do?'

Blacklock shook his head. 'Nothing.'

'There must be something. Doesn't that paddy photographer want to catch this bastard even more than you do? I could follow Porter for a while. He doesn't know me, and Phelps has only seen me once.'

'Never underestimate Phelps. And what would that achieve beyond spying on him and Tilly?'

'You've said it yourself: elimination. I'll start tonight. Come with me to Barts, point him out. I can least do that. Maybe you could set McCormac after Gordon.'

Forty

The Caldecott Residence, 17 Belgrave
Square, Knightsbridge, London
Saturday 9th March

Matilda's personal maid snivelled into her handkerchief.

'For the love of Pete, Ruby, stop bawling and tell me what's the matter. I don't have time to waste on sobbing girls,' snapped Mrs Osman, the Caldecott's housekeeper. 'Sir Edmund is hosting a grand dinner this evening and I've more important matters to attend to. You have no idea how much work I have to do.' She picked up her teacup.

Ruby dabbed her eyes with the corner of her apron. 'Miss Matilda hasn't ... had her monthly.'

'It's none of your business. When you're older you'll understand that Mother Nature doesn't have a strict calendar. Didn't that orphanage teach you anything? Go on. Away with you.'

'But... Mrs Osman – I don't think she's bled since before Christmas. She could be ill. Perhaps you should call Doctor Price?'

The teacup shattered as it struck the floor. Ignoring it, Mrs Osman snarled 'Not a word of this to anyone, Ruby, or you'll be out. Do you hear me?'

Forty-One

Blacklock's lodgings, 64 Pellerin Road,
Stoke Newington, London
Tuesday 12th March

The messenger stood before Blacklock, soaked to the skin and steaming like an exhausted stage horse. 'Sir,' he gasped between ragged breaths, 'please come with me. Inspector says it's Jack. I've a hansom waiting.'

Blacklock glanced at the clock. Barely ten p.m. *Surely too early for Jack?* 'How far?'

'Ten minutes in the cab, no more.'

Blacklock was confronted by a tableau uncannily like the last, albeit with one significant difference. A man of at least forty years lay before him, opened like something from an anatomy class. He stood over the body, trying to imagine what had happened. This was no frenzied attack – he must have been unconscious when the assault took place. He checked the cut and saw the hallmark he hoped would not be there. A sly upward glance revealed the tell-tale post mortem throat cut, with its trademark paucity of blood. *You fool no one.*

'Does that look normal to you?' asked Duncan over his shoulder.

'What?'

'The cut throat. I've seen plenty and people generally bleed like stuck pigs. The past couple of tarts have shed barely a drop. What's going on?'

'It is not without precedent,' lied Blacklock with an ease which alarmed him. 'Trauma and shock can seal even arteries on occasion.'

'Oh. Alright. How does he look ... down below?'

Under other circumstances Blacklock would have been amused by Duncan's uncharacteristic coyness.

'There appears – admittedly this light is very poor – to be no genital trauma although the post mortem will confirm that. Again the abdomen is open and again there are clearly some organs or pieces of organs missing – sections of the large intestine, probably more. It seems–'

'I'm don't bloody care how it *seems*! Are there any fucking *clues*, Blackmore? I'm past caring about what this pervert has taken or left. Is there anything which will tell us *who he is*?'

'Not that I can see, Inspector. Unless he has left other clues which come to light when the body is moved, or perhaps in the post mortem ...'

Duncan looked to the heavens and puffed his cheeks. 'Jesus! What a fucking mess.' He turned away, then swivelled back on his heel. 'Do you think he knows what he's doing?'

Blacklock frowned. 'What do you mean?'

'Could he be a professional – a medic? Does he seem to know his way around when he gets ... in there?'

Blacklock felt his colour rising and turned quickly back to the body. 'Anything is possible, I suppose, but much of the ... work, if you term it such, is crude and lacks skill.' Lying to Duncan became easier with every sentence. 'You could be looking for a butcher or abattoir worker, perhaps. I cannot imagine a medical professional being part of something like this.'

'You can't imagine that because you ain't been a copper for the best part of five and twenty years, that's why. You never want to see what I've seen, hear what I've heard, and God forbid smell what I've smelt. A sick bastard can achieve great things when he puts his mind to it.' He smiled humourlessly. 'So, thanks for the advice but I ain't ruling medics out, Prof. After all, who the hell would choose to cut people up for a living? Beats me.'

Blacklock decided in that instant not to argue, unwilling to highlight his profession by defending it. 'I am sure you are right, Inspector. I bow to your experience.' He fervently hoped he had not sounded sarcastic.

After a pause Duncan clapped his hands and said, 'Onward! When do you think we could move this poor bugger's body to the station?'

'I have sent for McCormac. As soon as he has finished making his photographs the body can be relocated. I have seen all I need to see, although I will wait for McCormac to ensure I get the images I need.'

'Very well. I expect to speak to you in –,' he consulted his watch, '– Jesus. Later today. The honourable Mrs Duncan will kill me one of these late nights or early mornings, I'm sure.'

Blacklock wanted to avoid prolonging his discourse with Duncan, so that he might have some time to examine the scene without the requirement to explain anything he might discover.

He bent down to examine the incision, racking his brains in an attempt to recall any important, specific differences between the Musketeers' scalpel work. Porthos was cavalier almost to the point of butchery – on cadavers, at least – but there were no clear memories of either Priestley or Gordon, whose work – much like his own – was neat, efficient and anonymous.

He sighed and exhaled deeply, trying to master his sense of despair. *Such waste.* He sighed again, before inhaling deeply to regather himself. What was that? *Ether?* Surely not. He rose and sniffed at both the door and window, which had presumably been opened to spare the attending officers' stomachs. He knelt down again and leaned as close as he dared to the man's mouth. He sniffed, tentatively at first. The victim's halitosis was typical of the general population, but years of experience had inured him to the worst of its effects. He closed his eyes and inhaled slowly. There was no doubt. The victim had been etherised. But why? Was the killer beginning to show signs of humanity? It made no sense. He inhaled again, continuing the line of thought.

'You don't have to go that far, Blackmore. I doubt if he'll kiss and tell.'

He started. Duncan had returned so quietly that he had not broken his concentration. 'For a few bob – or less, if you're lucky – there's many a girl who will pucker up for you.'

Blacklock jumped up, blushing furiously. 'It is not funny! And I thought you had left?'

'I don't know that it isn't hilarious, Prof, and I hadn't. But, if I was looking for a pervert with knife skills I might reasonably conclude that I had found one. So, what was you doing? Exactly. And don't try to pull the wool over my eyes. I might not be as stupid as you think.'

'I was trying to detect any unusual chemical traces.'

'Were you indeed? Fancy that. Why?'

Blacklock's mind was racing, desperately seeking a titbit which might satisfy the detective. 'I–I have been developing a method for ... determining the time of death based on ... the level of decompositional bacteria present. They generate methane as a by-product of their biological processes, you see.'

'I don't see but I'll take your word for it. We should use all our senses, so why not?'

'What did you come back for? I thought you were in danger of triggering domestic disharmony.'

'Listen, Blackmore, I'm going to be absolutely straight with you. I need you to find something – anything – new in this butchery. I can't fob Wren or the local mob off with vague promises for much longer. I need a result and you're the man that needs to light the tinder, so to speak. If you need more help, just tell me. I haven't the foggiest about what a scientist needs to solve such a puzzle, so if you don't ask I can't guess. Understand?'

Blacklock nodded. 'A clean room with better lighting is a must. Any tiny clues our murderer may be leaving could be lost because I am basically expected to work in a century-old dungeon with a couple of candles. Beyond that I think I have all the knowledge and tools I need.'

Duncan offered a tight-lipped smile. 'As you wish. I'll have Cargill try to find you somewhere more suited to the practice of your delicate art.' He turned and walked away, not even pausing to check that his latest sarcastic dart had hit its target.

Blacklock smiled. *He finally understands. It is a delicate art.*

Forty-Two

Blacklock's lodgings, 64 Pellerin Road,
Stoke Newington, London
Thursday 14th March

'Ye Gods, Blacklock! What is that feckin' *smell?*' McCormac was struggling not to vomit. 'Did something die in here?' He looked around Blacklock's small living area. 'Your landlady will have you on the streets if you don't do something about it.'

Blacklock shook his head. 'That, McCormac, is the aroma of science. Of evidence.'

'Evidence of what? Rats decomposing in a sewer full of leper's diarrhoea?'

'The few goods and chattels of Daniel Bernard Bainbridge, the latest victim of a Musketeer.'

McCormac held his handkerchief over his mouth and nose. 'It – he – didn't smell like this when I made my photographs.'

'Ah, but he did, Francis. You see, the *entire slum* smells like that, albeit marginally ameliorated by the occasional breeze from the estuary. You – we – simply do not notice it when we are there. I think it may be some form of protection function. Under other circumstances that alone might make for an interesting study.'

McCormac swallowed hard. 'But why is his crap *here*, in your *home?*'

'I thought I caught a whiff of ether in the room when I examined him, which made me think our murderer was at least an iota more humane than we might previously have thought. It also supports the hypothesis that it is a Musketeer – when we were training in Edinburgh ether was commonly used to anaesthetise patients. Of course, it is in fairly widespread use down here now, but still by no means the default position for all surgeons.'

McCormac shook his head. 'So this pile of stinking garbage is something you brought into your own lodgings from the crime scene to prove a theory you were already sure of?'

Blacklock rested his head on his hand and sighed. 'You are right, of course. This has to *mean* something, surely. There *has* to be a reason, no matter how warped.'

'Perhaps,' shrugged McCormac. 'Or perhaps not. Madmen do mad things, by definition.'

Blacklock sat back. 'Do you have any contacts in any newspaper offices? Journalists, in particular?'

'A few, maybe. Why?'

'I wondered if there was any unpublished information about Jack from '88. Perhaps I could compare his "work" – for want of a better word – with our man. Maybe there would be something to rule in or rule out the original killer?'

'Why bother? You already know who it is, within reason.'

'Perhaps I am mistaken. Perhaps Jack coincidentally made the same incision.'

'That sounds ludicrously improbable based on what you've told me. Besides, you don't need the press, you oaf.'

'Why not? It is not as if I can walk in Stoke Newington Public Lending Library and ask for it, is it?'

'Sometimes, Doc, you can be as thick as that chair you're sitting on. Thicker. You are *employed* by the feckin *Metropolitan Police*. You should have access to the first-hand records. If you don't, you can claim you need it. There's no point in replaying the work of some hack who was probably drunk or harassed or both, under the whip to churn out some sensational history of events. Go see Duncan. If that frightens you – what's his underling's name?'

'Cargill.'

'Ask *him*. It's bloody obvious. Or take a holiday. It's equally bloody obvious that you need one.'

Forty-Three

The Mermaid Inn, East Tenter Street, Shadwell
Friday 15th March

The inn was unfamiliar to Blacklock, despite being close enough to Leman Street to attract a large early evening police contingent. At least, he thought, he should be safe from robbery here – unless he were then only to succumb to the effects of inhaling tobacco smoke so thick that it was impossible to see from one end of the room to the other. It seemed that every soul bar him was smoking a pipe or cheap cigar.

He ordered a brandy and water while he waited. Several officers nodded in recognition, but it was clear that they were not entirely certain where they might know him from.

'Sorry I'm late, Doctor,' panted Cargill, emerging from the smoke. 'The guvnor wouldn't shut up. Still, I'm here now.' He looked pointedly at Blacklock's drink long enough for him to get the message.

'I am sorry, Sergeant, what will you have?'

'Pint of mild, please.'

The barman, hovering nearby, spat on a glass before polishing it with his apron and pulled the pint.

'So what can I do to help, Doctor? Your message was a bit cryptic.' He downed the first third of the pint, leaving a froth on his moustache that he smeared off with the back of his hand.

Blacklock sipped his own drink. 'Could you obtain the files for the Whitechapel Murders of '88? I am happy to read them in the station if that makes things easier.'

Cargill shrugged. 'Don't see why not. What are you looking for?'

'Similarities – or differences – between the recent cases and the older ones. I want to determine for certain whether we are dealing with a new perpetrator or the original ...

Jack.'

Cargill downed his pint. 'I'll see what I can do. The records will be at Scotland Yard now, gathering dust or fading or both. I'll get as many as I can recalled to Leman Street. Call in in a couple of days. Should I mention this to the old man, or are we meeting here because you don't want him to know?' He stared at his glass for several seconds.

Blacklock's heart sank. More unbudgeted expense, and not even spent on himself. He started to gesture to the barman who almost instantaneously began refilling Cargill's glass. 'To be honest, Albert, I would rather keep it from him for the time being. He might jump to conclusions the next time the Leman Street mob comes calling and we are not talking about six weeks, six months or even six years in prison for an innocent man – I keep thinking about poor Solomon Thurber – we are talking about the gallows.'

Cargill winked, then drank half the fresh pint in a single draught. 'Fair enough.'

As he reached for the glass again, Blacklock jumped in, desperate to avoid buying another drink. 'Can you send word when the files arrive, please?'

'Of course, Doctor.'

The glass was barely half way to Cargill's lips when Blacklock wished him a good evening and fled for the door.

Forty-Four

Leman Street Police Station, Shadwell, London
Wednesday 20th March

'This way, Doctor.' Cargill pushed the uncooperative door open and stood to one side, allowing Blacklock in first.

Blacklock ducked into the small room and looked around in bewilderment. 'How many...'

'Boxes? Eighty-three, sir. Enough to keep you occupied for a little while.'

The bankers' boxes were piled high around two of walls of the tiny room, with the remainder stacked precariously on an ancient desk in the corner. 'Is this the best available room, Albert? There is not even a window. It hardly lends itself to study.'

'I'm sorry. It's the best room that I could find that was empty *and* not somewhere the Inspector might amble into. You've seen the fat bugger – he might not even be able to make it up that final flight of stairs. You should be undisturbed here.'

'A small mercy, I suppose. Thank you for your consideration.'

'Let me know when you're ready for more.'

'*More*? There are more than this?'

'Heavens, yes. There are one-hundred and seven further boxes in the stores, but we didn't have a big enough wagon to carry them all at once. A little over half a million pages.'

'But I cannot–'

'Ah!' Cargill raised his hand. 'Be careful what you wish for.'

Forty-Five

Blacklock's lodgings, 64 Pellerin Road,
Stoke Newington, London
Friday 22nd March

'I followed Robertson home,' said McCormac, 'when his shift finished. He went straight there, via the most direct route. No detours, no dalliances. Got home about 7.30 a.m.'

'That seems remarkably ordinary,' replied Blacklock.

'I thought he would go to bed, but no. He changed his clothes and took his daughter – an invalid – to school.'

'An invalid?'

'Yes. She seems to be mostly confined to a bath chair. She can manage a few awkward steps, but only a handful. Ten at most.'

'Any other clues? Any deformations? Signs of mental feebleness or impairment?'

'I couldn't get close enough to determine such details but she appeared to be a bright enough little thing.'

'How old?'

'Hard to tell. I have little first-hand experience in such matters, but I would guess she is between eight and twelve, but really – I'm no expert. Robertson seems like quite the devoted father.'

'Thank you. How do we locate Gordon? With Robertson working overnight suspicion naturally falls on others.'

'No.'

'I beg your pardon?

'You're implying that Robertson works every night, and has done for the entire period during which these women have perished. Not so. Don't you think he has days off? St John's must have a rota system so he probably only works overnight on occasion. No one could work at night indefinitely, surely?'

'An excellent point. How could I forget so soon? So..?'

'So you still have a full set of suspects on the field of play.'

'Thank you. I sit corrected.'

'I haven't finished yet. If you want to meet Gordon simply invite him and Robertson out for drinks, or perhaps dinner. What have you to lose? Assuming he attends with Robertson, someone could follow him home afterwards and you would have all three addresses.'

'And if he declines the invitation?'

'You're no worse off.'

Blacklock stared into the fire, deep in thought.

'Just write to Robertson, Doc, and invite him and Gordon to dinner one evening. We'll take it from there.'

Forty-Six

Champion's Chop and Ale House, Hampstead, London
Tuesday 26th March

Champion's Chop And Ale House was a down-at-heel place that McCormac had recommended due to its proximity to St John's and cheap fare. It did not serve to present Blacklock as he wished to be perceived, but it was inexpensive and his accounts were almost exhausted, leaving him little choice. He and McCormac arrived early, a few minutes apart. McCormac took a stool at the bar and ordered mutton stew, which he ate absent-mindedly whilst feigning interest in his newspaper.

Without any acknowledgement of the Irishman Blacklock entered and procured a table for three. He ordered half a pint of dark ale, ostensibly to maintain a clear head, although the reduced impact on his finances did not go amiss.

Robertson arrived punctually at seven thirty. He strode to the table and offered his hand enthusiastically. 'Pathos – Nathaniel, I'm sorry – it's so good to see you. How are you, old man?'

'Very well, thank you,' lied Blacklock, hoping his smile was not a rictus. 'Such a coincidence our meeting like that. What will you have to drink?'

Robertson thought for a moment or two. 'Gin please. A small one. One should always keep one's wits, don't you agree?'

Blacklock held up his half-pint and smiled. 'Most of the time, certainly. I seem to recall you as a teetotaller?'

Robertson smiled wryly. 'Not anymore.'

'Is Gordon joining us, or should we order some dinner?'

'No, no, we should wait. I saw him yesterday and he definitely intends to dine with us.' He coughed into a dark handkerchief. 'Perhaps he has been delayed by a difficult case. You know how it is.'

'Indeed. So ... tell me about what you've been up to during all these years.'

'Not a lot. I married Maud soon after we left Edinburgh. I was on missionary service in the Shire Highlands – now the British Central Africa Protectorate – you must have heard of it?'

'Of course,' lied Blacklock.

'Good. God blessed us with a daughter on our first wedding anniversary. Life and the Mission were wonderful, until Maud fell ill and we had to return.' He exhaled. 'Enough of that. This is a celebration! Remind me again, where are you practising?'

Blacklock looked at the table. 'Nowhere, at present.' He saw no point in hiding the truth. 'I am currently serving a licence suspension.'

'Oh no! Why?'

'A patient had an unknown renal arteriovenous malformation. Two arteries, instead of one. She had already lost a good deal of blood during the procedure, albeit nothing from which she could not have recovered in the normal run of things.'

'As they do. That's always a messy procedure, I very dimly recall. I now only work in pharmacy and diagnosis - my surgical skills were never really up to snuff, as I'm sure you recall.'

'I am equally sure you would have prevailed with more practise and confidence. Anyway, I dissected out the original tumour but nicked the second arterial branch to the kidney. I tried to save her but by the time I had secured a decent field of vision and repaired the damage ... she was gone.'

Robertson shook his head. 'And they *suspended* you? How could you – how could anyone – possibly have known? You cannot be held responsible for abnormal structures. You have appealed, of course?'

'Naturally I have done so, and their decision has to be

given by August – at least in theory. I will not hold my breath. The decision has already been deferred more than once already.'

Robertson shook his head. 'There but for the Grace of God and all that. How long has this been going on?'

'Thirteen months.'

'How do you subsist?'

'I–.' He stopped himself, just in time. 'I lecture in pathology. Strictly part time, just until my licence is returned.'

Robertson held up his glass. 'To relief!'

'Relief!'

A period of awkward, circular conversation followed, as the chop house continued to fill. Eventually the inn door swung open, banging against its stops.

Robertson raised his hand. 'Over here!'

Gordon, unlike Robertson, had aged more than seemed possible over the intervening period. He was gaunt, ashen and even though his head was shaved Blacklock could see that his hair had been falling out in clumps before the application of the razor. Nevertheless, he seemed energetic enough as he worked his way through the crowd.

'Ye Gods, it's true!' He held out his hand. 'I assumed that Aramis here was suffering from delusions when he claimed that he had come across Pathos sitting on a bench outside the hospital, but here you are, Blacklock, large as life and twice as ugly.' He returned to the bar, collecting a glass and a bottle of wine.

He sat down opposite Blacklock. 'It really *is* you. Where have you been?'

Blacklock recapitulated his recent history.

'You poor beggar! I hope the RCS sees sense quickly.'

'And what about you?'

Gordon glanced quickly at Robertson before he replied. 'Not too bad, I suppose. A touch of ill-health – which you've already kindly been too polite to mention – but nothing that a dose of death won't put right.'

'Really?' stuttered Blacklock. 'I am so sorry. I had no idea.'

'Don't worry about it. I have more or less come to terms with the situation and made my peace. It would be easier if some bugger could diagnose the problem, but we aren't magicians, are we?'

Blacklock shook his head. 'If only we were. I suppose – you have no – prognosis, if you are undiagnosed?'

'Correct.'

They lapsed into silence as each searched desperately for something to say. When Gordon stepped away to relieve himself, Blacklock said, 'Does Gordon have ..?'

'Yes–'

Gordon returned to the table.

'Tell me more about your daughter, Aramis,' said Blacklock.

Robertson's face lightened. 'Her name is Eliza, ten years old and beautiful – but what father doesn't say that? She's very ... capable, and resilient. She's had to be. She lost her mother when she was three, and a year or so later she contracted poliomyelitis which affected her legs. Still, she's always smiling. A beacon for me – my guiding light.'

A second embarrassed lull was avoided by the approach of the landlord to collect their meal orders.

After the arrival of Gordon, Blacklock had sensed a small but definite shift in the conversation. Robertson and Gordon spent a disproportionate amount of time talking to each other about events he could know nothing of, subtly excluding him. Were they? Was the chip they had so often accused him of carrying on his shoulder really that, a paranoid little voice in the back of his mind, watching for examples where their behaviour matched his expectation?

When the food eventually arrived it was cold, something else for which he felt absurdly and unreasonably responsible.

He was rudely dragged from his reverie.

'Hey, Pathos, wake up!' Gordon was clicking his wasted

fingers in Blacklock's face.

'I am sorry, Charles. I was miles away.'

'With the fairies, eh? We always had our suspicions didn't we, Arthur?'

The pair laughed uproariously while Blacklock wondered how he had forgotten the point of the evening. 'So, Charles, are your lodgings far from St John's?'

'No, not at all. They're much more convenient than poor old Aramis's here. Five minutes from the hospital. Three minutes from the Nurse's Home.' He grinned in a manner which Blacklock found repulsive.

'Some people never change,' replied Blacklock with counterfeit humour.

'He lives in a veritable palace, Pathos,' said Robertson. 'You and I could but dream of such a place.'

'One day, *petit garçon*, I will settle down,' said Gordon. 'Or up. Or rather I would do, but as you can see I'm done for. Until that fateful day I shall continue to live by the example you set in Edinburgh – a life of ceaseless study and monastic celibacy.'

Gordon and Robertson managed to keep straight faces for only a couple of seconds before exploding into raucous laughter. As the tears rolled down their cheeks, Blacklock quietly put his cutlery on his plate, dabbed his mouth deliberately with a napkin and got to his feet. 'Goodnight, gentlemen,' he said.

'Please, Pathos, don't be so bloody sensitive. I hoped you might have outgrown this by now. Stay,' said Gordon. 'It's just an old joke amongst old friends. Where's the harm? Come on, sit down. I'll get another bottle, this time something more like wine and less like medicine.'

Forty-Seven

Blacklock's lodgings, 64 Pellerin Road,
Stoke Newington, London
Tuesday 26th March

'What the hell did you think you were doing, running out like that?' McCormac jumped to his feet and looked out of the window. 'I couldn't very well follow anyone after your performance, could I? You lost our opportunity because of a fit of pique. Are you mad?' He sighed. 'I thought you wanted to catch the killer.'

'I do not know any more. What does it matter? They are all alike in their unpleasantness and one of them is a murderer. At this moment I do not much care which of them goes to the gallows. I have half a mind to go to Duncan, as you and Starling rarely stop suggesting, and lay out the evidence – such as it is.'

'You know you don't mean that, Doc. You could no more let an innocent man swing than you would let a patient die who could be saved.'

Blacklock shrugged. 'Do not be so sure.'

'And don't you be so ... petulant. Childish. Choose your own adjective. You're supposed to be a grown man but you insist on lugging around their comments like you're in school. I've been there when Duncan has said far worse to you and you don't overreact like this. There are times, Blacklock – which I fear are becoming more frequent – when I simply fail to understand your behaviour. I swear to God there's some button they push and you lose all self-control. You need to get a grip on yourself.'

'I have an idea, McCormac. You try losing your career, then the temporary position you took in lieu of your career *and* your fiancée to an old acquaintance. When you have managed all that, by all means feel at liberty to return and lecture me on self-control. Until then I will thank you to keep your opinions of my mental state to yourself.'

McCormac shook his head. 'I'm not passing opinion on anything of the sort, Doc. I don't doubt that this combination of events has been especially painful, but in the context of four dead bodies it's nothing – an irrelevance. I'm not in the habit of issuing ultimatums–'

'Then I suggest you do not start now.'

'–but people are *dying*, and you have critical knowledge which would see the perpetrators removed from circulation, certainly pending trial. It's the twenty-sixth of March. You have two weeks from today to determine who is responsible.'

Blacklock started to speak but McCormac continued talking over him. 'If you have not done so, I'll go to Duncan and tell him what I know. Unless there's another death in which case time's up.'

'But the risk–'

'If you're about to bleat something about an innocent man going to the gallows, don't forget that women are at risk *right now*. Every night that you prevaricate risks another completely innocent life. You have immense responsibility, and by association with you so do I. My cousin was murdered – you can't imagine what that's like. The loss of a career or fiancée is nothing by comparison.' He picked up his hat and walked to the door. 'Goodnight. I am going to do something substantive. I am going to act against this murderer. Wallow in self-pity as much as you wish, Doc, but there *is* no time to waste.'

Blacklock stared at McCormac for a few moments before looking down, apparently examining some invisible flaw in his hand. 'I appreciate your sentiments, Francis, but my temperament is fundamentally at odds with this sort of work, this subterfuge, if you will. If someone shows me less than the respect I am due then I must stand up for my principles – as any gentleman would. It is easy for you–'

'Sorry? Why? Because I'm not a *gentleman*?'

'No – no. I did not mean that.'

'What did you mean?'

'Our backgrounds and education are different, so it is only natural that we should view the world from differing perspectives.'

McCormac mumbled, 'Is that so?'

Blacklock nodded, unable to meet his gaze.

'I see,' said McCormac, curtly. 'You present me with a dilemma.'

'I do? How so?'

'I feel, naturally enough, slighted by your attitude. If I were to behave as you would, were the tables turned, I would storm out now and leave you to rot, because as one of the final few souls left on God's green Earth who can bear to spend time with a moody prick like you even I have my limits. And that's exactly what you are, Blacklock, before you take umbrage. A moody prick who expects everyone to assist him in his Arthurian quest for justice whilst he simultaneously continues to denigrate them. You can forget my deadline – not because I will not take what I know to Duncan, but because I am no longer going to factor your views into my decision making. I take my leave, *Doctor Blacklock*. I may perhaps encounter you at the scene of the next horror, but that might be avoided if I elect to have Duncan incarcerate the suspects. *All* of them. No exceptions.'

Blacklock drew breath to reply but McCormac turned and left.

Forty-Eight

Leman Street Police Station, Shadwell, London
Thursday 28th March

Blacklock consulted his watch for the third time in his first hour in the sweltering garret at Leman Street station. He was already on the verge of despair. Each box was simply labelled "Whitechapel Murders" with a number.

The box contents strewn before him were the contents of the first box opened today, depressingly identified as 'Box 2 of 190'. He had started these studies irritated that he could not locate box number one; it had taken great willpower to ignore the sequence and open the second.

His dismay at not starting with the first box was as nothing to his current state. There was no order inside the box either, as if the contents of a disordered office had simply been swept into it with no concern for those that may follow. Perhaps there was not – after all, had not the unsatisfactory end to the Whitechapel cases been an embarrassment to all involved? It was likely that those responsible for the investigation were heartsick of the whole terrible episode.

He scanned the top of the desk. A mixture of cheap paper, written in myriad individual hands – some vaguely intelligible, most not.

He sat back and rubbed his eyes. This already appeared to be a fool's errand but it was all he had to do. There had been no word from McCormac since their argument two nights before. Blacklock had not spoken to a soul other than his landlady and the station desk sergeant, who clearly viewed him as some kind of harmless eccentric who spent time in the station because he had no other place to go – a view closer to the truth than he cared to admit.

When Blacklock finally left the airless room he was horrified to discover that he had been ensconced for fifteen hours and discovered nothing he did not already know from the seven boxes fully examined. He would not – could not – admit defeat. What else was there which would inform his "investigation"?

He stepped into the cool darkness of Leman Street, now peopled solely by those who were homeless and those that preyed upon them. A sudden despair overcame him. There was nothing more hopeful at his lodgings, nor to be found at The Unicorn. Any hunger he felt had waned long ago.

After a few irresolute moments he walked back into the station, where the relative warmth was free, and returned to his Sisyphean quest on the mountain of paper.

Forty-Nine

Leman Street Police Station, Shadwell, London
Thursday 4th April

After a week and more than a hundred hours of labour his painstaking examination of only thirty-three boxes was complete, with little of note to show for it. There was still no word from McCormac and his sense of isolation grew.

In these lonely hours his thoughts irresistibly turned to Tilly, his imagination relentlessly serving up the most unsavoury images of Porthos' conduct with her. There was enough evidence to remove Porthos permanently as a rival, and try as he might to reject such unbecoming and unjust thoughts they were not as easily dismissed as he would like. He was also troubled to discover that he could harbour such notions; distressed that they could even *occur* to him. *What kind of man – let alone what kind of doctor – could conceive of such ideas?* With the final thought came the realisation that he could forgive himself because he would not act on them. One of the Musketeers had far worse thoughts and under some unimaginable compulsion chose to act upon them. He hoped he was better than that.

Fifty

60 New Square, Lincoln's Inn Fields, London
Monday 15th April

The summons to Marlow's office was both brief and unexpected. Whatever news there was only merited two neutral sentences which Blacklock read and reread endlessly, searching for nuances which his solicitor, although competent, was probably incapable of achieving. *"News from RCS. Need to discuss your pointless campaign."*

'Sit down, Nathaniel. Tea?'

Blacklock waved away the offer. 'What is the problem?'

'This.' Marlow picked up a letter and balanced his antique pince-nez precariously on his bulbous nose. 'They have requested – no, they have commanded – that you stop your *"orchestrated campaigning forthwith or they will remove you permanently from the Surgical Register in ten days".'*

'*What*? I do not know what they are talking about.'

Marlow's quizzical eyebrow spurred Blacklock on. 'I give you my word of honour, Abraham. I have no idea what they could be referring to as "a campaign".'

'Do you know anyone called Porter?'

'Yes.'

'Gordon? Robertson? Presley?'

'Certainly. Spell the last one, please?'

'P-r-e-s-l-e-y.'

'Strange spelling of Priestley but otherwise, yes I know them.'

'Well call them off. Their vociferous letter-writing campaign for your reinstatement will backfire if they don't pull their horns in. Now.'

Fifty-One

Porter's lodgings, York Street, Marylebone, London
Monday 15th April

Furious that Porthos had found yet another way to damage his life Blacklock vaulted up the steps to the flats where Porter lived and ran through the front door, barely stopping to open it first. Inside, a set of deeply-polished mahogany post-boxes were numbered - which one was Porter's? One was overflowing, unable to accommodate the influx of mail. He removed the topmost letter. It was addressed to *Doctor Geo. Porter, Flat 17*. Blacklock stuffed the letter back in, but not before noticing that the one immediately underneath bore Miss Caldecott's unmistakably florid hand. It was thick; several pages long at least. *She never wrote to me at such length.* He glanced around. Seeing he was alone, he inserted his finger underneath the flap.

He stopped, conflicted. To read this would be theft, and what else? Pointless self-torture. He easily recalled the romantic phrases which had filled Matilda's letters to *him*. What good would be served by inflicting the pain of seeing the same empty words addressed to someone else?

None.

A waste-paper bin stood below the letter boxes, already host to myriad rejected missives. After pausing for a couple of seconds, he tore the envelope and contents into tiny fragments and dropped them like so much confetti into the bin. Before the last piece had completed its fall he was overwhelmed with guilt at his own behaviour but, like so many realisations he had had recently, it was too late.

The door of Flat 17 was identical to the others he had passed on the way up; anonymous. Undaunted, he rang the bell. He felt himself blushing, and cursed himself for it.

No matter; whatever contemptible scheme Porthos and the others were playing was going to end now.

There was no reply. Again checking he was alone – like a housebreaker – he crouched down and peered through the keyhole, only to be thwarted by the escutcheon on the other side.

'Are you here on official business?'

Blacklock jumped to his feet, blushing even more fiercely. His interrogator was an elderly lady, obviously well-to-do. At her side sat an enormous Alsatian, silent as The Sphinx, which stared at him as if contemplating which limb it might consume first. 'I–'

'Well, are you? I don't see too well. I suppose you're a bailiff? Colonel Hardy has been threatening young Porter with eviction – and not before time.'

'I am a – a bailiff's agent. I have been sent to discuss matters with Doctor Porter to see whether some less litigious route might be found to avoid any further unpleasantness. May I ask who you are?'

'Miss Roget. Flat 18. Next door.'

'I see. Can you recall when you last saw Doctor Porter?'

The old lady frowned. 'At least ten days; perhaps a fortnight. I used to hear him almost every day, coming and going at all hours. Most unbecoming of a resident here.'

'Thank you, Miss Roget.' Aware that the old lady was squinting – she clearly had cataracts – Blacklock pulled out his wallet and pretended to make some notes. '"*At least ten days, perhaps a fortnight.*" You have been very helpful. I can see I must return with a locksmith. Good day.'

Fifty-Two

Robertson's lodgings, 84 Grenville
Street, Vauxhall, London
Tuesday 16th April

Thoughts of the mysterious letters apparently bombarding The College whirled uncomfortably around his head as the hansom clattered through the streets towards Robertson's address. The streets grew poorer after they had passed St John's and continued their steady decline towards Vauxhall.

Robertson's house was a mean one, almost tumbling down in the centre of a terrace of similarly dilapidated properties. Blacklock paid off the cab – there was no point in paying waiting fees – and slowly approached the house. Lamps burned in both the ground and first floor windows, which he assumed meant that there was more than one person at home.

He rapped smartly on the door, which had neither a bell nor a knocker.

He was startled as the door opened almost instantly. An elderly woman bustled by without a word. 'Pathos!' said Robertson. 'Come in, please. Pay no attention to Mrs Rosebery – she's the very definition of shyness. She sits for Eliza when I have business elsewhere,' He stepped back to allow Blacklock to enter the tiny parlour – the street door opened immediately into the room without even the smallest of vestibules. 'Excuse the mess, Nathaniel. We live on top of each other.'

'Rosebery? As in..?'

'No relation, I'm sure,' laughed Robertson.

'Papa, who is it?' called a gentle voice from upstairs.

'An old college friend, Eliza. When you complete your needlework please call and I will bring you some hot chocolate.' The house was so small that he barely needed to raise his voice.

'Thank you, Papa. Good evening, Papa's friend!' She signed off with the most girlish of giggles.

'And to you too, Miss Robertson,' replied Blacklock.

Robertson sat down on an old dining chair. 'Well, Nathaniel, I must say this is a surprise. I thought we might never see you again after the pantomime at Champion's. To what do I owe this pleasure?'

'Have you written to the College?'

Robertson frowned. 'About ..?'

'Me.'

'*You*? Why should I?'

'That, Arthur, is what I am trying to determine. So, have you?'

'Of course not.'

'Has Gordon, do you know?'

'I couldn't possibly know, could I? What do these ... letters refer to?'

'They call for my reinstatement.'

'A worthy enough cause.'

Blacklock chose to ignore what he believed was an empty compliment. 'All I ask is that it stops. It is not that I am not grateful–'

'But you are ungrateful. Clearly, or you wouldn't be in my home, berating me.'

Blacklock shook his head. 'Please do not misunderstand or misinterpret my motives. I need this to stop, so if you have any idea who might be responsible please let them, or me, know. Whilst I am pleased that some persons may wish to intervene on my behalf, unfortunately it is having quite the reverse effect of that intended and is further prejudicing the process. To my considerable detriment.'

Robertson nodded sagely. 'I see. That won't do.'

'Indeed it will not.' Blacklock stood and picked up his hat. 'Could you give me Gordon's address? I might as well see him whilst I am at this end of town.'

Fifty-Three

Gordon's residence, Glaister Villas, Hampstead
Tuesday 16th April

Gordon's lodgings were several grades up from both Robertson's and Porter's. The door to the building, which presumably contained apartments, was guarded by an imposing uniformed doorman.

'Can I be of assistance, sir?'

'I am here to see Charles Gordon.'

'Are you? Is Doctor Gordon expecting you? He has not informed me of any visitors.'

'No, it is ... more of an impromptu visit. I was in the area and thought I would call in. My name is Blacklock. I went to medical school with Doctor Gordon in Edinburgh.'

'Do you have a card? I will ask a footman to present it.'

Blacklock patted himself down. 'Darn it! I changed coats this afternoon and neglected to transfer my card holder. I feel so foolish.'

The doorman remained implacable as he examined Blacklock's attire. It clearly did not meet with his approval. 'I understand. Please wait here and I will determine whether Doctor Gordon is receiving.' He locked the door with unnecessary emphasis to ensure that Blacklock knew he was an untrusted outsider.

Blacklock cursed quietly, hoping his voice had not carried.

In a few moments the door opened. 'Doctor Gordon has acceded to your request. Please follow me. May I take your coat and hat?'

'That will not be necessary, thank you. I will not detain Doctor Gordon for long.'

Gordon's apartment was palatial in comparison to anyone else's that Blacklock knew. A long hall ran the length of it, perfectly-polished floor tiles reflecting the dazzling electrified chandeliers overhead.

'Come in, old man. Brandy?' The bright lighting made his ill-health all the more apparent.

'If it is no trouble.'

'Not for Pathos! Take a seat by the fire and I'll be there in a jiffy.'

The brandy was rich and perfectly balanced. 'Thank you, Charles. I would not be surprised to encounter a butler in a place like this.'

'It's his night off, so one must fend for oneself. Life can be *such* a trial.'

Blacklock laughed. 'Very good. I was almost convinced.'

'Of what?'

'Of your retaining a butler.'

'But I do, Pathos. It really is Armstrong's night off. I believe he visits his sister in Clerkenwell.'

'Oh.' Blacklock stared into his glass. 'Of course.'

'Why are you here, Blacklock?' Gordon's tone cooled abruptly.

Blacklock matched it. 'Have you written to the College on my behalf?'

'Why on earth would I do that? You're merely an acquaintance from a lifetime ago. I assure you I have no interest in your uninteresting life.'

Blacklock's face reddened. 'It is not amusing, you know. You, Aramis and Porthos can play your childish games but you fail to understand that my whole bloody career is at stake. We never have to meet again but in the name of all that is holy please stop these games. I have tried to take my blows and concede defeat. You all win, I lose – as ever.' He put on his hat. 'Please be satisfied with that. I do not know why you would persist in this, and frankly I do not care to know. I suppose that casual malice can be its own reward.'

He left without a word.

Gordon poured himself another drink and wondered briefly what letters the clearly unhinged Pathos could be referring to.

Blacklock walked home, bitterly resenting his lot. Stupid jealousy from The Musketeers could kill him and they would care not one jot. Schoolboy games to last an eternity.

Fifty-Four

Frog's Island, Woolwich, London
Friday 19th April

McCormac's absence ended as he and Blacklock arrived simultaneously at the crime scene behind a long-abandoned warehouse on Frog's Island. They nodded curtly to each other and walked in silence to the police cordon, where Cargill was waiting.

'Doctor, Mr McCormac, thank you for turning out once again.'

'Where is she?' asked Blacklock, keen to avoid small-talk.

'This one's a little different, sir.'

'How so?'

'It's best you see for yourself, Doctor.'

Cargill led them through a distressingly familiar maze of dereliction. Litter clogged every pathway, and piled high in the dark corners which personified this place.

Eventually they reached a small courtyard, perhaps only ten yards square, although its precise dimensions were difficult to ascertain, so full was it with police officers.

Cargill pushed through to the bottom of a rusting iron stairway. 'Up there. Third on the right.'

Blacklock tested the handrail with his stick; a grey dust tumbled from where the supporting bracket was affixed to the soot-blackened brickwork. 'Is this safe?'

'Sure,' said Cargill, albeit without conviction. 'We've had a few lads up there already and they're still with us.'

Blacklock mounted the first step, which flexed in a way that he preferred it would not. He hesitated briefly before moving on, his hand following but never actually touching the handrail.

A single officer guarded the door. He glanced up as Blacklock reached the top of the stairs. 'Go steady there. This landing is pretty rickety if you ask me, and plunging to our deaths in that shitten mire below wouldn't be a great way to go for either of us.'

Blacklock raised a hand in apology and tiptoed the rest of the way, trying and failing to block out the creaking of the ironwork. The third door opened directly into a mean room in which there were no facilities and no furniture to speak of beyond a straw mattress on the floor.

A child?

The room was windowless. He gently closed the door behind him and sniffed. *Ether.*

He reopened the door to admit what was left of the fading light. In contrast to the previous scene there were no piles of bloody rags, no gruesome bowls.

He crouched down and lifted the child's frock. It was a boy. *What?* With infinite respect he continued rolling back the filthy covering. The incision was the same, albeit with much less local damage. He shook his head in disbelief as he gently – almost reverently – replaced the makeshift shroud.

A figure blocked the light. 'What do we have, Doc?' asked McCormac in the same tone of voice as if they had been together all evening.

'It is a young boy, Francis. I do not think he can be more than eight years of age.'

'Ah. Not our man then?'

Blacklock rose slowly to his feet. 'On the contrary, I believe it is,' he said in a whisper which he hoped would not carry to the officer outside.

'Oh my God, Doc. This *has* to stop. If only I had gone to Duncan this would not have happened. I've been such a fool!'

Blacklock gently rested his hand on McCormac's forearm. 'I understand completely. Looking at this half of me wishes you had.'

McCormac jerked his arm away. '*Only half?* Christ alive, this has gone too far. This child's blood is on our hands.'

'Please, Francis, try not to overdramatise–'

'Overdramatise?' hissed McCormac. 'Can't you bloody see

what's in front of you? How is it possible to "overdramatise" the murder of a *child?*'

The officer at the door leaned in. 'Is ... everything alright here, gentlemen? You seem to be getting a little hot under the collars, if I might be so bold.'

'Just a ... professional disagreement, constable,' said Blacklock. 'Are you sure this room is undisturbed?'

'I was the first here, sir, and I ain't left my post since. It's different when it's a kiddie, don't you think?'

'Yes, yes. Of course.' He turned to McCormac. 'He was not murdered here. There is no blood, no rags, none of the paraphernalia we are used to.'

'Blackmore!' Duncan's voice rang out from the end of the walkway. 'This mountain ain't coming to Mohammed, so you'd better come to me.'

'In a moment,' called Blacklock. 'Just a few exposures, Francis. I do not think there is much to help us here. I will try to placate Duncan. Please find me before you leave.'

Duncan was pacing the uneven cobbles at the base of the fire escape. 'Ah, Blackmore! About bloody time. There's no way on God's green earth that I am going to set foot on that pile of rusting iron. Now, what did you see?'

'A child, Inspector. Under ten years of age. A boy.'

'What the *hell?*'

'I do not think the child has been ... violated. The abdominal wounds are less extensive. I will know more later. I am not sure whether this is even the work of our man.'

Fifty-Five

Leman Street Police Station, Shadwell, London
Saturday 20th April

The boy looked even younger under the bright lights which had been installed at Blacklock's behest. 'How did you end up here, boy?' asked Blacklock.

Duncan had delivered on his promise of better facilities for Blacklock, but under the bright gas lamps the child looked especially pathetic. Beyond the familiar incision there were no hallmarks – no post-mortem throat cut, no wholesale destruction within the abdomen.

Duncan lurked close to the door, rattling his change. 'So, Blackmore, is it our man?'

'I do not think so. The appendix has been removed, but I believe the child died of peritonitis – I cannot prove it now but I believe the mite's appendix burst.'

'Natural causes?'

'Er ... yes. I think this pseudo-surgical intervention came too late to save the child, although the intent was humane.'

'Why abandon the body?'

'I cannot fathom that. I can tell you how the boy died, but the events that preceded his death are a mystery, to me at least.'

'Bottom line – not murder?'

'No. Not even manslaughter, although I have no clear understanding of the legal definition. I think somebody intervened to save him and they were too late. In the eyes of the law I have no idea how this would appear, but to me it is a failed surgery. How sanitary or otherwise we do not know. It certainly did not take place where his body was found – but your investigation is really limited to why they should discard him, who he belongs to, and who tried to save him.'

Duncan bit the end off a cigar and spat it onto the floor. 'Bugger. There's nothing here for me. Us.'

'But a crime has clearly been committed, surely?'

'Without doubt. Crimes are committed on every corner of every London street, every hour of every day. This–' – Duncan pointed at the small corpse on Blacklock's table – 'this is a crime. A child who has not been reported missing has died under the knife of a wannabe surgeon whose reach exceeds his talent. I would love to catch the bastard – don't think for half a second that I condone this – but this poor child was going to die anyway if what you tell me is correct?'

'He was. I believe his appendix was removed too late – after it had burst. He would certainly have perished as a result of the ensuing infection.'

Duncan stared at nothing then spoke in an uncharacteristically low voice. 'Someone tried to help this mite. No one else would. If I caught the man that did this I'd give him twenty-four hours to move on before I called looking for him.' He focussed on Blacklock again. 'You're surprised at how magnanimous I'm being. Don't count on it lasting, Blackmore. I can't sustain a hunt for the knifeman that did this because I have another one slicing up tarts left, right and centre across the East End which is starting to feel like a shaken barrel and once you lose control of a poor area it takes an awful lot of broken bones to get it back in line. I've seen it too many times.'

'That is a great speech, Inspector, but this poor child died due to someone's negligence. Does that not matter to you?'

Duncan tilted his head in thought before walking very deliberately over to Blacklock. 'But if he had died in an operating theatre, I'm sure that would have been absolutely fine. No criminal charges because a man with a sharp knife and a God complex cuts someone open in a hospital?' He stabbed his fat forefinger into Blacklock's chest. 'Watch your step, sonny. Watch your step.' He stalked away.

Within moments Cargill walked in. 'What did you say to the old man? I haven't seen him that angry for months.'

'It does not matter. A few home truths, perhaps, but they

were water off a duck's back. The boy is dead and Duncan does not care. If he had children he might feel differently about it.'

'He does. Did. He had a son, but he died.'

'*Murdered?*'

'Nah. Drowned in The Thames. Fell off a bridge parapet pretending to be Blondin. Every copper east of Hammersmith went looking for him but too late. He washed up the next day.'

'I was unaware of that.'

'He doesn't tell anyone. His wife topped herself a few days later – stepped off the same parapet with her pockets full of stones.'

'I had no idea.'

'It's not something anyone would want to shout from the rooftops, is it?'

'What did he do?'

'Nothing. Reported for duty the next day. Took a couple of hours off for the funeral – double funeral – and never mentioned it again.'

'Wait – he told me he had a wife to go home to, just a few days ago. That he was going to be in domestic strife.'

Cargill shook his head. 'Sometimes he forgets. Poor bugger.'

Fifty-Six

The Olde Bell and Unicorn Inn, Shacklewell Lane, Stoke Newington, London
Monday 22nd April

Blacklock slammed the ale on the table in front of McCormac. He had not bought himself one. 'I am sorry.'

McCormac was sitting back in his chair, arms folded. He raised an eyebrow but said nothing.

'Really. I am. If you had gone to Duncan it is possible – probable – even likely that the boy would have died a different death at the same sort of time.'

McCormac, unmoved, showed no emotion.

'He *would have died anyway*, Francis. The peritonitis would have killed him. Please believe me. It is not some ... convenient untruth.'

McCormac leaned forward and sipped his beer. 'Is that it?'

Blacklock, determined not to lose his temper, restricted himself to nodding.

'It may well not be a "convenient untruth", but it is without doubt an extremely convenient truth.'

'It is?'

'Of course. By dooming the wee kiddie to die regardless, you reduce the circumstances of his actual death to a mere coincidence. As if it doesn't matter. As if ... he didn't die at the hands of someone who uses you and your cronies' trademark incision. Five people have died – the last two of which, maybe even three, would not have done so had you reported your suspicions to Duncan.'

Blacklock flushed but did not reply.

'Mary Guiley died at Jack's hands. Two of the recent victims were mothers. You have no conception of the effect that has on a child. I shouldn't have been persuaded by your arguments before but I won't be now. I'll see Duncan first thing in the morning.' He reached into his pocket and threw some pennies onto the table. 'Don't be too proud to take them.' He turned and walked away, leaving the inn without a backward glance.

Blacklock waited a few moments to ensure that McCormac did not return before he scooped up the filthy coins and scurried out through a side door.

Fifty-Seven

Pickard's Bank, Lombard Street, City of London
Tuesday 23rd April

The manager bowed obsequiously. 'My colleague tells me you wish to close your account, Doctor Blacklock.'

'That is indeed my wish. They are my funds, after all.'

'I do not wish to pry or appear in any way forward, but you have been such a valued customer of our humble institution for several years and we would obviously like to retain the custom of an eminent physician such as yourself. May I ask why? Has our service fallen short?'

'I am going abroad,' replied Blacklock. 'Missionary work in Madagascar. I may not see these shores again.'

'Well, my goodness. So far afield! A brave choice, if I might be so bold, but a calling to God's work is not something one can refuse. When do you depart?'

'I have a train booked to Southampton at 7 a.m. tomorrow, hence the urgency of my request. There has been much to organise is a very short period.'

The manager bowed again. 'Very well. Who are we to stand in the path of the Lord's work?' He turned to his clerk. 'Mr Rockwell, please be so kind as to tally the good doctor's accounts and refund him the balance. Good day, Doctor, or perhaps Bon Voyage.'

The clerk returned twenty minutes later with a folio emblazoned with Pickard's logo. It contained the last few pounds which Blacklock had to his name.

As soon as he set foot in Lombard Street, Blacklock began to imagine that every man was a robber, aware of the contents of the slim folio he gripped so tightly. He stopped at a traveller's emporium, where he purchased a good-sized leather portmanteau before heading back to his lodgings.

It took him almost no time to pack. His landlady's furnishings were generous, so he had few personal effects beyond his instruments, his small library, clothing and toiletries. He packed his books into a box, with instructions to forward them to his aunt, placing the rest of his belongings into his portmanteau and briefcase.

Standing in the vestibule he reflected ruefully that this, his accumulated wealth, was scant return for a lifetime of study and medicine.

He glanced at his watch; almost ten. If McCormac had made good on his threat it would not take the police long to arrive. He left four weeks' rent and a brief note of apology for his landlady, wrapped a scarf around his lower face and hurried to a workmen's café across the street.

He did not have to wait long. Before his coffee had cooled sufficiently to drink three uniformed police officers approached his digs. After a brief consultation the largest of them made his way briskly around the corner, presumably taking station in the alleyway that ran behind the terrace. The others allowed their colleague sufficient time to get into position then walked up the steps and rapped on the door. Mrs Mason opened it, at which point the officers barged past her into the house beyond.

Blacklock realised that he was shaking only when he spilt some coffee onto the back of his hand. As he wiped up the mess the policemen emerged from the house, closely followed by a clearly enraged Mrs Mason who appeared to be upholding her tenant's honour extremely vociferously. He smiled in spite of his dire situation.

Eventually the police dispersed. With the excitement over, Blacklock's adrenaline level plummeted and he was overcome with a combination of melancholy and malaise. He had no notion of what to do. He obviously could not return to Mrs Mason's in the foreseeable future. He could not beg a bed with any of The Musketeers, who had presumably been apprehended at the same time as his attempted capture.

His anger at McCormac grew, but even this dissipated quickly. Logically, the Irishman's actions made sense – and the boy's death had been the justifiable last straw. Of course, McCormac wanted to save lives. Blacklock's career was built on the same premise, so he understood its powerful drive.

His thoughts turned to flight. Where might he go? Scotland made some sense, but surely Duncan would deploy men at the railway stations? Even if he broke that cordon, there was little doubt that the other Musketeers would betray him and what little they knew of his background and favoured haunts, at least those in Edinburgh. Fleeing via a port would be equally risky. The Caldecotts would not shelter him. Miss Henry would not assist either.

The waitress tapped him on the shoulder. 'If you ain't drinking, sir, I'd be grateful if you could free up the table.'

Flustered, he took a few moments to collect himself. 'I am sorry. Please excuse my distraction.' He moved to the window and looked up and down the street.

'There's no Peelers about if that's what you was looking for.'

He looked round in alarm.

The waitress smiled. 'I seen you watching.'

'No,' he said. 'I was just idly curious. I was supposed to meet a friend here but he has evidently been delayed. No matter.'

He paid his bill and left. Outside, he suddenly felt much more exposed – every pair of eyes was watching him, every pair of hands ready to detain him. He backed into a doorway and observed the crowd. No one was paying him the slightest attention. He was, he assumed, wanted for murder and yet not one person spared him a second glance.

With renewed confidence he stepped back into the flow, the mass of humanity fixated on their individual needs to the exclusion of all others, not unlike the spawning salmon he had seen so often in Scotland. As he put more of the East End's tangle of streets between himself and Stoke Newington he realised he was starting to feel just a little less paranoid.

His savings began burning a hole in his pocket, determinedly undermining his frugal intentions. When he felt a little footsore he hailed a hansom. The driver would only take him as far as Aldgate, which was close enough for his purposes.

Clutching his luggage tightly he forced his way eastwards through the bustling crowds in search of accommodation, aware that selecting the most circuitous routes might help to throw off any pursuers.

After a few minutes he noticed that the majority of men were bare-headed so he donated his hat to a hawker on a street corner. Each hotel or boarding house seemed meaner that its predecessor, not merely down-at-heel but actively decrepit. More importantly, the police presence thinned noticeably as he ventured further from the city.

At length he entered the margins of the East End proper, where he fell into quiet contemplation. His earlier sorties had been from the perspective of an outsider, a separate entity. Now that his intent was to hide here, all his new attitude brought with it was the realisation the people about him were not merely cardboard cut-outs from the works of Dickens but individuals in their own right, struggling to exist.

There was little accommodation that advertised itself as such but he was unconcerned – in a few days or even hours when the police had determined which Musketeer was responsible he might be able to return to his lodgings, albeit to face some awkward questions, but not a kangaroo court. His greatest hope was that Duncan would manage to control his impatience and take the guilty man, rather than the first he encountered.

Blacklock began by rejecting the first dozen establishments he saw, whilst gradually realising that he was not going to randomly wander into some grimy court and find a cheap outpost of Claridge's for a shilling a night.

Even with these lowered expectations he continued rejecting premises out-of-hand. His portmanteau grew heavier, and the awareness that his life savings were about his person with no Phelps to protect him began to erode his confidence.

Eventually he came to 22 Tewson Road in Woolwich, a dingy – but cleaner than most – property, which promoted itself rather grandly as "a hotel for the discerning travelling gentleman. Rooms by the hour, day or week".

After an unconscious check over his shoulder he knocked on the door.

'Old yer 'orses!' yelled a voice within.

He waited but no one came to the door. He thought about knocking again but decided to move on and look elsewhere. As he turned away the door opened.

'Yes?' The elderly woman had a clay pipe clamped between her ochre teeth.

'I saw you had a vacancy, madam, and I wondered whether I might see the room?'

'I ain't got no rooms,' drawled the woman.

'Thank you,' said Blacklock, not a little relieved.

'But this ain't my 'ouse. I just chars it. Mrs Evans will be back directly. Tell you what, step inside. No point in freezing your nuts off. And take them boots off. This 'ere's a clean 'ouse.'

With great trepidation Blacklock stepped into the darkened hallway. With the exception of the char's pipe smoke it smelled remarkably fresh. A match flared nearby. 'I'll light a candle while you're waiting. Want tea?'

Until the char asked the thought of tea had not crossed his mind; now it was all he could think of. 'If it is not too much trouble I would be very grateful. Thank you.'

'So, you're a jock. Edinburgh or thereabouts?'

'Yes. You have a fine ear.'

'My 'usband was from Linlithgow. The old bastard's long dead now but 'earing you's like 'earing him. I'll get the kettle on.' She looked down. 'Boots.'

Blacklock had removed one boot when a key rattled in the front door lock. Keen to oblige, he opened the door. A woman bustled in, her face hidden by the enormous brim of her hat.

'Mrs Mathers, I do wish you would remember to lock the street door. You never know who–. Oh. I'm sorry. And you are?'

'Nathaniel Blacklock, madam. Pleased to meet you.'

'Hello, Nathaniel Blacklock. How can I help?'

'Doctor Blacklock. I am a surgeon. Looking for lodgings.'

A frown creased her brow. 'A surgeon, you say? Hatless, with a portmanteau and a briefcase, seeking a room in the depths of the East End? You'll forgive my scepticism.'

'Well, Mrs–'

'Evans.'

'Mrs Evans, it is something of a long story. I–'

Mrs Evans held up her hand. 'Spare me the sob story,' she said, tartly. 'Do you intend to murder us in our beds, *Doctor?*'

It was Blacklock's turn to frown. 'Of course not!'

'A good answer. The room is seven shillings a week, four weeks in advance, with a three pound deposit against damages. Can you afford that?'

'Yes.'

'Another good answer. Alright, Mrs Mathers, please show our esteemed surgeon to his room.' She looked at the mantel clock. 'I shall serve tea in sixteen minutes. I shall expect your rent advance and deposit at that time.'

Blacklock followed Mrs Mathers meekly to the room which, although small, was spotless. 'Door's locked at ten p.m. sharp. No visitors after seven p.m. No unaccompanied lady visitors full stop. I serves breakfast between 6 and 6.15

a.m., Monday to Friday, weekends off. Questions?'

Blacklock did not dare. Mrs Mathers nodded approvingly and bustled out.

Mindful of his appointment for tea Blacklock quickly unpacked his few belongings and hung his clothes in the wardrobe before exploring the rest of the meagre furnishings. The washstand was filled with fresh water, so he had a cold sponge bath in order to aspire to what he assumed would be Mrs Evans's high standards of grooming.

Mrs Evans held court in the tiny front parlour. He guessed, correctly, that he should hand over his rent and deposit before taking a seat. Mrs Evans favoured him with a regal smile. 'Thank you. Please sit.'

He took the only free seat, an ancient wheelback dining chair.

'A surgeon, you say? Convince me.'

He recapped his career prior to his suspension, certain that continuing beyond that point so soon would muddy the water. Mrs Evans nodded encouragingly between murmurs of approbation. When he finished all she said was 'Interesting.'

He squirmed uncomfortably on his chair, as if waiting to be dismissed. Mrs Evans counted the money, which offended him until he remembered which part of London he was in. At length she reached into her handbag and retrieved a small notebook, into which she entered some figures in perfect copperplate and totalled them. 'Everything appears to be in order, Doctor Blacklock.' She smiled. 'Is there anything else? Would you like a receipt?' She smiled again, but her eyes were appraising him.

'No, no, not at all. If you are content with our arrangement I shall withdraw to allow you to enjoy your evening in peace, Mrs Evans. Will your husband be home soon?'

Without changing her expression or dropping her smile she said 'He should be back in five years, give or take, if he behaves himself. Ten if he can't keep his nose clean.'

As the evening light died and the streets were once again benighted, in their gloom Blacklock lay awake on his bed. He was lodging in a criminal's house, whilst he himself was a fugitive from justice. Although the sheets were freshly laundered and his accommodation spotless, the incessant voices and movements in the street feet from his window seemed determined to ruin his rest, aided and abetted by his own returning sense of peril.

Fifty-Eight

22 Tewson Road, Woolwich, London
Wednesday 24th April

Blacklock went down to breakfast at six sharp, famished. The aroma of bacon permeated the house. To his surprise Mrs Evans was already sitting at the dining table.

'Mrs Evans? What a pleasant surprise. I thought Mrs Mathers served breakfast?'

'She would. Under normal circumstances.'

'Under normal circumstances?' He felt himself flush. 'Do we find ourselves in abnormal circumstances?'

'One of us does, it would seem.' She took a newspaper from her lap and placed it on the table. The front page headline shrieked *"FUGITIVES FROM JUSTICE!"*

Blacklock's senses failed him. He heard nothing, felt nothing, smelled nothing. His mouth was instantaneously as dry as dust. All he could see was the headline. Compelled, he read on. Below the headline there were sketches – Porter on the left, him on the right. Both would have been laughably inaccurate caricatures under different circumstances. The subheadline read *"KILLER SURGEONS AT LARGE!"*

He managed to look away.

'You aren't a very skilled fugitive, Doctor Blacklock,' said Mrs Evans with a smile. 'Most people would at least have used an alias when taking lodgings. On the more positive front, it would appear that you are indeed a surgeon, which I frankly doubted when you arrived.'

'What are you going to do? Have you already called the police?'

'Oh, bless me, no. The police and I do not share an especially congenial relationship. You do, however, present me with a problem.'

'I am not a murderer,' stammered Blacklock. 'It is one of my medical school colleagues - one of four survivors. I fear it must be Porthos – Porter since he is also clearly on the run. I know it is not me so it must be him. Or one of the others.'

Mrs Evans laughed. 'A watertight defence if ever I heard one. "Another boy did it and ran away." Your grasp of legal matters is touchingly naïve.'

Blacklock sniffed. 'I have no knowledge of such matters.'

'That much is obvious. You have one piece of luck on your side, and that is that you landed up here. It's a clean little spot in the midst of the filth, but that is not where your good fortune lies. On no. You're lodging with the wife – alright, common-law wife – of a man who has also historically had some difficulties with the law. Mind you, I don't doubt that he's clocked a few fellas on the head as part of his profession, but at least he hasn't killed any doxies. No, you differ from him in that respect.'

'Madam, I assure you that you are mistaken.'

'Of course I am. And I used to be a nun. The question is what should we do about our little conundrum? Do I hand you over to the Peelers tonight? Tomorrow? Perhaps I should wait and see whether they offer a reward? Or do I risk you taking one of your knives and gutting me? Tricky, eh?'

Blacklock blushed. 'I will leave this morning. I am no murderer but I would not tolerate you or anyone else living in fear of me.'

'Alright. Suit yourself.'

'Thank you, Mrs Evans. If I might have my deposit and advance lodgings returned to me I shall depart without delay.'

'Hmmm. Your skipping out early breaks our contract and I get to keep all the monies paid to date. It also makes sure that if anyone comes calling with an inquiring mind I have never seen you.'

'But without that I cannot hope to secure any other accommodation.'

'Life can be hard on the run, Doctor. Everybody wants their pound of flesh. A month here and you'll be Jack Sprat.'

He watched as she painstakingly tore his picture from the newspaper, balled it up and threw it into the fire. It glowed brilliantly for a couple of seconds before bursting into flames. 'Oops,' she said. 'Pity they didn't publish a picture of this monster in the paper.' She tore the front page off and consigned that to the fire also. 'No story. No names. I have no idea what's happening in the outside world, Doctor Blacklock. It's like we don't exist, this far east.'

Blacklock remained silent, uncertain how to respond.

Mrs Evans got to her feet. 'I assume you will be staying with us, at least for a little while longer, Doctor. I'll have Mrs Mathers bring your breakfast in.'

'Thank you.' It seemed a wholly inadequate reply.

'One more thing, Doctor.'

'Yes?'

'Do you have the tools of your trade with you?'

'I do, Mrs Evans. A surgeon would never part with them. My instruments are an extension of my–'

'I think I will take them into safe keeping – perhaps as an additional deposit. I would hate for you to have an accident with them in my house. Someone might get hurt.'

Blacklock opened his mouth to object but did not speak, an indication of his tacit acceptance of Mrs Evans's proposal.

'Do you agree, Doctor Blacklock? I'm sure you must see the logic of my request.'

'Of course. From your perspective it makes perfect sense. Will they – my instruments – be safe?'

Mrs Evans smiled broadly. 'If there's one thing this house isn't short of it's secure hiding places. When you're in my husband's line of work you can never be sure who is going to call, or when, so it's best to be prepared.'

Blacklock thought it politic not to enquire further. 'I shall bring them down to breakfast tomorrow.'

Mrs Evans shook her head. 'I don't think so, Doctor. Given

your alleged trade – I know not all allegations are true but some are – I think we would all sleep a good deal more soundly in our beds if I took them into safekeeping rather sooner than that. Immediately, for example.'

He nodded his assent and retreated to his bedroom.

When he returned Mrs Evans was seated back at the table, the only addition to her ensemble being a sizable pistol which she pointed squarely at his chest. 'No need to panic. I merely want to make it abundantly clear that I can protect myself.'

He put the case of instruments onto the table and backed slowly away.

Mrs Evans smiled again. 'Thank you, Doctor Blacklock. Enjoy your stay.'

Fifty-Nine

22 Tewson Road, Woolwich, London
Thursday 25th April

During the first few days of what he rapidly came to view as his imprisonment Blacklock hardly slept, imagining that every footstep in the night was a police officer, every whisper that same officer searching the house. On those rare occasions when someone passed with a lantern he held his breath, watching the shadows dance across the ceiling. Gradually – imperceptibly – he began to relax. He remained vigilant, careful to stay back from the windows during the day, as he had been advised to by his hostess. It seemed that Mrs Evans and Mrs Mathers were well used to sheltering fugitives. Without further murders or arrests the newspapers' interest also waned, the hunt for the missing surgeons subtly relegated with each edition, first further down the page, then to the inside pages, with ever-reducing column inches dedicated to the story. Gordon and Robertson apparently remained in custody, while Porter was presumably still at liberty. Blacklock committed to waiting until Porter had been detained, at which point the murderer would in all probability be in custody – he continued to discount Priestley – and he would be able to reveal his evidence – assuming McCormac had not already done so.

The question of what precisely McCormac *had* told Duncan was critical, but there was no point in risking capture – or betrayal – through a visit.

'You need an emissary,' said Mrs Evans as he discussed his quandary one evening.

'A what?'

'A go-between. Someone without medals who can track down this McCormac character, ask the question, and disappear before returning to our fold.'

'Medals?'

'Warrants for their arrest, outstanding convictions. Someone who couldn't melt butter in their mouths.'

'I do not think such people grow on trees, Mrs Evans – even if the East End *had* any trees.'

She smiled. Blacklock thought she was being deliberately enigmatic.

'On the contrary, Doctor, an extensive network of such individuals is available if you know how to use it. For all the apparent lawlessness of this area – it isn't as bad as you imagine it to be. By the same token we aren't, as a whole, as pure as the driven snow. Nevertheless, there are ways and means to get to the Peelers. Most justice here is dispensed – how should I phrase this? – at a local level. On occasion, however, it still suits us to have more constructive relations with people like your friend Duncan, although neither side can be seen to be colluding with the other.'

'I see. Perhaps.'

'It's not cheap, though. A message and reply with this man McCormac of yours can be arranged for five shillings.'

'*Five shillings?* That is daylight ... robbery. Sorry.'

'Apology accepted.' She smiled again. 'It takes three messengers, you see, none of whom know both the start and destination address. It works well. Do you want to ask your question?'

Blacklock was briefly lost in thought. 'You implied this chain can also reach the police?'

'If absolutely necessary, yes, but I wouldn't recommend dropping Duncan a friendly note. He will not be amused by your disappearance. Seven and six for the Peelers.'

Blacklock snorted. 'Of course it is. I know to whom I will write. How do I establish this connection?'

'Write your letter. Seal it in an envelope addressed to whomever you trust enough in the police. I will deal with the rest. I would not recommend trusting *anyone* in the police, but ultimately that is your prerogative.'

With little hope of success and a terrifying certainty of discovery Blacklock wrote a short letter and submitted it to Mrs Evans's underground postal service. He watched as she sealed it into a larger envelope with a number of others, some sealed, some open, with a series of what he presumed were coded addresses upon them.

About an hour later a filthy boy came to collect the envelope, disappearing almost instantly into the throng.

'How long?' asked Blacklock.

'If your man deigns to reply – the delivery messenger allows him an hour to do so – so you might hear something tonight. If you don't hear anything within twenty-four hours you're never going to.'

He sat down, pallid.

'Mrs Mathers! Please bring Doctor Blacklock a cup of your strongest tea – with a drop of something in it to calm his nerves.'

Blacklock was chasing cold peas around his dinner plate when the reply arrived, courtesy of the same urchin.

Mrs Evans sauntered in. 'Cargill has returned your affection, it seems.'

With a hesitancy only eyes as acute as Mrs Evans's would have noticed, Blacklock opened the envelope. A piece of filthy paper was inside. One side contained several games of Hangman, the other a few lines in Cargill's uncertain, almost childish hand.

Nathanyel,

Im sorry to hear from you on the thiefs telegraph. We had Gordon and Robertson in for a while but their alibis stood up. They was quick to point the finger at you and Porter, too. Porter still at large. duncan is pozz that your his man and is telling all the lads here about how heel cheer when your strung up. I dont think you did it, but that means nowt around here. If you was to hand yourself in I reckon that suspicion would fall on

Porter. You better hope that no one gets killed the same way as them others. McCormac says you have a way to prove who is responsibal but that you didnt tell him what it was – only the names. When we arrested Gordon he swore that if they were all suspects you was naturally the most likely because youve been suspended and always had some axe to grind. Also something about you turning up at his flat and threatening him. Robertson mentioned something similar which makes duncan think your off your rocker.

Just come in. Itll look better for you than if we have to come and find you. I aint put your letter into evidence yet, but if this comes to light before I do Ill be for the high jump and no mistake. Ill give you 24 hours to get yourself into Leman Street before I hand your letter over.

Please come in. Every day that you dont makes you look more guilty.

Yours,
Al Cargill.

He sighed as he shoved the letter dismissively back into the envelope.

'So?' asked Mrs Evans. 'What's the story?'

Blacklock shrugged. 'McCormac did not give them all the evidence so Duncan and his cronies do not know *why* the people he named are suspects.'

'Ha! What about the other one that took to his heels?'

'There is no sign of Porter yet.'

'What are you going to do?'

'Sit tight, I suppose.'

'You can't hide forever.'

'If it is Gordon or Robertson then they have their man and once he has been dealt with I can get back to something approximating to a normal life.'

'I applaud your optimism, Doctor.'

'What do you mean?'

'No smoke without fire. You ran. They won't forget that, innocent or not. Peelers are like elephants. Long memories.'

'Then I would appear to have no options at all.'

'Do a runner. Abroad. I know some people–'

'You do surprise me.'

'– who can spirit you away – for a fee, naturally. You would have to go way up the north-east coast, somewhere between Alnwick and the Scots border. They would take you across when they're on their way to … collect some liquor to import from the continent. Makes their journey pay both ways.'

'Smuggling? *Contraband?*'

'That's the beauty of it. You wouldn't have to worry because they run empty eastwards. No evidence whatsoever. Easy. Cheap too, for your life. Perhaps thirty pounds, perhaps fifty. Not a lot more.'

'Thank you, Mrs Evans, but running is not my choice at the moment.'

'I beg to differ, Doc. You're here, aren't you?'

He could not suppress a smile. 'Touché, Mrs Evans.'

She scrutinised him out of the corner of her eye. 'You could make yourself useful out this way, so to speak.'

Blacklock frowned. 'How so?'

'You're a doctor. We don't have many.'

'I am not a general practitioner, Mrs Evans. I am a surgeon. In the general way of things I am not much of use in the community.'

'"In the general way of things", as you say, we see quite a few men getting injured. We had a medical sort who used to visit us but we haven't seen him for a little while now.'

Blacklock sat forward on his chair. 'Did you ever see him?'

'No. Fortunately this house has mostly been spared such occupational miseries. However, there are many in this neighbourhood who may occasionally need to avail themselves of your needlecraft. The occupations which people follow here sometimes bring them unavoidably into contact with sharp edges, the explanation for which would be complex and easily misconstrued.'

'Are you trying to say they get into knife fights? I dealt with one a few weeks ago; two men died. It is no more than they deserve.'

'Perhaps. Sometimes they might get cut when a window they're cleaning breaks, or a bite from a dog which suffers from insomnia and chooses to spend its nights patrolling its master's premises.'

'And a surgeon used to perform these services? Until how recently?'

'Until a few weeks ago. Rumours are that he met a woman and found that a better way to spend his time. He was a good man, by all accounts. Treated the working girls for nothing.'

'Really?'

'And he took nothing in kind, either. He was a gentleman. Don't think that because a girl has to work on her back for a living that she's any less decent than you. An empty stomach – or worse, your child's empty stomach – drives a person down a route they might not otherwise take. Poverty isn't romantic.'

Blacklock ran his fingers through his hair. 'Do you know any of the premises he may have consulted at, Mrs Evans?'

'I don't know what you're trying to imply, Doctor Blacklock, but I have never worked in that way.'

'I did not mean to suggest that you ever had, Mrs Evans.'

'Do you think that it's your man Porter? *Your fellow fugitive?*'

'Perhaps. I went to ground in the East End knowing no one. With Porter's local knowledge he would have a vast choice of potential boltholes.'

Mrs Evans became thoughtful. 'You "went to ground in the East End." An interesting analogy. Tell me about these murders you are alleged to have committed.'

'Three women, a man and a child, all of whom bear the hallmarks of a very particular surgical style. As far as I know there are only five surviving surgeons who operate in such a distinctive manner. I am one; Porter and the other two under arrest make four. Priestly – missing for years – makes five. I regret that I cannot prove my innocence to you, Mrs Evans, or indeed the police.'

Mrs Evans reached into her handbag, retrieved a manicure kit and began to absent-mindedly shape her nails. 'If someone wants to hide out this way, he can stay hidden. The Peelers don't even have an up to date map of this place. No one does.'

Blacklock sighed. 'So Porter may remain beyond their reach indefinitely.'

'Beyond the Peelers' reach, yes. However, local resources go deeper than simple anonymous mail delivery. I could put out some feelers if you like. Many people will know you're here – it's just a fact of life. The other side of that coin is that many people will also know where Porter is if he's here.'

'If so many people know my whereabouts, why have the police not already battered down your door?'

'East End honour, plain and simple. No one rats to the Peelers. Ever. Sometimes, when there's a large enough reward, tongues get loosened but you do that and you had better have your escape plan and a better life far away in place because you wouldn't last five minutes when you came back.'

'If Porter can be found ... I would then surrender myself. It would be a case for Duncan to reconcile the others' accounts and identify the guilty party.'

'Not a great plan, Doctor.'

'Oh. Why?'

Mrs Evans looked at him as though she was an exceptionally patient schoolmistress. 'You believe, do you not, in justice?'

'Yes.'

'Fairness?'

'Yes.'

'Science and logic?'

'Of course.'

'That's the typical mistake of the educated man. None

of those things exist in practical law – the law as actually applied, as opposed to the theoretical idyll you're clinging to. Duncan will go to trial with the man with the weakest alibi, the most fragile defence. It's getting a conviction that counts.'

'I cannot agree with you, Mrs Evans. Perhaps you are biased by your husband's experience?'

'Not at all. John's as guilty as sin. More so, probably. I hate that he's in Wandsworth, but I can't complain. He did what he was accused of – and more – and so he pays the price. Part of the game.'

'How magnanimous of you.'

She shook her head. 'Not at all. Simple facts.'

He nodded in agreement.

'Now, back to your problem. Don't imagine that the guilty one of you will definitely be the one strolling to the rope. Unless someone confesses it's a lottery. Duncan knows that the killings will probably cease whoever swings, reasoning that the murderer will be intimidated into stopping when there are only four suspects left to choose from.'

'What if he is not? What if there is some perverted sickness driving him?'

'No matter. Enter the copycat. Duncan will see to it that whatever it is that tied you four into this appears in the newspapers. Anyone – everyone – will know how to replicate the crimes. He's a sly dog. I only know him by reputation but you don't get to be an inspector by paying attention to the rule book. Don't hope to outthink him. Many's the East End boy that's tried. I can't recall any that's succeeded.'

'I am not an "East End boy", Mrs Evans. That aside, you have created a long list of things which will not work, which will not improve my situation. Can you tell me anything that will?'

'Stay here. Keep your head down. Hope that Duncan sends one of your friends to trial before another murder is committed.'

'That is not action. That is passivity.'

'Call it what you like, Doctor, but do it anyway. One of my brothers-in-law swung at Littledean Jail, which is out west somewhere. The hangman hadn't much practice and got the drop wrong.'

'I am afraid to ask…'

'You should be. The drop was too long and his head came clean off. At least he didn't suffer, I suppose.'

Blacklock snorted derisively.

'In the meantime I'll see if we can't rustle up this man Porter.'

'You said the East End is the perfect place to disappear.'

'It is. From the outside. Or for an insider. But you can't hide from the murders indefinitely, even here.'

'And if you are successful and find him?'

'We grass him up.'

'What?'

'We grass – we inform against him. Duncan will have a host of suspects and crack one of them. You'll be in the clear, the killings stop.'

'I suppose this will cost me money?'

'Everything has its price out there, and nobody is going to feel charitable towards some surgeon from up west. I'll put the feelers out to see who's available at what rate. I'll negotiate for you: you're clearly no match for the average commercially-minded character around here. It would be good sport, in the way that a cock fight is – unless you're the cock. Which, around here, you are.'

'Hardly the most persuasive argument, Mrs Evans, but I do not see many alternative options.'

'Such wisdom,' smiled Mrs Evans.

Sixty

22 Tewson Road, Woolwich, London
Tuesday 7th May

A few days later, as he was taking his breakfast, Blacklock was surprised when Mrs Evans entered with his meal rather than Mrs Mathers.

'Four pounds, Doctor Blacklock.'

'Pardon?'

'That's now much it is expected to cost to find Porter.'

'Uh-huh. A tidy sum.'

'Cheaper than a broken neck? It doesn't appear that he is looking for you. I suspect he doesn't know how.'

'This man ... you have found ... is he any good?'

'She is.'

'She?'

'Women aren't noticed. A strange man in an area can be seen as a threat. A strange woman is pitied, or abused, or protected – but is certainly never considered a threat.'

'How long would this take?'

'There is no way to tell. It depends on how well your friend has managed to hide.'

'Very well. Please instruct ... this woman–'

'Mrs Strathern.'

'Please instruct her to start work. I would appreciate at least weekly progress reports.'

Sixty-One

22 Tewson Road, Woolwich, London
Tuesday 21st April

Two weeks passed without any further light being thrown on Porter's whereabouts. The newspaper speculation increased around both Blacklock and Porter. Robertson and Gordon were released without fuss, allegedly due to lack of evidence. On the fourteenth day of what Blacklock hoped were genuine investigations Mrs Evans called him down to the dining room shortly after lunch.

She gestured to the chair. 'How are you?'

'Is there some news, Mrs Evans?'

'I will not waste either your time or my own. Porter is not in the East End.'

'But – but how can you be so adamant?'

'A red-headed Scotsman, soft as putty, hiding here without being seen? Not possible.'

Blacklock examined his hands. 'Damnation! Oh – sorry – please excuse my language.'

'I hear worse on my doorstep every day. I'll have Mrs Mathers bring some tea in. That should tide you over until dinner.'

'No thank you, Mrs Evans. I must undertake an errand.'

'Are you sure that's wise, Doctor? You're on every lamppost in town. Faded, rain-soaked, but nevertheless some sort of likeness survives.'

'Perhaps, but I have neither shaved my whiskers nor visited a barber since I absconded. I am sure that I must be less recognisable. It is imperative that I speak with someone who may know of Porter's whereabouts. I shall not wear a cravat. I look so slovenly that I doubt anyone would recognise me.'

Mrs Evans shook her head. 'If you must, I suppose you

must. Wait here and I'll see if I can find something more suitable for you to wear.'

She quickly returned with an old suit and shirt, which Blacklock noted with some distaste was missing its collar. 'They're my husband's,' she said. 'They're a little on the large size – he's a muscular man and you ... aren't – but then nobody here can really afford decent clothes. You step out there and everywhere you look you'll see folks wearing dead people's clothes.'

'Thank you,' said Blacklock, slightly affronted by Mrs Evans's withering allusion to his physique.

She took a bowler from a hook. 'And wear this. You stand out more without a hat. Stick to the busiest streets. It'll be harder for the Peelers to spot you in a crowd. Look at the pavement. Avoid eye contact. It's a hare-brained scheme but on your head be it. I will see you this evening, assuming you make it back.'

Sixty-Two

*The Caldecott Residence, 17 Belgrave
Square, Knightsbridge, London
Tuesday 21st May*

Blacklock felt horribly conspicuous as he threaded his way through the crowded pre-dusk streets. Every police officer he saw chilled his blood, but there was no sign of interest, let alone recognition. He concentrated on being furtive without appearing so, an onerous task which stretched his nerves taut and wearied him in equal measure. *How do criminals live like this?* At one point he passed within a couple of feet of an acquaintance from Prince Albert's, but Blacklock did not register with him at all. Relieved at surviving this close encounter he quickened his steps to Belgrave Square. The crowds became sparse, and his working-class garb stood out as much as a Savile Row suit in Walthamstow. Fortunately there was a scattering of tradesmen going about their business too, and where he could safely do so he fell into loose step with them.

As before he approached the house from the far side of the square, using the gardens to ensure he remained obscured from any alert eyes from within the Caldecott household. Blacklock hesitated as he approached the gate. His disguise, perfect camouflage when he set out, was a liability here. He tried to shrink into himself a little and pressed on. Only yards inside the park he met two ladies promenading. He nodded respectfully, tilting the brim of Mr Evans's bowler over his eyes, but the women passed by as though he was invisible.

'The working classes hardly know their place these days,' said one, ensuring she would be overheard.

No one else paid any attention as he crossed the small park. He hung back from the fence, uncertain how to proceed.

'Hello, friend.' The voice nearby almost startled Blacklock into a shout. 'I didn't expect to see you back so soon. Still pining after the girl, eh?'

He turned and immediately recognised the itinerant who had come to his aid on his last foray here. 'Mr–.' He stopped. 'Please forgive me. I cannot recall your name.'

'That's usually the case, but thanks for calling me mister. Paulinus Stewart, at your service, once again. Over the top again, is it?'

'Goodness, no. I need to speak with Miss Caldecott but I am certain that Sir Edmund's lackeys will have a contrary view.'

Stewart smiled. 'Why don't I see if I can't help true love run a little smoother, eh? 'Sides, I ain't seen Phelps for a few days. This lad is easier to handle.' Stewart fished in his heavily-loaded pockets and dragged out a dog-eared envelope. 'Dirty pictures. He loves 'em. Ten minutes enough for you?'

'Ample, I would imagine.'

'Alright. I'll see what I can do.'

Before Blacklock could say anything else Stewart vaulted nimbly over the railings and crossed the street. From there he made his way nonchalantly towards the coachman, who had moved to the street-side horse. Stewart stood on the same side, shielded from the house by the carriage. With a furtive glance around, the coachman moved towards Stewart, who reached into his coat and produced the envelope which he handed to him.

The coachman opened the packet and glanced inside. He turned and walked away with Stewart in his wake, who looked across to Blacklock's hiding place and gave him a subtle thumbs-up.

As soon as the unlikely duo were out of sight around the corner of the wall Blacklock clambered over the railings and ran to the pavement below Tilly's window. The pavement was dusted with fine grit, the sweepers behind with their daily commitment. He scooped up a handful and threw it at her window. His attention darted from window to window, terrified that he might have attracted someone else's attention, or worse that the coachman would hear and return to brutalise him.

The sash opened above him. 'Who is–? *Nathaniel?* What are *you* doing here? The police have been here only this morning.'

'I am sorry to disturb you, Miss Caldecott, but I need to ask–'

'Don't worry about that. You can be seen loitering outside the house. Meet me at the servants' gate. I'll be there directly.'

She closed the window and hurried away from view.

Blacklock made his way to the gate. It was locked. After a few moments came a barely audible whisper. 'Nathaniel?'

'I am here.'

'Oh, thank goodness. I didn't know whether you would ever come. You ignore my letters.'

'I–'

'No matter. You're here now.'

Blacklock frowned at his own confusion. 'Can you open the gate?'

'No. Only Papa has a key during the evening. Papa and Phelps, actually, but Phelps is away in France on some business for Papa.'

'I think we meet at cross purposes, Miss Caldecott. I–'

'Please, you may call me Tilly if you wish. As you used to.'

'Miss Caldecott, I have received no correspondence from you. I have lately changed my lodging arrangements.'

'Oh. I thought as much after that awful to-do with the other Musketeers. I wrote to the university too.'

'I regret to admit that I am no longer engaged there.'

'I'm sorry, Nat, I had no idea. Perhaps I should speak first.' Her voice fell back to a whisper. At first he could not comprehend what she was saying, before he realised she was sobbing.

Tilly sighed loudly. 'Please Miss Caldecott, I do not mean to cause you distress, but alas I cannot understand what you are saying.'

'Nathaniel, I am disgraced.'

'Pardon?'

'George has ... ruined me.'

'I do not follow.'

'Please, Nathaniel, don't be so cruel. I am ... I ...' She began weeping once more.

'Whatever is the matter, Miss Caldecott? Matilda? Has Porter deserted you? If so, I am sorry.'

Matilda's crying became deeper, more heartfelt. 'Nathaniel, what am I to do?'

'Try not to fret. You will surely meet someone else. I understand only too well that circumstances may feel difficult now, but it will pass, I promise.'

Blacklock thought his words appropriate but beyond the gate Matilda broke down completely, her weeping becoming a keening wail. 'It's too late for that, you fool!'

'Do not be so silly, Matilda.'

The sobbing reduced. 'Don't you understand, Nathaniel? Is it not obvious? I'm ruined. No man would look at me now.'

'Ruined? I do not–'

'For God's sake. Do I need to spell it out? I'm ... I'm ...' She struggled to speak between her hitching breaths. When she spoke again, she whispered. 'I am *ruined*, Nathaniel, because I am *with child*. George's child.'

Blacklock recoiled from the gate. 'How? I–'

'It doesn't matter. I am disgraced.'

'And Porthos? What is he going to do?'

'He has fled. I don't know where.'

Blacklock did not know what to say, but ventured, 'And your father?'

'Is angrier that I have ever known him. He is making plans to send me away. He has a cousin in Ireland.' She paused, then continued in a hesitant whisper. 'Can you – could you – do you know someone who could ... end my difficulty? Medically, I mean.'

'That is illegal,' he hissed. 'I do not. There is no safe way to complete such ... a procedure, if I understand your implication.'

'You, Nathaniel? Surely you ..?'

'No. Never. I am not even a licensed surgeon any longer and even if I were I would never undertake such a procedure.'

'But perhaps you will be licensed again soon. I have written often to the Royal College in support of your reinstatement.'

'*You?*'

'Yes. I thought if you were a surgeon again we might try to reconcile our differences and even – I hope against hope – renew our engagement. I used the Musketeer's names and disguised my handwriting.'

Blacklock swallowed hard but said nothing.

'Nathaniel? Are you there? Please say something. We could still be together. I don't care about your mother, or the workhouse or anything else from your childhood–'

He became simultaneously hot and cold. '*What?* What did you say?'

'About your mother. I–'

'Did Porter tell you that? Pillow talk, was it?'

'Nathaniel! How could you?'

'How could *you*, Matilda?'

'Papa retained a private investigation agent when we became engaged, and he found out your mother was a fallen, drunken woman who – who couldn't keep you, and died in the workhouse. With Papa keen to enter Parliament I obviously couldn't be permitted marry someone so ... low, so he forced me to break our engagement. But now I'm so terribly sorry, and–'

Blacklock heard no more as walked silently away, unable to summon a gentlemanly response.

Sixty-Three

22 Tewson Road, Woolwich, London
Tuesday 21st May

'It seems that whichever way I turn, Mrs Evans, I am betrayed.' Blacklock stared into the bottom of his teacup, as though the leaves might guide him.

'It is rare that one is truly betrayed,' she replied. 'People have their own lives to lead, that's all. This girl – Matilda? – she's with child, unmarried, and the father's run for this hills. That is not a situation which leads to sound decision making for anyone, least of all a young girl who's been sheltered for her entire life.'

'But–'

Mrs Evans raised her hand. 'I'm not condoning what she has done – far from it. Desperate people do desperate things. Human nature.'

'Nonetheless–'

'Have you never thought me a little too well-spoken, a little atypically articulate for the East End, Doctor?'

'I rather thought the others were simply less so.'

'Oh dear. So much to learn. I am here for the same reason as Matilda. I had every advantage – perhaps not quite to the extent of your Matilda – but not far short. Cheltenham Ladies' College, a Finishing School in Zurich, even a minor Grand Tour. But then I attended Ascot with my family and I met my husband – and fell for him. Consumingly so, truth be told. My family were appalled and tried to separate us, but we still found ways to meet. Eventually nature took its course, as it has with your ex-fiancée, and I fell pregnant. I told my father and I was – quite literally – thrown from the family home and cut off without a penny. I lost the child and never became pregnant again. I was even barred from my father's funeral. My husband, although he may well lack refinement by others' standards, at least stood by me.' She looked directly at Blacklock. 'I understand what it is to fall, and how easy it is to do so. Goodnight.'

Sixty-Four

22 Tewson Road, Woolwich, London
Friday 24th May

The following three days passed in a daze for Blacklock, who felt the four walls of his room in the Evans house becoming more like those of a cell. On Saturday morning, as he lay in bed after a fitful night's sleep he was roused by a knock on the door.

'Doctor Blacklock?' said Mrs Evans, 'I think you should come down to the dining room as soon as you are able.'

He stared at the newspaper, dumbfounded.
'I'm sorry, Doctor Blacklock.'
'But a *reward?* How could she?'
'Who?'
'Matilda, of course.'
'Not Miss Caldecott. Her father.'

He looked at the quarter-page panel, which again featured the same inexpert sketches of Porter and himself. '*A thousand pounds?* For "information leading to the conviction of the murderer"? That is a sum which will have the whole of London looking for me. Courtesy of Mr Caldecott's largesse. I do not doubt that Matilda influenced this.'

'Forget him. He's irrelevant; just trying to improve his position in society. No one will care who stumped up the money. The fact that the reward exists is the problem.'

'Where can I go now, Mrs Evans? What about those people you mentioned who could help me get abroad?'

'Too late, I fear. It would be expensive, and will be more so because of this reward.' She thought for a moment then shook her head. 'No, the risk is too high. If someone can take fifty pounds from you to get you across The Channel, then simply deliver you into the hands of the Peelers and pocket twenty times more, they could afford to retire somewhere far away.'

'A rat in a trap,' murmured Blacklock. 'There is no way out. I must throw myself on the mercy of the court.'

'No. Absolutely not. All you can actually do is sit tight. I don't have an answer, Doctor. We must both think, and think hard. If you run now you'll get caught. If you're caught running, you'll swing. If you hand yourself in, you'll probably still swing. If you're caught here, I will also find myself in custody for aiding and abetting. You must go to your room, draw the curtains and stay there. Don't come downstairs. Don't be seen through the window. Keep everything – clothing, toiletries, whatever – packed, so that you can depart at a moment's notice. If it was anyone else I would simply eject them but I don't see you coping at all well with confinement, and I believe your story. Of course, I enjoy having some intelligent company too.'

Before the reward was offered Blacklock had not thought it possible that his nerves could be stretched any more tautly, but even in that he was misguided. The huge incentive, courtesy of Matilda's father, posed an enormous risk. He was incensed because he felt blameless – surely this was all Porthos's doing? He had not slept properly in days, further weakening his already exhausted mental reserves. When he did eventually sleep that night it was almost dawn, and he plunged into the dreamless sleep of the dead.

The stinging blow to his cheek would have drawn a shout were it not for the hand over his mouth. 'Wake up, Blacklock! The Peelers are on their way!'

He sat up, instantly alert. 'Mrs Evans, where shall I go?'

'The box room has a loft hatch. Up through there. To the left of the chimney breast is a hinged panel which will take you into the attic next door. Close the panel behind you. Don't make a bloody sound. Wait there until someone comes for you. Pray it isn't too long.'

'But how did they–?'

'That old bitch Mathers. The grand was too much to resist. She had better run far and fast, that's all.'

'I–'

There was a hammering on the front door. 'Metropolitan Police! Open up!'

'I'll be right there,' shouted Mrs Evans. She pointed urgently at the box room. Blacklock needed no second bidding and ran to the room as Mrs Evans made her way nonchalantly down the stairs. By the time she opened the door he had the hatch open; he was pulling it closed behind him by the time the police gained entry.

There was a clear path to the wall hatch. He crawled to it in the darkness which was only alleviated by shards of light shining through the occasional misplaced roof tile. As feet thundered up the stairs below he opened the second hatch and crawled into the adjacent loft space.

Sixty-Five

24 Tewson Road, Woolwich, London
Friday 24th May

He sat with his back to the panel, panting. Stinging sweat ran into his eyes. He wiped them with his hands, which in turn were covered in whatever detritus covered the loft floor, irritating them further.

The loft hatch he had closed less than a minute earlier flew open. He held his breath, certain of discovery.

'Nothing up here!'

He rested his head against the panel and sighed.

'Hold on...'

His heart and breath stopped again.

'No, it's alright.' The loft hatch slammed closed again. He listened to the raised voices teeming below for a few minutes until they gradually reduced in both quantity and volume.

For what seemed an eternity he waited in the darkness, straining both vision and hearing. He expected Mrs Evans to call but she did not. *Was she in custody?* He thought about his next steps under such a circumstance, mindful of her advice against surrendering himself. *Surely that would be better than hiding in a pitch-black attic which was probably teeming with rats?*

Untold hours passed before he heard fingers fumbling with what was presumably a bolt below the hatch in this house. He opened the hatch back into Mrs Evans's, preparing to retreat.

'Down you come, Doctor,' she said. 'Where are you?'

'Here, Mrs Evans,' he replied. 'I was not certain it was you so I thought it prudent to move back into your attic.'

'You're learning. Come on.'

The landing below was illuminated by only a single,

heavily-shaded candle. 'Careful, Doctor. We aren't showing any lights. It would make sense if the Peelers posted a lookout, although I can't see one about. I know where they'd hide.'

'Where have you been?'

'Having a long – very, very long – chat with the boys in blue. The old cow Mathers had told them quite a tale, which needed careful unpicking. I think I bored them into releasing me.'

'I am terribly sorry.'

'Don't be. Occupational hazard. I live with a robber when he isn't doing stir. I've seen the inside of enough police stations to last me the rest of my natural. Anyway, it was almost refreshing to hone my verbal skills again.'

'What is next?'

'You sit even tighter than before. I will move you into the box room. It's not so comfortable but an escape route is always useful. For the moment we're staying here. Later on we will both go back the way you came.'

Sixty-Six

22 Tewson Road, Woolwich, London
Friday 31st May

Mrs Evans's box room quickly became a cell in all but name. The community grapevine thrummed with word of Mrs Mathers's treachery. In her absence community vengeance was visited on her family. Her son would surely have died from his beating had it not been for the intervention of a passing clergyman.

In a few days Blacklock's story once again fell from the newspapers altogether, after a period of migration from the front page to the inner pages as successive political and sexual scandals superseded it. Never had he been so grateful for tittle-tattle.

His preoccupation shifted too, from fear of capture to his dwindling finances. With no opportunity for employment of any form he simply decanted his cash from his bag to Mrs Evans's. There was a question in the air between them that it took him a long time to summon the courage to ask, fearing the answer.

'Mrs Evans, can you tell me what will happen when my funds are exhausted? To my lodgings here, I mean.'

'I am afraid I will have to ask you leave. It is already an enormous risk keeping you here. Without any form of compensation the scales would not tip in your favour. I'm sorry.'

'Perhaps if you were to pawn my surgical instruments?'

'Listen to yourself, Doctor. You still aren't thinking carefully enough about your situation. It is widely known that the police have searched my establishment for one of the "murderous surgeons". Mrs Mathers's story will also be common knowledge. If I were to try to pawn a set of surgical knives it would not take Sherlock Holmes to identify the source, would it? The same if you pawn them.' She sipped her sherry. 'What funds have you got left?'

'Enough to last two weeks, perhaps. Three, if I stretch things.'

'Oh dear. That is most unfortunate.'

'But–'

'No buts, Doctor Blacklock. A contract is a contract. It could be argued that I have already stepped significantly beyond the scope of duties expected from a landlady. The furore around you will die down more quickly than you might imagine; even the reward will slip from people's minds. By the time those two or three weeks have passed you should be perfectly safe. Sa*fer*, anyway.'

Blacklock's shoulders slumped. There was nothing wrong with her logic, or her commercial acumen. 'Of course. I understand.'

Sixty-Seven

22 Tewson Road, Woolwich, London
Sunday 2nd June

Blacklock was startled into wakefulness by distant screams. In his time in Tewson Street such sounds were not unusual; indeed, he had heard enough to inure him. But these cries were different – and coming closer. He mentally prepared to scurry up into the attic, and rose from his bed to pack his scant belongings into the case he kept ready.

The screams continued to draw closer and with that become clearer. An adult male was obviously grievously hurt. Whomever or whatever was transporting him turned into Tewson Street. Blacklock could hear the hooves of a single horse and the wood-rimmed wheels of a small cart. A dog cart, perhaps.

The cart stopped underneath his window, the cries dying away as the movement stopped. Someone tapped on the street door. Mrs Evans – evidently waiting up – answered immediately. Several hushed voices engaged in urgent conversation before Mrs Evans said, 'Right. Bring him in.'

Another scream rent the night as the injured man was carried into the house. Blacklock realised that his skills were likely required and dressed himself more neatly while he waited to be summoned.

After a couple of minutes Mrs Evans shouted, 'Doctor Naismith, would you please come downstairs? Your opinion will be of great value.'

Doctor Naismith? He checked his appearance in the wall glass and hurried downstairs.

The tiny parlour was full. On the table lay a large man in his forties, pained and shaking. His face was painted with perspiration.

'Doctor Naismith,' repeated Mrs Evans. 'Thank you. This

is my brother-in-law, Ernie, who has fallen from a roof he was working on and I fear he may have sustained a significant injury. His companions are Charlie, Jack and Barney, who have done a great service by bringing him here.' They shrugged off the thanks.

'I see,' said Blacklock. 'Mr–?'

'King,' replied Mrs Evans. 'But he prefers Ernie or Ernest.'

'If everyone could stand back so that I might examine him, that would be very useful.' The men pressed themselves back against the wall, which left Blacklock just enough room to circulate. Still again, King seemed calmer. His right foot lay unnaturally flat on the table, his knee aligned with it. 'It appears as though you have broken your femur – your thigh bone – or perhaps your hip. Either injury requires great force in a fit man such as yourself. How far did you fall?'

'About twenty feet, maybe twenty-five, Doctor,' whispered King. 'From the roof of a three-storey house.'

'That is a long way,' muttered Blacklock. 'I must check for other injuries before I attend to your leg. Did you hit your head, Ernie?'

'No.'

'Did you lose consciousness?'

'Don't think so. It's all me bloody leg, Doc. Jeez, it hurts.'

'Alright.' Blacklock quickly checked King's neck, back and other limbs. 'Nothing else appears to be broken. So, to your leg. Mrs Evans, I must remove Ernie's trousers to examine him further, so if you would kindly leave the room I can continue.'

'Don't mind me, Doctor,' replied Mrs Evans. 'There won't be anything I haven't seen an example of before.'

Blacklock bit his tongue; he knew better than to argue. He unbuckled King's belt and unbuttoned his fly. 'This is going to hurt, Ernie, but they have to come off. I will cut them off as much as possible, but there will still be some movement of the broken limb.'

Mrs Evans reached into a basket near the hearth and

withdrew a small piece of kindling wood. 'Bite on this, Ernie,' she said. 'Otherwise your girly screams will bring the house down.'

Blacklock carefully unlaced King's boot and slid it tenderly off. The kindling splintered in King's teeth.

'Mrs Evans, if I might have my instrum–'

Mrs Evans already held Blacklock's instrument case open at his elbow.

'Don't cut me bleedin' leg off, please Doc!' said King.

Blacklock smiled. 'At this moment all I want to do it cut your clothing off so that we can see what we are dealing with. We can take a view but obviously any further intervention will be the decision of the hospital staff.'

'I ain't going to no hospital.'

'But you must.'

'I can't.'

'Of course you can. If it is about money–'

'He's wanted, Doctor,' interrupted Mrs Evans. 'Any and all treatment he needs has to happen right here. If he goes into hospital this leg'll be the least of his worries.'

'I cannot promise–'

'You don't have to. Just do your best. Please?' With the last word Mrs Evans's voice lost it usual assured tone.

Blacklock shook his head and began to split King's trouser seam up from the ankle. In seconds he reached the waistband. 'I regret, Mrs Evans, the Ernie is not wearing any undergarments.'

'Do get on with it, Doctor Naismith. I expect he has a penis and testicles under there. I am familiar with the concept.'

Blacklock blushed profusely, for once grateful for the dim lamp. 'As you wish.'

He finished cutting King's trousers off, before slicing a section off the bottom and placing it over King's genitals.

Even King laughed at this, before the pain of movement silenced him again.

'Good Lord above,' said Charlie, 'It's Adam, complete with

figleaf.'

King laughed again, then winced. 'Shut up, Charlie. I can't laugh. It hurts too bloody much.'

Blacklock carefully cut King's sock off. The foot revealed was white beneath its grime, and flopped back onto the table. 'This foot has no radial pulse,' he said. 'Without an adequate blood supply it will die – it is already dying, in fact, as we speak – but whatever the injury is, it has at least pinched the artery closed. Bite the wood hard, Mr King.'

King complied.

Blacklock pushed down hard on King's hips but there was no movement. 'Your pelvis appears to be intact, which is great news for you. Therefore I fear the femur is broken, which takes tremendous force. The fracture must be reduced immediately. Have you any spirits in the house, Mrs Evans?'

'Of course.'

'Please give them to Mr King; with no anaesthetic to help him we must improvise, and getting him profoundly drunk may be the best we can do.'

'Good whisky? Gin?'

'Whichever is strongest. You, Ernie, need to get as drunk as a lord as soon as you can.'

Charlie and Barney made as though to leave. 'Please stay,' said Blacklock. 'Our next task requires great strength and I cannot do it on my own.'

It took thirty minutes for King to drink himself into a stupor. Even in the poor light his foot grown even whiter – almost ghostly – and cold to the touch.

'I think we should start now,' said Blacklock. We cannot afford to wait any longer. We need to realign his femur, which requires that traction be applied so that the broken bone ends can be pulled past each other, against the immense strength of the thigh muscles. With a displaced fracture such as this we must pull the lower leg down and then manipulate it into its correct position. Two of you must hold his torso; I will pull the lower leg away with Jack's assistance. As it extends, we must rotate his foot clockwise – into a vertical position – then reduce the tension. If we are lucky the bones will meet and join in the correct manner, restoring the blood supply to the lower limb.'

'And if we're unlucky?,' whispered Mrs Evans.

'Then either we cannot do it, or there are multiple fractures in the femur which render a simple reduction impossible.'

'And?'

'He loses his leg – in hospital. Otherwise he may lose his life should gangrene set it when the foot dies.'

Mrs Evans looked at Blacklock's gleaming assortment of instruments. 'Do you have what's required to take it off, if you have to?'

Blacklock turned to her, horror-struck. 'That is not a viable option. It would be barbaric.'

She looked at King and gently brushed away a lock of hair which was stuck to his forehead. 'As would handing him over to the Peelers.'

Blacklock removed his jacket, unbuttoned his cuffs and rolled up his sleeves. 'Let us hope that it does not come to either of those choices.' He pointed at Charlie and Barney. 'You two, take him under the arms. Jack, take a firm grip on his ankle. You and I must *pull* the leg as far down the table as we can, and then *turn* it. When I say so, we release it. All clear?'

The men nodded.

'Mrs Evans – I know your brother-in-law is very intoxicated but I fear that even as much whisky as he has had will offer but scant relief from the pain as we start this procedure. You may even need to clamp his jaw around the kindling if he makes too much noise. Are we all ready? Good. Now *pull*.'

Despite King's near-unconsciousness Blacklock felt that his patient's screams would be heard at Westminster. The men faltered but Blacklock egged them on. King's thigh muscles were in spasm, intensifying both the pain and effort required to stretch them. Although Blacklock could cope with King's screams, it was clear the others were distressed.

'Let us all rest,' said Blacklock. The men shone with sweat, and were almost as white as King's dying foot. Mrs Evans provided more gin-and-water; her water was brackish but Blacklock drank it anyway.

'I am sorry, gentlemen,' he said after a few minutes, 'but this foot cannot wait any longer for its blood supply. It is now or never. Whatever noises Mr King makes you must ignore if we are to save his leg.'

They renewed their efforts. After what seemed hours of screaming but was only minutes King finally passed out; seconds later Blacklock manipulated the femur back into alignment. He checked the foot; the pulse was restored. 'Progress! Thank you for your efforts.'

Mrs Evans poured out large tumblers of whisky. Blacklock tried to refuse, already feeling light-headed, but could not defend himself against Mrs Evans's insistence.

'What do you think, Doctor Naismith? Has this operation been a success?'

Blacklock leaned forward and felt King's thigh. 'It seems to be properly aligned. We must now turn our attention to immobilising the leg. Do you think it would be possible to obtain any gypsum plaster?'

'Anything is possible, but not immediately. I'm sure I could get something tomorrow.'

'This leg must be immobilised before he regains consciousness. If he wakes before we do so he could easily displace the fracture again, setting us back to square one or possibly even further if he were to chip the bone ends.' He sipped his whisky. 'We must fashion a splint, although from what I do not know.'

'What about chimney rods?' asked Charlie. 'I'm a sweep and have plenty of spares. A few of those would hold it straight if they was bound on well enough.'

Blacklock nodded. 'Are they nearby? Time is of the essence.'

'On me cart outside. 'Ang on.' He darted out and was back in seconds. 'Any good?'

'Perfect.'

Mrs Evans sourced some webbing, stripped unceremoniously from an armchair, and in twenty minutes a functional splint had been applied. As Blacklock was finishing King woke up.

'How does it feel, Mr King?'

'Sore as buggery, but still a lot better than when I came in.'

'Good. It looks to be a simple fracture which we have successfully reduced. If left to rest properly it will heal well. I think you were fortunate that these fine men were here and able to assist. Realignment took an immense physical effort.'

'When will I be out and about again? I've got mouths to feed.'

'It is a big bone, Mr King, and the fracture will take a long time to knit back together. At least twelve weeks, perhaps sixteen. The right time will be about four weeks after you think it has healed. If you overstress it too soon the setback may prove worse than the break now. You must stay here until Mrs Evans has managed to procure some gypsum plaster so that I might make a cast.'

'Twelve weeks is a bloody long time.'

'Perhaps, but you were perilously close to losing this leg tonight – and may still do so if you neglect my warnings. I cannot stop you. To begin with, the pain will. After that the period of maximum danger occurs, when patients believe the fracture is held firm but the reconnection is only tenuous. Early rebreaks can easily occur in the femur of active individuals – and could even sever an artery. You would bleed to death in twenty minutes or less, and no one could help you. I am not your keeper, Mr King, and your recovery is entirely subject to your patience.

King nodded. 'How much do I owe you, Doctor?'

'Nothing, Mr King,' replied Blacklock. 'I am glad that I was able to help. Spend some of the money on good milk. The calcium will improve your chances.'

'If you're sure?'

'I am.'

'Leave it to me, Ernie,' said Mrs Evans. 'I will provide some recompense for Doctor Naismith.'

By lunchtime King's leg was in a cast; his pain greatly reduced. Once the gypsum plaster was set, Charlie returned with his cart.

King held out a huge hand. 'Thank you.'

'My pleasure, Mr King. The only payment I need is to hear that you are resting properly. If you do not, you place the leg and quite possibly your life in peril.'

Blacklock watched with Mrs Evans from his upstairs window as the cart pulled away.

'Thank you, Doctor Blacklock,' she said, with a peck on his cheek. 'I'm extremely grateful.'

Sixty-Eight

22 Tewson Road, Woolwich, London
Wednesday 12th June

The remaining time with Mrs Evans passed with bewildering speed, even with Blacklock confined exclusively to the box room. He had not been entirely open with her, so even when he was evicted from her premises he would have sufficient funds to secure a few weeks in another sanctuary, albeit of a lower standard than hers. He hoped he would find something suitable further into the East End.

Every day brought a frantic search of the broadsheets – and even the tabloids – but to no avail. There was no news of Porter's capture and as far as he could ascertain Gordon and Robertson were no longer suspects.

He checked his wallet again, as if more money might have materialised within by the force of desire or magic, but to no avail. It was time to leave Mrs Evans's box room.

'Are you sure this is wise, Doctor?' she asked as she returned his instrument case. 'If you get your collar felt while you're carrying them it would only make things worse for you. You can leave them here until you need them. They won't get half-inched.'

He looked at the mahogany case, dusty now, lacquer starting to flake, with the same expression as the day when his uncle had presented the set to him. *'Your aunt and I are extremely proud of you, Nathaniel. Your mother would have been so too. Some milestones in life deserve to be appropriately marked.'* He wiped a finger across the inlaid brass plaque. "To Nathaniel Blacklock, M.D., with all best wishes on the occasion of your qualification. Aunt Moira and Uncle Leonard. 31st December 1881." He knew instinctively that Mrs Evans was right, but he did not want to abandon them.

'Thank you, Mrs Evans, but that will not be necessary.'

'Are you positive? You could send for them later, or come back to collect them. Even the box marks them as something special, *and* it has your name engraved upon it – the name of someone wanted for murder. If your next lodging is shared with others you will be asking for trouble. They will be as safe as The Bank of England itself here. Cross my heart.'

There was undeniable sense in what she said. He looked heavenward for a moment, then sighed. 'Of course, you are right. They are only an unnecessary encumbrance now. I shall return in due course, Mrs Evans, and pay an appropriate storage fee.'

She waved him away. 'It's the least I can do. You've brought an excitement to my days which is lacking when Mr Evans is absent, and freed me from Doreen Mathers – the habit I seemed to have developed of mislaying small items of jewellery and trinkets seems to have cured itself in her absence. Remarkable.' She smiled and offered her hand. 'Good day, Doctor, and good luck. I am sure we will meet again under less trying circumstances.'

Sixty-Nine

Woolwich, London
Wednesday 12th June

The East End Blacklock ventured into was its familiar grey self; the air rank with the filth in the streets, decaying fish discards from the myriad landings and the yellow fog from fires fuelled by cheap coal. Nobody paid him any attention – the small fortune offered by Matilda's father superseded in collective memory by the need to survive in the here and now. His feet, unused to exercise, quickly grew sore and his once-precious hands blistered from the nervous grip he kept on his luggage.

The sound of hawkers yelling above the din merged with one another as he escaped into thoughts of the past and the future, subconsciously redacting his present. Every few moments he scanned his surroundings, looking for a place to shelter, but there was nothing. True vagabonds would probably be able to identify such premises without the need for signs, he mused, but he was not a vagabond. A small but insistent voice added "yet", but he strove to disregard it.

Despair settled upon Blacklock, as if everything and everyone was determined to conspire against him, but still he trudged on. It was some miles before he realised he had stopped looking for somewhere to stay. The stench of decay was stronger than ever when he chose to notice it. There were few stone buildings now. Most of what stood around him were little more than shacks constructed of salvaged materials from wrecked or retired river-craft. In some, portholes acted as windows, complete with brass fittings. The light was waning and cheap candles could be glimpsed here and there, guttering on deal tables and shelves. Some of the dwellings even had open fires on their dirt floors.

He turned back the way he had come, miles from the

relative comfort of Mrs Evans's. A weaker man, he knew, would sob but he determined that he would not succumb. His limbs were so fatigued that even one more step seemed impossible. He stood his portmanteau on one end, ignoring the filth in which he had placed it, and sat down for a few moment's rest.

—+—

'Is he dead?' The voice seemed distant. A small boy.

'Don't think so. Give 'im a poke.'

'Ferk off! I might catch summat.'

'If he's dead he won't care if you poke 'im with a stick. 'Sides, he might have a few bob on 'im.'

Blacklock jerked to wakefulness as a small hand tried to steal into his coat. 'Get away!' he shouted. 'Wretches!'

The boys laughed and ran away, disappearing into what was now the night.

His brief rest had served no useful purpose – indeed, he felt further enervated rather than refreshed. Nevertheless, where the young boys had ventured older criminals were sure to follow and it would not do to encourage them with a further display of vulnerability. He hoisted his luggage and stumbled on, every step a minor trial.

The streets, or rather the populace in them had become noticeably more sinister; too many people paid more than a passing interest in him. After about a quarter of an hour a garishly illuminated inn came into view. The Three Goats Inn was too lively and too loud for his taste but he hoped he might find a seat and some sustenance. Without hesitation he went in. Unlike their neighbours the customers displayed no interest in him, and the barman only a little more. Eventually Blacklock managed to procure a pint of ale and the promise of a mutton sandwich. He took a seat in the corner. Most of the customers were absorbed in a game of cribbage played with bewildering speed between a pair of old men. Wagers were made, and remade, at every turn of a card. Voices rose, mirroring the increasingly febrile atmosphere.

His attention was disturbed by a serving girl, delivering his sandwich on an ancient wooden platter. 'Cook was just finishing for the night so she's put the rest of the spuds on there for you too. T'would only have gone to the pigs otherwise.'

The bread was stale and the mutton tough but his hunger would have driven him to eat anything placed before him. The food was probably mouldy too, but the few candlesticks scattered around the room mercifully produced too little illumination to be sure. The ale went almost immediately to his head and he started to nod off again. His stupor went unnoticed by the other patrons. He shook his head and widened his eyes in an attempt to clear the fog which seemed to engulf him, but to no avail. He felt nauseated as his stomach roiled, threatening to reject his supper. He sat back and closed his eyes in an attempt to regain control.

Seventy

Ballast Wharf, Erith, four miles east of London
Thursday 13th June

A rat scampered across his legs, rousing him. He was lying on a mixture of gravel and rubbish. Forcing his eyes open he saw several larger rats staring implacably back at him. He sprang upright, only for the crushing pain in his head to force him back to his knees.

He took a few deep breaths to steady himself before tentatively opening his eyes again. Before him was a mass of rotten boats, dismantled rigging, broken masts and smashed carts, as though he had awoken at the scene of some naval tragedy. Behind him rose a cliff of crumbling brick and powdery mortar, the wall of a massive soot-blackened warehouse. He struggled to orient himself, confused by both his location and the haziest recollection of the night before. He climbed gingerly to his feet, thankful for the support of the grimy wall. He tried to take a step but was immediately overcome by a rush of dizziness, almost losing his balance. Without warning scalding bile erupted from his stomach in a fetid gush. He reached automatically for his handkerchief but it was not it its usual pocket, nor the opposite one. He patted himself with rising panic as he realised that all his pockets were empty.

My wallet.

He became frantic, even tearing off his soiled jacket and shaking it upside-down – but it was gone. Not lost, but stolen. He sank to his haunches and settled against the wall. *Hadn't there been an inn?* Yes. *What was it called? The Red Lion? The Bear? The Barley Mow, perhaps?* He felt even sicker as he realised that he had no recollection of its name. He tried running through the alphabet in the hope that concentrating on an initial letter might trigger a memory but still nothing came.

A solitary tear formed, which he wiped unconsciously away.

He tried to stand again but each attempt was accompanied by a flood of nausea and painful dry heaves. He used his sleeve to wipe his watering eyes and the perspiration from his forehead. *You are an intelligent and resourceful man.* He filled his lungs and stood up, defying his stomach and headache. He was in an area of wasteland between two derelict warehouses. After a couple of stumbling steps he vomited again, although less severely. Through the tall undergrowth he could see some people walking past so made his way towards them.

'Excuse me, sir,' he said to a cleanly if not smartly dressed old man, 'but is there an inn nearby? I cannot recall the name, but I may have left some important papers there.'

'Sober up, you fool,' replied the man. 'It's barely eight o'clock in the morning and you're looking for a drink? You should be ashamed.' He stalked off, turning once only to scowl.

Blacklock, aware that his appearance was beyond dishevelled, elected not to approach any women. The next man he asked was less complimentary than the first.

There was nothing for it but to commence his own search of the area. He methodically walked in a widening pattern of streets, with the warehouse at the centre, but without success. The public house was nowhere in the vicinity.

Realising that his money, spare clothes – in fact everything he had left – was gone, several hours later he found he was back at Mrs Evans's table, drinking tea and eating bread with all the restraint of a starving Labrador. She had waved away his embarrassment at falling foul of a robber so quickly after his departure.

'You'd better keep this,' she said, offering her husband's suit again. 'It's a little more presentable, at any rate. I'll tell him moths got it.'

'Thank you. I feel almost human again. Now, I would like my instruments, if I may.'

'Of course. Why?'

'I need to pawn them.'

'It wasn't a good idea yesterday and it's still not a good idea today. Do you honestly believe you can pawn such a set without arousing suspicion? The pawnbroker need only recall you during the next police appeal and you're done for.'

'Could I impose upon you to pawn them on my behalf? My position is desperate.'

'Still no. Same reason. How much are they worth?'

'About twenty pounds. They are excellent quality.'

Mrs Evans whistled. 'They must be.' She paused, deep in contemplation. I'll give you ten pounds – as an honorarium for your efforts on Ernie's leg – and an additional two pounds ten as a loan against the instruments. I won't sell them on. They are of no use to most of the people I know. And the ones that could find a use for them are safer without too many sharps about them.'

Blacklock hesitated.

'Two pounds ten, no interest. That's the best I can do.'

'Very well. Thank you. I would be most grateful. It is only until I can redeem them, of course.'

'Naturally.'

Seventy-One

Belgrave Square, London
Thursday 13th June

Blacklock set off with a veneer of confidence which he did not feel. His plans encompassed nothing more than leaving the East End as far behind as possible. Securing accommodation in any conventional sense was out of the question, given that all he possessed was Mr Evans's suit and twelve pounds ten, which was securely stowed in one of the many hidden pockets which the thief's suit afforded. His destination, under normal circumstances, would represent a huge risk – but normal circumstances were barely a memory now.

In all this time only one person had extended any kindness in a purely altruistic manner.

He arrived at his destination just as it closed, which was perfect timing. Although the park was closer to Matilda than he would have wanted, he had little choice. He watched as the keeper threaded a heavy chain through the penultimate gate and secured it with a massive brass patent padlock. As the man bent down to insert the key Blacklock stepped smartly through the remaining unlocked gate and sidestepped into the bushes nearby. All he was aware of was his heart pounding as the elderly keeper dawdled to lock the gate.

'All out! All out! Final call, ladies and gentlemen!' shouted the keeper. Blacklock felt his nails digging into the bark as he gripped a tree. After a minute or so the keeper locked the gate and whistled as he walked away, rattling his keys like a cheerful jailer.

Blacklock waited for a few minutes before he dared to move, venturing nervously into the centre of the park. There was no one in sight as he perched on the rim of the ornamental fountain, unsure what he was doing there, disbelieving that his life had come to this.

'Well, well – look what the cat's dragged in,' said a gruff voice he did not recognise. 'Nice threads, too.'

Blacklock gripped the marble ledge, although he felt ready to fight if the need arose. There was nothing left to lose.

'Leave 'im be, William, he's a friend,' warned Paulinus Stewart, seemingly appearing from nowhere.

William muttered something unintelligible but obviously crude under his breath and moved away.

'What brings you here, Nathaniel? Back to see the young lady?'

'No.'

'Phelps then?'

'Neither, Paulinus.' He swallowed before continuing in little more than a hoarse whisper. 'I wondered whether I might stay here this evening?'

'*What?*'

'I must admit to a run of misfortune which has made my situation ... difficult. I can go elsewhere if you would prefer.'

'No, stay. You seem a decent sort and most of us are too. Where's your pack?'

'My what?'

'Bedding? Any grub?'

'I have nothing.'

'Hmmmm. You can't sleep outside without cover, even at this time of year.' He scratched his stubble absent-mindedly. 'Got it! Danny French ain't been around for a few days – maybe he got collared pilfering – but his bedroll is under the bandstand. Should be pretty dry. It'll do until you get your own stuff.'

'But I will not need any–'

'Ahh. Don't say that, friend. We all said that to begin with. Best to accept things as they are.' He led the way to a clearing underneath some towering rhododendron bushes. The earth was scoured clean by the many that spent their nights there. 'This is the bedroom. You can have this spot, Nathaniel. My bedroll is the one wrapped in them GWR sacks. Now, follow me.' Stewart led the way to the bandstand. 'The third trellis panel to the right of the stairs is loose. This is where you stash your stuff when you're out during the day. The parkies know full well it's here but they're mostly decent enough fellas and they turn a blind eye.' He removed the panel and crawled in, returning seconds later with a bundle wrapped in a filthy sheet. 'Here you are. Danny wouldn't mind. Come on, take it.'

The stench of sweat, damp and filth brutally overwhelmed Blacklock's senses, reminding him of a months-old drowning victim he had dissected in medical school. He tried to mouth breathe, but years of self-training to do the opposite for the sake of etiquette kept defeating him.

'Sorry,' smiled Stewart. 'It's a bit ripe, ain't it? Danny's never been one for soap and water. You'll get used to anything when it's all you've got.'

Later that evening, as the group of outcasts were gathered around a fire so small that he could barely fathom how it remained alight, Blacklock regaled his edited life story to an eager audience keen to escape their daily struggles. They listened attentively, with only occasional interruptions for clarification until one, silent until that moment said, 'With respect to your suspension from surgery, why did you not simply invoke Tompkiss vs. Regina, 1856, or Adams vs. Regina, 1862? Obvious precedents!'

Blacklock turned to the questioner, open mouthed. 'I beg your pardon?'

'You have two clear-as-day precedents which would absolve you. A surgeon acting in good faith cannot be held responsible for unnatural anatomical features.'

Blacklock's dumbstruck perplexity was clear.

'Don't worry, Nathaniel,' said Stewart. 'The Judge is

harmless enough. He's read every legal book under the sun during many years spent at Her Majesty's pleasure, ain't ya?'

The Judge shrugged and turned away, muttering.

'So he made that up?' whispered Blacklock.

'Oh no. He'll be absolutely right, you can count on that.'

'Then why on earth is he..?'

'Here?'

Blacklock nodded.

'Bad luck,' said Stewart. 'Add to that an insatiable appetite for the company of young men and you end up here. People could say the same about you, Nathaniel.'

Blacklock started to reply but stopped short as the truth dawned. Stewart was not talking claptrap, no matter how hard he might try to persuade himself otherwise. He examined the men he now grudgingly admitted were his companions. Each was lost in the flames, each had a story. Such people had been invisible before now – but they were the only ones to extend a hand of friendship.

'Penny for them?' asked Stewart.

Blacklock waved him away. 'Nothing interesting, my friend. Nothing at all.'

Seventy-Two

Belgrave Square, London
Friday 14th - Saturday 22nd June

Blacklock's last conscious thought as he lay down to rest was that he could never sleep in such squalor, only to awaken more rested and refreshed than he had done for many weeks.

The others were already gathered around the long-dead fire in the pre-dawn light. 'Morning, Nathaniel,' said Stewart. 'Sleep well?'

'Like the dead. Perhaps the air is cleaner here.'

'Maybe. Gather up your bedding and stow it neatly underneath the bandstand. We have to be out of the garden the moment it opens at dawn. We're only allowed to stay as long as we remain invisible.'

A few minutes later Blacklock stood bleary-eyed on the pavement, at a loss as to how he would fill the next fifteen hours. He set out in the opposite direction to the others, unwilling to be associated with such a down-at-heel band. Even as he did so, his conscience pricked him; these men had shown him kindness and acceptance which no one else had; on more than one occasion he wondered whether he might now *be* one of them and struggled ineffectively to push such thoughts aside.

In the event the day passed more quickly than anticipated, although he did not understand how. He fell into some form of disconnected reverie which sustained him throughout the day, allowing the hours to pass almost unnoticed. When he returned to the garden at sunset it was with a mix of guilt and pride over how little he had achieved and how easy it had been to do nothing.

The first few days passed with the same mixture of

apathy and indolence, coupled with a gnawing awareness that this "lifestyle", such as it was, might prove indefinitely sustainable. His initial revulsion over both the washing and – more particularly – the toileting habits he had to adopt quickly subsided. He noted their loss with bemusement but little else, since his life circumstances were now largely defined for him. Realising – and fearing – how comfortable he had become stirred occasional thoughts of escape and justice, but they remained simply thoughts without action. This, in its way, further irked him and he reacted against it, only for the more positive feelings to subside in their turn. His feelings oscillated between these poles, seemingly of their own accord.

It took some time before he could lower himself to attempt to beg. His pride got the better of him initially, trying to demonstrate his need with a laissez-faire attitude which appeared to others as belligerence. Once, in Piccadilly – recommended by Stewart for its practical combination of wealthy patronage and multitude of escape routes should he attract police attention – someone approaching him crossed to the other side of the road, making it obvious that it was simply to avoid him. His outrage almost drove him to pursue them.

In the night, often shivering beneath the stars, Blacklock occasionally thought of Miss Caldecott, sleeping within a few tens of yards. Had she remained pregnant, and if so how far along was she? Had she found the means of termination? He hoped that her father doted upon her as much he pretended to; any less and her changing appearance might lead to her clandestine deportation to the distant Irish relatives so that nature might take its course, far from the million watchful faces of London. It would not do for a prospective MP to have a bastard in the family. He was frequently tempted to peek at their house but feared Phelps's preternatural protective instincts.

Every day some new and unexpected depth was revealed within his companions, most of whom were homeless by mischance rather than indolence. There were exceptions, of course – William being a particularly unwholesome character – but they were few. Stewart had been a master stonemason working on great buildings throughout the city but an accident had damaged his back, and with it his ability to stand for the long periods required for his work. Blacklock pledged to have him seen by a specialist as soon as his own "crisis" had passed, but despite the smiles and assurances neither man believed it.

Seventy-Three

Belgrave Square, London
Sunday 23rd June

Stewart shook Blacklock into wakefulness. 'Wake up, Sleeping Beauty. There's work to do.'

'Really? What?'

'Time for you to gain some education, Nathaniel. Get over to the fountain, wash your face and especially your hands. Pretend you're about to wield a scalpel.'

'But–'

'Come on, chop chop. We've an appointment to keep.'

Confused but keen to retain his place within the group he headed to the fountain. William was already there. 'I will only tell you this once, new boy: If you get in front of me today, I will kill you as surely as we stand here. Don't think for a moment that I won't. You wouldn't be the first.'

Before Blacklock could reply William stalked away into the undergrowth that served as their latrine. He was still looking where the thug had gone when Stewart startled him. 'Come on man, scrub up. It's almost time for us to leave and you need to be ready for the show.'

With an uncomprehending shrug Blacklock plunged his face into the frigid water, the shock of the cold driving the breath from his lungs. A hand fastened onto the nape of his neck; he tried to raise his head but his assailant was too strong. After what seemed minutes, by which time he was sure he needed to fill his lungs with water, his head was lifted from the pond by the hair. William pulled him close. 'Remember what I said. Always behind me.'

William strode away without a backward glance. Blacklock took a minute or two to regain his breath and allow his pulse to slow before following him.

When the assorted "gentlemen", including Blacklock,

left the garden it was almost dawn. A chilly morning mist shrouded the square, softening its edges and further isolating the wanderers from the wealth around them. They walked the short distance to the canal where they settled as comfortably as they could, all quiet. The clocks struck six, seven, then the half.

'Right,' said Stewart, 'time to take our positions.'

Blacklock struggled to his feet, hindered by both his cramping muscles and freezing toes. He joined the train, limping as the blood tried to resume its flow and still in the dark about the proceedings.

After a couple of turns along unfamiliar byways he realised with horror their destination. He slowed down, keen to fall from the pack, but Stewart noticed him and jollied him along. Blacklock did not wish to insult his fellow gentlemen so fell unwillingly back into step, keeping his head down. His sole consolation was that the Caldecotts attended the ten o'clock service, so he was not in danger of meeting them, cementing his disgrace. A line of women, in similarly straitened circumstances, ran from near the front door of St Aidan's. 'It's our turn to be first this week,' said Stewart, 'so we stand nearer to where the coaches arrive. The closer you are to the church, the less money's left as pockets empty. You need to stand at the very end of our line, next to the first woman. Her name's Viv. Lovely gal.'

Blacklock moved along the line, William scowling as he passed. 'Viv? My name is Nathaniel. Pleased to make your acquaintance.'

Viv turned and offered a modest smile. Blacklock congratulated himself at not recoiling from her smallpox scars.

There were eleven men before Blacklock; Stewart at the head of the queue, then William, then everyone else who had fallen into their places with little rancour. To his right, seventeen women.

He checked the clock. Nearly eight. He was tortured by the fear that the rector may come out to minister to the poor, at which the point the depth of his fall would become public. His feet were still numb and his knees were becoming even stiffer. If the carriages did not arrive soon he was convinced that he might simply collapse to the pavement.

A procession of coaches, not dissimilar to the Caldecott's, swept into the far end of the square.

Viv nudged him. 'Them's the Caldecotts. We should do well today.'

Blacklock's stomach flipped. 'The Caldecotts? It cannot be. They attend the ten o'clock service.'

'Not today, love. Ten o'clock's cancelled. Everybody'll be at this one. We'll be on our way home by ten past.'

Blacklock tried to run, even as the carriages began to slow only a dozen yards away, but his legs refused to cooperate. Reason told him that fleeing now would also draw unwanted attention from both sides of the divide.

As if on cue the line of beggars shuffled forward as a collective until they were arrayed along the kerb. Blacklock dare not look up; Phelps would spot him in an instant. Sir Edmund's carriage had now slowed to a snail's pace as he doled out alms. Blacklock recalled the dice rolls. Had he thrown eleven or more that morning? Would he have tried again to secure a lower number?

Sir Edmund continued working along the line, bestowing his threepenny pieces as though they were papal wafers. Blacklock held out his hand, which shook doubly with cold and fear. Two hands remained extended before his. A small gilt coin was dispensed, then another to the hand next to his ... He kept his head bowed in supplication as he waited for his coin ... in vain. He glanced up, just as Caldecott displayed his empty purse. 'Sorry my man, nothing left. Perhaps next week, eh?' He looked Blacklock full in the eye; there was no hint of recognition. Beyond him, Tilly was looking steadfastly in the other direction from below a heap of blankets.

The Caldecott convoy moved on without further charity.

The one which followed – Blacklock thought they might be called the Knoxes – had obviously been observing the Caldecott's progress for the point at which Sir Edmund's purse inevitably ran dry. Their carriage stopped in front of him and an elderly woman peered out, squinting over a half-moon lorgnette. 'A sixpence for you, my man. Be sure to observe The Lord's day and refrain from alcohol.' Blacklock thanked her and bowed his head and she continued along the line of women, who received a shilling each with the same benediction.

'It ain't always good to be at the front of the row, mate,' said Viv. 'Caldecott's a bloody miser. Money goes to money but it don't often come back. See you next week, if we're both still above ground.' She smiled and walked away.

Blacklock was still watching her absent-mindedly when William spoke. 'You got sixpence?'

'Yes. I was fortunate that the Caldecotts ran out of funds before they reached me.'

'Give it 'ere.'

'What?'

'Give it 'ere, if you want to keep those pretty teeth of yours.'

'But–'

'Give it. I'll give you my threepence and we'll say no more about it. Unless you'd rather lose your teeth as well?'

'N-no.' Blacklock held out his sixpence.

'Attaboy.' William took the coin.

'My threepence piece? You said–'

'Forget what I said, cretin, and be happy you've still got something to smile with. Now get out of my sight.'

Seventy-Four

Belgrave Square
Thursday 27th June

Blacklock woke, fighting for breath. A huge weight crushed his chest; his mouth and nose were blocked. In the failing light of the dying campfire William's face swam into view inches from his own. The keen edge of his knife glinted.

'One word – one sound – and I'll slit your throat,' whispered William. 'Get it?'

Blacklock nodded, wide-eyed.

To underline his intent William pushed the point of his knife into the side of Blacklock's neck. He felt his skin part under the pressure.

William took his hand from Blacklock's mouth. 'We're going to take a little walk,' he continued, hoarsely. 'Me and you's got an appointment.'

William's knees pinned Blacklock's arms; he sat on his chest. Blacklock nodded again, mindful of the knife. 'Alright.'

'And don't try nothin'.'

'I will not.' Blacklock's voice was barely audible. 'You have my word.'

'Good boy. 'Tween you and me I'd rather stick you but you're worth a fortune to me alive.'

Blacklock caught a flicker of movement in the corner of his eye, a fraction of a second before William collapsed to one side, unconscious.

Behind him, Stewart held a club. 'I don't know what his game was, but you need to move on or I think he might do for you. There's a good bunch of lads in the corner of Regent's Park, near the zoo. Ask for Tommy and tell him I sent you. If I were you I'd make tracks sharpish. You don't want to be here when William wakes up. And get that neck seen to – it'll draw too much attention.'

'What about you?'

'I can handle myself - don't you worry about that.'

'Thank you.' Blacklock offered his hand which Stewart shook with the crushing grip of an ex-stonemason. He nodded in the direction of the main gate. 'Be off with you, Nathaniel. Godspeed.'

As Blacklock pushed through the undergrowth the church clock began to chime. Three o'clock. Still hours before dawn .He wasn't fully clear of the bushes when he heard the first police whistle, followed immediately by several others, a wall of noise surrounding the park. He ran back to the centre, hurdling the now semi-conscious William.

There was nowhere to go.

He spun around, desperate for cover, bewildered by the cacophony of myriad whistles. *The bandstand.* He ran to it, and in a single movement pulled aside the loose trellis and dived inside. In a couple of seconds he had the trellis back in position.

He peered through. Police lamps were closing on the centre. Stewart hopped onto the edge of the bandstand's deck, legs dangling in front of the loose trellis.

A moment later the first constable arrived. He pointed at William. 'What's up with him?'

'Too much ale last night, I'd imagine. That's his normal trick,' replied Stewart. 'Can I help you fellas?'

'Where's Nathaniel Blacklock?'

'Dunno who you're talking about. Blacklock, you say? Don't ring a bell.' He swept his hand towards his assembled companions. 'Anyone else heard of him?'

As the others vociferously denied any knowledge of him, Blacklock retreated to the centre of the bandstand underfloor, where the absent travellers' packs were piled high. The stench was overpowering – he thought he might retch but steeled himself as he made a small opening in the middle of the pile. Satisfied that he could not be seen from any direction he pinched his nose and waited.

'Maybe he's under the bandstand,' said another recently-arrived officer. 'I'll have a look.'

'Good luck,' said Stewart. 'Plenty of rats to keep you company.'

Blacklock shuffled further into the packs. The light of a lantern flashed about the underfloor. 'Just a pile of tramp crap. Nothing to see.'

'You'd better get in there to check,' said the first officer. 'Duncan'd have your guts for garters if you missed him.'

Blacklock listened as the officer walked around the bandstand, the surrounding ornamental gravel crunching at every step. 'There's no way in.'

'There must be,' replied the first. 'Otherwise the tramps couldn't pile up all their shit under there. Come on, Jonesy, look sharp.'

A trellis panel splintered. 'See? There's a hole. In you go. Better get this done before the guvnor arrives.'

'Why not you?'

'I'm a martyr to my back. I can't go crawling in there.'

Jonesy sighed. "Spose so.'

Blacklock tensed. *He was caught.*

'Jeez,' said Jonesy. 'The bloody smell. I can't go in there. Let's wait for the dogs. If he's in there he ain't going nowhere.'

'What's wrong with Price?' Duncan's voice further alarmed Blacklock.

'And who might you be?' asked Stewart.

'Inspector Duncan. Leman Street. Now answer.'

'William had a proper skinful last night,' replied Stewart. 'I'm sure he'll be up and about soon.'

'Hmmm,' mumbled Duncan. 'Perhaps.'

Blacklock watched as two more pairs of uniformed legs strode into the clearing. 'No sign anywhere, Inspector.'

'Makes no sense. He was supposed to be here. Clear all these stinking tramps out of here. They disgust me. And find out where the bloody dogs have got to.'

The police shepherded out the night sleepers, including Stewart, who dragged William away with him. Duncan climbed deliberately up the bandstand steps and walked slowly around the perimeter, each board squealing in turn.

Blacklock barely dared to breathe – the threat from above and the stench surrounding him conspired to force him to surrender. Occasionally Duncan paused and Blacklock *did* hold his breath. After a while the inspector would resume his patrol.

During one of the pauses a constable returned. 'Dogs are just coming, sir.'

"Bout bloody time. Get them under here as soon as they do.'

Blacklock closed his eyes; the chase was over. The hounds would pick up his scent and in seconds he would be done for. Unless – *I'm in a hell of competing scents.* There was half a chance – if that – that they might *not* detect him. He began to move packs and bedrolls from underneath him to above, gradually burying himself. The reek was close to overwhelming him, but anything instead of Duncan's dubious form of justice would be preferable. All he wanted to do was vomit; his eyes watered and his whole body trembled from the effort to bury himself. What was in all likelihood only a couple of minutes' effort seemed like hours, but eventually he felt the soft, dry earth on his face. Even the dirt itself was rancid from the decades of contact with the filthy belongings of innumerable homeless, but at least he was now entirely buried. It would take a remarkable dog to find him.

Forehead on crossed forearms he tried to breathe through his mouth, but nothing could disguise the stench of decades of filth.

He listened. The dogs – two or three, he estimated – were barking nearby whilst Duncan yelled unintelligible orders.

Another trellis panel was smashed. They would soon be upon him. It had come to this, a pitiful end.

One, then two, then uncountable further dogs entered

the space under the bandstand.

Blacklock tensed, waiting for his inevitable discovery. The dogs were running around the space, their yelping filling his ears – but second by second, minute by minute, their intensity decreased. The yelps became whimpers, then simple snuffling. Still he was undiscovered, in a space three feet high and twenty yards in diameter.

He dared to hope that even at this, the final minute of the eleventh hour, he might still be spared. Someone shouted, and one by one the dogs left as quickly as they had arrived. 'There's nothing under there but tramp shit, guv,' said another disembodied voice.

'Fuck!' shouted Duncan, then sighed. 'Alright. Take 'em away. We did our best. Cargill!'

Blacklock heard someone fighting through the undergrowth. 'Yes sir?'

'We're going to wait for another couple of hours or so, then call it a night. The Prof might still come back. Have the men keep as much out of sight as possible, and make sure those other tramps don't warn him off.' There was a pause. 'Go on then! Do you want me to write it down for you? Jeez!'

Cargill, Blacklock presumed, scurried away. *Two hours. Only two hours and I will have beaten Duncan.*

Something lapped at his neck wound, waking him. As he started he almost called out, but managed to resist the impulse. The animal ran away. He opened his eyes. The light seemed brighter, but he did not dare disturb his camouflage to check.

The animal ran back across his neck, heavy and sharp-clawed. *A rat!* He shuddered, which was enough to make the rodent withdraw again. Above him, Duncan started another stately circuit of the bandstand, jingling the change in his pockets. *How much longer?* Perhaps Duncan would finally get bored and – something bit Blacklock's finger; he snatched his hand back. He could not see but knew that it too was bleeding.

The rat bit deep into his forearm. He reached out instinctively and grabbed for the creature. The animal's smooth body writhed in his hand. It twisted to bite him again; without thinking he grasped its head with his other hand. It squealed, a keening shriek.

Above, Duncan stopped.

The rat squirmed in Blacklock's hands, threatening to escape his grip. Beneath his fingers he could feel the muscles tensing, every sinew taut. Under that, bones.

He closed his hands even more tightly, squeezing with all his might.

The rat twisted, arched, fought. Blacklock tried to crush it.

A bone gave, then another. The rat fought back, still threatening to escape his grip.

Still he squeezed.

More bones splintered. *Ribs?* He twisted his hands, wringing the creature. A louder crack – the spine, he hoped – and the rat was still.

He let it go and rolled it away from him. It was not dead, not quite. If he held his own breath he could still hear the rat's laboured attempts. There was a faint whine to it.

Blacklock was overcome by a profound sorrow – no, guilt. He did not want to kill anything, and try as he might he could not convince himself that he had had no choice.

He came back to his senses as Duncan resumed his patrol on the deck above.

After what seemed like several hours of panicked speculation about the possibility of contracting bubonic plague or rabies from the rat Blacklock heard the church clock strike five.

The clock striking six woke him. Duncan's vigil continued, his spare change rattling like Jacob Marley's chains. Blacklock heard him yawn expansively.

'Cargill,' he barked. 'I've had enough of this. Stand every

man down – and take those stinking dogs back to wherever they came from. He ain't here, and he ain't coming back. What a waste of a bloody night!'

Blacklock listened with relief to the sounds of the police operation being dismantled, as the voices of men and dogs faded away into the morning. He committed to waiting until eight before venturing out and somehow putting distance between himself and London. There had to be a way.

The clock struck finally eight. Blacklock extracted himself from the wretched pile and crawled towards the loose trellis. The rat was glassy-eyed. He was relieved that he did not need to put it out of its misery, although he had steeled himself to do so.

He reached the trellis and looked around. The park was deserted. He clambered out, stretching gratefully as he rose to his feet.

'Morning Prof. Hell of a shaving cut.'

Seventy-Five

Belgrave Square, London
Thursday 27th June

Duncan jumped from the bandstand, smiling triumphantly. 'Doctor Blacklock, I presume.'

Blacklock froze. 'Inspector.'

Duncan glanced over his shoulder then nodded at Blacklock. 'Cargill, if you'd be so kind as to do the honours.'

Cargill stepped from the undergrowth, blushing profusely and handcuffed Blacklock. 'Sorry,' he whispered.

'Come along, Blacklock,' said Cargill with a counterfeit authority more aimed at Duncan than his prisoner. Blacklock complied, only to find himself in leg-irons almost immediately.

'Is this really necessary?' he asked Duncan.

'You've been running too long, Blacklock,' said Duncan. 'You're quite the escapologist. Not a risk I'm willing to take.' He turned triumphantly to a uniformed officer. 'Take him away.'

Seventy-Six

Leman Street Police Station, Shadwell, London
Thursday 27th June

His cell was at the most remote extreme of the abandoned sub-basement, devoid of natural light. Even so, Duncan's henchmen had deemed it necessary to blindfold him as he was brought down. A bare pallet served for a bed, a bucket without a handle for a latrine. Blacklock sat back against the damp wall, the condensation frigid through his shirt. He idly wondered whether pneumonia could enter through the skin, perhaps a souvenir left by a previous inmate of this desperate place. When he called or listened for other prisoners there were none. *Of course*, he recalled – the cells lined only one side of the basement, so he could not see whether anyone else was incarcerated alongside him. It was obviously a forlorn hope when he remembered the detritus stored in the neighbouring cells.

His sole visitor was the taciturn custody sergeant who had nothing to say but exuded a knowing insolence, as if he was enjoying Blacklock's fall from grace. *And why shouldn't he?*

Seventy-Seven

Leman Street Police Station, Shadwell, London
Friday 28th June

Blacklock did not see anyone until after what passed for breakfast on his second morning of imprisonment. He was pretending to nap on the pallet, hoping that appearing comfortable would irritate his jailer, when there was a barely audible tap on the bars. 'Blacklock,' – a hoarse whisper – 'it's me. Al.'

Blacklock decided not to open his eyes in order to maintain his affectation of comfort. 'To what do I owe this rare pleasure?' It was a line he had been rehearsing.

'Duncan doesn't know I'm here. I just wanted to see how you're bearing up.'

'I will not dignify that with an answer, Sergeant.' He tried to calm himself before continuing in a more measured tone. 'What happens next?'

'You'll be questioned in due course. I don't know when that will be. Duncan likes to let suspects stew. He says that time to think frees the tongue.'

'Does that work?'

'Sometimes. On weaker minds, or with people minded to construct ever more complex stories that they eventually lose track of, which is when he springs his trap. I don't know how long he plans to keep you down here.'

'How long *can* he leave me here?'

'As long as he likes. He's the guvnor.'

'But surely–'

'No. He's the king of the castle. Anyway, I'd better go.' He rummaged inside his jacket and retrieved a small package wrapped in brown paper. He unwrapped it. 'Here,' he said, handing over a doorstep cheese sandwich. 'He'll starve you if he can. Get this down you sharpish. It'll be bad for both of us if you're caught with it. Got to go.'

Before Blacklock could thank him Cargill wheeled away, his heeltaps echoing in the damp confines.

Blacklock sat down on the pallet. The sandwich was fresh and tasty, the best meal he had had since ... he thought back, and laughed. It was certainly the most welcome meal since the debacle at Fortnum and Mason's, which seemed more than a lifetime ago, like a bygone age when his biggest concern had been the preservation of his hands and therefore what passed for his reputation. He examined them in the guttering candlelight. Blackened nails, split to the quick. Blisters on his palms, chaps open in his fingers. The hands of a tramp, which he supposed he now was. What next? The gallows? Certainly, if Duncan got his way and offered up a sacrificial lamb to the baying crowds, to be hung, drawn and quartered by the locals.

It was a greater shock to realise that he no longer cared.

Seventy-Eight

Leman Street Police Station, Shadwell, London
Sunday 30th June

Another three days dragged by before Duncan favoured him with a visit. Sitting opposite Blacklock he had a predatory glint in his eye, a cat playing with a mouse instead of ending its misery. 'How have you been keeping, Blacklock? We were starting to miss you. We wondered what we had said or done to so upset you. We began to think we might never see you again, and what a disappointment that would have been – but here you are, large as life, safely ensconced in the very bottom of our little police station. Indeed, it's an honour to have you with us.'

Blacklock said nothing.

'I don't know why you even tried to run; I was always going to find you. Where have you been? Where did you hide?'

Blacklock maintained his sullen silence.

Duncan sighed. 'Am I going to have to persuade you to talk, Blacklock?'

He shrugged. 'So, suddenly I am Blacklock?'

'You always were. It needles people into action if they believe you cannot even be bothered to remember their name. And, as a bonus, I find it amusing. A simple game of superiority.'

'It is pathetic.'

'Aha! A bite.' Duncan stopped smiling. 'When I want your opinion I'll ask. Right now – well, tomorrow morning – I will want facts. You can muse on that overnight. I want to know which ones you killed, whether there are any we don't know about yet and *why the fuck you killed the child*. You should clear your conscience before you hang and spend eternity in an unmarked hole in the corner of Wandworth's yard.'

'I did not kill anyone. The child died – not at my hands – because his appendix burst. Someone tried to intervene but it was already too late.'

It was Duncan's turn to shrug. 'A pretty enough tale, but save it for tomorrow.'

'Do not count on my breaking down too easily, Inspector. I have been living rough for the past few weeks and as you can see I am far from being a gibbering wreck.'

'You'll come round. Are you getting enough to eat?'

'No.'

'Good.'

Seventy-Nine

Leman Street Police Station, Shadwell, London
Monday 1st July

It seemed as though he had barely closed his eyes to sleep when he was startled into wakefulness by the custody sergeant running his truncheon along the bars of his cell. 'Wakey, wakey! Rise and shine! It's time for your chat with the Inspector.'

Blacklock rubbed his eyes. 'What time is it? It is still dark.'

'It's just after midnight – I'm a few minutes late. *Sorry*. And it's always dark underground, moron. Duncan'll be here at four a.m. but he likes to make sure that prisoners have enough time to attend to their toilette and get dressed comfortably before the day's work begins. Ain't he the considerate one?'

Blacklock yawned and rubbed his face. 'This is madness. Four hours' notice? Please, let me sleep.'

The sergeant laughed hollowly then stopped abruptly. 'You get no say in this, you shitty little perv. Get used to it.' He turned on his heel and strode away, once again running his truncheon along the bars.

Blacklock rested his head on the straw mattress and fell asleep instantly.

'Two o'clock already and you're not even properly dressed yet?' bellowed the sergeant. 'What have you been doing? Playing with yourself, no doubt.'

Blacklock forced his eyes open. 'For God's sake, man. This is torture.'

'Two things, sniveller. One – I'm Sergeant Pettifer to you at all times. Two – torture is against the law and has been for many years. I'm simply giving you adequate opportunity to clear your head and gather your thoughts. What's wrong with that? We're giving you every chance to shine...' He smiled, revealing rows of rotten yellow pegs which had once been teeth.

'Please, sergeant, I–'

'Sergeant *Pettifer*. Christ, you're slow.'

'Please, Sergeant Pettifer, I–'

'Shut your slimy mouth. There's nothing you're going to say that I won't have heard before. I don't give two shits about what you think. Three women, one fella, and a kiddie. They're who I care about – and you butchered 'em. Don't expect any favours from me.'

He walked a few paces before turning back. 'Bless my soul, I've had more tea than's good for me on this shift, that's for sure.' With a smile he unbuttoned his fly and emptied his bladder onto Blacklock's mattress. 'That's better. See you in a couple of hours. Try not to nod off again, my brave little soldier.'

Blacklock was sitting disconsolately on the floor when Pettifer returned two hours later. He pulled a huge key from his belt and unlocked the door. 'Out you come, Tinkerbell.'

Blacklock dragged his aching body upright and walked from his cell.

The policeman smiled and half-bowed, extending his arm towards the stairs. 'After you.'

Blacklock had taken only three steps when he heard a rush of air and pain exploded in his knee as Pettifer's truncheon connected, felling him. The agony consumed his consciousness; it stopped his breath even as it nauseated him. He rolled onto his side but before he could regain his breath the officer buried his boot in Blacklock's stomach. When he did manage to inhale it only seemed to release more pain, allowing it free rein to course throughout his body. Pettifer lifted him by his hair and slammed his head against the wall, moving so close that his nose almost touched Blacklock's. 'That, you nonce, is for the kiddie. There's plenty more where that came from, so don't count on getting too comfortable here. By the time I've finished with you you'll be glad to hang. Now walk.'

Blacklock had managed a handful of faltering steps before he heard the jingle of Pettifer's keys then felt an intense pain in his bicep. He looked at the livid wound which started to bleed belatedly as he watched, as if the flesh itself was taken aback.

'I'm pretty good with a keychain too, perv. Never forget that,' said Pettifer.

Blacklock slumped into the chair opposite Duncan, still breathless, while Pettifer manacled his hands to the table between them.

'You seem a little out of sorts, Doctor?'

Pettifer interrupted Blacklock's reply. 'He stumbled as he was making his way up from the cells, Inspector. I was too slow to catch him. Sorry, sir.'

'I'm confident you did your best, Sergeant,' said Duncan, dismissing him with a nod of his head.

Blacklock waited until Pettifer had closed the door. 'He attacked me, Duncan. Completely unprovoked. He beat me and whipped me with his keys.'

'I see.' Duncan drew a small penknife from his jacket and began cleaning his nails. 'That's a very serious allegation. It's the word of a respected officer nearing retirement versus a murder suspect who has spent a couple of months on the run. I'm sure any complaint would get a fair hearing though. I'm impartial, after all.'

'I wish to make a formal complaint.'

Duncan yawned and rubbed his temples with one hand. 'Of course you do. So be it.' He stood up. 'Here's my pen. I'll fetch some paper.'

He returned moments later with several sheets of ruled foolscap. 'Here. I'll look in on you in a while to see how you're doing.'

Blacklock struggled against the short wrist chains which tethered his arms to the table but eventually managed to scratch out a short statement. He called out and Duncan returned.

The Inspector read Blacklock's account through and placed it gently back on the table. 'Very interesting. Smoke?'

'You know I do not.'

'There's no telling what habits a fugitive might pick up on the run.' Duncan lit a cigar butt and dropped the match, still burning, onto Blacklock's statement. Yellow flames spread quickly from the match-head, consuming the paper in seconds. 'Ooops,' smiled Duncan. 'Silly me. Want to write another little fairy tale?'

'I do not believe there would be any point in my doing so.'

'Attaboy. That's the wisest thing you've said all morning.' He stubbed out the cigar on the tabletop. 'Alright, Blacklock,' Duncan continued, 'Before we get embroiled in the whys and wherefores of your crimes allow me to paint you a picture of how our little tête à têtes are going to work. That's Frog for a chat but a man of your boundless intellect would know that better than me. I'm going out of my way here, because I would hate for someone of your delicate disposition to find themselves confused or upset.' He took a huge drag on his cigar, then blew the smoke towards Blacklock. 'The duty overnight custody sergeant will wake you at midnight and 0200 to make sure you're ready to play. Sergeant Pettifer will retrieve you from your cell at 0400 sharp. You could set your watch by him – if you still had one. Be careful of the stairs on the way up; they're treacherous. There have been more accidents than I care to recall over the years and I'd hate for you to have another tumble. Then,' he pointed at Blacklock, 'we'll have our friendly chat, except if I feel that you're not keeping your end up it gets ... unfriendly. If you've done your bit to my satisfaction we'll shake hands and you can go and get some rest.'

Duncan rose and walked to the interview room door. It had a small observation grille in it, which he briefly peered through. 'If you foolishly choose not to play ball, which is your bizarre right under the law, we'll have to do it all again the next day. You're a bright boy and I'm sure you'll soon work out what's best for you.'

He retook his seat. 'We keep going until you break. You can save us all a lot of time – and one of us some pain – by telling us the whole story at the outset. Is all that clear to you?'

Blacklock nodded.

'Good.' Duncan consulted his watch. 'Good Lord! It's ten to five already – the sun will be up soon – I'm almost sorry you can't see it from your lodgings. Doesn't the time fly when you're having fun?' He became suddenly serious. 'Let's get down to business. Why did you kill Jenny Greaves?'

'I did not kill her. Or anyone else.'

'I won't pretend that your lack of candour doesn't disappoint me.' Duncan shrugged. 'Pettifer?'

The sergeant entered.

'Take Doctor Blacklock back to his accommodation. I think that nasty bump on the head from his previous accident seems to have dulled his memory, poor chap. He needs some rest, although I think you'll need to perform hourly welfare checks from 0500 until further notice. If I were you, Blacklock, I wouldn't get too cosy.'

Eighty

Leman Street Police Station, Shadwell, London
Tuesday 2nd July

Although disturbed on schedule at midnight and two it made little difference to Blacklock, his putrid mattress unusable and his only alternative, the damp flagged floor, impossible to sleep on. At four he steeled himself for a casual assault that never came. Pettifer was a model of politeness, which confused him even more.

Duncan stood as Pettifer led him into the interview room. 'Nathaniel! I do hope you're well rested. Please, take a seat.' He smiled broadly. 'And here's some bread in case you're hungry.'

Blacklock frowned. 'I assume it is poisoned, or at least tainted in some way?'

Duncan appeared affronted. 'Not on my watch, Doctor. Look.' He tore off half and ate it greedily. 'See? Would I do that if there was anything in it?'

Blacklock's stomach cramped at the prospect and he reached for the bread.

'Goodness me!' cried Duncan, pulling the plate beyond Blacklock's reach. 'The sergeant has forgotten to secure your bonds. I despair of him sometimes.'

Pettifer stepped forward and shackled Blacklock to the table.

'Thank you, Sergeant, that's better. I was in fear of my life for a moment there. By the way, the good Doctor here fears that this bread may have been tampered with. Can you taste it to assure him that it's not tainted?'

'No,' said Blacklock, a little too quickly. 'That will not be necessary. I am sure it is fine. I will eat it.'

'We take no risks with our hospitality, Doctor.' Duncan shook his head and nodded to Pettifer, who picked up the bread and finished it. 'Delicious, sir.'

'He's a brave man, that sergeant of ours.' Duncan grinned. 'Before we proceed to business do you have any questions?'

Blacklock shook his head, defeated.

'Why don't you start at the beginning and tell me why you killed the women? Thrills?'

'I did not kill anyone.'

'Your university chums beg to differ. Said you were a grasping outsider, and – I quote – "clinging to the tails of our morning suits." Safe to assume you didn't win them over.'

'Have you caught Porter?'

'No. But we have you. Remember that the smart fox doesn't need to run faster than the hounds. He just needs to outpace another fox. You're the slow fox.'

'But ... I have been *helping you*.'

'An excellent ruse. Quite brilliant, although you're not the first and you certainly won't be the last to try that.'

Blacklock shook his head impatiently. 'You are not listening. It is right what they say about you. You do not want to solve a damned thing. You do not want to see justice. You just want someone to pay.'

Duncan was on his feet in an instant, leaning over the table towards Blacklock, a bull about to charge. '*What?*' Anger strangled his words. 'Who says that? *Who?*'

Blacklock looked at his hands to secure some thinking time. He could sacrifice Cargill which would distract Duncan, but the detective sergeant had so far been his only ally. 'I overheard a couple of uniformed PCs discussing you at one of the scenes. I do not clearly recall who or where. Sorry.'

Duncan lowered himself slowly back onto his chair like failing automaton. 'If you remember who you'd better tell me. They need some education.'

'Do they? What about Solomon Thurber? Did you not throw him to the mob? An innocent man sacrificed without evidence?' He looked evenly back at Duncan, who had veins bulging in his forehead, his face so red that Blacklock thought he could feel the heat from it.

'You don't have a *fucking clue* about how poverty affects Whitechapel – and the whole of the East End – it's just a tinderbox. It's always on the edge of revolt. Always on the edge of violence, of riot. Always waiting to blow, like the fuse is already lit. Sometimes to stop a war the innocent are sacrificed. You should count yourself lucky that I don't throw you to the wolves now, Blacklock. Don't think for a second that I've ruled it out. Maybe I should let Pettifer discover you trying to escape. That would save the cost of a trial.'

'You would not dare. There is too much attention on this case, and the unexplained death of a suspect in custody would raise all manner of unwanted scrutiny I imagine you would rather do without.'

'Don't try to blackmail me, you jumped-up little shit. You're a failed surgeon, failed teacher, failed pathologist, failed fiancé. You wouldn't be the first such loser to end his life suspended from their own bedsheet.'

'I do not have the luxury of bedsheets in my cell.'

'They could be arranged, Blacklock. And just so we're clear, my friend, I'd be more than happy to accept your suicide as an admission of guilt. Nothing for either of us to worry about after that.'

At this Blacklock determined to remain silent. Duncan had obviously made his mind up and any evidence to the contrary would clearly be irrelevant.

'Tell me about the killing of the boy. That was depraved, even by your standards.'

Blacklock bit his lip and stared at the edge of the table, counting the knots in the wooden beading.

'Alright, a simpler one. How did McCormac know that your nonce Scotch bedfellows were all suspects?'

There were twenty-seven knots in the beading.

'You aren't helping yourself. You could at least deny something.'

There were eleven panel pins holding the beading to the table top.

Without warning Duncan leapt forward and slapped Blacklock's cheek, hard enough to stun him. It burned briefly then transitioned into a dull ache. He could taste his own blood, metallic, where he had been gripping the inside of his cheek between his teeth.

'You're doing well, Blacklock, I'll grant you that. Your pal Gordon gave you up straight away – he didn't need any persuasion. He was simplicity itself to break; he spent most of the time weeping like a baby. He blubbered from the moment he was arrested. Truth be told I was glad to see the back of him in the end.' Duncan stood up; Blacklock flinched, but the inspector made no move to strike. Instead, he opened the door. 'Sergeant Pettifer, please come in. I fear that the good doctor may need to meet with another small accident. I think he is unbalanced by his guilt.'

''Appens all the time, sir.'

'I think ... a finger, Sergeant. Such a small bone, so easily broken–'

'No, please.'

'Feeling cooperative? What a pleasant change. Shoulder, Sergeant.'

The blow was swift and precise, the pain intense, radiating from his shoulder like an earthquake. He felt close to vomiting, but fought not to give Duncan and Pettifer the satisfaction. A few deep breaths caused the pain to relent a little.

'Sore shoulder?' asked Duncan. 'Perhaps you slept awkwardly. Take your mind off it by telling me all about the evidence you've been suppressing.'

'I have not–'

'Sergeant!'

Pettifer stepped forward.

Forgetting he was manacled Blacklock tried to slam his fist on the table. 'For God's sake, Duncan! For the last time *it is not me*.'

Duncan sat back and folded his arms. 'You can either confess or tell me who did it. I don't care which, and I'm much more patient than you might give me credit for.' He stood up. 'Sergeant Pettifer will take you back downstairs, and please watch your footing this time. I would hate for you to have another fall, Blacklock. You might break your neck before the hangman gets his chance, and deprive us of a jolly morning out. When you have something different to say just let the sergeant know. Until then, I'll be seeing you at the same time every day, so make sure you aren't a dirty little stop-out. We want you as fresh as a daisy for the morning, don't we?'

Eighty-One

Leman Street Police Station, Shadwell, London
Thursday 4th July

By the evening of day seven of his incarceration Blacklock's mattress had either dried sufficiently to allow him to lie on it, or he had become so accustomed to the stench of Pettifer's urine that he no longer noticed it. Regardless of the cause he managed to get some sleep, despite the combined efforts of the night custody sergeant and Pettifer to keep him awake. Even as he laid down his head he heard – or perhaps felt, or imagined – something scurrying into the mattress. Only a few months before such an outrage would have rendered him incandescent with rage. Now, he had fallen so far that he smiled and wished the unidentified rodent a good night. After each wake-up call he was now able to get back to sleep immediately – in spite of the hunger which was trying to transform his intestines into a Gordian Knot.

The time he had spent sleeping rough in the park with Stewart and the others had obviously toughened him more than he had realised.

Eighty-Two

Leman Street Police Station, Shadwell, London
Friday 5th July

Pettifer was content to start the day's proceedings by merely spitting on the sleeping doctor to wake him. Blacklock was pathetically grateful that that was the limit of his warder's morning tyranny. There were no pushes or punches or trips on the way to the interview room. He flinched whenever Pettifer reached for his keys but no assault, physical or verbal, ensued. He tried to determine the rules of today's game was but could not sufficiently order his thoughts.

Pettifer delivered Blacklock to the interview room with no drama of any kind. The room was empty. 'Inspector Duncan will be along directly – something has delayed him. I'm terribly sorry but I must once again manacle you to the desk. If you'd be so kind, sir ..?'

Blacklock held out his arms without a sound to allow Pettifer to route his shackles through the iron rings welded to the table.

'Not too tight, Doctor?'

The cuffs had been so gently refastened that Blacklock imagined that he could simply pull his hands from them. 'Not at all. Thank you, Sergeant.'

'If you'll forgive me, Doctor, I must take my leave.' Pettifer left.

Blacklock was at a loss to explain Pettifer's uncharacteristic solicitousness. He had not reached a conclusion when the door opened gently behind him.

'Good morning, Doctor Blacklock,' said Duncan. 'I must apologise for my tardiness but something cropped up – unrelated to your case.' He sat down and carefully straightened the sheaf of papers he had brought with him. 'So, are we treating you well? Are you fed, watered and rested?'

Blacklock did not know how to answer; he was acutely aware that this must be some new kind of trap and he did not want to trigger it. 'I am a little hungry, I must admit, but otherwise quite well, thank you.'

'Oh dear,' replied Duncan. 'I'll have to give the overnight waiting staff a bollocking if they insist on forgetting our guest in the dungeon. Sergeant!'

Pettifer answered from outside.

'Please fetch Doctor Blacklock an apple. It seems that his catering arrangements have failed again.' Duncan turned back to Blacklock. 'Where were we? Ah yes, of course – have you remembered anything which might be useful in your defence? You've next to nothing on your side of the scales of justice, whilst those nice chaps Gordon and Robertson can give full accounts of their conduct at the times these crimes were committed. You, on the other hand, have no such advantage. Do you keep a journal which might jog your memory?'

'Everything I own has been stolen.'

'Of course. A ... convenient misfortune which–.' Duncan was interrupted by a deferential tap on the door. 'Come!'

Pettifer entered with a cloth-covered plate. 'An apple, sir.' He placed it in the centre of the table and left.

'If I might further delay your breakfast – just a moment or two longer – your continuing forgetfulness is most troublesome,' continued Duncan. 'Disappointing.'

'I did not know that I *would* later be forced to remember anything,' replied Blacklock. 'Who does? Do *you* know what you were doing on the evenings in question, Inspector?'

'A point well made, Blacklock. I do, as a matter of fact. I could simply consult my diary.' He smiled as he lifted the cloth from the plate with the flourish of an amateur magician.

A couple of wasps walked drunkenly on the decaying remains of a half-eaten apple.

'Whoops!' Duncan sniggered. 'It looks like someone got

to your breakfast before you.' He pushed the plate within range of Blacklock's chains. 'Tuck in. Don't stand on ceremony, Doctor. You must be famished.'

Duncan's expression was a combination of glee and evil. Blacklock blew the wasps away and they flew off lazily to a safe distance, almost as if they knew the chained man was no threat to them. He closed his eyes. The desire for the mean sustenance was offset with the hatred of giving Duncan and Pettifer their petty satisfaction. His guts knotted as he struggled to control himself, but hunger suddenly overwhelmed him. He picked up the rotten fruit which began disintegrating even as he moved it towards his mouth. The apple was more bitter than any he had any he had ever tasted. He tried to swallow but knew that even if he succeeded he would be unable to keep the rotten flesh down. He spat the mouthful back onto the plate as he blinked away a tear.

'We could only get a Bramley, I'm afraid,' said Duncan. 'It might be a tad on the sour side. Go on, eat up. I can wait.' He sat back, armed folded.

Blacklock wiped the remains from his mouth with a shaking hand. 'I am less hungry than I thought.'

'After all our efforts? You ungrateful swine. I'm minded not to bother again.' Duncan picked up his papers. 'Anything to add to your comments to date? Confession's apparently good for the soul, you know. I could be your priest and rabbi and vicar all rolled into one lovely package. Whaddya say? You must be as tired of this pantomime as I am.'

'I have nothing to add. I am innocent.'

'Then who is guilty? You must know. Robertson? Gordon? Porter? The mysterious Priestley? Some other freak who likes to slice people up?'

'I do not know. It must be one of those three. Bear in mind – this I know you are apt to forget – that two of them are innocent.'

Duncan rolled his eyes. 'Gordon and Robertson have

decent alibi. Gordon's family also appointed a QC, which got Commissioner Wren's attention. On top of that his trust fund's in payment so he's only working a couple of days a week to amuse himself. When he was not at the hospital - we've checked his timesheets - he was at his Club. Robertson's timesheets – ditto. A couple of the murders occurred when he was on duty. Porter and Priestley are still missing, but we'll find 'em. We always do. You don't have an alibi. To be straight with you, Blacklock, even my renowned patience is wearing thin. I might press charges anyway, because there's no doubt of a connection between you and the murders, even if it's not you. All that's stopping me is some inexplicable fraternal affection I have for you, which although troubling for a man in my position is fading faster than a tart's smile.'

'So Gordon's alibi is based on his rich friends and servants of the club vouching for him? Surely you cannot let that stand?'

''Twas ever thus, Blacklock. Money and power talk. Scum such as you and me – well, we make our way as best we can.'

'But the man has *syphilis!* If it infects his brain he might do anything...'

'And how on earth would you know that? Your fanciful exclamations are getting increasingly tedious.'

'I recognised the symptoms and Robertson confirmed it.'

'If that were so he'd hardly be practising medicine would he?'

Blacklock puffed out his cheeks. 'He will until the disease becomes too debilitating to continue. It is an unwritten part of the profession's unofficial code of conduct.'

'You people are a bloody disgrace! You hold yourselves up as little Gods among us but you're ... pathetic, the lot of you.' He gathered up everything he had brought with him. 'Enough of this blathering; I'm a busy man. Maybe you'll change your tune tomorrow. Who knows? I'm sure you'll find the next twenty-four hours as fun-filled as the previous hundred or so. Let's get you back to your suite, shall we?

I need to be somewhere else. Sergeant Pettifer will do the honours in a couple of minutes.'

Pettifer escorted Blacklock back to his cell, as courteous as before. 'It's a little lonely down here, I dare say.'

'Not really. I have the promenades with you and the philosophical conversations with the Inspector to sustain me.' As they reached the cells, Blacklock was surprised to see Duncan waiting there. In the half-light, just for a moment, he also thought he saw a giant crouched on his bed.

'I thought perhaps a little companionship wouldn't go amiss,' said Duncan. 'This gentleman is Samuel Wainwright. We're out of space above so he'll be bunking with you. I'm sure you'll get along famously.'

Pettifer motioned Blacklock to stay where he was and moved to the side of the cell. 'Now, Sam, be a good boy. This here is Doctor Blacklock, and you'll be sharing a cell with him for a little while. I want to open the door to let him in. You know what to do, don't you?'

With a grunt Wainwright put his hands through the bars, reminding Blacklock of a dancing bear he had once seen in Covent Garden.

'Good lad,' said Pettifer, cuffing Wainwright to the bars. As he moved to open the door he turned to Blacklock and said, 'He's had a difficult life and can be a tiny bit violent from time to time.' He waited while Blacklock entered the cell, then slammed the door closed with unnecessary vigour and locked it.

'Thank you for securing him, Sergeant,' said Blacklock.

'It was only temporary while I had the door open. Sam's prone to rages and it's always better to have bars between you and him, believe me.' He started to remove Wainwright's cuffs.

'But–'

'Don't thank me, Doc. The Inspector doesn't want you to be lonely down here. Best thing for you to do is make friends. It's fair to say that Sam's conversation isn't of the most sparkling variety, what with being dumb and all. I won't visit you overnight – laddo here can get a bit feisty if he's disturbed. There are some bedsheets in the corner, too. The Inspector said you might need them.' He winked. 'See you at four.'

Pettifer stalked away, swinging his enormous key chain and whistling as he did so. Duncan leaned against the opposite wall, beaming.

'What did he do?' Blacklock whispered.

'I thought you'd never ask,' replied Duncan. 'Killed a cellmate. Damn near tore his head off. Cheerio.' With a grin he followed Pettifer.

Wainwright slowly drew his hands back into the cell, as though it had taken him that long to register the removal of the handcuffs. He turned and stared at Blacklock, who backed into the opposite corner as though he was striving for invisibility. Wainwright made no sound beyond a strange, low humming which created an undertone to his mouth breathing.

'I am Nathaniel,' hazarded Blacklock. 'I hope you are well. I mean you no harm and I am no threat to you, sir.'

Wainwright frowned, then chuckled.

'I am pleased to make your acquaintance, sir.'

The giant chuckled again but made no other gesture.

'I understand that you are unable to speak?'

Wainwright nodded.

Blacklock was at a loss. He was keen to maintain some form of dialogue because Wainwright seemed calm and if Duncan had told the truth it was wise to keep him so. Every thought that crossed his mind for his next line was almost absurdly polite. While Blacklock was engaged in desperate thought Wainwright simply looked at him with an expression more akin to an incurious Labrador Retriever than a sentient human. Before Blacklock could say anything Wainwright pointed first at the slop bucket then signalled Blacklock to turn away.

Deep embarrassment gripped Blacklock, who had managed to limit himself to making water so far, no doubt in part to the starvation rations Duncan had decreed. Wainwright was already loosening his belt as Blacklock turned to face the cell corner, mortified. As soon as Wainwright started it was immediately clear that his diet was either insufficient or primarily liquid, as the sound of his evacuation splashed into the bucket; the accompanying stench almost caused Blacklock to vomit, a horror only avoided by pinching his nose. Even so, the sound brought goosebumps to his arms and shivers to his spine. It seemed as though the purging might never end but eventually everything ceased. Blacklock allowed a few moments for his cellmate to dress himself before he turned back.

The bucket had overflowed slightly, the pooled excess being slowly absorbed by the corner of the mattress. The *only* mattress, Blacklock realised. He had given no thought to their shared sleeping arrangements but the prospect of using the mattress now turned his stomach again. He shook his head is despair. It was only now that he spotted his handkerchief floating in the bucket, clearly used by Wainwright to clean himself.

'For God's sake, Wainwright, are you an animal? What did you think you were do–.'

In that instant, Wainwright was upon him, Blacklock hopelessly outmatched. The giant hoisted him up against the bars with a hand around each of the doctor's biceps. Blacklock fought back, punching and kicking, but to no avail as Wainwright's expressionless eyes stared implacably back at him. Blacklock's blows achieved nothing, the giant apparently impervious to his best efforts. 'I'm sorry,' he croaked, 'sir.'

In that instant Wainwright released his grip and let Blacklock fall to the floor. He chuckled again.

Is it "sir" that calms him?

Wainwright, meanwhile, stretched on the putrid mattress and stared at the ceiling as if the preceding incidents had never occurred and indeed that Blacklock was invisible. Discretion guided Blacklock back to the opposite corner of the cell.

The day passed with glacial slowness. Around midday the duty sergeant threw a couple of dry crusts into the cell. Blacklock secured his share by simply asking politely and adding "sir" to his request. This new-found understanding between the cellmates enabled Blacklock to relax, albeit partially. Wainwright's frequent use of the overflowing pail moved Blacklock to briefly consider confession and escape via the gallows.

Eighty-Three

Leman Street Police Station, Shadwell, London
Sunday 7th July

Two further interminable days had passed with only a single visit each day from the duty sergeant, who again flung a couple of stale crusts through the bars. Day and night were indistinguishable below street level. The cheapest tallow candle burned twenty-four hours a day, its foul stench simply another dimension added to the smells of the damp, the rotting mattress, Blacklock's own filthiness combined with Wainwright's and the slop bucket, which Sam had contrived to upset during a particularly vivid dream. The flood of urine and faeces which lapped around Blacklock's feet barely registered with him.

He took a deep breath and before he understood what he was doing, started speaking. 'God,' he said, 'if you are there and could extend your infinite compassion to one of your creatures, albeit a faithless and unworthy one, I will ...' His voice trailed off as he found himself unable to strike a bargain of sufficient sacrifice from his side of the scale. 'Dear God,' he continued, 'I have nothing to offer. My life has been, I realise, of little merit. I may have helped others, even saved lives, but only as a side-effect of my own quest for advancement and status. If you can hear me, Lord–'

'Enjoying a little pointless superstition, Blacklock? I thought prayer was the last resort of the uninformed?' asked Duncan.

'There might be something there, Inspector. It cannot do any harm.'

'You're closer to hell than heaven, and when you swing you can make it all the way. Congratulations on surviving these nights with young Samuel, by the way. Did you get Doctor Jekyll, Mr Hyde, or a little of both?' Duncan nodded at Pettifer who was lurking nearby. In a couple of minutes the process of Blacklock's introduction to the cell was reversed, leaving Wainwright's wrists once again manacled through the bars.

'Be sure to release him, Sergeant,' said Blacklock. 'He deserves respect.'

Pettifer glowered and looked at Duncan, who shrugged. With another of his trademark petulant sighs Pettifer released Wainwright.

'Good,' said Duncan. 'If the custody arrangements now meet with the good Doctor's approval perhaps we can proceed upstairs?'

'Well,' said Duncan. 'I must say that I find your attachment to Sam most affecting, and so quick-blooming too. I could almost shed a tear, both for that vision of love and regret because I fear someone else may have replaced me in your affections.'

Blacklock said nothing.

Duncan took a deep breath and smiled. 'Anything new to say? Beyond, of course, your surprising conversion, which was another privilege to witness.'

Blacklock sighed, betraying his exhaustion in a single breath. 'I really do not understand what you expect from me. I am innocent. I did not kill any of these poor people. You already have what I believe is a complete, closed list of suspects. Six men, one of whom is dead, one missing. Your choices are therefore Porter, Robertson, Gordon or me. You tell me that Robertson and Gordon have watertight alibis. Good for them. Which leaves just two. Porter and me. I know I am not the killer, but cannot prove it. The burden of proof should not lie with the accused, but with the accuser. The logical conclusion is that Porter is the murderer. I will continue to proclaim my innocence until hell freezes over because *I am innocent.*' He sat back and bowed his head. 'I have nothing more to say. Nor will I tomorrow. Or the day after. Set your dog Pettifer on me and I will still have nothing to add. Set any other troll that serves in this station on me and I will have nothing to add. Now, if I may I would like to return to my cell.'

A long silence stretched between accuser and accused. Blacklock stared at his shoes. Duncan lit a cigar.

After a couple of minutes Duncan snorted and began a slow handclap. 'Bravo! Ten days underground and you think you're Sydney bloody Carton and Joan of Arc rolled into one. A good speech, Blacklock. Not good enough, naturally, but sufficient to buy you another few days downstairs. You've overlooked your key advantage, or disadvantage, depending on which way you look at it.'

Blacklock looked up. 'I have?'

'Oh yes. Absolutely.'

'What is it?'

'You're my bird in the hand.'

Eighty-Four

Leman Street Police Station, Shadwell, London
Thursday 11th July

'Look sharp, Blacklock. I have something for you to do which doesn't involve sitting around cooling your lazy arse in pools of piss.'
'What is it?'
'You'll see.'

Duncan offered Blacklock a coffee which on this occasion he could drink easily because his chains weren't fastened to the table. 'What is in this concoction, Inspector? Opium? Anthrax? Perhaps digitalis to conveniently trigger a cardiac arrest and thus solve the case without unnecessary expenditure and, God forbid, paperwork?'

Duncan swapped the cups and took a sip. 'Really, Doctor? I must confess that I'm disappointed that you think so little of me.'

'Exchange them again.'

Duncan laughed. 'You seem to be developing some form of paranoia, Blacklock.' He swapped the cups and drank again. 'Happy?'

Blacklock sipped the coffee. It was glorious. 'Thank you.' He glanced up at the clock. 'It is eleven p.m. Is this not a little early for another interrogation, or merely another stratagem to further undermine my resolve? Coffee will not make me falsely confess to these horrors, simply because I am not responsible for them.'

'Blah, blah, yawn, yawn. Then at least tell me how you knew that the Blacklock Five, as we now call them – catchy, I think, something for everyone to remember you by – were all victims of one of your Scottish butcher friends?'

'There is not anything specific, Inspector. More of a feeling for the style of work.'

'I see.' Duncan drew on his cigar then examined the glowing tip. 'Are you sure about that?'

Before Blacklock could reply he was interrupted by some shouting from the street above. 'What is that?'

'*Shit*,' spat Duncan. 'Wait here. Don't do anything stupid because whether you know it or not you're on a knife-edge, Doctor. The only person between you and the gallows is me.' He jabbed a dirty finger into Blacklock's face. 'Don't forget that. You're in deep shit and I'm the only bloke you know who might – *might* – lend you a shovel.'

Duncan ran from the room and moments later the shouting outside turned to uproar. Beyond the interview room door Blacklock could hear hobnail boots running along the corridor. Duncan's voice boomed above that of the crowd, but too indistinctly for Blacklock to make any sense of what was being said. Amid the jeering the Inspector continued to expound with considerable passion. Blacklock surmised that the riot was somehow related to his unscheduled recall from the cell but could draw no further conclusions. He finished his coffee with no apparent ill-effect, then Duncan's, half-listening to the quietening crowd outside. He mused on his prospects for escape, given that he was handcuffed but not manacled to anything else, but quickly dismissed any such notion; Pettifer or one of his ilk would beat him, probably to a convenient death, before he could clear the confines of Leman Street.

He was still mulling over these unpleasant notions when he realised that the street was silent. At that instant Duncan re-entered. 'Come on, Blacklock. You've got work to do. Pronto.' He grasped the chain connecting Blacklock's wrist shackles and dragged him to the temporary pathology room.

The harsh lights revealed a covered body on the table.

'I need you to find the cause of death and determine whether this is the work of one of your knife-wielding surgeon friends. No funny business – I'll be watching you like a bleedin' hawk, matey.' He nodded at Pettifer who dropped the now-rusted instruments clumsily onto the table.

Blacklock took a deep breath and cautiously lifted the sheet, which was covered in florets of dried blood absorbed from below.

The scene was a return to the earlier carnage. Pettifer ran from the room and vomited noisily outside. The young woman's abdomen was open, the incision running from almost hip to hip. Blacklock reached for the wound, but halted. 'For God's sake man, how can I work in chains? This is delicate work and this woman deserves no additional defilement.'

Duncan thought for a moment before he sighed heavily and removed the handcuffs with unnecessary vigour. 'Be careful,' said Blacklock, massaging each wrist in turn. He began his examination slowly, not touching the body. He pulled the sheet further back. There was no wound, post-mortem or otherwise, to her throat.

'Can you tell whether it's our man?'

Blacklock's mind drifted, against his will, to the prospect of freedom. A simple word would cast suspicion on one of the other Musketeers whilst his own alibi would be unimpeachable. Just one word.

Blacklock picked up the rudimentary forceps which had been provided and attempted to draw the wound closed. The skin had lost much of its elasticity and slipped from the forceps as he increased the tension. Undeterred he pinched each side of the wound with his bare hands and pulled them together.

No Edinburgh Incision.

'The incision doesn't bear the hallmarks of the oth–'

He was interrupted by the blushing Pettifer re-entering the room.

'Apologise to Doctor Blacklock, Pettifer,' said Duncan. 'And then get lost. There's no place for such weakness here.'

'But–'

'Did you hear me, Sergeant? Apologise now, get out, mop the corridor. If you do not immediately do each of those things, in that order, I shall see to it that you lose those stripes. Understood?'

'Sorry, Blacklock.'

'Sorry Doctor Blacklock,' said Duncan.

'Sorry *Doctor* Blacklock,' repeated Pettifer insolently.

Before Blacklock could respond Pettifer left.

'You were talking about hallmarks, Blacklock. By that, I take it you mean the Edinburgh Incision?'

Blacklock dropped the forceps. The echo in the bare room filled his ears. 'You know about that?'

'Of course I do. It's my *job* to know, Blacklock. You underestimate me again.'

Blacklock sighed. 'McCormac.'

'No, not your Paddy mate. The good doctor Gordon tearfully shared the gory details with me. I'd already had an amateur squint at this poor woman before you and couldn't see what he was talking about, and would have got Gordon himself to double-check my opinion if it hadn't been for the local savages outside. I'd've got him anyway if you'd said otherwise.' He nodded. 'Full marks, though. I thought you might lie to get yourself out of this hole and drop one of the others in it, but your misplaced sense of justice or honour or ... whatever bollocks it is ... is both impressive and informative. The more important question, Blacklock, is not how long I have known. It is why you did not tell me.'

Blacklock shrugged. 'That is simple. Solomon Thurber. The first Musketeer you laid hands on – which might be me – could be the next poor soul torn to shreds by your not-so-tame mob.'

Duncan raised an eyebrow before he continued. 'I'll let that pass. He was probably guilty of something, anyway.' He pointed at the victim. 'So, what *has* happened *here*? Do we have another mad surgeon on the loose? That's all I fucking need. And give me your version of the Edinburgh Incision story. Remember that I've heard it twice already.'

'The six of us – *The Musketeers* – developed it. No, that is too grandiose – as a group we came across a small modification to the opening incision which seemed to reduce the incidence of follow-on infections. To the best of my knowledge only the six of us ever used it.'

'But if it–'

'I know. If it works, why not share it? Simple. Surgeons are amongst the most competitive men you will ever meet. One becomes expert at keeping advantages to oneself.'

'Really? Why?'

'Possibly. Probably. It is simple economics. If my fatality or complication rate is less than the next surgeon's, you are more likely to employ me. The more I am employed the more I am promoted, the more I earn. Surgeons in a nutshell. Not pretty, I know, but that is the unfortunate reality. Much like the police beating confessions out of innocent men.'

'Watch that mouth, Blacklock. It could yet be your death warrant.' He cleared his throat before continuing is more measured tones. 'What's this, if it's not that?'

'I believe this was a backstreet Caesarean delivery. This cut was made with a fine, sharp blade – possibly or even probably surgical. You wouldn't get margins like these with a household knife, or even a razor. The incision is direct and positive, with no signs of hesitation or deviation – see how the navel is circumscribed? Not the work of someone full of bloodlust.'

'This is no use to me, Blacklock.'

'What?'

'Another psychopath, slicing the innards out of young women, even harder to catch than Porter? I don't believe in coincidences – this has to be our man. Shame there's no sign of your favourite cut, but maybe you were all wrong about that; last thing I heard was that only the Pope's infallible. All I can know for sure is that it isn't you. You're a conceited ass, obviously, but I don't dislike you. I would have been moderately disappointed to see you making the big drop.'

Blacklock smiled, trying to appear appreciative of Duncan's back-handed compliment. 'Thank you. I think. God knows it is hard enough to keep a bleeding mother alive in hospital, let alone in some windowless tenement by candlelight. You must find out who is responsible, but it is not a heinous crime. And not a Musketeer.'

'Bad luck. I'd hoped you might get out of here.'

'Me too,' sighed Blacklock. 'There is probably a baby which needs saving somewhere. Perhaps a search party–'

'Do you know how many newborns are fished from the Thames each day? On average?'

'No. One or two a week, perhaps?'

'Eight. A day.'

'*Eight?*'

'Yep. Most of them are stillborn or whatever, but some are healthy but unwanted or unaffordable. If this poor girl's kid has survived this *operation* then its fate has already been long decided, one way or another. It's either been adopted by a relative or friend or it's jetsam.' He checked his watch. 'We've both had a late night, Blacklock. It's almost three. I think I'll let you get an extra dose of beauty sleep and we'll skip our morning chat – unless you've something new and useful to say?'

'I am innocent.'

'Neither new nor useful; I feared as much. And, of course, no alibi.'

'There must be a hundred thousand people in this city without alibis.'

'Perhaps. But there ain't a hundred thousand people who also perform the Edinburgh Incision. Pettifer! Please escort Doctor Blacklock back to his suite. I'm sure young Sam will be pining for him by now. See you tomorrow, Nathaniel.'

Eighty-Five

Leman Street Police Station, Shadwell, London
Friday 12th July

'How has your garrulous cellmate been? Has he behaved?' Duncan smiled.

'Of course. Impeccably. I find that if you treat a man with a modicum of respect, even the basest individual can behave. Perhaps you should try a similar approach sometime,' replied Blacklock.

'I'm so glad you've enjoyed your time together. Sadly, that must end.'

'Why?'

'We're letting Sam out this morning.'

'But he killed a cellmate! You cannot let a murderer run free!'

'Murder? Sam? Whatever gave you that idea? Has a little time underground driven you mad?'

'You told me–'

'I said no such thing, Blacklock. I think that your brief period of incarceration has scrambled those mighty brains of yours.' He grinned again, wider than before. 'Sam's a good sort, until he gets a drink or two inside him.'

'Ah, a violent drinker?'

'Good God, Blacklock, you do like jumping to conclusions, don't you? When young Samuel has had a bevy he likes to steal ladies' foundation garments from washing lines and hoard them for his dubious pleasures. You were pretty safe all along.'

'But he did attack me. He held me up against the bars. I have bruises–'

'Gosh, Sam's good, isn't he? He wouldn't hurt a fly, although a word in his ear from a voice of authority can induce erratic behaviour.' He winked. 'You look punch-drunk, Blacklock.'

'How ironic. It has been several days since your gorilla *actually* punched me.'

'Touché. I can arrange for that oversight to be rectified.'

'I do not doubt it. Your physical interrogation techniques must be very effective when someone has something to confess – which we both know I do not.'

'What about this man Porter? Could he have done this?'

'Of course. As could Gordon, Robertson, Priestly or I. It is someone who was at Edinburgh when we were all there, who understands our infection control theory. To the best of my knowledge there are just five of us left. Including Porter.'

'We found Porter.'

'At last! Is he being interrogated too?'

'He's in Paris.'

Blacklock's eagerness betrayed his excitement. 'But being deported?'

'In a manner of speaking. Want to dob him in now?'

'No. I will let you do your job and see if he confesses.'

'He won't.'

'But you and Pettifer can be so ... persuasive.'

'Won't work. Guaranteed. I think he'll be impervious to even the Sergeant's dubious charms.'

'Why? How can you be so sure?'

'He's dead. We're good. But not that good.'

'*What?*'

'Porter is dead. Washed up on the bank of the Seine just outside Paris with his pockets full of stones. Looks like self-murder. He had his passport on him which had survived the water better than he did and the Frogs sent a wire.'

'But he would not–'

'He ran to France while you were running to the East End. Looks pretty suspicious if you ask me.'

'What is the evidence for suicide?'

'A letter was found about his person.'

'A confession?'

'No idea, but let's assume so. The river water had erased

it. I like to think I'm a fair judge of a man – you have to be in my job – and I don't have you in the frame for this. With Porter dead under such circumstances I intend to let you go.' He paused. 'But I'll still be watching you.'

Blacklock was confused. 'Is this a trick? And how does it help you?'

Duncan shook his head.

'Ah!' said Blacklock. 'I understand your scheme. I start to leave and you have Pettifer beat me to death for trying to escape?'

'You have my word, Blackmore.'

'Black–'

Duncan raised an eyebrow. 'You're free to bugger off, Prof. Go about your business – if you still have one. Porter's flight and self-murder is good enough for me. I'm tired and want all this done with.'

'How do I get out?'

'What sort of idiotic question is that? I thought you medical types were supposed to be intelligent. You get up and walk out.'

Blacklock held up his hands, chains rattling.

'Pettifer!'

The sergeant opened the door, pulling out his truncheon as he did so.

'There will be no need for that, Sergeant,' said Duncan. 'Professor Blackmore is free to go.'

'He is?'

'Just do the honours, Pettifer. We no longer need our friendly chats with the Prof.'

Eighty-Six

Leman Street, Shadwell, London
Friday 12th July

Blacklock stumbled blindly into the dawn light of Leman Street, still rubbing his wrists where the manacles had been clasped too tight by the overzealous Pettifer. Though in theory no longer a fugitive he still felt watched, but as he anxiously scanned the crowds no one was looking back at him. This only increased his unease, as though everyone was his pursuer – when he looked at anyone in particular, the others were watching him. He berated himself for this paranoia, but even to his own ears his voice was pathetic.

After half an hour of aimless wandering his nervousness eased and his thoughts turned to accommodation and sustenance. It was barely eight in the morning. The streets were thronged but most of those using them knew where their next meal and next bed were coming from. He had neither clearly in mind. He started out towards the garden in Belgrave Square but realised that he had probably outstayed his welcome. His money had disappeared from his personal effects while in custody in Leman Street. Mrs Evans would not consider him when he was without funds; neither could he redeem the loan secured against his surgical instruments.

Eighty-Seven

*Starling's lodgings, 19 Colvestone
Crescent, Hackney, London
Friday 12th July*

Blacklock made his way slowly to Starling's lodgings in Hackney, only to discover that his friend was of course at work. He did not wish to loiter outside, and no one would let him enter, so with an air of hopelessness he set out for McCormac's.

McCormac paled when he opened his door to the shabby apparition that Blacklock had become. '*Doc?* I thought you were–'

'Languishing in the Leman Street dungeons? No longer. I am a free man and therefore no longer a fugitive who could bring the massed hounds of the legal system baying to your front door.'

'Listen, I–'

'If that is the beginning of an apology there is no need. You did what needed to be done.'

'But–'

'No buts. Really, if anyone should apologise, it is I. You were right and I should have told Duncan everything.'

'And now you have?'

Blacklock hesitated, not wanting to lie but unable to frame a truthful sentence. 'I ... did not have to.'

'Why?'

'Porter is dead. It appears that he committed suicide in Paris, Duncan assumes in a fit of guilt. Case closed without recourse to the courts – kangaroo or otherwise – or the hangman.'

Suddenly flustered, McCormac realised that the consultation had taken place on his doorstep. 'Please forgive me. Come in, Nathaniel.'

Blacklock was pleased that McCormac had used such a familiar name.

'I hope the food parcels I sent at least helped a little.'

Blacklock frowned. 'I do not follow.'

'I sent food in, almost every day. Just a sandwich or a pie, sometimes a bit of fruit?'

'The bastards,' spat Blacklock. 'I did not see any of that. Not a morsel.'

McCormac sighed. 'Good old Duncan, ever trustworthy. So, what are you going to do next?'

'I do not know, Francis. I have the clothes I stand in and nothing in my wallet. I will go to an employment agency, I suppose, as soon as I secure a permanent address.'

'You must stay here.'

'If it is not too much of an imposition?'

'I wouldn't have it any other way – it's the least I can do. Tomorrow we'll see if we can't get you smartened up. An agency, you say?'

Blacklock shrugged. 'I have no occupation I can pursue. Even if I had a licence my instruments are still in hock.' He looked around the room at the disorderly collection of photographic plates, prints and chemicals. 'What have you been doing?'

'Getting by. The work with the police has all but dried up – I'm not Duncan's favourite photographer – but my artistic work sells well to my existing clientele.'

Blacklock smiled and raised an eyebrow. 'Of course it does. I am sure it must be both popular and educational for men with little knowledge of the female anatomy.'

McCormac sniffed. 'Some think it art.'

'And you do think that?'

'I find it primarily profitable, with aesthetics a distant second.'

Eighty-Eight

McCormac's lodgings, 25 Barnabas
Street, Kensal Green, London
Saturday 13th July

Blacklock had not had access to clean water or soap for many weeks. At McCormac's pointed insistence Saturday began with a visit to a public bath house. Blacklock found the water so comforting that he had two baths, delighting in the sensation of the horrors of Leman Street washing away. McCormac also took him to a shop where he was able to purchase a second-hand suit, shirt and new undergarments which made him feel part of decent humanity again, although he did not replace his hat, aware that his financial resources were both finite and wholly inadequate.

Over lunch at McCormac's local alehouse conversation turned to Blacklock's quest.

'Has it crossed your mind that Porter *was* the murderer? Occam's Razor and all that?' McCormac's exasperation was evident. 'You have nothing to gain by resuming your amateur investigations.'

'His death is not ... conclusive, is it? It is Duncan's *assumption* that Porthos was responsible, an assumption which suits *his* agenda.'

'I don't really care about this but no doubt you will enlighten me.'

'It is all too easy, too pat, too ... convenient – and I remain convinced that Porthos was not that kind of a man.'

'And Gordon or Robertson is? Or the mysterious Priestley?'

Blacklock slumped. 'Not exactly. Not at all. But one of them *must* be the guilty party.'

McCormac yawned expansively. 'And no doubt you have a hare-brained scheme to catch the culprit.'

'I have a plan.'

'And?'

'I follow one of Gordon or Robertson until something happens which proves – or disproves – their innocence. If you were to follow the other one–'

'No! No no no. Helping you has cost me the greater part of my income and forced me to expand my other pursuits. I will gladly provide board and lodgings but that's the absolute limit of my involvement this time.'

'Of course.'

'How will you choose? Is it to be Gordon or Robertson?'

'Gordon.' He paused. 'No – Robertson.'

'Sure?'

'No.'

'I'll decide for you, Doc. Heads it's Gordon, tails Robertson.' He tossed the coin almost to the ceiling before catching it expertly. 'Heads. Gordon.'

Eighty-Nine

St John's Hospital, Hampstead, London
Saturday 13th July

Blacklock's first evening of surveillance at St John's began badly. He arrived in time to see first Gordon then Robertson arriving for a night shift. He had slept as much as possible during the day to preserve his energy so was not keen to return to McCormac's and try to sleep again. He set out to wander the East End more from idle curiosity than for any other reason. He ambled through the labyrinthine back streets, alleys and courts until he happened across the brothel he had so regrettably blundered into previously, prompting a question to return to his mind. He took a deep breath and knocked on the door. Within a minute he found himself in the lounge area, trying to look at anything except the girls and women arrayed before him in their undergarments.

'See anyone you fancy?' asked the old woman, presumably the madam. 'Have you overcome your shyness?'

'I–I am sorry,' he said, 'but on this occasion I am not here for pleasure. I–'

'Don't worry love,' said the woman. 'I can arrange a little pain if that's more your cup of tea.'

Flustered and reddening he continued to stumble over his words. 'I am a doctor – a surgeon – and I wondered how you obtain medical care for your ... ladies.'

'If you're touting your services we don't need them. There's plenty in your line will swap one favour for another, if you get my meaning.' She leered expressively, which only heightened Blacklock's embarrassment.

Undeterred, he continued. 'What about more serious complaints, which might for example require a surgical intervention?'

'You're still out of luck and you can pay like anyone else. We don't negotiate.'

'I am not here for...' He searched desperately for the right word. 'Services. If you can tell me anything you know about any surgeons who may be operating in this community I will be on my way.'

The woman sighed. 'Alright. If it will end this time-wasting and get you out my hair there's a Doctor Adava. He's been around for a while now, helping people out with their problems.'

'Adava? Are you sure?'

'Yes. A–D–A–V–A. He should be easy to find. First name Clement, I think. Now, sling your 'ook.'

Blacklock walked back to McCormac's with his mind racing. *Could this Adava be the man responsible for these atrocities? But why would he use the Edinburgh Incision?*

When he arrived, McCormac was minutely examining a number of postage stamp-sized photographs of women in various states of undress.

Blacklock eagerly shared his news.

'So,' said McCormac, 'what does this mysterious surgeon look like?'

'I ... neglected to ask.'

'For Pete's sake, Doc. He's working under a patently fake name and you didn't even get a description?'

'How do you know it is an alias?'

'Tell me you're joking. *Please?*'

Blacklock shrugged.

McCormac rolled his eyes. 'Clement Adava? C. Adava? *Cadaver?*'

Blacklock put his hand to his forehead and sighed deeply. 'How could I be so–'

'Because you *are* that stupid, Doc.' McCormac shook his head. 'Who else? Mr D. Edbody? Dr C. Orpse? Dr–'

'Shut up McCormac! When you are perfect, please feel free to criticise. At least I am not some morally bankrupt pornographer!'

McCormac raised an eyebrow. 'Yet you're happy enough to live off my immoral earnings?'

'I am sorry, Francis. These past weeks have taken their toll on both my patience and my conduct. My remark was born of frustration and was both unkind and untrue. I apologise unreservedly.' He paused but McCormac did not respond. '"Doctor Cadaver" was what we called the bodies we were assigned during training. I cannot believe I missed that. But it does provide further evidence to suggest that we seek a Musketeer.'

'So it's back to Duncan with this?'

'And tell him what? Some more "evidence" has come to light in the form of a students' prank name for corpse? I would bet you a pound to a penny that it is not a unique nomenclature either.'

Ninety

The Olde Bell and Unicorn Inn, Shacklewell
Lane, Stoke Newington, London
Saturday 13th July

Blacklock stared at his empty glass, oblivious to the payday revellers in The Unicorn. 'I have to disprove one of their alibis, Jon. One of them is still out there, operating for whatever reason they have justified to themselves.'

'Priestley?'

'Porter assumed he had drunk himself to death by now. I'm inclined to agree.'

'Alright.' Starling examined his wallet as if he was a magician expecting something to appear. 'There'll be no more ale tonight, Nate. Shall we take a little air? It's stopped raining.'

Blacklock shrugged and followed Starling, who was already wending his way to the door.

It was barely quieter outside, the narrow lanes filled with the penniless drunks who, like them, had exhausted their meagre funds. They walked together in silence for a while before Starling spoke. 'Alright. First Principles. Why were their alibis sufficient to see them released?'

'Cargill was not keen to go into any specifics, Duncan even less so, but from what I could gather they can both prove that they were somewhere else on at least two of the nights when deaths occurred.'

'Hmmm,' replied Starling, his vacant tone one of someone deep in thought. Blacklock had learned better than to interrupt.

'Presumably,' ventured Starling after several minutes, 'there must be some overlap between these alibi periods?'

'An overlap? I do not follow.'

'In Eulerian Circles, there must in this case be an

intersection.'

'I trust this makes sense to you, Jon, but I have no idea what you are talking about which leaves me at a considerable disadvantage.'

Starling smiled. 'My apologies. You have set my mathematical brain in motion, something which isn't required any longer in my actuarial work. My premise is that on at least one of the dates in question *both* Gordon and Robertson *must* have been able to prove their whereabouts to Duncan's satisfaction. If there wasn't one coincident night within the set they could both be guilty. Is that clearer?'

Blacklock frowned. 'Not particularly. I could blame the ale but I fear I might struggle even with a crystal-clear head.'

Starling stopped and faced Blacklock. 'For at least one of the killings they *both* had to have proven where they were at that time. Otherwise one could deduce that Gordon had killed some and Robertson the others, operating either independently or in concert.'

'That's preposterous!'

'Is it? With coincident alibis, it isn't even a possibility. Even you've been unable to tell whose handiwork these cuts have been. I admit it's a rather fanciful – or more technically improbable – explanation. But it is ruled out by the proof.' He resumed walking. 'Such as it is.'

'Such as it is?'

'Logic, Watson. Pay attention, dear boy. If *everyone* from your Edinburgh cohort has an alibi then *none* of them could have done this and you're barking up the wrong tree. If the others all have alibis and it's *still* someone from Edinburgh then it's you: QED.'

'But–'

'Unless.'

'Unless what?'

'Unless one of the alibis is a fabrication.'

It was Blacklock's turn to stop. 'It is hopeless, Jon. Duncan's men have examined Gordon's and Robertson's alibis and determined them to be sound.'

'Perhaps.'

'No, Jon, not "perhaps", you irritating pedant. Cargill told me, and Duncan repeated it.'

They had reached a rare bench, one not occupied by a vagrant. 'Sit, Nate. Time for your second lesson.'

Blacklock obeyed, although Starling remained on his feet. 'People – even actuaries, hard as that is to believe – make assumptions. All the time. Consciously and unconsciously. Conscious assumptions are fine, and can be documented for later examination if necessary. Unconscious assumptions, by definition, are much harder to identify. We have to make them all the time, otherwise we couldn't function.'

'Speak for yourself. I do not.'

Starling laughed. 'So it's only you who is free of such failings.'

'Apparently.'

'I see. You *assumed* that the slats in that bench were not rotten and further *assumed* that they were strong enough to support you. I didn't see any tentativeness as you parked your skinny arse on it. You *assumed* that the ale we just drank at The Unicorn wasn't poisoned. You *assumed–*'

'But those are far from critically important assumptions. I meant that I did not make assumptions in my work. You do not, in yours. The police, I assume, do not in theirs.'

'Ha! You *assumed* the police do not make assumptions! You're making this too easy.'

'Wordplay, Jon. Inelegant sophistry, nothing more.'

Starling became serious. 'Tell me again, why are you suspended?'

'Because–.' Blacklock stopped short, then sighed. 'Point taken.'

'Sorry. That was underhand of me, but now you understand what I'm trying to say.'

Blacklock nodded.

'Good. Tell me everything you know about their alibis.'

'Not a great deal. I know that their timecards were checked and that therefore they were accounted for.'

'So the underlying assumption is?'

'That ... they were on duty at the time of the deaths.'

'Alright. What's the assumption that's supporting that one?'

Blacklock paused for several moments. 'There is no assumption. It is a factual dead end.'

'Wrong. Dunce Cap for Blacklock. Stand in the corner.'

'But–'

'No. The assumption is that the timecards accurately reflect their attendance. How would you falsify a timecard?'

'I would not.'

Starling inhaled deeply. *'Give me strength.* How would someone who is not a paragon do it? Someone like the late-lamented Porter, for example?'

'They cannot. There are checks and balances throughout the system. I am sure I do not need to lecture *you* on checks and balances.'

'Touché.' Starling slumped heavily onto the bench. 'I assumed this would hold my weight.' He looked out over the river. 'You're the murderer, Nate. Nice knowing you.'

'Wait–'

'If the timecard system is as flawless as you claim, and no one else makes this incision, then you're the last man standing. Porter could not reach across the channel from his compromised position, floating in The Seine like a dead horse. Likewise Ballantyne floating down The Ganges or wherever the hell it was that he died. How sure are you that it's not this Priestley character?'

'Like you, Jon, I am thinking of the probability,' replied Blacklock. 'Four of us are – or were – already in London. Add to that the fact that he has dropped from even the RCS's sight. Something tells me – instinct – that he is dead or as good as.'

They lapsed into silence again, watching the boats' lamps playing on the dark water.

Without looking away from the water Starling asked, 'Why do you even have timecards? Overtime?'

'Ha,' laughed Blacklock. 'Doctors are not paid overtime, Jon. Whatever next? Medicine is a vocation, so we receive something more akin to a stipend than a salary.'

'So whatever hours you work you get paid a fixed sum?'

'That is the tragic case. Locums do a little better, when they are working, but a common-or-garden doctor gets paid whatever is stated in his contract and not a penny more.'

'And not a penny less?'

Blacklock laughed again. 'I admire your optimism, or perhaps naïvety. Absence is not paid. Woe betide the doctor who falls ill, even if the poor soul contracts his ailment from a patient.'

'That's not fair.'

'Vocations are not fair. Apparently.'

'So in essence the timecard system exists to ensure that people receive the minimum possible payment.'

Blacklock shrugged. 'Absolutely. Look at the scene before us, or any of the vast "improvements" the Empire has brought us. We live in the age of joyless efficiency, Jon. Everything must be refined to within an inch of its life. A machine should have no unnecessary parts. A hospital should have no one paid for labours they do not complete, whilst making absolutely certain that it does not pay for all the work that people *do* complete. The industrial age is fully upon us.'

'Nice speech.'

'I have simply paraphrased the chief accountant's "welcome address" at every hospital where I have ever worked. They fail to see the irony.'

'I can't understand why anyone would bother.'

'We probably started out wanting to heal the sick.'

'Let's walk on,' said Starling. 'It's bloody cold and I think better on my feet.'

They walked upriver, passing frenetic dockyards and warehouses, the sound of the river a chorus of horns and cursing. It was getting light, and the banks were teeming with hordes of children, some barely more than toddlers, combing the flotsam for anything which might fetch a farthing.

After perhaps half an hour Starling spoke. 'Why do locums "do a little better?" Surely they would earn even less?'

'Do you not know anything about what I do, Jon? They earn a little more to compensate for the fallow periods when they earn nothing. In point of fact, the extra they are paid gets predominantly creamed off by their agents, so it is not a great position.'

'Interesting.'

'Not really.'

'Don't be so sure. Sounds like something you should do.'

Blacklock tutted. 'Do not be ridiculous. You appear to have forgotten I am suspended. I could not get onto any agency's books. Even Garrett's would not take me on. *I cannot practise.*'

'I know that. You might have mentioned that before. Want to hear a foolish plan?'

'I fail to see how a foolish plan would differ from one of your usual plans, Jon.'

'Be a locum – at St John's.'

'Why on earth would I want to do that?'

'To examine the timecard system, and to determine whether it works on the principles you have described from your other engagements. It's the only way to clear your name. And who is or are Garrett's?'

'They are the largest locum agency in London. But why me?'

'Because *even you*, Nathaniel, should be able to impersonate a doctor.'

Ninety-One

The Hawk Inn, Hampstead, London
Wednesday 17th July

Blacklock and Starling were waiting in a small inn a couple of hundred yards from St John's, the only sheltered spot to be found to keep them from the unseasonable summer storms. With any luck Robertson would pass this way between the hospital and home. If they were unfortunate he would pass them in the opposite direction, towards a night shift and their journey across town would be wasted. They guessed that the chance of encountering Gordon was minimal, since it appeared that he was at his club far more often than he deigned to work, his trust fund and his illness exacting competing tolls.

Starling nudged Blacklock. 'There's your cue, Doctor Frankenstein.' Robertson hurried past on the opposite side, apparently intent on getting home before the rain soaked through his overcoat.

'This is a bad idea, Jon.' Blacklock could feel his pulse quickening.

'You'll be fine. Hop to it.'

Blacklock downed the remainder of his ale and headed for the hospital.

He had brushed down his clothing as best he could, and McCormac had even shined his boots, but still Blacklock felt oppressed by his shabbiness as he walked with false confidence into St John's.

Just inside the entrance a porter was fussing with a clay pipe.

'Excuse me, porter,' asked Blacklock, simulating an imperiousness which he was not feeling. 'Where is the physician in charge? I am a locum for tonight's shift.'

'If you say so,' replied the porter, sucking desperately on

his pipe which was refusing to light. 'First floor. Ask for Mr Kelly.'

Blacklock's heart stuttered as he realised he had *already* made a mistake by departing from the approach which had been so painstakingly fashioned with Starling and McCormac. They had drilled him in the need to avoid meeting another doctor and he had immediately failed. At a sudden loss he walked slowly towards the stairs, desperately trying to dig himself out of this pit of his own making.

He glanced back at the door. The watchful porter, with smoke finally pluming from his pipe, used it to point at the stairs. Blacklock raised a hand of thanks and started to climb the staircase. After half a floor it turned back on itself, obscuring him from both the porter's view and the floor above.

On the first floor the double doors were open onto the ward. He glanced in but no one was looking in his direction. He continued climbing the stairs until he reached the fifth floor, the first one in full darkness. He walked along the corridor, his pace quickening as his eyes adjusted to the meagre light which entered through the glass doors.

He sat on a bench and closed his eyes. *Idiot!* After several minutes of irresolution he developed his plan to escape, which was to continue along the corridor, away from the stairwell, hoping to eventually find an alternative route down. In time he reached an unlocked service stairwell. There was no lighting so he felt his way down, aware that his sense of peril was disproportionate to the actual risk but nonetheless unable to control it. His shirt stuck to his back; the acrid stench of his perspiration filled his nostrils; salt stung his eyes. Even his hand began to ache because he gripped the bannister as though he might plunge to his death at any moment.

He had no idea how long his descent took; it was probably only a minute or two but felt interminable. At last he reached the bottom of the staircase. He fumbled in the pitch darkness for a while before he found a door handle. With huge relief he grasped it to step out from this premature burial. He rattled the door, tried to shake it off its hinges – nothing. Unwilling to admit defeat he redoubled his efforts but to no avail. Close to despair he felt his way back to the base of the stairs and sat down. For an instant he felt like weeping but chose instead to berate himself – such weakness had no place here. The only direction was back up to whence he came. He started slowly, feeling his way, but soon realised he was able to climb much more quickly than he had descended. He stumbled once or twice, but the potential penalty was psychologically less severe than falling on his descent.

Once he reached the fifth floor again he crossed easily to the other stairwell. He almost scampered down. Sensing that escape was only seconds away he paused on the second floor to check that the coast was clear before continuing. As he turned on the first floor landing, studiously avoiding a look at the ward, a voice called out. 'There he is!' From the country burr he knew it was the porter.

He ignored it.

A woman's voice, more strident and authoritative, followed. 'You there! Locum! Where the hell have you been, and where in the name of heaven do you think you're going now?'

Blacklock buckled under the voice of authority. He turned, hoping he was suitably composed. The nurse's headdress and uniform made it clear he had already made a powerful enemy. 'I am sorry, Matron. I lost my way looking for the timesheet office.'

'Honestly, Garrett's men are so greedy that I scarcely understand why we bother. Each is worse than the last. Might I suggest that you perform some actual medical duties before you extract payment from us? Come! You're needed in Room 12. There'll be time enough to claim your pieces of silver before you go.'

Blacklock's fear rooted him to the spot.

'For God's sake man, Room 12. It has the number one adjacent to the number two on the door. Even you can find it. I don't have all night!'

He complied with this most direct of orders, years of matronly obedience overcoming his dread. He rushed past the matron, who muttered something under her breath, and the porter who glared a warning at him.

The stench of corruption in Room 12 stopped his breath. Even the nurse, clearly an experienced campaigner, looked green.

'Thank goodness you're here, Doctor,' she said. 'This is Mr Garmonsway. He has a problem with his groin. I have other patients to attend to. Mr Garmonsway, this is Doctor–'

Blacklock's mind regurgitated the first name that occurred to it. 'Priestley. Douglas Priestley.'

'Doctor Priestley will help you.' Without another word or even a glance the nurse made good her escape.

Blacklock composed himself. This was not an impersonation. This was his vocation. 'Mr Garmonsway. How can I help?'

'Call me Reg.'

'Alright, Reg it is. What has brought you to us today?'

'I've got this, Doc.' He pulled back the sheet. His nightshirt was gathered about his waist, leaving him naked below that point. In his left groin a gross abscess had formed, the size of half a grapefruit.

Blacklock managed to suppress his revulsion. 'How long have you been suffering with this?'

'A few months now, but this past fourweek it's got much worser.'

'Why did you not seek treatment earlier?'

'I have, doctor. Been in the free queue every day for the past fortnight but no luck 'til this afternoon.'

Blacklock rinsed his hands in the basin of murky water on the nightstand. 'May I examine it?'

'Long as you don't grab the old meat and two veg. My missus claims rights over them. Used to, anyway.'

Blacklock smiled. 'Trust me, Reg. I will not be tempted.' He paused to change his tone. 'Mr Garmonsway – Reg – this may hurt, but it is important to understand the consistency of this mass. Before I do that, can you tell me what it feels like to you?'

Garmonsway shuddered. 'Makes me sick to even think about touching it. A donkey once kicked me in the bollocks and that hurt like the shit for weeks after. This'n's ten times worser. Fifty times worser.'

'In that case I am very sorry that I need to palpate – feel – this mass to determine its consistency.'

Garmonsway drew in a deep breath, bit his lip, and nodded.

With a confidence he did not feel Blacklock reached forward and began to palpate the growth. At first glance he had feared that it might be a massive hernia, but the consistency was wrong. He glanced at his patient; Garmonsway was shining with sweat and tears stood in his eyes.

'All done, Reg,' said Blacklock, standing back. 'I think this is a simple, albeit large abscess. It will need to be drained.' He looked around. An old lancet, blood-encrusted, lay near the basin. 'If you will please excuse me for a moment.'

Blacklock stepped outside, gulping the fresher air in the corridor.

'What do you think, Doctor Priestley?,' asked the nurse, who was still waiting outside.

It took a moment for Blacklock to recall that *he* was Priestley. 'It is an abscess which needs to be drained as a matter of urgency. Given its location I am surprised that it has not already ruptured its sac and killed the poor man via sepsis. Can you assist? I will need sterilised instruments, clean lint to pack the wound, bandages and of course some carbolic acid.'

'You realise he's a free, don't you?'

'Yes.'

'There's none of that for a free. I can find some spare lint, perhaps, and some towels, but nothing else.'

'For God's sake!' He paused. 'I am sorry, nurse. I did not mean to offend you. Rules are rules, eh? Please do the best you can. Oh, and the wound will need suturing.'

He stepped back into the room. 'The nurse is gathering the necessaries and then we will get this out of you. You will be as right as rain in a few days.' He smiled again, hoping to instil a confidence in Garmonsway that he did not feel within himself.

'Can't I just leave it and see if it gets better by itself?'

'This *will not* get better of its own accord, Reg. It just wants to kill you. You can leave if you wish and you will be dead inside a month. I cannot force you to do anything.'

The nurse entered, bearing some ancient towels and stained bandages. She smiled apologetically. 'Best I could do.'

'Thank you,' said Blacklock.

'I found a little carbolic, too.'

'You are an angel.' He picked up the lancet, trying not to imagine how many procedures it had already performed. He smiled at Garmonsway. 'Ready?'

Garmonsway nodded, even as he said 'Not really.'

Blacklock moved to open the abscess but stopped short. 'Nurse, is there a commode available?'

'Yes, doctor.'

'I have an idea to give Mr Garmonsway the best chance. Could I trouble you to fetch it, please?'

'I ain't gonna shit meself. Honest, doc.'

'It is not that, Reg. You will not be able to leave the bed for at least a few hours after this is treated. I do not think it will help anyone for you to sit or lie in what we are about to release.'

The nurse returned with a commode as filthy as everything else. Blacklock helped Garmonsway edge gingerly onto it. 'If you will open your legs as wide as you can, Reg, then I suggest you look around and count something – like the ceiling tiles. It will take your mind off this. I will start when you get to three.'

'One–,' started Garmonsway.

Without any further hesitation Blacklock made a deep incision – an Edinburgh Incision – into the abscess.

'–Ahhhh!' Blood and pus flooded from the wound, splashing noisily onto the porcelain below. Blacklock worked with two fingers to squeeze the growth, trying to eject as much of the corruption as he could.

Garmonsway whimpered but did not flinch.

'You are doing brilliantly, Reg. There are not many people that could bear this so stoically.' He freed what he hoped were the final clots and pus, then bathed the wound with half the carbolic. 'Nearly there, Reg.'

Garmonsway was close to fainting.

Without further delay Blacklock sutured the wound – quite passably, he thought – then washed the area with the remaining carbolic. He looked up. Garmonsway had finally passed out.

'A blessing,' said the nurse. 'Well done, doctor.'

Blacklock nodded then said, 'We must get him back into bed. Please do all you can to keep him here as long as possible.'

'I'll try, although between Matron and Mr Kelly I don't think he'll be allowed to stay long after he wakes up.'

Even as she spoke, Garmonsway began to regain consciousness. 'Am I done?'

'You are indeed done,' said Blacklock. 'You will feel much better soon.' He glanced back at the nurse. 'It will be good for you, Reg, to pretend you are asleep for as long as possible. Good man.'

The next couple of hours passed in an invigorating whirl, with Blacklock called from patient to patient with no opportunity to make good his escape – even if he had wanted to, so engrossed was he. He delivered a baby which had its cord securely wrapped around its neck but was able to resuscitate it and stem the mother's post-partum haemorrhage; two lives saved.

Seemingly without a pause for breath he was called in to suture another wound, this time for someone who claimed to have slipped whilst adjusting a window, an injury forecast by Mrs Evans so long before. Throughout all this hectic activity he had not even glimpsed the mysterious Mr Kelly. Every time he asked about him he was answered with either a shrug or a knowing smile. Blacklock, although fearful of exposure, was more thrilled than he thought possible by the simple act of discharging his professional duties again. It was only when the clock struck one that he realised he had already worked half a shift, helping a variety of people, most of whom would otherwise have received no care at all. He was struggling to leave, even though he had no right to be there, when Kelly breezed in.

'Everything under control, Priestley?'

'Yes sir.'

'Excellent. Sorry I haven't been around. Had a tricky delivery with a member of the gentry.' He touched the side of his nose. 'No names, no pack drill, what?' His breath reeked of whisky, which Blacklock did his best to ignore. 'You're a Garrett's man, aren't you?'

'Yes.' For once Blacklock resisted the temptation to embroider.

'Well, you certainly seem to be a cut above the usual no-hopers they inflict upon us. I've heard good things, even from Matron – which is remarkable. Well done. Carry on. I must return to her ladyship.'

Before Blacklock could draw breath to reply Kelly was gone, striding away to what Blacklock suspected was an empty private room and a bottle of Johnnie Walker.

'Doctor?' called another nurse. 'We need you. Urgently.'

'A whole bloody shift?' cried Starling.

'Yes.'

'And yet you didn't sign in?' You only had to find the timecards and in twelve hours you didn't manage to do that?'

'It was not as simple a situation as you are trying to describe, Jon.' Blacklock paused, partly to gather his thoughts and partly to add emphasis. 'Patients there *needed me*. I actually practised real, useful medicine, at its most satisfying ... its most visceral. For the first time in over a year I was doing something of value.'

'Of course you were. I can't argue with that. However. Of *more* value might have been to do something to distance yourself from the gallows. If you enjoyed your dozen hours of blood and gore so much you can sign up for more *when you're not a suspected murderer.* It's all well and good doing a Florence Nightingale act but that's not why you were there.'

Ninety-Two

St John's Hospital, Hampstead, London
Tuesday 23rd July

Blacklock had to wait until the following Tuesday before he was able to report for duty again. He watched Robertson leave then entered the hospital immediately. A different porter manned the desk, apparently close to expiring from boredom.

'Hello. I am a locum from Garrett's. I have not worked here before. Where do I sign my card?'

The porter mumbled unintelligibly and pointed along the corridor.

'I am afraid I did not quite catch that.' Blacklock produced a threepenny piece. 'Perhaps you would be kind enough to show me the way?'

The porter eyed the coin, almost too lazy to take it, then relented with an exaggerated sigh. 'This way.'

They walked along to a doorway which opened onto a descending staircase. The porter led the way, walking more slowly than a tired glacier. He showed Blacklock into a room lined with filing cabinets.

'Top drawer, left-hand side. Blanks are at the back. File yours under Garrett. Make sure it's complete by Friday morning – that's when they check them.'

'Thank–,' replied Blacklock but the porter was already gone. With a guilty glance over his shoulder Blacklock began rifling through the drawer, which was so full of cards that they were jammed into position. It was impossible to withdraw one without removing a few either side along with it. It was equally difficult to simply flick through them. He pulled a set of cards at random – they were connected with treasury tags – Strickland. An inch further forwards – Robins. A few seconds later he had Robertson's thick sheaf of dog-eared cards, which were more white space than ink, even though the range covered more than a year. He extracted a scrap of paper from his pocket which listed the dates of the deaths: Robertson had signed in at 1900 on at least three of the nights in question. At the end of each entry there was a small red tick, in a column headed 'Absence return checked?' Sporadically – not more than half a dozen occurrences across the year – the column was stamped ABSENT: NOT PAID. None of these dates coincided with the dates of interest. As he slipped the cards back into place a thought occurred to him and he pulled them out again. *Robertson had not signed in that morning, yet he had left not more than ten minutes before.*

Gordon's much larger collection of cards was in a different drawer. Blacklock checked the dates, and all but one tallied with his list. It was a surprise to discover that Gordon was in fact more conscientious than Robertson about such dreary paperwork. More for curiosity than any other reason Blacklock flicked through the stack of cards to the latest. Gordon had signed in less than thirty minutes before.

Barely able to breathe, Blacklock grew suddenly hot. Gordon? Here? He made a frantic copy of Robertson's and Gordon's latest cards before he searched for an escape route. Every nearby door was locked. There was no alternative but to head back the way he had been brought in, with the risk of encountering Gordon at any point. He tried to concoct a reasonable explanation for his presence but nothing came; the possibility was one he would have to deal with should it arise.

He had no sooner returned to the hallway when he spotted Gordon heading towards him, perhaps only thirty yards distant. Fortunately – for Blacklock – the lecher was fully engaged with a young nurse whose blushes and giggling made Blacklock fear for her wellbeing. He looked around – a room with a door marked LINEN was his only place to hide. He dashed in. The cupboard was a large one, with several runs of shelving stacked with fresh linen, more akin to a library. He listened at the door, his own breathing drowning out anything else he would otherwise wish to hear.

The nurse's laughter grew louder, then – horror – the door handle began to turn. He stepped back behind the first row of shelves and Gordon entered, nurse in tow.

Before Blacklock could form any plan or frame an explanation the door opened again and the matron entered. 'Doctor Gordon, you are needed to treat patients, not to audit bedlinen or impregnate silly girls who should know better. As for you, Nurse Tolliver, report to my office in ten minutes so that I might reacquaint you with your duties.'

'Sorry, Bridget,' whispered Gordon. 'I'll see you later.' He stepped out, leaving the nurse sobbing. Blacklock thought of intervening but could not think of any way in which such an action would improve the situation. A couple of minutes later she had composed herself and left.

Blacklock followed a short while afterwards and was able to make good his escape. He left a folded note with the porter, addressed to Nurse Tolliver, urging her to avoid Doctor Gordon in order to maintain her health.

Ninety-Three

McCormac's lodgings, 25 Barnabas
Street, Kensal Green, London
Wednesday 24th July

With Starling in attendance for the first time McCormac's messy lodgings seemed even more oppressively crowded than before, something Blacklock would have previously thought impossible. The introductions between the two had been curt and businesslike, as though an immediate mistrust had formed between them.

'You'll be as amazed as I was, Mr McCormac—'

'Frank, Mr Starling.'

'Jon, Mr McCormac. You'll be amazed that our dear Nathaniel here has managed not once but *twice* to enter St John's without either revealing his identity or even arousing suspicion, as far as we know.'

'A remarkable improvement,' replied McCormac.

'The better news, Frank, is that we have learned how easily Gordon or Robertson could have circumvented the time recording system to provide an alibi. It is to be regretted that Inspector Duncan was unable to reach the same conclusion before he set them both free.'

'How did they do that?'

'Simplicity itself, Frank,' replied Starling. 'The cards are only collated and checked on a Friday. Everyone and anyone has free access to the card system. It seems clear that one of them was completing timecard entries after the event, to provide some cover. It didn't raise any eyebrows because pay is only docked for absence, which is only notified if the staff member is rostered for work and doesn't show up. The reverse – turning up to work when you're not scheduled to be there – isn't checked because overtime isn't paid. That's the hole one of them has potentially exploited. If Duncan took the timecards at face value without checking the roster Bob's your uncle.'

'And did he?'

'If whatever underling was sent to do that didn't ask how the system worked, they might think it foolproof. As Nathaniel did.'

'I see. What's next?'

'We find ourselves with three-and-a-half suspects.' He smiled. 'The half is of course our beloved Nathaniel.'

Blacklock rolled his eyes but said nothing.

'He counts for half because *we* believe he is innocent - it's just that the daft bugger can't prove it.'

McCormac nodded.

Starling stood up. 'Now all we need to do is work out which of the others is responsible.' He tried to take a step but was thwarted by the clutter and was forced to retake his seat. 'This environment makes thinking difficult.'

'It is not your bloody legs, Starling, but your head that is the more appropriate part of your anatomy for thinking,' said Blacklock, chafing to make at least one contribution to the conversation.

'Steady on, Nate. Mens sana in corpore sano and all that. It's your neck we're trying to save. Let's assume that one of them has faked their timecard. What *else* do we know about the perpetrator?'

Blacklock shrugged. 'Apart from his alias, very little.'

'An alias?' asked Starling.

Blacklock glanced at McCormac. 'Dr C Adava.'

'Cadaver?'

'Well spotted, Jon. It would take an idiot to miss that,' said McCormac.

'Indeed' sighed Blacklock, getting to his feet. 'I will continue following Gordon. It has to be–' He did not speak for several moments.

'Doc? You alright?' asked McCormac.

'It's Aramis – Robertson.'

'Why him all of a sudden? Why not Gordon?,' asked

Starling.

Blacklock clapped his hands. 'I have just remembered. *Robertson named the specimens. He invented Dr C Adava.*'

'It's possible – before we get carried away – that Gordon could of course use Adava to incriminate Robertson,' said Starling.

'Let's inform Duncan,' said McCormac, 'and let the police do their own feckin' work for a change.'

'I would rather see this through, Francis,' said Blacklock. 'Aramis deserves some sort of hearing, which is more than he'll get when Duncan unleashes the hounds. I will wait at the hospital and confront him.'

Ninety-Four

St John's Hospital, Hampstead, London
Friday 26th July

For the second time, the beard that Blacklock had grown since fleeing from Mrs Mason's a lifetime ago proved useful, providing a semblance of disguise. On his second night of vigil he wondered idly about the small boy waiting nervously at the hospital door, ignored by everyone flowing past.

Almost everyone.

A few minutes after the day shift ended Robertson emerged and was immediately accosted by the boy, who forced something into the surgeon's hand.

Robertson opened them – they were clearly notes – and scanned them quickly. He consulted his watch, said something to the boy and summoned a hansom. The boy ran off in a different direction.

A change from Robertson's usual routine, but what could it mean? Blacklock hailed a hansom for himself – they were always plentiful around the hospital, and he had a pocketful of Starling's loose change – and set his driver in pursuit of Robertson's cab.

The convoy quickly reached the East End, and as the cab traffic began to thin Blacklock feared discovery. 'If he alights,' called Blacklock, 'please stop well short. I would like to avoid detection.'

The cabbie grunted noncommittally. As events transpired Blacklock had made his request only just in time. At the next junction Robertson stepped down and hurried into an alleyway. Blacklock paid off his cab and followed Robertson on foot.

The court they entered was as dispiriting as any Blacklock had seen in all the time he had spent at this end of the city. Robertson proved to be surprisingly conversant with the layout of the narrow conduits here, turning left and right in the maze of paths and buildings without either hesitation or seeking guidance. Blacklock struggled to match Robertson's pace, and was further delayed when a brawl spilled out of an inn between them, filling the alley. He passed the altercation with some difficulty, by which time Robertson was out of sight. Blacklock paused at a cross-street, unsure which path to take. A small boy stared at him with naked curiosity. 'Did you see a man in a black cloak pass this way, only a moment or two ago?'

The boy's expression did not change.

'A man? Running? With a big bag?'

'Joseph!' screamed a mother's voice from somewhere nearby. 'Leave that gen'leman alone and get in 'ere.'

After regarding Blacklock for a few more seconds the boy turned tail and ran into the darkness. Blacklock looked around impatiently but there was no one else to ask.

Somewhere to his left, a woman screamed. He hastened to where he believed the cry came from but was faced once again with a featureless tenement.

Another scream, from the doorway directly ahead. Within, a lantern burned dimly but he was able to discern a man standing outside a room, peering in. Blacklock dashed forward. He was a few feet away when the man turned to him. 'What do you want? Get out!'

'I am a doctor,' said Blacklock, attempting to push his way past.

'We already got one, so bugger off!' The man, obviously distressed, took a couple of menacing steps towards Blacklock.

'Leave him be, Mr Race,' said Robertson from the room. 'He can assist me. Come in, Pathos. I need all the help I can get.'

Race stood aside to allow Blacklock to enter.

'I knew someone would find me in the end,' said Robertson, 'but for now I'm particularly grateful that it's you. This woman has suffered a traumatic birth and as you can see is bleeding profusely. There is ether there - please administer it whilst I try to locate the source of the bleeding.'

The combination of Robertson's authority and his own instinct set Blacklock into action almost before he realised he had become a conspirator. He administered the ether without argument, keeping one hand on the woman's wrist to monitor her pulse, which was slowing as she slipped mercifully into anaesthesia.

Robertson worked fast but clumsily, stemming the bleeding quickly. 'Try to bring her round, Pathos.'

Ignoring the slight Blacklock slowly reduced the ether level, the patient responding quickly and regaining consciousness almost immediately. An older woman, presumably her mother, entered. 'How is she?'

Robertson smiled at her. 'She's lost a lot of blood but I think we have managed to stop the bleeding now. She needs rest and plenty of water – and liver if you have it – will help because it fortifies the blood.'

'Can't afford the liver, Doctor, but the rest I can manage.'

Robertson reached inside his jacket and withdrew his wallet. 'Here's half a crown. *Please* spend it on wholesome food for her, especially liver if you can find it.'

'I can't never pay this back.'

'It doesn't matter – forget it. Just keep her warm and fed.' He looked around. 'Where is the baby?'

'It weren't a baby, Doctor. 'Twas a ghoul, some kind of monster. Born dead, thank the Lord. It's been taken away.'

'I see.' Robertson looked at Blacklock as if he had forgotten he was there. 'You can go, Pathos. Thank you.'

'But–'

'Please, Nathaniel, go. We can discuss all this another time. I need to ensure this girl remains well.'

Blacklock faltered.

'I'm not going anywhere,' sighed Robertson. 'You have my word. Besides, you know that if you were to call the police now this girl would almost certainly perish.' He brandished the second note, which Blacklock could not read. 'I have another woman to attend to a few streets away immediately after this patient stabilises. She may also die. I know you don't want that. You have a conscience.'

'Then I will go.'

'And what will you work with? Your bare hands? Are you some kind of faith healer who can open a patient with their fingers?'

'Will you return to your home?'

'Of course. Eliza needs me.'

'You cannot continue with this, Arthur.'

'We took an oath, Pathos. These people can't afford any form of medical care, so should they simply be left to die, doomed by their circumstances, as we stand aloof? I know you don't think that way. Gordon, yes. Porter perhaps leans more to charitable thinking when he can see something in it for himself. But you and I, Nathaniel, remember where we came from.' He started to walk away.

'Porter is dead,' called Blacklock, but Robertson did not hear. Blacklock watched him disappear into the dark maze, then hesitated for a few moments before he turned for home.

Ninety-Five

McCormac's lodgings, 25 Barnabas
Street, Kensal Green, London
Friday 26th July

'You let him go?' screamed McCormac. 'What in the name of actual flying fuckery is wrong with you? *Jesus!*'

'But McCormac, I have to let him make his case.'

'You found him disembowelling a woman!'

'Do not be so melodramatic, man. He was preventing her bleeding to death. I was there a few seconds behind him – he had no time to *attack* her before I caught up with him. *He saved her life.*'

'What about the others? The child?'

'I will do nothing until I hear his side of the matter.'

'Your delays cost lives last time.'

'Did they? I am not so sure. Robertson was clearly trying to save them, but they were beyond help.'

'And cutting their feckin throats would assist their recovery, I suppose? Another advanced Edinburgh technique, I assume?'

'Those wounds were post-mortem, Francis, to cover his tracks.'

'And you honestly believe that? Why should he even need to cover his tracks if what you're claiming is true?'

'I do not know.'

'Just yesterday you suspected him of murder, and now he's transformed into some kind of saviour? Really? I don't know which of you is the most deluded.'

'Very well. Your point about delay is well made. I shall leave for his home immediately.'

'I'll come with you.'

'As you wish. I thought you wanted no part of this.'

McCormac pulled on his coat. 'I didn't, but I can't let

your warped sense of justice or duty allow him off the hook again. I want this madness over, and you don't seem capable of behaving rationally. I'll tie this Robertson to a bloody tree if I have to. And we'll get Starling on the way. Maybe the two of us can control you too.'

The hackney – which McCormac had paid for – pulled up close to Robertson's house.

'I cannot see any lamps or candles,' said Blacklock, peering from the cab, 'but it is barely dusk. His daughter will be at home, anyway.' The three alighted.

It was only when the hackney was too far away to be recalled that they realised the house was empty.

Not only empty, but deserted.

McCormac cupped his hands against the parlour window. 'There's nothing, Doc. Not a stick of furniture in the place.'

Blacklock crouched down to peer through the letterbox. 'Damn him. He said he was returning home!'

The door of the adjoining house creaked open. An old man shuffled out, wearing only old trousers and an ancient, stained singlet. 'Can I help you fellas?'

'We are looking for Doctor Robertson, mate,' replied McCormac.

'E's gorn,' said the old man. 'Moved out when he come back from jail. Couldn't get a moment's peace after that, poor beggar.'

Blacklock exchanged glances with McCormac. 'Do you know where he has gone, sir?'

'No. Moonlight flit. The blokes as collected the furniture a few days later had nothin' to say neither.'

'I do not suppose you recall the name on the removal cart?' asked Starling.

'Nah, sorry. Readin's never been my strong suit, as my old ma used to say. "Alfie Flynn, you'll be the death of me." Every day she said it.'

'Thank you anyway,' said Blacklock. He turned to

McCormac. 'It appears that we are back to square one.'

'Perhaps. Perhaps not. How did you find him last time?'

'I waited outside the hos ... pital. Of course. If he is still practising there we should pick up his trail.'

They made their way immediately to St John's, where Blacklock strode to the Records Office without hesitation. The last few days on Robertson's timecards all bore the same legend: ABSENT: NOT PAID.

McCormac tutted as they waited for the kettle to boil back in his room. 'If I was in his shoes I'd be a hundred miles away by now. Further if I could – America even.'

'I do not think that Eliza can travel any sort of distance. He said as much himself.'

'So he's gone to ground,' said Starling. 'In London there are myriad places. It took Duncan and his cronies weeks to find you and you're famously useless at subterfuge.'

Blacklock shook his head. 'If you recall I was betrayed by an associate. They did not *find* me, as such.'

'His wife is dead, correct?'

'Yes.'

'And the daughter's a cripple?'

'Yes, apparently with some kind of additional degenerative condition of the digestion system which is clearly reaching a crisis.'

'He has to be in London, then. What do you think, Frank?'

McCormac nodded.

'Let's assume,' continued Starling, holding his palm up to Blacklock, 'that he has stayed close to where he was last seen. He's not earning at the hospital. If he's here he must be depending on acquaintances or strangers. Gordon?'

'No,' replied Blacklock. 'I would not risk any female family member under the same roof as that syphilitic lecher.'

'I'm sure he speaks highly of you, too,' said McCormac. 'If he needs to do this ... thing that he does, backstreet surgery or whatever, does the daughter tag along too? What is she, ten? Not old enough to fend for herself, especially if she's so poorly.'

'A woman childminds for him,' said Blacklock.

'Who? You've never mentioned her before,' said Starling.

'I do not know – I only met her once, in passing. She was leaving Robertson's as I arrived.'

'Did he introduce you?'

'I assume so.'

'So what was her name?'

'I cannot recall.'

'You *must*, Nate. What's the first letter? A? B?' Starling ran through the alphabet several times, stressing Blacklock.

'For God's sake, man, give me a little peace. Stop mammering me.'

'I'm not,' replied Starling. 'I couldn't care less whether you get yourself out of this mire or not. Frank and I are doing our level best to extract you but you seem perversely committed to staying put.' He put on his hat. 'When or if you feel differently, you know where I am. Good evening, Frank. Nate.'

Blacklock could not think of anything to say before Starling left.

'Not a bright move, Doc,' said McCormac.

Blacklock shrugged again. 'It's difficult to remember anything when someone is shouting at you. It is like being back in Duncan's bloody dungeon.'

'My accommodation may be a little on the mean side, I'll grant you, but I resent you likening it to a dungeon. Drink?'

It was long past midnight. McCormac had deprived Blacklock of all his matchsticks in a card game the surgeon could not grasp the rules of. At some point Blacklock had furnished McCormac with an IOU for a million pounds. After several hours Starling had returned, somehow even more drunk than when he had left.

Blacklock's head pounded, and the room was slightly

unsteady on its foundations, feeling more like a ship's cabin than a bedsitting room. 'I need some fresh air, gentlemen,' said Blacklock. 'I need to think.'

'Don't overtax your brain cells, Doc,' said McCormac. 'You'll regret it if you kill off the both of them.'

Blacklock half-walked, half-fell into the street. McCormac lived in a permanently busy part of the city, where half the neighbourhood worked at night in occupations on both sides of the law. There was always someone around. At this time the late inns were turning out, so the drunken Blacklock struggled to make headway against the equally intoxicated people all around him.

He chose his route whimsically, turning left if he saw a cat, right if he saw a dog and heading straight on if neither was present. In no time at all he was refreshed, more sober – and utterly lost.

He wandered aimlessly for a while, hoping that he might recognise a landmark or even a junction but to no avail. At a loss as to whom to ask and unwilling to show his vulnerability he strode on in his most confident style. His lessons from being previously lost in the city weighed heavily. On the verge of losing hope he sought someone less common to ask but saw no one until a constable emerged from an alley.

'Excuse me, officer, but I seem to have lost my way.'

'Where was you wanting to go, sir?'

'Barnabas Street, Kensal Green.'

'Are you sure? It's not really the sort of place where a gentleman would wish to find himself.'

'I am sure; an Irishman of my acquaintance – no, a *friend* – lives there.'

'Ah. I see, sir.' He pointed over Blacklock's shoulder. 'Back the way you came, straight down here for a couple of hundred yards, turn right into Tower Lane. A couple of chains along there, turn left into Larkhill Lane, then left again into Roseby Court. That'll bring you into the High

Road and you'll be almost there.'

'Thank you, officer. Rosebery?'

'No, Roseby, sir.'

'No, Rosebery – that is it! You are a godsend, officer.' He shook the constable's hand with both of his and sprinted into the darkness.

The officer shook his head. 'Mad as a bag of frogs.'

Starling and McCormac were sound asleep when Blacklock burst back in, McCormac face down on the table, head resting on his arms, Starling leaning back in his chair, mouth agape, drooling.

He shook Starling. 'Wake up! Wake up, man! It is Rosebery!'

Starling squinted at him. 'What or who is Rosebery?'

'The woman's name. Rosebery.'

'Like the PM?'

'Precisely. Robertson even joked that she was no relation.'

McCormac sniffed and opened his eyes. 'Time?'

Starling checked his watch. 'A little after three.'

'Too late to go now. We'll go in the morning. Now shut up, Doc, and we'll try to get the rest of our beauty sleep.'

Ninety-Six

McCormac's lodgings, 25 Barnabas
Street, Kensal Green, London
Saturday 27th July

Blacklock hardly slept and spent most of the remaining hours of the night wondering how the others could do so. When dawn broke he could no longer contain himself. The others were woken by the smell of burning bacon and eggs from the pan on McCormac's tiny spirit stove.

'Morning, gentlemen,' said Blacklock. 'Today we find Robertson. Mrs Rosebery will show us the way.'

'Not so fast,' said McCormac. 'We don't want to spook her. If he has any sense Robertson will have told her to keep quiet if anybody comes looking for him.'

'On the other hand, Frank,' said Starling, 'we're all getting a little bored with standing in the cold. Or, at least, Nate is. She might even tell you his whereabouts if you ask nicely. Otherwise she might run straight to him. Either way you'll find him without freezing your nuts off. Technical term. What do you think, Nate?'

'Ha. A dilemma. Speaking as one who has on more than one occasion come perilously close to losing his testicles to frostbite I am not keen to wait, but equally find myself unwilling to risk losing Robertson's trail again. If our hypothesis is correct and he has not already flown from London, flushing him out now will certainly cause him to flee further.'

'You can't play this by ear, Nate. It's one or the other.'

'I shall therefore talk to Mrs Rosebery and see what she is willing to divulge.'

'No, Doc, you won't. I'm the trained bloody journalist here and there are ways and feckin' means to get people to talk to you. Based on the last few months of our acquaintance I would respectfully suggest that you know none of them.'

'As you wish. Francis.'

'Just an honest observation, Doc. Let's go back and see Alfie Flynn.'

'*Who?*'

'Jeez, Doc, do you listen to *anyone?*'

Ninety-Seven

82 Grenville Street, Vauxhall, London
Monday 29th July

'Mr Flynn? I do not know if you remember me, but–'

'I do. You was looking for the doctor.'

'That is correct.'

'And I told you I don't know where he went.'

'Indeed.' Blacklock paused, then said, 'Do you know a Mrs Rosebery at all?'

Flynn's eyes narrowed. 'Why?'

'I need someone to sit for my young son and Doctor Robertson recommended Mrs Rosebery very highly. With his moving elsewhere I was hoping that she might have time available to help me. Times are hard for all of us.' Blacklock was relieved that he had recalled the story Starling and McCormac had drilled into him.

'No mistake there. Irene lives a couple of streets back – Arndale Terrace. Number seventeen, I think.'

Arndale Terrace was as run-down as the rest of the area, with only occasional houses showing any signs of cleanliness or even basic care. Mrs Rosebery's was one such beacon. Little more than a one-up-one-down, it fronted a street ankle-deep in mud and backed onto a litter-strewn alley.

Blacklock and Starling stationed themselves in the yard of an abandoned manufactory which opened onto the back alley while McCormac went to speak to Mrs Rosebery. Starling peeked into the alley every few seconds, reminding Blacklock of a manic cuckoo clock.

After a couple of minutes they heard a distant shout. McCormac was beckoning them furiously from the end of the alley. They ran towards him but he did not wait.

When the turned the corner he was already waiting ahead at the next junction. This game continued for a couple of further streets, each darker and more impoverished that its predecessors. Finally they dashed around another corner to find McCormac sauntering along as if he did not have a care in the world. They caught him and matched his pace.

'She's over there – rusty orange headscarf. On her way to Robertson's. An older girl – maybe a granddaughter – said I'd just missed her and gave me a description.'

'I don't understand how Flynn got word to her so quickly,' said Starling.

'He didn't; she's going to watch the daughter. He lives somewhere in The Rookeries, in a place called Blind Row.

The Rookeries was a dark maze of semi-derelict tenements in streets so narrow that the gutters – had they still existed – might have touched across the street. It was hosting a pathetic kind of market, filled with produce obviously rejected elsewhere and every variety of hawker selling equally woebegone goods. Nevertheless the street, barely wider than the barrows and tables and suitcases the vendors brought, was thronged with people. It was impossible for the three men to remain together, so they were more often than not separated in the crowd. Blacklock concentrated on the elderly woman's headscarf whilst simultaneously trying to maintain his distance. He glanced around and could see neither Starling nor McCormac, but dared not wait for them; they would have to find him. He looked back as Mrs Rosebery turned into the narrowest of side alleys. He followed her into the labyrinth seconds later but she was already nowhere to be seen. Panicking at the thought of another lost opportunity he rushed ahead, looking into side turnings as he went.

Robertson, carrying a black Gladstone, was heading away from him, perhaps only thirty yards ahead. He was being led by a small girl, who was pleading with him to keep up. They sped through the labyrinth, Blacklock giving chase, eschewing politeness for once to maintain his pursuit.

Ninety-Eight

The Rookeries, Old Nichol, London
Monday 29th July

For once fortune smiled on Blacklock and it was Robertson who was delayed by the crowd. When a brief gap opened Blacklock ran a few steps and grabbed Robertson's wrist. He looked round in alarm but his expression softened immediately; he made no attempt to pull away. 'What the hell do you think you're doing, Pathos?'

'I am making a citizen's arrest. This madness has to stop.'

'I will explain everything, in due course. But right now, by detaining me, you are risking another life. Rosie here needs me to tend to her mother. Are you going to stop me?'

'You gave me your word last time and it proved worthless. I cannot trust you.'

Robertson turned to the girl and crouched down. 'I'm sorry, Rosie, but this man wants your mother to die. Please go home and tell your parents that Doctor Nathaniel Blacklock will not permit me to help her.'

The girl began to run away.

'Wait, child!' cried Blacklock. The tearful girl turned back and regarded him with a combination of hatred and hope. ' I will help.' He glared at Robertson. 'When we have done all we can we must attend to other business. Is that not correct, Doctor Robertson?'

Robertson nodded.

Minutes later both men were at the patient's bedside. The woman lay tangled in sweat-soaked bedlinen, struggling to breathe.

'Could you be pregnant, Mrs McBurney?' asked Robertson.

'No, Doctor,' she panted, teeth gritted. 'My youngest is still on the breast.'

'But–,' said Blacklock.

'Alright,' interrupted Robertson, shooting a warning glance at Blacklock. He pushed gently on the woman's abdomen, eliciting a squeal of pain. 'I'm sorry to ask you to do this – it may hurt – but could you cough for me?'

Mrs McBurney complied, with more obvious distress.

'I think you have an appendicitis, Mrs McBurney, and we must operate. It we don't–'

'You will die,' said Blacklock.

'The consequences may be very severe,' continued Robertson, opening his bag. 'My colleague will help you to sleep.'

Blacklock administered the ether and Mrs McBurney quickly fell into unconsciousness. 'Do you need any other assistance?' he asked.

'No thank you, Pathos. I know what I am doing.'

Robertson made an initial Edinburgh Incision. Blacklock frowned. 'Are you not going to enter via the external oblique aponeurosis? You might wish to start a few inches farther to the left–'

'It doesn't matter what it's called,' hissed Robertson. 'Shut up and let me do my job.'

Blacklock watched Robertson's work as closely as any student's. It took him several attempts to adequately secure the ligature at the base of the appendix, after which he almost lost the severed organ within the open abdomen. His sutures in each muscle layer were adequate – albeit barely – and by the time he reached the skin his hands were trembling so badly that Blacklock forced his way in and took over. He stopped the ether application and they waited in tense silence for Mrs McBurney to regain consciousness. After a further half hour Blacklock thought her sufficiently well that they could leave her.

They had only walked a few yards through the slums before Blacklock could hold his tongue no longer. 'That was abysmal work. How can you even show your face in St

John's?'

'I don't operate there, as I've already told you. Besides, you were breathing down my neck, Pathos, and you saw the conditions for yourself. You could do no better.'

'You just watched me close the final wound. I *did* do better – far better, in fact.'

Robertson snorted. 'Well, we're not all blessed with your God-like skills, Blacklock.'

He tried to walk away but Blacklock clasped his shoulder. 'Just answer a straight question, Arthur. Did you kill all those people – the child, the women and the man?'

'No.'

'No?'

'They died, but would've done so anyway without my intervention. You know that as well as I do, no doubt. You've autopsied them. There are myriad other people alive and well in this cesspool who would not be if it weren't for me.'

'And you can prove that?'

'If need be.'

'I want to believe you, Arthur, but it seems so far-fetched. Why have none of these ... survivors ... come to light?'

'Because I bought their silence for a few pennies a week. I didn't want anyone finding out about this until I was ready.'

'*Ready*? Ready for what?'

Rain began to fall, gently at first but in seconds becoming a downpour. 'Let's get a cab,' said Robertson. 'I'll pay.'

They made their way to the nearest thoroughfare and hailed the next available hansom. 'I think you can let my arm go now, Pathos.'

'Blacklock. Doctor Nathaniel Blacklock.'

'You used to revel in that Musketeers nonsense.'

'Tell me about these back-street surgeries of yours, if that is what they are. What are you trying to get ready *for*?'

'My wife – Maud – had a congenital abdominal condition which worsened steadily until she was completely debilitated by it, requiring surgery just to enable her to perform the most mundane of activities. As you well know

I was not a very capable general surgeon so was of no use to her. In Bristol, where I was practising, there was a general surgeon of great repute – Sir Geoffrey Storie. He assured me that the surgery was routine and I believed him. Maud bled to death on his table and he wasn't even slightly remorseful.'

'I am very sorry, Arthur.'

'It's not your fault. Now, I'm convinced that Eliza has the same condition, but obviously I can trust no one to operate on her but myself. I was rather out of touch with surgery given my hiatus from theatre work so I have been volunteering to help the poor–'

'You have been using them as guinea pigs? For practice?'

'I've been *saving* them, Blacklock.'

'And cutting the throats of your failures?'

'You know very well they were already dead when I disguised them.'

Blacklock shook his head wearily. 'I ... do not know what to say. This is appalling.'

The cab stopped; the traffic had come to a temporary standstill. 'There are more than fifty men, women and children walking around the East End who would not have stood any chance of survival without my intervention. My fatality rate for surgery is around one in ten. I bet that's a darned sight better than yours, eh? I'm not the one suspended due to my ineptitude.' He shook his arm free of the distracted Blacklock's grip. 'Now leave me be. None of this stops until Eliza is safe and well. Can't you see I'm ill?' He coughed, once, twice. His hand flecked with blood. 'See this?' he yelled, holding it aloft. 'I know my time is short, Nathaniel. Consumption, cancer – I don't know which but we both know I won't live long enough to hang. I have little enough time left to save her, even without your bungling interference.' He jumped down from the cab and started to stride away.

Blacklock followed and grabbed him by the shoulder, ignoring the unpaid cabbie's cries behind.

'I said *no!*' shouted Robertson as he turned and brought his knee up to connect squarely with Blacklock's testicles.

The pain flashed through Blacklock, followed by a burst of heat as he fell to his knees. He recovered a little of his senses and looked up in time to see Robertson hailing another hansom. Swift anger overcame the nauseating pain radiating through his abdomen. He struggled to his feet and staggered back to the cab from which they had just alighted on the opposite side of the street. He could barely speak. 'Please,' he gasped, 'follow that hansom ahead, being drawn by the palomino. It is of the utmost importance.' He clung to the cab to prevent himself collapsing again.

'I dunno what your game is, mate, but I don't take no pissed fares in my cab. Now leave go before I take the whip to you. Besides, my horse is dead beat, and I can't get him no further than the stable.'

'Please,' gasped Blacklock, 'wait.' He fished in his pocket and found a guinea, emergency funds provided by Starling. 'This will be yours. I am not inebriated – you must have seen him assault me.'

The cab driver snatched the coin and examined it closely. 'Get in. I'll give you your change when we stop.'

The first mile, perhaps two, passed in a daze and Blacklock stared through the dirty window, eyes still watering. As the unremittingly drab scenery rolled by his breath returned as the pain in his groin reduced to a dull but nevertheless intense ache. With returning focus he swore to avenge his attack, simultaneously aware that it would be worthless against a dying man.

He lowered his window and peered out. 'Driver? Can you still see him?'

'Yes guv, two cabs ahead. Unfortunately for you the traffic is flowing well – when they get jammed up I'll give you a knock. Now get your bloody head back in before somebody or something knocks it off.'

Blacklock mopped his brow on his shirtsleeve. He had been perspiring profusely since the assault, although his discomfort was easing. As he pulled his jacket over the yellowed cuff there was a sharp double knock on the cab roof. 'Look sharp, squire,' shouted the driver. 'Your man's taken to his heels.'

Blacklock jumped down and set off in the direction the cab driver was pointing. The traffic flow had ceased because the road deck of Tower Bridge was opening. 'Keep the change,' Blacklock yelled, without looking back.

At the sound of Blacklock's raised voice Robertson glanced around and spotted him. He searched desperately for an escape route; with the bridge open and Blacklock running towards him he had no option but to run to the Tower staircase, where as usual there was a queue of sightseers waiting to ascend. Without hesitation Robertson elbowed his way past them, ignoring the ticket seller, and began to run up the stairs two and three steps at a time, belying his poor health. With everyone in the queue looking after Robertson it was easy for Blacklock, approaching from behind, to overtake them and continue the chase. The aftermath of Robertson's blow began to tell once again as Blacklock ascended the confined staircase; he had to stop every dozen steps or so for respite. Indignant shouts from above told him that he was not far behind his quarry, the man's frailty obviously beginning to tell. This reinvigorated Blacklock, and after a few more turns of the staircase he could hear Robertson's steel heel taps ahead, tantalisingly out of reach.

How could an invalid maintain such a pace? More than once Blacklock came close enough to grasp Robertson's coattails, but missed each time. The stairway was lightening ahead, not a moment too soon for Blacklock whose thighs were burning, his heart and lungs feeling fit to burst.

A few steps from the top a giant of a man took a sidestep to block the stairs. 'Wait your turn, oik, or I'll knock ya down every bleedin' step to the bottom.'

'Please,' panted Blacklock, 'I am pursuing a fugitive – a

murderer.'

Easily persuaded by Blacklock's earnest desperation the man moved to one side, allowing him to run the final few steps unmolested. The wide gantry was greatly crowded. Most people were pressed against the sides of the walkway, craning to see London from a new perspective. Blacklock pushed through the centre, eager to prevent Robertson's access to the far staircase and with it yet another escape. He caught sight of him a few yards ahead, also delayed by the crowd. Blacklock was gaining on him, even as the escape route loomed. There was no queue to descend, nothing to impede Robertson. With a final effort Blacklock grasped his quarry's coat.

Robertson spun around; Blacklock caught his wrist and gripped it so tightly that he could feel the bird-like bones within. Mindful of his recent low blow, he turned sideways to protect himself.

'Let me go!' snarled Robertson, trying to pull his arm free.

Blacklock was determined not to release him. 'No, Arthur. Not this time. You–' His words were cut short as Robertson stopped resisting and relaxed a little. Blacklock, caught off guard, followed suit as Robertson bowed his head in surrender. Blacklock moved towards him. In an instant he was reeling backwards, his nose broken by a head butt. Robertson was now free again, but Blacklock retained his wits sufficiently to position himself to block the exit.

The crowd drew back, forming a circle around the men. Robertson howled, trapped by the dense wall of onlookers. Blacklock, wiping his nose on his sleeve, felt no pain, heard no shouting. Flooded with adrenaline, his focus narrowed; all he could see was Robertson. He lunged after him; the crowd parted as the two men grappled, breaking through the circle.

Robertson's breathing was ragged and he coughed. He stared at Blacklock like a fox at a hound, backing slowly away, eyes fixed on his pursuer. A trail of blood ran from one corner of his mouth. This bloody revelation of sickness served to fracture the crowd around them – even the chestnut vendor abandoned his post.

'Robertson – Arthur – please, give this up. You cannot run any further. You have nothing more to lose, and what about Eliza? You can explain what you were doing, make your case to Duncan. With the survivors–'

Robertson laughed hoarsely. 'You've met the man. He's a pig. I was trying to save people who had no chance. Now I must *save my daughter*. Don't you understand that?'

'Of course I do, Arthur. I will support you and Eliza in any way I can. You have my word.' He risked a look around. 'The police will be here shortly.' A movement in the corner of his eye made him turn back. Robertson was pushing the chestnut vendor's cart towards him. Blacklock, with the crowd tightly packed behind him, could not back away any further so he put out his hands and pushed the cart hard back at Robertson. The weakened man, no match for Blacklock's strength, fell backwards. He reached out to save himself and grasped the cart, which overturned onto him, spilling its burning coals as it did so.

For Blacklock time slowed. The hot coals ignited Robertson's trousers. The flames spread rapidly up his legs. He managed to stand but could only stagger a few steps before the fire engulfed his torso too.

Blacklock pushed Robertson to the ground and began to roll him, beating at the flames with his bare hands as he did so. The pain was excruciating but he carried on, trusting that water was on the way. A few seconds later – no more, though it seemed like a decade – a man began pouring a keg of beer over them both. The screams Blacklock heard were either his own or Robertson's, perhaps both. His nervous system took pity on him and his world went black.

Ninety-Nine

Barts Hospital, London
July-August

Blacklock awoke in a netherworld of disconnected voices he could not understand, delirious unfocussed images occasionally looming in his field of vision. Bewilderment. Pain from his hands, with no capacity to express it. At other times euphoria made him believe he was driving a chariot across the heavens, white horses in the surf or simply taking flight from one of the pinnacles of Tower Bridge.

Someone – a woman – murmured gently as she moistened his lips or mopped his forehead with a blissfully cool cloth. He could not resolve her words into a coherent form. He could sense, rather than hear, the soothing monologue.

At other times the pain in his hands seemed enough to shatter his sanity. Even then he could still hear the distant words of comfort but they were no match for the agony.

Somewhere a clock chimed irregularly. Sometimes it would sound the hours consecutively, at others missing a number out as if an abyss had opened in the day and swallowed time itself.

Days passed. His head began to clear hour by hour, day by day, sense by sense. His hearing became more acute, occasionally catching the start of words or sentences in a way that made interpretation easier. He came to understand that he was in a hospital; the way these strangers addressed each other, faceless blurs taking observations, changing his dressings. His hands – they were injured, but he did not know how – were infected, the smell of corruption strong when the bandages were removed.

More often he was alone, with his thoughts and piecemeal memories which made little sense. He had had an accident of some sort, on a bridge. Was there a fire? Piecing the fragments together led him to the conclusion that he had been involved in some form of conflagration ... Of course! The locomotive had plunged into the river after a ship had struck one of the bridge piers. But ... fire? Perhaps the engine had fallen to one side, rather than entering the river, its coals falling onto the oil-soaked sleepers.

Chestnuts. Something about chestnuts ... *really?* Obviously nonsense – the product of an overheating imagination trapped in a body fighting infection.

A woman, reading. To him or to an audience? What was she reading? Her voice was so soft that try as he might he still could not discern what she was saying, interrupted as it was by the rustle of ... newsprint! This lady was reading the newspaper to him. What nurse has time for such an indulgence? She could not be a visitor because he did not know any women who would do so. Who could it be?

"Matilda" was on the tip of his tongue. Did he know a Matilda? No, not Matilda – *Milly*. That was it. He lay back, trying to shut out the world and recover her memory, to construct an image of this "Milly".

His memory proved a stubborn adversary. No image of "Milly" was forthcoming, but kaleidoscopic images of mutilated women and children appeared at every turn. He tried to reject these visions each time, only to find himself confronted by another, more bloodied, more torn. In his torment he writhed but found himself soothed by cool bedclothes and the continued flow of kind, indistinguishable words. When he eventually opened his eyes he would see Milly and all would be well, his world set back upon its axis.

Not Milly. Tilly. That was her name. Tilly. Matilda Callicott. No – Caldecott. Her father was ... a carriage driver, grooming black horses outside a large house near a park. The memory fragments – wherever they came from – at least coalesced into clear memories. Tilly - *his* Tilly - with her beautiful French Plait.

They were changing his bandages again. *That smell ... nauseated.* The doctors were whispering amongst themselves. Amputation? Did they say *amputation*? He wanted to cry out, to scream, to explain how he would be unable to – what? He needed good hands, fine motor skills, to do his job, but what *was* he? He scoured his memory and images passed through like a lunatic's magic lantern show. He remembered that he was a detective looking for Jack the Ripper.

No, not a detective. A photographer. Everything was monochrome. *Naked women?*

His attempts at speech, although sounding perfect to him, only elicited bemused requests to repeat himself. He hoped that the hospital staff were not as stupid as they seemed and that the problem therefore lay within him. *Perhaps a problem with the larynx* – had that been burned too? *Larynx? I'm a doctor.* Once he had had this realisation, this ... epiphany – more memories returned, memories he felt could be relied upon. There was an unsettling vagueness about how he practised – or whatever he did. Why would he be a doctor and not practise?

His thoughts were interrupted by another bandage change. What was happening to time? Surely it was only minutes ago that they had last tortured him in this way? As the nurse unwound the dressings from his fetid hands, the pain pulled him back to himself as if it was the skin itself she was peeling away. The tell-tale acidic stench of infection filled his nostrils again. 'Wash them in an iodine solution,' he said. 'That should help.'

The nurse stopped. 'At last, he speaks. Welcome back, Doctor Blacklock. Do you know what happened to you? Where you are?'

His mind reeled momentarily. He had been *understood*.

'I burned my hands on ... some chestnuts... No, that cannot be right. Why would I do such a thing? I do not even like them.'

'You're not a million miles away, Doctor Blacklock. You tried to apprehend a murderer on the Tower Bridge. There was an altercation and he apparently upset a chestnut roaster, setting himself alight in the process. You tried – foolishly, if you ask me – to put him out with your bare hands. Burned them almost to a cinder. Certainly medium-rare beef, at least.'

'And Aramis?'

'Who?'

He scoured his memory. 'Arthur ... Robertson? The man who burned.'

'Ah. He passed away a few days later. There was nothing to be done for him.'

Blacklock fell silent.

'Your lady friend was here this morning. She'll be very sorry to have missed you. She's been here every spare minute.'

'It would be good to see her. Miss Caldecott – Matilda – is a good sort, and–'

'I don't think that's her name. Let me think...'

'Tilly. She is called Tilly for short. Informally, I mean. She's my fiancée.'

'No, not Tilly, either. My God, why can't I remember?' The nurse tutted. 'Something French. Cecille? Camille, that's it! Camille.'

'Are you sure?'

'Yes. Miss Henry. Showed up a couple of days after the event. You made the front pages. She has been here reading to you ever since.

'How long..?'

She picked up the clipboard which was hanging on the end of the bed. 'This is your thirty-fifth day in our company.'

'Thirty-five days?'

'Your doctors have been administering sizable doses of analgesia – morphine – and the anaesthetic effects have been very marked in your case.'

He pushed himself up, wincing as he forgot his injuries and took his weight on his hands. 'This room,' he said, looking around. 'It must be ... quite expensive. I have no funds to speak of.'

'I'm given to understand that a gentleman from Belgrave Square is taking care of your expenses, Doctor.'

Blacklock smiled in spite of himself. Clearly Sir Edmund was desperate to distract either himself or more likely distract others from Matilda's plight and repair the family's reputation. His nascent political career would only benefit from the publicity.

Later that afternoon there was a gentle knock at the door and it opened an inch or two. Camille peeked through. 'Goodness, Doctor Blacklock, you're awake. How do you feel?'

'Very well, Miss Henry,' he lied. 'Thank you.' He flushed in spite of his best efforts not to. 'Please excuse my ... indisposition.'

Miss Henry entered the room, smiling broadly. 'There is nothing to apologise for. You have been very ill and one should excuse an invalid everything, don't you think?'

'You are very kind.'

'Nonsense.'

'But why are you here at all?'

He thought he detected the merest hint of additional colour in her cheek.

'What are friends for? Given the torrid time you've had – and the hard times you temporarily find yourself in – well, I thought someone should help you. Anyway, now you're awake and so clearly on the mend my time here is done and I should go.'

'Please – no,' replied Blacklock, more quickly than he intended. 'Some intelligent company would be very agreeable, if you could spare just a little more time.' He cleared his throat. 'Of course, if you have to go then please do not let me detain you. Please accept my heartfelt thanks for your tender ministrations. My sole regret is that I was not sufficiently conscious to more fully appreciate them.'

Miss Henry's colour flared again.

One Hundred

3 Augustus Street, Marylebone, London
Friday 6th December

The marital home which Nathaniel and Camille shared was small but impeccably clean, as befitted a couple of their mutually scrupulous habits. It had been bought not with an exhausting mortgage which would yoke them to the wheel of labour for decades but with a portion of the reward which The Honourable Sir Edmund Caldecott – now the Member of Parliament for Peterborough North, who had swept into office on a wave of sympathy after his daughter had perished during an unspecified surgery in Ireland – had posted. A reward, which – after much harassment from Starling and McCormac – Blacklock had reluctantly accepted. When Caldecott had presented the reward privately to Blacklock it had, of course, been delivered with an accompanying threat from Phelps that any mention of the reason for Matilda's journey to Ireland – ostensibly for the "benefit of her constitution" – would be injurious to Blacklock's health. Unwilling to be beaten, the dogged McCormac had eventually determined Priestley's fate. He had been struck off years ago, unable to control his drinking, and died after a fall in a bleak Glaswegian vennel half a decade before.

The Henry-Blacklock nuptials had been held in the late autumn, a small affair, once again in keeping with their modest means and equally modest aspirations. Camille had worn a simple but elegant gown, with Miss Ellis as her Matron of Honour. Nathaniel had finally been persuaded to purchase a new suit and hat. Charles Gordon had been invited but had not acknowledged his invitation. Cargill had accepted without hesitation and enjoyed the limited free alcohol offered to the utmost extent. With Starling as his

Best Man and McCormac as chief usher and photographer the wedding breakfast had quickly degenerated into an event which was memorable for all the wrong reasons. The only other guests were Paulinus Stewart, Viv, Mrs Evans and an overly-grateful Ernie King who presented the happy couple with a dramatic piece of unboxed Waterford Crystal that they did not dare put on open display.

Blacklock was marking some papers from his students of Basic Human Biology. He had been quietly reinstated to an expanded role within the School of Medicine after Salvadori had unexpectedly been sent abroad after breaching some unknown family rule. Justice had been swift and absolute. He ignored the knock at the door, wrestling as he was to craft an appropriately supportive summary for a student who seemed forever to be struggling with the most basic of concepts.

Camille entered his small study. 'Two letters, Nathaniel. I took the liberty of opening the letter from Eliza's governess. Her post-surgical recovery continues without any setbacks.'

'Thank you, dear. Such good news. Please leave them on the side – once again I am grappling with some of Hughes Junior's most error-prone work.'

'I think you may care to read the other missive. Perhaps sooner rather than later.'

Blacklock put down Hughes's script and turned to her. The envelope's return address was 57 Harley Street. He raised an eyebrow. 'Aha. I wonder if the College has finally reached a decision? Am I acquitted or condemned?' He anchored the envelope onto his blotter with the back of his left hand, the two remaining fingers of which were fused uselessly together by scar tissue. With his right hand he manoeuvred his letter opener into what now passed for a grip, where his fourth finger could still close almost to his palm. 'Are you ready for the verdict, Camille?'

'Of course, Nathaniel. Your exoneration is long overdue.'

He tutted. 'It may remain so.' He split the envelope

open, for despite his scarred hands and virtually useless remaining fingers he could manage such simple tasks as well as the next man – at least, he often joked, as well as the next man with turtle flippers for hands.

'*Dear Doctor Blacklock,*' he read, '*it gives me the greatest pleasure to inform you that the Disciplinary Committee of The College has cleared you of all charges arising from the death in surgery of Mary Banville on Monday, 5th February, 1894. You will therefore be duly readmitted to The College as a licensed surgeon with effect from Wednesday, the first of January 1896.*'

He examined his hands. 'An excellent decision, Camille. I am free to pursue my cutsmith's calling again.' He cast the letter into the small fireplace, where it flared briefly, the heightened flames flashing off the dulled brass fittings of his dusty surgical instrument case which lay abandoned, long forgotten, underneath his bookcase.

THE END

Afterword

Thanks for reading this book. I hope you enjoyed it.

I've played a little fast and loose in places with the chronology - anaesthetics were more widely used and the poor (slightly) better served by hospitals at the tail end of the nineteenth century. Anybody who was practising medicine in the period and objects to something - contact me for a refund.

Duncan's use of 'Tinkerbell' is unapologetically anachronistic; Tinker Bell didn't appear until 1904 with Peter Pan - but I liked the line.

As always, feel free to drop me a line at antony.guntrip@gmail.com.

See you with a ghost story next!

Tony Guntrip
October 2022

Acknowledgements

Of course, none of this happens – or anything else I do of any value - without Supergirl. Thanks also to our myriad children who are more supportive than The Brady Bunch and The Partridge Family combined.

Printed in Great Britain
by Amazon